Promises of Mercy

Montana Promises

Book 1

Vella Day

PROMISES OF MERCY

Print Edition

www.velladay.com
velladayauthor@gmail.com

Cover Art by Sloan Winters
Published in the United States of America
E-book ISBN: 978-0-9899759-0-2
Print Edition ISBN: 978-0-9899759-2-6

Dedication

To Dr. Charley and Dr. Rebecca Lynn for all your help.

Without Olivia Jaymes and Kennedy Layne this book might never have been written.

To the best proofreaders and editors around: Maureen, Anne-Marie, Carol, Corinne, and Erica. You ladies rock!

Chapter One

As oncology nurse, Amber Delacroix, stepped from one of her patient's room, her boss, Tammy White, headed toward her with tense shoulders and a haunted expression. She hesitated only a moment before wrapping an arm around Amber's shoulders. Amber stiffened at the unexpected contact—and feared what it might mean.

"We need to talk," Tammy said in a soft voice. And Tammy didn't do soft.

Those ominous words "we need to talk" swam in Amber's head, and her stomach tumbled. Something horrifying must have happened. Tammy never approached her unless it was serious.

"What's wrong?" Amber's voice shook.

Her boss escorted her down the hall into the break room. "Let's sit down."

Tammy motioned to the sofa. She sat next to Amber and inhaled deeply, the lines around her eyes and mouth appearing more pronounced than usual. When Tammy picked up Amber's hand, an ugly sludge oozed through Amber's veins.

She couldn't stand the suspense. "Tell me." Her voice cracked.

"I'm sorry to have to tell you that your brother was in a very bad motorcycle accident an hour ago."

Amber's heart stopped. That couldn't be true. Intense pressure crushed her from all sides. "But he's okay, right?" She needed to go to him. "Why didn't I find out sooner?"

"Amber. Chris ran a red light. The paramedic on duty did everything he could to stabilize him, but his spinal cord was compromised and his spleen may have been damaged."

Amber shook her head. "No." Chris was a bit careless, but he was a good driver. She rubbed her temples, but Tammy's words still stampeded through her brain. "I have to see him." When she tried to stand, Tammy gently pulled her back down.

"He's in good hands. Let the doctors do what they do best."

Having their standard saying apply to her made Amber realize what her patients' family members truly went through. *Living Hell.* A sob bubbled up and escaped.

Tammy rubbed her back. "It'll be okay."

No, it wouldn't. Amber's shoulders trembled. Poor Chris. She dropped her face in her hands and cried. When the tears finally stopped, Tammy stood. A few minutes later, she was back with a cup of tea and some crackers.

"Drink this. It'll make you feel better." She placed the package next to her.

Amber shook her head. Nothing would make her feel better. Upon Tammy's prodding, Amber sipped the hot tea, but it didn't dull the ache racing through her.

For over an hour, her boss remained by her side trying to comfort her, but nothing helped. The door had opened a few times and whispers sounded, but her boss must have shooed her coworkers away.

Tammy's pager then went off, and when she looked at it, her jaw hardened.

Amber wiped her cheeks. "Go ahead and take it. I'll be okay."

"I hate to leave you."

"It's okay. You have a job to do."

Tammy appeared torn. "I'll check up on you." She gave

Amber one last hug and hurried out the door.

No longer able to sit, Amber stood, wrapped her arms around her stomach, and paced. She couldn't believe this was happening.

She halted. *Oh, God.* She had to tell her mom. The thought of delivering the bad news made her stomach churn even worse. She wasn't even sure she could say the necessary words.

Just do it.

Inhaling, she punched in her mom's number, hoping she'd be free to talk. As head cardiac surgeon at the Oklahoma City Memorial Hospital, her mother could be with a patient or addressing a group of doctors somewhere in the country.

"Amber? Can I call you back? I'm having lunch with someone important."

I'm not important? The hurt and anger from the past, combined with this recent blow, nearly drowned her. There never would be a good time for her mom, so she blurted out the terrible news. "No, Mom, you can't. Chris was hit by a car." She choked out another sob and rubbed her palms down her pants, trying to dry the perspiration. "He might be paralyzed."

"Oh, my God. Was he driving that damned motorcycle of his? How many times have I warned him of the danger?"

"Is that all you can focus on? This is your son we're talking about. Chris. Remember him?" Then she recalled that everyone grieved in different ways.

"Amber, don't be insolent."

Then don't shut me out. "He was on his bike when a car ran into him." The horrific part was that he was speeding and had run a red light, but she wasn't about to share that bit of information now.

"What's his prognosis?" Her mother's tone came out cool and controlled. A far cry from Amber's emotional reaction.

"It's too early to tell. Can you come and be with him? He'll want to see you when he wakes up."

"Oh, darling, you know I would if I could, but there's a huge benefit this weekend to raise money for the cardiac unit of the hospital, and I'm running the event." Chatter and the clinking of glasses sounded in the background, implying she was at a restaurant. "Call me when you know more, and I'll try to get up there."

"You have to come. Chris needs you."

"I'll try." Her mother disconnected.

You better do more than try. Amber sagged against the edge of the break room counter, her gut clenching. Every bit of pent up frustration shot to the surface. Why was she so disappointed at her mom's response when she'd never been any other way? Once her older brother, Thomas, became a doctor, her mother's mission in life had been fulfilled, and it seemed as if she'd said to hell with the rest of her kids.

One of the reasons her mother insisted Amber's younger brother move from Oklahoma to Rock Hard, Montana was because she thought Amber might be able to tame him. Now apparently she'd failed at even that.

Amber shook the phone. "Fuck you, Mother."

She didn't know whether the dismissal or the hint of blame her mom seemed to be placing hurt more. Amber turned back around and looked in the mirror over the small kitchen sink. "It's not my fault." *Christ.* She looked like shit. The person with the red eyes, sunken cheeks, and brown wavy hair that had escaped its tie, mocked her.

Before she could do anything about her ragged appearance, the break room door burst open and Jamie Henderson rushed in. "Oh, Amber, I just heard."

Her best friend, a hospice nurse at the hospital, embraced her, and the comfort helped unbind some of her muscles.

Jamie tried to soothe the hair around Amber's face. "Maybe you should go home and rest. You need to be strong for him."

Amber shook her head. "I can't leave him."

Jamie leaned back and squeezed her hand. "I found one of the doctors who worked on Chris." Her smile looked forced. "He's going to live."

The words should have comforted her, but Chris's definition of living might be different from Jamie's. Amber sniffled. "Did they say when he'd be back in Intensive Care?"

"The doctors are looking at the CAT scan now."

That didn't answer her question. She hoped Chris needed surgery. If his spinal cord had been severed, there'd be nothing the doctors could do.

Amber wiped the moisture from under her eyes. "I should let them know where I am in case one of the doctors needs to get a hold of me." For the first time, she noticed the small table wedged in the corner of the break room. It looked as lost as she felt.

Jamie gave her another hug. "I'm staying with you."

"What about your patients?"

"Marla and Cherise are covering for me."

"Tell them thank you."

She followed Jamie out of the room and located one of the emergency room nurses. Amber told her she and Jamie would be in the waiting room until they received news of her brother's condition.

"I have to call my older brother Thomas," Amber said, the crack in her heart widening once more. "He's a doctor."

"I remember." Jamie stood. "I'll give you some privacy. I'll grab some snacks from the machine. They don't have tea, so do you want a Coke instead?"

"Sure." The caffeine might help with her headache. Dread swirled as she called Thomas, but his phone went straight to voicemail. *Shit.* She hated to leave the terrifying news on a message, so all she said was for him to call her back. That it was important.

Less than a half an hour later, after downing two packages of crackers and a Coke, he returned her call. Because the waiting room was freezing, she stepped outside into the sunshine and told him the same thing she'd told their mom. At least her brother sounded upset even though by the time Chris was old enough to talk, Thomas had already left home for college.

Pinching the bridge of her nose for relief, she returned to the waiting room.

"So?" Jamie asked.

Her best friend knew of her rocky relationship with the rest of her family members, outside of Chris. "He sounded genuinely upset, and I don't think it was his doctor's persona either."

Jamie rubbed Amber's arm. "I'm glad."

Over the next two hours, people came and went and yet there was no news about her brother's condition. Amber stared at the endlessly ticking wall clock and prayed for someone to bring good news fast. Chris *had* to survive. She'd be lost without her brother.

Without him, she had no one.

At 5:25 P.M., a doctor entered the waiting room, his gaze cast downward. She recognized him, but she'd never spoken with him before.

"Amber?"

"Yes?" She stood and crossed her arms over her stomach. "How is Chris?"

"Stable. I'm afraid his C7 was severed."

Her heart stopped. Her head spun. Everything between C3 and C6 was needed for the diaphragm to work. Everything below C7 was for moving the rest of his limbs. "He has no movement at all from the chest down?" She didn't know why she asked. Was she hoping the doctor had made a mistake?

Jamie stood and wrapped an arm around her, and Amber dropped her head on her friend's shoulder for a moment. Her temples pounding, she faced the doctor.

"I'm afraid not. He can breathe on his own, so that's good."

His cheeks sagged. "He'll be able to shrug his shoulders, move his wrists, and wiggle his fingers. With therapy, he might be able to peck out some words on a keyboard. His cord is still swollen, so we can't say precisely the full extent of his injury until after we test him."

Hope of a recovery evaporated. Chris would *want* to die. "When can I see him?"

"He's sleeping and needs his rest. We had to intubate him and give him a lot of pain meds, but you can go in and hold his hand for a few minutes if you want." He told her the room number.

"Thank you."

The doctor nodded and left.

Amber might be an oncology nurse who dealt with pain and death on a daily basis, but to see Chris crumpled and broken would take every ounce of courage she possessed not to let him see the horror on her face.

✧ ✧ ✧

Stone Benson, a paramedic for the Rock Hard Fire Department, jerked his attention back to what his roommate, Cade Carter, was saying. "Sorry. What?" Stone had been off work for four hours, yet he hadn't been able to get the image of that poor kid sprawled at an odd angle next to his cycle out of his head.

Stone's mind had wandered to when he was in Iraq holding his best friend, Heath, in his arms, helpless to save him. Heath's legs had been badly mangled by a bomb, whereas this young man's spine had been contorted by the wreck. Both had life altering injuries. He'd been unable to save Heath. At least this kid had lived.

"I asked if you'd heard anything about Emma Luther's case?" Cade brought Stone's attention back to their present conversation.

"No." He looked up at Cade. "You do remember I don't work at the hospital, right?"

"You socialize with the ER docs. One of them might have mentioned something about her death."

Stone blew out a breath. "Emma Luther was a late stage cancer patient. She might have died suddenly, sending the oncology wing into a tizzy, but the ER docs wouldn't have a reason to know about her except for hearsay." Had her parents not demanded an autopsy, no one would have known she'd been murdered. Stone held up a hand. "I did ask around for you, but either the emergency room guys want to protect someone or they don't know anything. Bottom line is no one's saying a word."

Cade stabbed a hand through his hair. "I'm at a dead end."

Stone stood, went over to the kitchen and retrieved a beer from the fridge. "I bet that's driving you crazy." Cade worked harder than anyone Stone knew—too hard in fact—though if Stone's father had been a criminal like Cade's, he might want to work extra hard to atone for his wrongdoings, too.

Cade stopped pacing and dropped onto the living room sofa. "I've spoken with every one of the nurses and doctors who cared for Emma as well as the family members, but I can't point a finger at any of them."

Stone sat back down across from him. "Weren't you convinced Emma's nurse was involved? What was her name?" Cade handled a lot of cases, and Stone couldn't keep up with who was who.

"That's the one I'm talking about. Her name's Amber Delacroix."

His heart pinched. "Delacroix?"

Cade's hand stilled. "You know her?"

"No, but I brought her brother in today." The emergency room doctor had told him the young man was Amber's younger brother and that she was a nurse at the hospital.

Stone blew out a long breath. At least when he'd delivered the kid to the ER, the young man had been alive. Too many motorcycle accident victims died before they got help.

"How is he?"

"Bad." He described the gruesome scene when he'd arrived. "You know how much I never like to resort to a neuromuscular blocker, but the victim was thrashing about so much, if I hadn't stopped him from moving, no telling what further damage he might have caused. From the angle of his head, his spinal cord had already been compromised."

"That sucks."

"Tell me about it. You think after six years of seeing this shit, I'd become immune."

Cade chugged half his beer. "Did you speak with the sister?"

Stone often tried to follow up with the family members. "Not yet, but I will after I visit the boy. There was something special about the way the kid looked at me that makes me want to be sure he's okay." It was hard enough to find the time to visit the injured let alone the relatives, but with Amber, he considered it a professional courtesy. Besides, when Cade first mentioned her, his eyes had lit up then extinguished quickly as if he didn't want to consider her a suspect in the other case.

"Let me know your impression of her. Amber stated that Emma suffered a lot and that she was terminal. When I interviewed Amber a month ago, I admit she seemed compassionate, and not really the type to be an angel of mercy, but she had the motive and opportunity." He hunched over. "I just need evidence."

"I'll speak with Amber because that's what I do, not because you want me to help with your case. If I think there's something screwy or unscrupulous about her, I'll let you know."

Cade nodded. "Thanks." He leaned back in his chair and stared ahead. "This case is kicking my butt."

"It's okay not to be perfect." Cade had lost weight in the

past month and his cheeks were a bit sunken. Stone suspected it was this case in particular. "You don't have to solve all your cases. No one does."

His roommate took another hit from his bottle, but he set it right down. He must have forgotten it was empty. The slightest hint of a smile appeared. "You think I'm perfect?"

His change in attitude cheered Stone up. The fun-loving side of Cade had returned, if only briefly. "In your mind, buddy."

"What do you say we head to Banner's Bar and tie one on?"

Stone's shift started at 4:00 A.M., and he needed to be sharp. "I'll take a rain check."

Cade nodded as if he'd expected Stone to turn him down. "You got it."

Stone finished his beer, dumped the bottle in the trash, and headed to his room to shower. His mind raced to that poor broken boy and his sister. Not that he believed in stereotyping, but he imagined that as an oncology nurse, Amber Delacroix would be a true caregiver who would give hell to any doctor who didn't do the best for her patient.

Once he undressed, he stepped into the shower and let the warm water cascade over his body. Too bad no amount of heat or scrubbing could erase the look on the boy's face from his memory. The least he could do was try to help Amber, small though his effort may be. After he finished his shift tomorrow, he'd stop by the hospital to see Chris, then find the sister.

Chapter Two

Amber spent her day off with Chris. Only when she couldn't keep her eyes open anymore, did she hug him one last time and return home. Her mom hadn't called to check how Chris was doing, which added to her depression. Amber kept telling herself it was because her mom was waiting for her to call and deliver the news.

With shaking fingers, Amber punched in her cell.

No answer.

Damn. Delivering the additional bad news about the hopelessness of Chris's condition sucked, but it she were honest, had they connected, her mom's insensitive attitude might have upset her more.

The beep sounded. "Hey, Mom. The news isn't good. Chris's spine was severed at C7. He's on pain meds, but maybe they can take him off the ventilator tomorrow. Call if you want to talk." Her mom probably wouldn't respond, but Amber harbored the slimmest of hope the accident might make her mother reach out for a change.

Amber pulled a leftover casserole from the fridge and heated it. She managed to eat a few bites, but as soon as she thought back to Chris, her appetite disappeared.

She had to get some sleep. After showering, she dropped into bed. Even after punching the pillow a few dozen times, she still couldn't get comfortable or turn off her mind. Around three in the morning, Amber finally dozed off.

By eight, she'd dressed and returned to the hospital. She probably wouldn't be at her finest for her two to midnight shift, but she wanted to be close to Chris in case he needed her.

As she entered his room, a fleeting rush of joy filled her. The ventilator was gone. Chris was asleep, his chest rising and falling gently. She pulled the chair next to his bed, lifted his hand in hers, and squeezed. "Hey, Chris. It's Amber. Can you hear me?"

When Chris didn't move, blood pounded in her head. "Come on, Chris." She pressed a palm to her forehead to help keep the impending headache at bay. "Wake up. You can do it."

If she had to sit there and carry on a one-sided conversation for hours on end, she would. He had to pull through. Chris was a fighter, and she'd be there for him every step of the way.

Amber squeezed his hand while she talked to him, trying to stimulate his brain into rousing. She recounted some happier times when they were growing up, like when Dad would take them to ball games, but even those memories failed to bring the usual joy.

It must have been close to noon when Chris finally groaned. Her heartbeat picked up. His lids fluttered and she placed a hand on his cheek and shook it gently.

"Welcome back, Chris."

At the thought of having him wake up in a hospital, her stomach tumbled. Now she'd have to break the terrible news to him. Finally, he opened his eyes, but it seemed to take forever before he recognized her.

"Amber?"

"Yeah. It's me, kiddo. You don't have to talk."

"What happened?" His voice sounded scratchy, but that was to be expected from the throat tube.

He tried to wet his dry lips. She reached for the water and placed the straw to his lips. When he sucked up the liquid, excitement bubbled through her. He nodded, and she put the pitcher back down.

"Do you remember crashing your bike?" He shook his head then winced. "A car hit you."

"How bad?" Pain sliced across his face.

"You messed up your back pretty bad."

He wiggled his fingers as if attempting to lift his arm. He grit his teeth then relaxed his hand. "I can't—"

Amber's pain cut so deep, she lost the courage to tell him what was in store for him. "I'll be right back." She never was a coward, but this was her brother.

She shoved back her chair and rushed out the room. She needed to tell the nurse he was awake, as the monitors wouldn't have alerted them. Tears trickled down her cheeks. As she rushed up to the nurses' station, she wiped away the moisture.

The woman's name was Sheri. The nurse looked up and smiled. "Can I help you?"

Amber explained Chris was awake. "I need his doctor to explain his condition to him. Now."

Sympathy poured across Sheri's face. "I'll page him immediately."

Amber's chin shook. "Thanks."

With her chin held high, she returned to Chris's room. His head was turning right and left, panic crisscrossing his face.

"I can't move." He gasped for breath, and she rushed to his side.

Be strong for him. "It'll be okay." She hated lying. "Shrug your shoulders. You can do it. It's going to take time to regain strength." That much was true.

A few minutes later, the doctor came in. He didn't look much older than she did. He introduced himself, and then told Chris about his limitations and what he was in for.

"This is bullshit," Chris said. He pounded the back of head into the mattress, the only part of his body he could really move.

Her heart broke.

The doctor asked Chris to move his fingers, his shoulders, and his arms. It hurt her to see him struggle so. The doctor then stepped to the end of the bed and ran a closed pen up and down his feet. When Chris didn't react, Amber had to force herself to appear calm.

After he checked Chris's breathing, the doctor placed a hand on Chris's shoulder. "I'll be back tomorrow to go over your prognosis. I know this is a lot to take in." He nodded to her then left.

She drew in a deep breath and slowly exhaled. "Sweetie, I know this is hard, but with therapy you'll be able to do some things."

"I can't live like this, Amber." He turned his head again. Tears shimmered. God help him. Her baby brother never cried.

She wanted nothing more than to hug him, but he'd think she pitied him. The sad fact was that a part of her did.

After another hour of trying to convince him that his life would get better, a knock sounded, and Jamie peeked her head in. "Hey, Chris."

Amber welcomed the interruption. Jamie and her boyfriend, Ben, had come by the house nearly every weekend after Chris moved in with her.

"Go away, Jamie."

Amber's patience snapped. "Chris, that's no way to speak to one of our friends." Now she sounded like their mom, but it couldn't be helped. The last thing he needed was to push people away, especially when he'd need help the rest of his life.

Amber stood, and keeping her back to her brother, she walked toward Jamie. "He's having a hard time coming to grips with the paralysis." She made sure to keep her voice too low for Chris to hear.

"Wouldn't you?" Jamie whispered back.

Amber had to be honest. "Yes."

Jamie moved to the side, looked at Chris, and slightly shook her head. Chris was a proud man. Having his friends see him this way would only add to his pain, but at some point he had to accept help.

Someone lightly tapped the door and a nurse came in. "I need to turn him and check his vitals."

"I can't do this," Chris said to no one in particular. "I can't live like this."

Amber strode over to him. "Don't say that, Chris. Please. You need to have patience."

"Fuck patience. What am I supposed to do now? I'll never be able to walk, never be able to ride my bike." A tear dripped down his face. "Never have a family." He looked up at her. "I know you always thought I was this irresponsible kid, but I didn't want to end up like Dad—always working, never having time for any of us."

His words cut. He spoke the truth and sympathy choked her. He clearly wasn't in the mood to listen to her rant about being strong, but she would have that talk with him at some point. "I know it's going to be hard. Let the nurse do her job. I'll step outside for a bit." She should call their mom again.

When Chris turned his head away from her, her heart finally cracked, and Amber had to work hard to keep from breaking down. Part of her wanted to shake him, and the other part wanted to hug him.

You have to stay strong.

She bet that would be her motto for the next few years.

From what Stone had heard from a few of the nurses, Amber would probably be by her brother's side. Since he'd been the first one to bandage Chris's legs and bring him in, he hoped the young man would remember him—at least the part before Stone medically paralyzed him in order to get him to stop twisting and flailing. Being unable to breathe, even for a few seconds, could emotionally scar anyone for life.

He first stopped by the ER to speak to Randy Carstead, the doc who'd worked on Chris. Stone waited until Randy finished with a patient.

When his friend spotted him, he tore off his gloves, dumped them in the trash, and came over. "I'm not used to seeing you here without a gurney by your side or not wearing your uniform."

"I just stopped by to find out about my trauma patient I brought in."

Randy shook his head. "It was bad. His C7 was severed."

"Fuck." He feared all that movement had done irrevocable damage.

They were only able to discuss the kid's other injuries for a few minutes because a gunshot victim rolled in.

Randy's shoulders straightened. "Gotta go. Let's hit Banner's Bar next week."

Stone could use a hard night of partying. "Works for me."

As soon as Randy disappeared behind the automatic door, Stone went up to the ICU, and spoke with the nurse on duty who gave him Chris's room number. She mentioned that Amber had been in earlier and said she'd be back.

"Thanks."

He walked to the end of the hall, knocked on Chris's door and opened it. The young man was stretched out on his bed with his eyes closed. At least he was breathing on his own.

"Hey, Chris."

The kid opened his eyes. He looked at Stone hard as if he was trying to recognize him. "Who are you?"

It was always hit or miss whether the victim would remember him. "I'm Stone Benson, the paramedic who brought you here."

He turned his head. "You should have let me die."

Christ. He sounded so much like Heath, Stone's heart squeezed. He pulled up a chair and straddled it. "Listen. What happened to you is a tragedy, but you ran the red light." Personal responsibility could be a bitch.

Chris's gaze shot right then left. "I don't remember anything."

"That's not unusual."

The kid's jaw hardened then trembled. "I'm sorry."

"You don't need to apologize to me. You have to live with the consequences." Stone found that by being tough, the patient could better cope.

"Was anyone else hurt?" Tears threatened to spill and he turned away.

"No. Only you. You're lucky you're not dead."

Chris looked back to Stone. "I'm scared."

That cracked his heart. Stone had two options. Be gentle and supportive or tell Chris his options. If the kid didn't face his reality like a man, he'd never find something fulfilling in his life.

"I know. It sucks, but you can make the best of what you have."

He shook his head. "I can't do it."

Stone had heard the same sentiment from many patients, especially from the critical ones. "Yes, you can. I bet your sister wants you to try."

"I don't want Amber to have to take care of me."

So that was at the crux of his issues.

Before he could address the situation, the door opened, and Stone turned around. A woman, who he guessed was Amber, along with another nurse, entered. Cade had described the sister as being about five feet four, having long wavy brown hair, a pert nose, and full lips. The fact one of the women was a blonde made identifying Amber easy.

He pushed back his chair and stood. "Ladies." He nodded to

both. "I'm Stone Benson. I was the paramedic on duty who brought Chris in. I just stopped by to check on him."

"I'm Amber, Chris's sister." Her shoulders sagged.

The blonde woman clasped Amber's arm. "I'll call you later."

Amber's lips pressed together as if she was working hard to keep it together. "Please do." They hugged.

Amber looked behind him at her brother. "May we speak outside?" She looked tired and quite disheartened though he could hardly blame her.

"Sure." He'd already switched his day off with Drake Longworth, so he had time to spend with her.

"I'll be back, Chris," she said.

Her brother didn't answer.

They stepped into the hallway. "How is he?" she asked.

"I'm not a doctor, but as someone who has seen his share of bad accidents, I've witnessed the whole range of reactions. Chris is scared, but that's not unusual."

Her eyes widened. "He told you that? That he was scared?"

"Yes, but Chris seems like the type who can overcome this."

She sucked in her bottom lip. "You don't know how happy I am to hear that. I need him to recognize what he's going through. He's been angry."

"I would be, too." He didn't want to deceive her. "I've seen patients go from angered to determined to depressed all in a span of minutes."

"So have I." Her stomach grumbled.

Given her red eyes, either she'd been crying, hadn't slept much, or both. Most likely she'd foregone food, also. "When was the last time you ate?"

She glanced at the ceiling and slowly shook her head. Amber wouldn't do Chris any good if she didn't keep up her strength. He placed a hand on her back. "Come on. Let's grab a bite. I need to eat." She hesitated and he cursed himself. She might think he was trying to pick her up. "I thought we could talk about Chris."

Her shoulders dropped a bit. "I'd like that. The doctor really didn't say much other than it will take time."

"That's true."

They took the elevator to the second floor and walked down a hallway plastered with photos of the hospital Board. The last door on the right led to the cafeteria. As if she was on a mission, Amber headed straight to the food line. The place was crowded and loud. Stone didn't know why the ordered chaos bothered him now. Maybe it was because he felt sorry for her and thought she'd appreciate the quiet.

Though her voice had remained calm when they'd been in Chris's room, he could tell from the way she'd crossed her arms over her chest like she was afraid she'd fall apart, that she was barely holding it together.

In relative silence, they pushed their trays through the line. While he piled the food on his plate, Amber picked up two small salads, one of which was a small bowl of cut fruit.

"These coming months will require a lot of your energy. You need to eat." He tried to keep his voice as soothing as possible.

"I know." She grabbed another bowl, this one containing green beans.

When they reached the cashier, she pulled her wallet out, but blocked her efforts to pay. "I'll get this." Amber would need to purchase a special bed for Chris, medications, and a host of other items.

"That's very kind, but no thank you."

He shrugged, not wanting to push her too hard and add to her stress. Amber seemed the type of woman who was cautious around men. He had no solid basis for his assumption, other than how she avoided his direct eye contact and was constantly fiddling with her uniform as if she believed he was judging her. Because he'd wanted to understand who he'd be dealing with,

Stone had asked a friend of hers if she was dating anyone or had family nearby for a support system. The nurse said she didn't.

They found a table toward the back of the cafeteria where the noise wasn't as loud. As soon as they sat, Amber picked up her fork then set it down. Her stomach was probably churning, and he really wanted to put her at ease.

"Tell me about Chris."

She looked at him, but it was almost as if she didn't see him. "What do you mean? He's paralyzed."

That was not what he'd meant. "Tell me what he was like, what he did for a living, what he enjoyed doing for fun. Stuff like that."

She sighed and the tiniest smile crossed her lips. "Chris is a dreamer. He hated school probably because our older brother was a superstar. Not that Thomas was around much since he was fifteen years older than Chris, but Mom bragged about him all the time." She looked down at her food and stabbed a piece of fruit. "In her eyes, Thomas could do no wrong. My mom is a cardiac surgeon and pushed her first offspring to be a doctor. When I came along, I wanted to be a doctor, too, but it wasn't to be."

Now he felt like a shit for asking. Dredging up bad memories hadn't been his goal. "So was Chris more into athletics? Or was he an expert at video games?" He figured that covered the gamut of what kids did who didn't like school.

"He was a daredevil. A real adrenaline junkie." Her lips quivered, and he had to urge to clasp her hand to give her comfort—but he didn't.

"So Chris lived life to the fullest."

She finally made direct eye contact. "Yeah, he did."

Stone leaned forward. "What were his goals?" None of which might ever be realized now.

She shook her head. "I'm not sure. If I had to guess, I'd say it was to have a good time." Her lips pressed together, and she looked up at the ceiling again as if she'd find her composure there. "When he came to live with me, I insisted he take at least one night school class and get a job, so he worked as a garage mechanic. He's really talented."

"I'm glad he found something he excelled at." He scarfed down part of his meal while he thought about her answers. "Were you and Chris always close?"

"Surprisingly, yes, even though we were opposites. I was always studying and figured when I was done with school, I'd have plenty of time to travel and enjoy myself." She sipped her tea.

"How's that plan working out?" He tried to keep his voice light.

A small chuckle escaped. "When I find the time to do the things I want, I'll let you know."

"I hear ya. I always dreamed of seeing the world, too. Finding the time and money seem to be my stopping points."

"Amen."

It was cool they had the same vision in life. "The ER doc said you're an oncology nurse." He wanted to hear about her passion.

"Yes."

"Why oncology?" He wasn't sure he could handle the depression day in and day out.

"It's where I believe I can help the most." She returned to her food for a moment before continuing. "When I see how quickly the doctors have to meet with so many patients, I'm glad I chose nursing where I can spend time with each person." A spark filled her eyes.

"What's the best part of your job?"

"That's easy. Seeing my patients' courage. I've never met more upbeat and wonderful people in my life." She inhaled, and then exhaled deeply. "Don't get me wrong, I do have many sad cases, but when some go home and live a full life, I'm so happy for them."

"It seems as if you really love what you do."

Her face softened, and she looked beautiful at that moment. "Yes." She sighed. "But now I'm not sure how I'm going to take care of Chris full-time and do my job the way I want."

He wondered why she thought it was her responsibility. "What about your parents?"

She shook her head. "My dad, who was a lawyer, walked out on us a long time ago, and my mom works long hours."

"As a cardiac surgeon, maybe your mother could hire someone to care for her son."

"She could, but I'm not sure she plans to." Amber's lips pursed. "I'll speak with her about it."

He hadn't expected such pain and bitterness to lace her tone. For today, he'd leave that conversation alone. No need to bring up something so unsettling.

For the next few minutes, they ate—or rather he ate and Amber picked. She'd bring the fork close to her mouth and hold it there for a moment as if she was lost in thought.

He glanced at the big clock behind the cafeteria line. "When do you need to get to work?" She was dressed in scrubs, so he assumed she was here for her shift.

Amber sucked in a big breath. "At two. If I have time, I want to stop back and see Chris once more. My boss said to take a few days off, but I figure if Chris's condition changes, I'll be close by." She closed her eyes tight for a moment. "You know what he said when he first woke up after the accident?"

Stone shook his head.

"He said he wanted to die."

Stone nodded. "He told me that, too, but it's the fear talking. It's going to take time to come to grips with the life-altering event."

She drew in her bottom lip. "How can I convince him that he can lead a useful life?"

Did she really believe he could? Fuck, if he got run over and couldn't move, Stone might elect to die, too. When Heath had been in his arms, he kept begging Stone to let him go. Stone had tried to convince his friend to hold on for the sake of his wife and newborn child, but Heath had shaken his head, claiming he didn't want to be a burden to his family.

"It's going to be up to Chris. All you can do is be there for him." She certainly didn't need to believe it was her responsibility to make Chris happy.

"I know, but my brother is going to be so miserable. This may sound callous, but perhaps he'd have been happier if he'd died in the crash. Chris is strong when he wants to be, but I don't see the fight in him this time around."

Cade's doubts regarding Amber resurfaced in his mind, but Stone refused to believe she really would lend a helping hand to end someone's life. Her belief in the human spirit seemed too strong.

Stone reached out and clasped her hand. "Give him time. Just be supportive in whatever he decides."

Her lips quivered. "Thanks. I know we'll get through this somehow."

They finished their meal and placed their trays next to the trash. Stone motioned her toward the exit. "I can't begin to imagine what you're going through right now, but I want you to know I'm a good listener."

Amber had struck a chord in him. He dealt with the injured every day, but he had a responsibility to help the strong and brave ones, too. When his sister had been diagnosed with acute leukemia eighteen years ago, it was his aunt who'd spent time with him when everyone's attention had been focused on Katie. Having Auntie Carol's support was what allowed him the ability to help his sister get through the chemo and the bouts of pain. Everyone needed an advocate.

He pulled a card from his pocket. "Here's my number if you

ever need to vent. I'll be back to check on Chris from time to time."

"Thank you."

When they left the cafeteria, he welcomed the sudden drop in noise. He placed a hand on her shoulder. "I mean it when I say call me."

She nodded, turned, and walked down the hallway. When she reached the elevator, she glanced back. The quick smile she gave him lodged deep in his chest. There was no way Amber Delacroix could take anyone's life. She was too pure and full of hope.

Chapter Three

Between visiting Chris, working her twelve-hour shifts, and barely sleeping, Amber's body was beginning to give out. If her mind would just stop drifting to her brother's worsening condition, she might be able to handle the fatigue better. She wasn't even sure if she was giving her patients the care they deserved.

Twice, she'd been about to give a patient the wrong dosage, when at the last minute, she'd snapped out of her daze. At least she had the wherewithal to double check herself from then on. As a medical professional, she understood that if she didn't rest, she'd have to tell Tammy she'd be using the remainder of her vacation days in the coming weeks, which meant she wouldn't always be close by should Chris need her.

Amber usually stopped in to see her brother during her breaks, but too often he was asleep. When she was able to wake him, she suggested he try to move his fingers, but he kept shaking his head, asking why he should bother. He just wanted to die.

She might have to ask Stone to have another talk with Chris. Somehow, the man-to-man thing had seemed to work—at least temporarily. The therapist said Chris was depressed, but everyone Amber spoke with told her that was to be expected. She and the therapist both were trying to find things for him to do that would stimulate him and give him a reason to live. But nothing had worked so far.

On the fifth night after Chris's accident, Jamie and Ben insisted they take her to dinner. Jamie had been Amber's rock these last couple of days. Her friend always seemed to know all the right words to say.

After eating a big meal and enjoying herself for the first time since the incident, she went home and crashed. She actually slept. Amber figured it was because her body knew she didn't have to work for the next three days.

When she awoke, she felt a little perkier until she called her mom.

"He's not any better?" her mom asked.

"Not mentally. Not physically, either. He's not exactly excited about physical therapy." She inhaled. "It might help if you visited."

"Has he asked for me?"

Amber didn't know what her mother hoped her response would be, but she wouldn't lie. "No, but that doesn't mean you shouldn't come and be supportive."

"I'm afraid if I walk into his room, Chris will become more agitated. I do want to see him, but not if it's going to upset him more."

Her mom had a point, but that wasn't a good enough reason to stay away. "Don't you want to see your son?"

Her hesitation said it all—no. "I'm afraid he'll see the pain on my face and know it's hopeless."

Amber opened her mouth, but nothing came out for a moment. "You're a doctor. You must lie all the time to patients to give them hope."

"Amber! That's a terrible thing to say. You know that's not true."

Amber wasn't in the mood to get into an argument. "Be there for Chris just this once. Okay?" This time, she was the one to hang up. "Aargh."

Sometimes she wondered why her mom bothered to have any more kids after Thomas.

Frustrated and pissed, Amber drove to the hospital to see him. This time, when he cracked open his eyes, he closed them again, probably not in the mood to listen to her badger him to move.

"Just leave," he said. "I don't need your cheery bullshit."

Ouch. That pierced her heart. "You have to stop feeling sorry for yourself. The physical therapist is coming this afternoon, and I want you to do what he tells you."

"Like his stupid exercises are going to do any good? That shrink lady stopped in today and that was a joke, too." He turned his head and firmed his lips.

"Dr. Donovan is a very competent psychologist. Zoey also happens to be a good friend of mine."

"I know."

Amber blew out a breath wishing he'd give Zoey a chance. "You do know you have to face this at some point? You're not doing yourself any favors by refusing help."

He didn't say anything, but from the way he pressed hard on his lips, he wanted to.

As usual, she failed to have any effect on him, but she wasn't ready to give up on her brother—nor would she ever.

As soon as she stepped outside the building, the bright sunshine seemed to mock her, and she wondered if she'd ever be truly happy again.

She inhaled the clean air as she headed to her car. When she stuck her hand into her purse for her car keys, she felt the card Stone had given her.

Stone. He might be the only one who could help Chris. She'd never met anyone who seemed so sincere, and as much as she prided herself on her strength, there were times when a person needed an unbiased opinion on whether she was pushing her brother too hard.

She unlocked her car door, slid onto the seat, and called him.

"Stone Benson."

"Hi, Stone, this is Amber." She figured since she'd seen him a couple of days ago, he'd remember her.

"Hey. So glad you called. I stopped by to see Chris yesterday, but he wasn't in a good place."

Relief washed over her. He'd understand. "By any chance are you free right now?"

"I get off at noon. Why? Has something happened to Chris?"

"No. I'm the one who needs to talk." He'd said he was a good listener. While she never just called a guy and asked to meet with him, this was an exception. "Do you think you could meet me for lunch?"

"I'll do one better." He didn't hesitate. "How about I pick up a few things and we can find some quiet spot for a picnic?"

He must be a mind reader. It was inevitable she'd break down, and it would be better if they were in a secluded area. "That sounds wonderful." The idea of getting away from it all lifted her spirits.

"I can pick you up at your place or, if it's more convenient, at the side entrance to the hospital."

She weighed her options. "How about the hospital side entrance at 1:15 P.M.?" That would give both of them time to get ready.

"Great."

"What can I bring?"

"Just yourself."

It didn't surprise her that he'd say that. "Perfect." When she disconnected, a small weight lifted off her shoulders.

Amber wasn't the type to take advantage of anyone, so she headed to the store to pick up some extra items, like strawberries for dessert and a few bottles of her favorite Arizona Tea. She had no idea what Stone liked to drink, but if he was off duty, maybe he'd enjoy a beer. She picked up a six-pack of the brand Chris drank and went home to change. This wasn't a date, so how had a trickle of excitement snuck into her veins? Maybe it was relief.

Once at her house, she took two beer bottles from the carton and placed them on ice in a small cooler. The strawberries, along with her teas, she kept out.

It was rather silly of her to care what she looked like, but it would make her feel better if she put some effort into her appearance. She changed into matching underwear, her good shorts, a rather form-fitting top, and light hiking shoes in case he planned on eating somewhere truly remote. It was sunny and warm outside, but in case the sun dipped behind a cloud, she'd bring a pullover.

She only had a few minutes to brush on some blush, redo her lipstick, and drag liner over her eyes. When she checked her appearance, her mood elevated. Pain resided in her eyes, but to the casual onlooker, she might look fine.

Not wanting to be late, she grabbed her small backpack purse and cooler and headed out to the car. When she arrived at the hospital employee entrance ten minutes early, she parked, ducked inside and rushed up to Chris's floor to check on him.

Yesterday, they'd moved him out of the ICU. Her friend Becky was at the desk.

"Amber!" She ran her gaze up and down her. "You look like you're ready to go on a hot date." Becky nodded to her cooler.

Yikes. She hadn't even noticed she had it with her. Her mind definitely had gone to mush. She hoped her clothes didn't suggest to Stone that she considered this a date. She didn't want him to think she was using the need to talk with him as an excuse. For all she knew, he was in a committed relationship. "Nah. I'm going out to lunch with a friend. If the doctor needs me for something or Chris becomes agitated, text me, okay?"

"Will do."

To make sure her brother was okay, she hurried down the hall and peeked her head in the room. When she saw he was asleep, she quietly closed the door. Satisfied she'd covered her bases, she strode back down the hallway. To avoid getting into a long conversation with Becky or having to wait for the elevator, she took the three flights of stairs down to the exit.

As soon as she stepped outside, she spotted Stone, leaning against his truck, looking wonderfully casual. Even in her frazzled state, she noticed that Stone Benson was one handsome man. His brown hair was short in back, but the front kind of flopped over his forehead, which drew her attention to his intense green eyes.

He looked up with a broad smile on his face. "You just visit Chris?"

Why her heart sped up at seeing Stone she didn't know, but if he could take her mind off her reality even for a half hour, she'd be forever grateful. "Yes, but he was sleeping."

He nodded to her cooler. "Whatcha got there?"

"I didn't want to arrive empty-handed."

He slipped the container from her hand.

When their fingers touched, it was as if an electric spark shot up her wrist. What was up with that? Her defenses must be *kaput,* and any stimulus affected her more than usual.

"You didn't have to, but I'm sure I'll be happy with what you brought. Ready?"

"Yup." She liked how he put her at ease no matter what she said or did.

He pulled open the covered back of his truck bed where he had bins stored between sections of bungee cords and placed her cooler snuggly between the taut lines. He walked her to the passenger side and opened the door.

He waited until she was seated before shutting her in. Maybe she'd gone out with the wrong type of man in her life, but rarely had anyone acted like such a gentleman. Come to think of it, the last date she'd had was when she lived in Oklahoma City, and that man never did anything nice. God only knew, her ex-husband surely wasn't the type to open a door for a woman.

Stone climbed in his side and smiled. She didn't know why, but her heavy heart lightened knowing he'd help share her burden, if only for today.

"So where are we going?" She wasn't even sure what to say to this nice man.

He glanced over at her. "Would it bother you if I said it was a surprise?"

She liked the idea. "No."

He exited the parking lot and headed west. "How long did you say you've lived in Rock Hard?"

"A year."

Stone nodded. "Have you explored Harmes River?"

She hadn't taken the time to do much. Other than dinner with friends, or having Jamie and Ben over on the weekends, she'd spent her evenings reading or brushing up on the latest oncology protocols. Of late, she'd worried about Chris. "Nope."

"Then you're in for a treat." He looked over and smiled. "I hope."

She hadn't invited him on a date but rather wanted to discuss her brother's mental and physical condition. "I know you're not a doctor, but any guess on how long it'll be before I can take Chris home?"

"That's hard to say. His leg needs to heal first."

She was about to say Chris hadn't complained about any leg pain, but why would he? He had no sensation below his chest. "What's your assessment of his leg injury?" The doctor hadn't been specific, and Stone had seen her brother before the doctors had patched him up.

"While the abrasions only required a few sutures, I'm betting the doctors will monitor him for clots."

"Good to know." While Stone seemed to have endless patience, maybe now wasn't the best time to drill him or ask him for more favors. "As much as I had planned on discussing Chris and his mounting depression, I think I'd like to discuss something else." Anything that would take her mind off her troubles.

"Like what?"

She shrugged. "Let's start with what brought you to Rock Hard."

"I was born here."

"Oh." *Crap.* He chuckled and the sound rumbled through her chest and made her smile.

"You want the scoop on Stone Benson? Here it is. My mom is your basic housewife who's the best cook in the world. My dad is the manager at USA Hardware. My mom wants him to retire, but I don't think that will ever happen." Stone turned onto Gold Avenue, which ran along the river. He tapped his fingers on the steering wheel. "I also have a sister and a brother. I'm the oldest at thirty-one, my sister, Katie, is twenty-six, and Craig is twenty-four."

"Do they live in Rock Hard?"

"Katie does. She had acute leukemia a few years back, but now she's in remission. Boy, was I a basket case, trying to console her while she went through chemo. Funny thing, Katie ended up being the strong one."

"The best ones always are." Though she believed Stone, too, was made of granite. His heart, however, was as pure as gold.

For the next few minutes, he leaned back and drove as if he was deep in thought. That gave her a chance to study his profile. He had a straight nose and a strong chin. What really held her appeal was his smile and his pretty green eyes that had long lashes she'd kill to have.

Not long after leaving town, he turned into the Harmes River National Park instead of continuing on to the National Forest. After a short trip on a gravel drive, he pulled into a parking space alongside several picnic tables.

Stone looked over at her. "It's not fancy, but I figure we'd have some peace and quiet here."

"It's perfect." She was a bit relieved that they weren't going to hike.

He cut the engine and walked around to her side. When he opened her door, he held out his hand, and she placed her palm in his. The warmth of his skin soaked into her. It had been a long time since she'd been touched by a man.

The sun was bright, and the air the right temperature. The sound of the rushing river created a wonderful serenity. He extracted two coolers from the back, and when she held out her hand to help him, he shook his head.

"Today, I want you to think of nothing but the beauty that surrounds you."

She smiled. That would include him. When he found a clean table, she opened her case and handed him his beer.

His eyes sparkled. "You are too sweet."

Sweet wasn't the best description, but it would do. *Why are you thinking of this as a date? You want him to help Chris.*

That isn't all.

As soon as he began to take out the contents in his container, her cell rang.

"Let it go to voicemail," he said. "You need to eat."

"It could be the doctor telling me something about Chris."

He nodded and she answered. "Hello?" She stepped away from the table and turned her back to Stone.

"Amber Delacroix?" The voice sounded ominous, and her heart jumped to the throat.

"Yes?"

"This is Dr. Almaguire. I'm very sorry to inform you that your brother has taken a turn for the worse."

Chapter Four

"Amber, what's wrong?" Stone slipped the phone from her fingers, set her cell on the table, and then clasped her shoulders in a gentle embrace.

Oh, my God. She'd said that standard phrase to too many families. She knew what it really meant, and her heart refused to stop banging against her chest.

"He's dead." Tears leaked out of her eyes, but there were no sobs—the shock prevented it.

"Who's dead?"

She slowly looked up at Stone. Compassion and tenderness filled his face. "Chris is dead."

He shook his head. "No one would have called with that message. Tell me what was said."

"It was Dr. Almaguire. He told me Chris had taken a turn for the worse."

He led her back to the bench and made her sit down. That was good because her legs were too wobbly to keep her standing for much longer.

Stone squatted in front of her and picked up her hands. His warmth helped. "Amber. Listen to me. Taking a turn for the worse doesn't necessarily mean he's dead. There could have been a blood clot lodged somewhere."

"Maybe." She wanted to believe it could be true, but in her

heart she knew the truth.

Stone stood and shoved the food back into the containers. "We need to get to the hospital."

The pain in his voice shook her out of her fogged world. "Yes." She was sorry he'd gone to the trouble of a picnic, but Chris had to come first.

"While I drive to the hospital, I want you to eat something." He kept out a sandwich container and set it aside.

As if time had slowed, he'd gathered what he'd brought and led her to his truck. After he handed over her lunch and made sure she'd snapped her seatbelt, he stowed their picnic gear. Seconds later, they were on the road to Rock Hard.

"Eat," Stone coaxed.

She couldn't for fear she'd throw it up. A horrible thought struck. "Do you think Chris begged someone to take his life?" Doctor assisted suicide was legal in Montana.

He looked over at her, his expression hard. "Let's not be premature. We need to find out the details first."

She choked back her grief.

Stone's hand reached out and grabbed hers. "It'll be okay. We'll get through this."

The word "we" rang in her head. Having someone by her side was more than she expected, but right now she'd willingly accept any solace.

Before she knew it, they'd arrived at the hospital. Had Stone not wrapped an arm around her waist and walked her up the steps to the hospital entrance, she wasn't sure if she would have made it.

As if by magic, Stone and she were suddenly standing in front of Dr. Almaguire. She couldn't recall the elevator ride up to Chris's floor or walking to his office.

Almaguire placed a hand on her shoulder. "Amber, I'm very sorry, but Chris stopped breathing a while ago. We did resuscitate him, but I fear it was too late."

Her chest seemed to crush her and when she opened her eyes, she was in a chair in a private office with Stone sitting across from her, her hands firmly held in his.

"Welcome back."

"What happened?" She prayed all of this had been a dream.

"You passed out."

Dr. Almaguire handed her a cup of water. "Drink this."

Stone let go and moved his chair next to hers. She wasn't sure if the doctor had laced it with a sedative, but she trusted him and sipped the drink until it was gone. "Why did Chris stop breathing? He was so healthy, other than his broken body." Bile rose to her throat and her gut twisted.

"I'm not really sure of the details yet. I do know that Nancy—she was Chris's nurse—had checked on him at eleven, and he was fine then."

"That's when Jamie and I were there."

Almaguire's lips pressed together. "When Nancy returned at one fifteen, he wasn't breathing. She had no idea how long his heart hadn't been beating, so she immediately called a code and intubated him. He's in ICU now."

She stilled, her mind spinning fast. "I don't remember, but wasn't he hooked up to a heart monitor?"

"Not after we took him off the ventilator."

Of course. She wasn't thinking clearly. "I stopped in a little after one and he was asleep."

Stone leaned close. "Are you sure he was asleep?"

Amber bit her bottom lip. "I think so. I didn't go into the room, so I can't swear if his chest was rising and falling." She tried to do the math. "I probably got there five minutes after one, and if Nancy arrived ten minutes later, Chris couldn't have been dead for long. He might not have much brain damage." She didn't really believe that. Even a few minutes would harm the brain stem.

"Let's not get our hopes up, shall we?" the doctor said.

"While we're not ready to pronounce him dead yet, I have to tell you he was unresponsive when we applied a noxious stimulus, and he had no pupil or corneal reflexes."

"Oh, no."

"I'm sorry. We'll remove the endotracheal tube later, and if he doesn't cough when we're suctioning, we'll check his PCO2 levels, but at that point, I'm guessing it won't be long before we'll have to pronounce him dead." His gaze lowered, as did his voice. "I'm so sorry, Amber."

She forced the medical part of her training to take over. "Why did he die?" Before the doctor even opened his mouth to respond, she wept and had to clamp a hand over her mouth to contain her anguished cries. *Damn.* Stone wrapped a comforting arm around her shoulder.

"I promise you we'll do everything we can to find out what happened," Dr. Almaguire said.

She wasn't sure it really mattered any more. If Chris was dead, nothing could reverse that fact now. *Chris. Chris.* One of his best qualities was his generosity. "My brother is an organ donor."

"We can talk about that later when we learn if his organs are viable. If not, he can be a tissue donor. I'd like to speak with your parents about that."

Her chest caved. Her mother would act strong, but deep inside, her mom did care—or at least Amber wanted to believe she did. "I'll give you her number, but she's hard to get ahold of." She told him what her mom did for a living. "My father hasn't been in the picture for years."

Once more, his gaze lowered. "I'll call her myself."

That would relieve a big burden off her shoulders. "May I see him?" She didn't know how those words erupted, but she needed closure.

"I'll take you to him," the doctor said.

Stone stood and helped her up. "I'm coming, too."

He was so kind. "You don't have to."

"Amber." From the stern look he shot her, he wasn't going to take no for an answer.

They followed the doctor out of his office. Stone leaned closer. "When I was in the service, my best friend, Heath Drandle and I were inseparable. We told things to each other we'd never dared tell anyone else. Then one day, while we were on patrol, Heath heard a noise and said he wanted to check it out."

Amber couldn't tell if he was telling this story to take her thoughts off Chris, or if he needed to rid his mind of his own bad memory. Regardless, she wanted to hear what he had to say. "It was bad, I take it?"

"Yes. I needed to finish packing the gear, so I told him I'd catch up in a second." Stone ran a hand down his face and his cheeks sagged. "Moments before I met up with him, Heath stepped on a land mind."

Amber gasped. "I'm so sorry."

He nodded. "When I got there, most of both legs were blown off. He was in shock and told me not to get help—that he wanted to die."

That sounded so much like Chris. "You couldn't let him, I bet."

"No, but the problem was I was helpless to do anything. I had no training. All I could do was hold him and tell him everything would be okay." Stone shook his head. "He died in my arms just as the medic ran up to us."

Now it was her turn to provide the comfort. She reached out, clasped his hand, and squeezed his palm. "Thank you for telling me."

He inhaled deeply. "What happened next, really changed me. After the medic shook his head, the man stayed with me and let me talk on and on about what a great guy Heath was." He looked over at her. "I knew then how important it was to have someone with you during those really hard times."

So this was his way of paying back. She said nothing. Words weren't needed. Dr. Almaguire opened the door to Chris's room, and as soon as she saw he was intubated, she froze for a second. Then Stone placed a hand on her back and pressed her forward.

She walked toward her brother. "Chris?"

She felt stupid calling his name, but she had to be sure he was really gone. There was the tiniest of hope that he would respond to her voice.

"If you need me," the doctor said, "I'll be in my office."

Before she could turn around to thank him, the door closed and she was alone with Chris and Stone. Amber edged near, willing to see her brother move. Though it was dumb, she shook his arm. "Chris? Can you hear me?" Her voice cracked.

Stone wrapped his arms around her from behind. "Don't do this to yourself, baby."

She shook her head as the tears streamed down her face. "Is he really gone?"

Stone let go of her, stepped to the side, and lifted her brother's eyelid. Even she could see that his pupil didn't register the change in light. Stone let go and stepped back.

"Oh, Chris. I'm so sorry." She hiccupped.

Stone gathered her in his arms and held her tight. "Go ahead and cry. Let it all out."

She didn't know why his words helped, but she buried her face against his flannel shirt. The material smelled fresh like her grandma had put it through the wash with her lemon-scented detergent. She fisted the material and cried. He rubbed her back using soft circular motions. Amber never let anyone see her breakdown, but with Stone, she sensed he understood.

She had no idea how long she was in his arms, but when she looked up, he bent his head close and all she could focus on was the tenderness in his eyes.

He straightened. "Come on, Amber. We both need to eat."

He must have noticed she hadn't eaten more than a bite of the sandwich he given her. "I'm sorry I fell apart."

He lifted her chin. "If you hadn't, I'd have been worried about you. It's healthier to grieve."

His sobering words helped her gain some control. Then why didn't she feel any better?

She probably should call her mom, but what if her mother hadn't taken Dr. Almaguire's call yet? The discussion would be difficult and one of denial.

Be honest. You don't want to hear your mom's response. When Amber did finally speak with her, she would ask her to break the news to Thomas.

"Come on. Take one last look at Chris and say goodbye."

He turned her around, and the sight of her brother tightened her throat. Her bottom lip trembled. As if a heavy blanket fell over her and caused her to suck in much-needed air, she spun around and quickly exited the room, plastering her back against the wall for support. She closed her eyes and tried to calm her ragged breaths.

When she finally had the courage to open them, Stone was there. He clasped her hand and led her to the elevator. She honestly didn't care where they went or what they did. Chris was dead, and her life had changed forever.

Thankfully, Stone didn't give her any platitudes about how much better off Chris was now, or that she no longer had to worry about taking care of him. Instead, he walked by her side and was there to help her when she needed him. He didn't bring her to the hospital cafeteria as she expected, but rather guided her outside.

As if she was on autopilot, she climbed into his truck. He cut down Gold Avenue to Second Street. In less than ten minutes, they arrived in town. Since it wasn't yet three, there were plenty of places in front of the Valley Café.

"You okay with this?" Stone's fingers hovered over the keys

as if he'd pull back out if she wanted to eat someplace else.

"This is fine." She didn't care where they ate.

This time she waited for him to open her door. When he did, she welcomed his strong grip as she stepped to the pavement. The fresh air filled her lungs, helping to blot out the despair.

They went inside the cozy café where only a few tables were taken.

"Hey, Stone," an older woman said from behind the counter.

"Hi, beautiful." He looked at Amber. "That's Bea. She's the owner."

Amber caught him wink at the lady. "You come here a lot I take it?"

"Sure do." His grin stirred something deep inside her.

He planted his hand on her waist and led her to a booth on the side. Once seated, Bea came over. "What can I get you two?"

"I'll have a sweet tea," Amber said.

Stone smiled. "I'll have a coffee, darlin', but be sure to add a double dose of sugar for me, will ya?"

"You're already sweet enough, good looking, but I'll make sure it's to your liking." This time it was Bea who winked before waddling back to the counter.

Stone turned his attention back to Amber. "I know this might be bad timing on my part, and a little premature, but would you like me to help you with the funeral arrangements? Or will your mom come down and help?"

Funeral? She blew out a breath. "I haven't had time to even think about that, but Chris would have wanted to be cremated." Everyone in the family had the same opinion.

"There still should be a service."

She nodded. "I think Chris would have liked that."

He shook his head. "Sorry. That was totally unsympathetic of me to bring that up."

"No. I'm glad you asked. I'm not thinking straight."

"You're doing great, but how about we talk about something

else." He sat back and laced his fingers behind his head, looking totally relaxed. "So tell me about your hobbies."

"My hobbies?" That actually caused a tiny bubble of laughter to emerge.

"Yes, hobbies."

Talking about something else would be refreshing. "Mmm." She had to think. "For the first few months after I arrived, I studied all the time. I had planned on going back to school for my masters, but then the job took over my life."

She almost didn't want to fully analyze what her life was like for fear she'd conclude she'd become too much like her mom. "Sad to say, I have about four girlfriends who I meet with on Thursday nights for drinks. Other than that, I don't do much." She unwrapped the silverware from the paper holder. "Unless quilting counts."

"It sure as hell does count. My Auntie Carol loved quilting bedspreads, place mats, and even pillowcases. Her whole house was filled with her craft stuff. As a kid I loved to visit her." His smile looked like it came from deep inside. "I always felt like I was at a country fair when I was visiting her." He lowered his arms and looked as if the mere mention of her name brought peace. "There's something warm and good about the love and attention to detail that goes into making a quilt."

She couldn't help but stare at him. "Are you sure you're real?"

He stilled. "What do you mean?" He looked around. "You think liking quilts isn't manly?"

Now he was yanking her chain. Stone Benson was all man. "Sure it is."

"Did I fail to mention my Auntie died a week after I turned eleven?"

"I'm sorry. She sounded like a wonderful woman."

"She was."

"What I meant about questioning if you were real was that

I'm not used to having a man come to my rescue. On top of that, you like quilts."

He delivered a fake scowl. "Just so you don't get the wrong idea, I'm like every other fireman. I like to party with the boys from the station and do my job the best I can." He held up a finger. "But you're crazy if you think you don't inspire a man to be his best around you."

She inspired him? His words almost made her uncomfortable. She didn't have much money, so there was nothing he could want from her. Amber leaned back in her seat. "You don't even really know me." That sounded like she was fishing for a compliment. Hell. Maybe she was.

Stone cocked a brow. "I don't know you? I've spent years around nurses and doctors, and I can tell which ones care and which ones only do the job for the money."

"I can usually tell the difference, too."

He leaned forward and placed his elbows on the table. "I'll give you my take on who Amber Delacroix is as a person."

She was surprised he'd taken the time to notice she was someone other than a grief-stricken woman. "Tell me."

"I can see you yearn for parental acceptance and considered yourself Chris's surrogate mother."

His words took her breath away. Was she that obvious? "Being Chris's older sister, I believe I understood him better than my mom did."

"You see? I'm right."

"You can't know someone in only a few days." Though she believed she knew Stone. He wasn't complicated. When he'd been with her, he'd always been good. There didn't seem to be any hidden agenda.

Bea came by and placed the drinks on the table. "Have you two decided or have you been too busy feeling each other out?"

Amber sucked in air. Did Bea think she was flirting? She was about to tell the woman her brother had just passed away, when

Stone nudged her foot.

"Give us a few minutes, Bea."

"Sure thing, cowboy."

The woman left and went over to another table. "She means well. Bea's been trying to fix me up for years. So far she's failed."

Amber had been so consumed with her brother's situation she hadn't taken the time to truly study Stone beyond how he'd acted with her. Seeing him flirt with the elderly woman, Bea, endeared him to her more.

Whoa. Now wasn't the time to consider dating, but if she were looking, he'd be the perfect man for her.

Chapter Five

Detective Cade Carter's boss, Dan Hartwick, tossed a folder on his desk.

Cade looked up. "What's this?"

"Another case."

He was juggling three of them already, but the one that still haunted him was Emma Luther's. "I already have my hands full. Give it to Trent Lawson." Trent had just closed out the burglary case he'd been working on for the last two weeks.

"Take a look at it." Dan's usually controlled expression was suddenly filled with concern. But there was something more. Excitement maybe?

Curious, Cade pulled the file toward him, and when he opened it and spotted the name, Delacroix, his gut churned. He scanned the comments. "They ruled Chris Delacroix's death a homicide?"

"The toxicology screen came back this morning. There was an excessive amount of Ativan in his system."

"Shit. That was the same drug Emma Luther had in her system when she died. I'm guessing his doctor hadn't prescribed that drug to him?" From what Stone had told him, Chris was quite angry and depressed, not anxious, which was the reason to prescribe the drug.

"No. Besides, the dosage was significantly more than what

would normally be given to a patient."

"Would that amount be enough to kill him?"

"It might, though Dr. Almaguire suspects succinylcholine. It's a—"

"Neuromuscular blocker. Stone uses it on rare occasions to sedate a victim and then has to intubate them." *Shit.* He couldn't imagine what it would be like to die by paralysis. With the blocker, the kid wouldn't be able to breathe.

He glanced at the report. "It doesn't say the drug was in his system."

"According to Almaguire, the blocker dissipates quickly, making it basically undetectable."

"Crap. Had the person not used Ativan first, he would have gotten away with murder—literally."

Dan's mouth twisted. "Looks like we might have an angel of mercy killer on our hands."

His thoughts shot to Amber. Was she so kind that she'd kill? His chest constricted. He hoped like hell she was innocent. Stone seemed quite taken by her, and Cade knew why. When he'd previously interviewed her, there was something about her that made a man want to get to know her better.

He scoured the report again and spotted Chris's nurse's name and was relieved it wasn't Amber's. Reason intruded. The hospital never would have assigned her to treat her own brother, but that didn't mean she didn't have access to Ativan. She'd admitted to giving the drug to Emma Luther.

He pushed back his chair. "I'm on it." If it killed him, he'd find the bastard who did this to Chris. No one had the right to say when a person should die. Not even a sister.

"From your reaction, I take it you think the Emma Luther case and this one are connected?"

"My gut tells me they are."

"Let me know what you find." Dan nodded and left.

Although Cade often worked with Ethan Harper, he wanted

to do a few inquiries on his own. He truly didn't like that Amber Delacroix's name had come up again—first with Emma and now with her brother. He didn't want Amber to be involved, but if the facts pointed to her then he'd have to bring her in. He refused to let his emotions blind him.

Cade hopped into his SUV and headed to the hospital. He probably should have first called Sandra Carr, the medical examiner, who did the autopsy, but if she wasn't available, he'd speak with the possible suspects, starting with Nancy Waldron, Chris's nurse. She'd been the one to find him not breathing and had resuscitated him. Cade wouldn't rule out the idea she'd brought him back in order to throw suspicion off herself. Looking at the timeline, she'd come in just quick enough to make it look like she wasn't involved.

When Cade entered the hospital, the girl at the reception desk smiled. She was Tanner Rand's little sister. Rock Hard might have close to fifty thousand residents, but he knew most of those who'd been here a while. Growing up in the town gave him that edge.

"Hey, Chelsea."

"Cade." She drew in her bottom lip and looked up through mascara-caked lashes. "You here for a case?"

If not a case, it would mean he was either sick or visiting someone, and he never was ill. "A case. Is Dr. Sandra Carr in?" He squared his shoulders to appear more authoritative, but that didn't seem to affect Chelsea at all.

She smiled. Poor girl always had a crush on him, but he had rules. Never date a twenty-one year old or a fellow detective's sister. Cade didn't need that kind of drama in his life.

She pressed a button to dial the morgue. "Hey, Dr. Carr. Detective Cade Carter is here to see you. Are you free?" She tapped a bright pink nail on the desk then smiled and hung up. "She is. Do you know where the morgue is? Or would you like an escort?"

That made him chuckle. "I've been there before."

Not wanting to linger, Cade spun on his heels and headed to the hospital basement. He liked Sandra Carr. She might be young for a medical examiner, but she was first rate. He stepped into the elevator. No surprise, he was the only one who wanted to visit the bowels of the building.

The disinfectant failed to mask the stench of death, but he didn't cover his nose. He was used to the smell. He approached one of the autopsy rooms and looked in. Although the lights were on, the place stood empty. At the next room, he spotted Dr. Carr and knocked.

She looked up, pulled off her face guard, and came toward him. Before she opened the door, she discarded her gloves and paper smock. He stepped back to let her exit.

"Well, well. Nice to see you again, detective." Sandra seemed to enjoy the break.

"The pleasure is all mine, though I'm here on official business."

"I assumed." He caught the sly smile. "Let's speak in my office."

He followed her. He could have sworn there was an extra sway in her hips just for him. Was it his imagination or was every woman trying to distract him today? Maybe it was because his mind was on one particular woman.

Fuck if he knew.

Sandra slid onto a cushioned seat behind a scarred mahogany desk that looked older than she was. "Have a seat," she said, nodding to the wooden spindled chair that angled toward her desk.

He didn't want to take up much of her time. "I'm here about Chris Delacroix. What can you tell me about his death?"

"Not much more than what was in the report."

"I didn't see a time of death. If his nurse resuscitated him around 1:15 P.M., could you tell how long he hadn't been breathing?" It was times like this he wished he'd been better versed in medicine.

"That's hard to pinpoint. He was almost brain dead when the nurse came in. From the cross section of the brain stem, I might put his time of death ten to thirteen minutes before that."

Stone had told him he'd picked up Amber in front of the hospital around 1:08 P.M. "Could you be off by five minutes?" Maybe the murderer came in before Amber arrived.

"Yes."

He asked her about the Ativan dosage, and she confirmed the amount as excessive but not deadly.

"The killer must have injected something lethal afterward—something that dissipated quickly so as not to be detectable," she said.

"Such as?" He wanted her to make the diagnosis.

Sandra Carr pressed her lips together then drew in her bottom lip. "My first guess would be succinylcholine. It's a neuromuscular blocker."

"Thank you." He placed his card on her desk. "If anything else comes to mind, call me."

His next stop was to speak with the pharmaceutical technician to see who'd checked out the drugs or determine how someone could gotten a hold of the drug without signing them out.

Even after more than a week, the pain from Chris's death hadn't diminished. Dr. Almaguire called the day before and said he'd ordered an autopsy because her brother's death had been suspicious. While the doctor had access to the results, when she'd asked him for the details, he said he'd handed everything over to the police. Which meant she was out of the loop. The cops would never release any information until after the killer was found.

The whole concept of someone wanting Chris dead boggled her mind. Who would want to kill a crippled man? Her thoughts shot to Emma Luther, and Amber's body trembled. Someone had wanted the girl dead, too. Right now, she didn't have the energy to think about who would want her brother dead or why.

Rumors had run wild in the oncology department about an angel of mercy, but the administration had ordered the staff to keep their comments to themselves. If the mercy killing theory ever leaked to the press, there would be widespread panic, and the hospital might be forced to close.

Amber made a promise to herself that as soon as she made her peace with Chris today, she'd find out the truth. His funeral was at four o'clock in the afternoon, and she worried about keeping her emotions in check during the service. Crying in front of her mom would make her look weak, and if there was one thing her mother hated, it was someone without a backbone.

Ben, a friend of the family, was giving the eulogy. Sometimes Ben's social skills weren't the best so Jamie promised she'd help him with what to say. If Amber honestly thought she could have kept it together, she would have spoken.

Jamie had told her right before Amber moved to Rock Hard, Ben's mom had died of Lou Gehrig's disease, a nerve disorder that attacked a person's muscles. Amber had witnessed the effects of the fatal disease and couldn't imagine a worse way to die. Jamie said Ben grieved for months afterward, and she feared when he went back to the funeral home he might not hold up well. Ben assured them that wouldn't happen, and Amber hoped he was right.

Mom and Thomas were flying in a little before two o'clock and should arrive shortly. Amber had offered to pick them up at the airport, but her mom had insisted on renting a car. They were only staying the day then flying out later that night. To Amber, a car rental made little sense, but that was her mom.

There wouldn't even be time for the three of them to have dinner together, though listening to Mom say how careless Chris had been for a whole meal would have turned Amber's stomach and caused her to say something she might later regret. While her mother claimed she was looking forward to seeing Amber again, her actions said something very different.

A knock sounded on her door, and she jumped. With a shaky hand, she opened up.

"Amber," her mother said.

"Mom, Thomas. Come in."

They weren't an affectionate family, so there were no grief-ridden exchanges, which suited her fine. Both of them walked in and looked around rather than focusing on her and how she was holding up.

"Come sit down. I'll make some coffee." Amber had caved and bought coffee from Starbucks. Her mom was very picky about what she drank.

"No, thank you," her mom said. "I'd like to wash up if you don't mind."

"Sure. The bathroom's the first door on the left." Given she lived in a two-bedroom apartment, her mom would have no problem locating the washroom.

She stepped up to Thomas and gave him a light hug. At least he returned the gesture.

"How are you holding up?" he asked.

"As good as can be expected. How's Mom doing?" She felt obligated to ask.

He cocked a brow. "Her usual self. I know I was deluding myself, but I really thought she'd at least act sad when she learned her youngest son had been murdered, but she went on as if nothing happened." His lips thinned, and he glanced to the ceiling as if he was seeing the real Margaret Delacroix for the first time.

"Maybe that's the way she copes." Amber didn't really believe that, but she didn't want to make this harder on Thomas.

He shook his head. "She's just cold."

Never once had Thomas expressed any kind of dissatisfaction with their mom's behavior, most likely because she fawned over him. "I'm surprised you see that."

"You'd be surprised what I notice." He glanced down the hallway before walking the short distance to the sofa and sitting. "Tell me what you know about Chris's murder."

She'd already explained what happened, but perhaps he needed to hear it a second time for closure.

"When I spoke again with Dr. Almaguire, he said the toxicology screens showed Chris had been murdered and that the police were investigating."

"What kind of drug was in his system?"

"He wouldn't give any details because it's an investigation."

"I know you. You'll find out."

Because she always had the patient's best interest at heart, she did have a tendency to bug people until they told her what she wanted to know. "I plan to."

Their mom returned looking a little more put together. "I'd like to go to the funeral home now."

The service wasn't for another hour, but maybe she wanted time to be with Chris. "Sure." Once she gathered her purse and coat, she ushered them out.

"We'll follow you," her mom said.

Amber wanted to suggest they drive the three miles together, to be a family once more, but now wasn't the time to complain. "No problem."

When they entered town, the traffic was minimal, allowing her brother to remain close behind her. Fortunately, the funeral home lot was almost empty as well. Amber parked near to the entrance, rushed out of her car, and strode over to their rental.

Thomas helped his mom out of the vehicle and then walked next to her down the tree-lined path to the funeral home. Amber followed behind, not wanting to be near her mom right now. She wasn't sure she could remain civil.

Inside, one person stood near the front of the room facing the open casket—Stone. Relief washed through her.

Her pulse sped up.

He must have heard the clickety-clack of her mother's heels because he turned around.

Her mother looked over her shoulder. "Who is that man, darling?"

"That's Stone Benson. He was the paramedic who found Chris."

Amber expected her mom to make some comment, but she dabbed at her eyes instead and said nothing. Amber softened at her mom's show of grief.

She moved in front of them both and led the way down the aisle. She stepped into the front row. Thomas followed, and then came her mom. Stone slipped into her row of chairs and stood next to her.

She leaned over and looked up at him. "Thank you for coming."

"You're welcome."

Amber really didn't want to see Chris in his coffin, but if her mom and Thomas went up, so would she. For ten minutes, both her relatives stared ahead as if they were trying to come to grips with Chris's death. Then, with bowed heads, both walked up to the casket.

Amber stayed behind for a moment as her mother grabbed a handkerchief and dabbed her eyes again. Thomas definitely seemed affected by his brother's death. His shoulders would shake and he'd bow his head.

When they turned to each other and hugged, a pang of what she could only describe as longing filled her. Growing up, she ached for that kind of embrace from her mom.

A second later, Stone's warm hand clasped hers. When she

looked up, he was facing forward, acting as if comforting her was the most natural thing to do. As Thomas and her mother walked back down the aisle, Stone squeezed her hand once before letting go.

"Ready?" he asked.

He must have recognized how hard this was for her. "Yes."

Together, they trudged up to the coffin. When she saw Chris looking so young and at peace, she almost smiled. Gone was his usual angry expression. She wasn't ready to admit he was happier not having to face life paralyzed, but maybe someday she would.

After she said her goodbye to Chris, more people entered, and the service began shortly thereafter. During the eulogy, Ben held it together beautifully, and she doubted there was a dry eye in the church. She wished her mind hadn't wandered as often as it had, but her heart was too heavy to stay focused.

When the service ended, her mom squeezed her shoulder and said she and Thomas had to be on their way.

"You're not going to hang around a bit and speak with Chris's friends?"

"I heard them all say nice things about my son. That was good enough for me. Maybe I'll come back under better circumstances. Seeing Chris like that has shaken me to the core."

Amber searched her mom's face for deceit, but she detected only sincerity. "You do that." Even though the words sounded nice, there wasn't much her mom could say or do to erase Amber's years of bitterness.

As soon as her mom and brother left, Jamie and Ben rushed up and hugged her.

"How are you holding up, Amber?" Ben asked.

"As good as can be expected. Thank you for those kind words. You were wonderful."

He nodded. "I needed to have closure, too."

Jamie grabbed her hand. "You know we're both here for you."

"I know."

When her supervisor, Tammy, walked up, Jamie and Ben hugged her one last time and left. Amber was totally blown away that almost the entire oncology staff had shown up, as well as some of her former patients. The support brought a ray of hope.

Throughout the rest of the gathering, Stone never left her side. There were times when Chris's friends actually laughed about some of his antics. She'd be forever thankful that Chris had led a full life.

Everyone left within a half hour after the service ended.

"It's close to dinner time," Stone said. "Let me take you out to eat. I'm betting you don't feel like cooking."

Was he always this good to the relatives of those who'd passed? Or had they really made a connection?

Stop obsessing.

"I'd like that."

As he led her out of the funeral home, the last person she wanted to see was standing there, his arms crossed and his stance wide.

Oh, my God. He thinks I did it. He thinks I killed Chris.

Chapter Six

Stone wrapped an arm around her waist and escorted Amber right up to Detective Cade Carter.

From the tight way Stone held her, he wasn't happy to see the man either.

"Cade," Stone said. "What are you doing here?" His usually calm demeanor turned hostile.

That was the question she wanted to ask. The next one was how did Stone know the detective? The answer came quickly. Stone grew up here. Maybe Cade had, too.

Cade shifted his gaze to her and her stomach tumbled. "I'm very sorry, Ms. Delacroix, but I need to bring you in for questioning."

Her heart pounded. That was totally ridiculous. "Why? You can't think I had anything to do with my brother's death, do you?" Or was he here because of Emma Luther?

"Please come with me." He held out his hand.

"Don't you have any decency? I just buried my brother!" She failed to keep her voice down. From the lack of sleep, the stress of having to cope with Chris's death, and dealing with her mom, she was exhausted and didn't have an ounce of compassion or patience left in her body.

The detective lowered his arm and moved his feet closer together. At least he looked a bit less threatening. "I'm aware of that, and I'm very sorry, but I've already waited two days to allow you time to grieve."

Two days? Is that all it took?

Stone moved between her and Detective Carter. "What the fuck are you doing, Cade? Give her some space."

"I'm doing my job."

They both leaned toward each other as if they were about to fight. A brawl was the last thing she needed.

As if a huge needle had flown down from the sky and pricked her, her energy deflated. "Stone. It's okay. I'll go with the detective. I'm sure there's some misunderstanding."

"Ma'am." Carter held out his hand again as if he was insisting he escort her. She liked it better when he'd called her Ms. Delacroix.

Stone stretched an arm in front of her to either prevent her from moving or to stop the detective from nabbing her. "I'll drive her to the station."

She didn't want to leave her car here. "I can drive myself."

"No," the detective and Stone said in unison.

Detective Carter frowned. "I need to escort you."

"I'll take her," Stone said.

She grabbed the hem of her short jacket and crunched it. "Am I under arrest?" Her tongue stuck to the roof of her mouth and fear radiated through her.

"No." It was as if Detective Carter didn't want to admit he had nothing on her.

"Then why can't I drive?" Her vision slightly blurred and the coffee she'd sipped crawled up her throat.

The detective ignored her and lasered Stone with a stare. "Don't take any detours."

"You think I would?"

"Of late, I don't know what you'd do."

Stone stepped within inches of the detective's face. "Sometimes you can be a fucking ass."

"It makes me good at my job. Bring her. Now."

As soon as the detective strode back to his car, Stone twisted her toward him. "I'm really sorry. Cade gets that way sometimes."

Confusion descended. "What do you mean? How well do you know him?"

"I'll fill you in on the way to the station."

After he helped her in, he jogged to his side, jumped into the truck, and started the engine. She would have liked to have driven, but in truth, being with Stone was comforting. He always seemed to be there when she needed him most.

And yet something didn't seem right. "What was all that macho shit between you and the detective?" Stone might be a fireman, but butting heads with the law didn't seem smart even if he was defending her.

He glanced over at her. "I guess I forgot to mention Cade and I live together."

Sludge filled her veins. "You're roommates?"

All sorts of terrible thoughts raced through her mind. She was quite aware the detective believed she had a hand in Emma Luther's death. While preposterous, she could see his point of view. She had administered one milligram of Ativan to Emma shortly before the killer gave her a lot more. It hadn't helped that the second person had used her code to sign out the drugs. What tormented her was she'd been in such a hurry, it was possible she hadn't signed out. Whoever came in after her could have pretended to be her. *Christ.*

He winced. "Yes. I should have told you sooner, but I was so focused on you that I forgot to mention him."

She studied her hands. "You're sure your sweet roomie didn't ask you to cozy up to me so you could find out whether I'd murdered Emma Luther?"

Stone's jaw tensed and he slammed on his brakes. He skidded to the parking lot exit and faced her. "You really think that?

That I'm some kind of monster?" His pinched brow and open mouth made her tremble. She'd never seen this side of him before.

His horror-filled words finally registered.

Shit. She'd made a huge mistake. "No, I don't. I'm sorry. I'm not thinking straight. I just don't understand why you would hold something like this back. You had to know that he questioned me in regards to a previous murder." Her brain had stopped working the moment she'd seen Chris's coffin.

He inhaled and studied her. Then sympathy swamped his face. "You're right. I should have told you. Honestly, I was afraid you would think exactly what you're thinking now. Cade and I do talk about our cases. But to put your mind at ease, even though I did know he'd interviewed you about Emma Luther's murder, my decision to meet with you had nothing to do with the case. I liked Chris."

That made sense or else she wanted to see his good side. "Oh." She twisted in her seat, feeling confused but wanting desperately to believe him.

"So we're good?" he asked.

She loved how he could put her slight aside so rapidly. "Yes." Pushing away that terrible misconception, she focused on the reason behind the detective's request. "Do you know why your roommate is dragging me into the station minutes after I said goodbye to my brother?"

"No." Stone headed out of the funeral home lot. "Cade's not the most open person. He's incredibly focused on his job, which means he won't let emotion get in the way of doing what he thinks is right. I know it may not seem like it now, but he's a good man."

She admired people like that, but if he was so good, why did he have to bring her in? She'd done nothing wrong.

A random thought crossed her mind about getting a lawyer. Would she need one? She prayed the answer was no.

The eight-block drive only took minutes. Before she knew it, Stone was escorting her inside. "Cade's desk is this way."

The detective couldn't have beaten them there by more than a minute, but the insensitive man was standing at his desk, looking through a file.

"Cade. We're here," Stone said.

Cade looked drawn and tense, like Dr. Almaguire had when he told Chris he'd never move again. However, she refused to have any sympathy for the man. "Come this way please, Ms. Delacroix."

The way he acted so formal scared her to death. She wanted to tell him to call her Amber, but she held her tongue. Both men flanked her as they escorted her down a dull hallway. The floors might have been highly polished terrazzo, but the walls could use a fresh coat of paint. Cade pushed open a door that said "Interrogation Room 2", and her heart dropped to her stomach.

She halted, refusing to take another step without getting answers. "Tell me what this is really about. I've already answered all of your questions about Emma. I don't know anything more." She refused to believe he thought she'd harmed her own brother.

"This isn't about Emma."

Bile shot into her mouth, and she swallowed hard. "You really think I had something to do with my brother's death?" Her mouth turned dry and her underarms moistened.

"Please step inside." His comment brooked no argument.

As if she was marching to her own death, she eased over to the sterile table and sat, her back ramrod straight. The place smelled of something distasteful—body odor and mold maybe. Her throat closed.

Cade looked over at his roommate. "Mind waiting outside?"

There was a mirror on one wall, probably a two-way, so Stone could watch from there.

Instead, he pulled out the chair next to Amber and sat. "Yes,

I do mind." Stone picked up her hand, and her blood pressure dropped a bit.

Cade bristled. "The only way you're staying is if you keep your mouth shut. One word and you're gone."

Cade had interrogated scores of criminals in his career, but never had he felt as much of a shit as he did now. But facts were facts. Amber Delacroix was his most likely suspect.

"Let me explain how I see this." He switched his gaze between his best friend and the woman Stone clearly cared for. "You are a highly competent oncology nurse. When I spoke with your supervisor, Ms. White, she attested to that fact."

"You did what?" She pulled out of Stone's grasp and fisted her hands. "Why would you go to her?"

He refused to let her accusation make him feel guilty. He waited for her to ask a follow up question, but when she didn't, he wanted to satisfy his curiosity. "Is that a problem?"

Her jaw loosened. "A problem? Why would it be a problem to have a detective ask my boss a question about whether she thought I was capable of a mercy killing?"

"I never said anything about a mercy killing."

She rolled her eyes. "Emma Luther was a vibrant seventeen-year old girl who had inoperable brain cancer. It made my heart ache every time I treated her. It killed me to see her pain grow more intense each day." She leaned forward. "Did I wish she were pain free? Yes. Did I wish the good Lord would take her sooner rather than later? Hell, yes. But, did I give her some huge dose of Ativan? No damn way."

She leaned back in her seat and glared. While he couldn't see her leg bounce, he heard the light whoosh of the material against the seat.

Sometimes this job sucked. Maybe he wanted to solve Emma's murder so much, he willingly grasped at anything. Her parents stopped by everyday begging for news. They kept saying Emma was braver than they all were. Not only was it terribly sad for anyone that young to die, but the young girl been a star athlete with colleges recruiting her. *Fuck*. Was he being too hasty bringing in Amber? No. A month was too long for any family to wait for closure. He was convinced that whoever had put Emma out of her misery had been the same person to kill Chris Delacroix.

He refocused his attention on the woman in front of him. Cade scribbled a note that she'd mentioned Ativan but not the neuromuscular blocker. Neither he nor Dan Hartwick had leaked that information.

"How do you explain your signature for Emma's second dose?" He'd asked her this before, but perhaps in her agitated state, she'd tell him more.

Five pharmaceutical technicians worked at the hospital. The one who gave out the second dosage swore there was no record of Amber having requested the first dosage. Clearly, someone was lying.

"Like I told you. I can't. But if I wanted to give her a dose big enough to kill her, why wouldn't I have signed out the usual small doses several times, instead of asking for a large dosage, which from what you told me, the killer did. Only a surgeon would have asked for that much, not an oncology nurse."

"I don't know, but then I'm not a medical professional or the one accused of murder."

Alarm raced across her face. "Are you accusing me of murder?"

He didn't have any concrete evidence. Everything was circumstantial, which wasn't enough to hold her. "Where were you between 1:00 P.M. and 1:15 P.M. the day your brother died?"

Her respiration increased, and she now looked pissed. "Do I need a lawyer?"

"Do you need one?" He shouldn't have been on autopilot, but the years of being with the scum of the earth had hardened him.

"I do if you plan on arresting me."

"Not yet."

"Cade," Stone said. "Why are you being such a dick?"

"Because I want justice for Emma Luther and Chris Delacroix." Cade shoved back his chair and stood. "Leave."

Cade's cousin had died in a hit and run when she was sixteen. It might not be the same as watching a young girl waste away from brain cancer or seeing a once vibrant man turn helpless, but he'd wanted justice. Tanya's family or his own hadn't healed until the man had been caught.

"Fine." Stone turned and faced Amber. "I'll be right outside." Without looking back, he strode out.

If Cade's boss got wind that he'd let Stone sit at the table with Amber, there would be hell to pay. But Stone was his best friend.

As soon as the door closed, Amber seemed to shrink before his eyes. *Fuck me, but rules were rules.* She inhaled and straightened her back. He admired her fortitude.

"Regarding where I was the afternoon of Chris's death, speak with Becky Andrews. She saw me come in a little after one in the afternoon. I rushed to Chris's room, saw he was asleep, and left. I didn't even enter the room. A minute later, I met with Stone. Becky should remember, because I had a cooler with me that I'd forgotten to leave in the car."

He made another note. "I will."

"Dr. Almaguire told me the timeline, too. Could I have killed Chris? Yes." Her face turned red. "I couldn't personally kill him, but the timing would fit. I never would have harmed him. I loved him too much."

"All the more reason not to want to see him suffer."

She grit her teeth. "You're a shit. No offense."

"I've been called worse."

She stilled. "Oh, my God. Did Chris have Ativan in his system, too?"

The shocked look on her face made him take pause. He saw no reason not to tell her the truth and judge her reaction. "Yes."

"A lot?"

"Yes."

She dropped her face in her hands. Amber admitted to giving one milligram of Ativan to Emma. The rest, she claimed must have come from the killer. Chris wasn't prescribed that drug, so the killer would have given him enough to calm him before possibly injecting him with succinylcholine to make him stop breathing.

She looked up. "What else did he have in his system?"

He wondered when she'd ask. "I'm not at liberty to say."

"Besides having two people I know die, having access to Ativan, and me being in my brother's room minutes before the killer, what physical evidence do you have against me?"

She had guts. He had to hand it to her. "You're free to go." He wasn't willing to show his hand.

Her gaze bounced around the room. "Tell me this, Mr. Detective. Was my signature on the Ativan dose for Chris, too?"

"No, but that doesn't mean you didn't have someone get it for you." He had checked the logs and all vials had been accounted for. How the killer procured the drugs for Chris remained a mystery.

She pushed back her chair and stalked out.

Crap. Now he'd be on Stone's shit list, all because he needed to solve this case. But just because he didn't have proof Amber Delacroix killed two people didn't mean she wasn't guilty.

Do you really believe that? He wasn't ready to answer.

Cade had looked deep into the eyes of many killers and his gut told him she wasn't one. *Shit.* It didn't matter. Cade wasn't going to stop until the killer was brought to justice.

Chapter Seven

Amber felt dirty and degraded. Add in hungry and tired, and she wasn't fit company for anyone. The problem was that as soon as she and Stone walked out of the station, she remembered he'd driven.

Stone slid her hand into his and guided her to his truck. He acted like her father used to when he wanted her to do as he said. She didn't know if she should be pissed that Stone thought she needed the help or be appreciative.

The latter required less effort. Stone had stood up to his roommate for her and insisted being with her during the interrogation. For someone who'd only met her recently, he'd been wonderful.

"In you go," he said, as he guided her onto the seat and once more secured her seatbelt.

She'd been about to swat away his hand, tired of people telling her what to do, but then refrained. It was clear her threshold for politeness had evaporated as soon as she found the detective waiting for her.

Stone climbed into the cab and started the engine. "How about delivery pizza?"

It took her a few seconds to connect the dots. She was hungry and needed to eat. "That sounds good." At least she wouldn't have to put up with restaurant noise. Then the concept of "delivery" finally registered. "Where are we eating it?" Her mind refused to remain on one subject. She kept alternating between the funeral and that terrible man who accused her of killing someone.

"Your house," he said.

She failed to figure out if that was a good or bad idea. They neared the funeral home. "Remember, I need to pick up my car."

"No."

"No?" Why was Stone suddenly being an ass? Okay, a nice ass, but still an ass. It was as if his roommate's attitude had rubbed off on him. *Be fair.* At least he'd kept his voice soft. "Why not?" This time, she didn't sound so challenging.

He glanced at her as he drove past the funeral home. "I don't think you'd get home in one piece. Haven't you noticed that you keep mentally drifting off?"

Her anger deflated. "Yes." *Maybe.* Not really, but the possibility existed. Perhaps after they ate, he'd be willing to drive her back to town.

He took a right on SR25. "How do you—"

He glanced over and smiled. "Know where your house is?"

"Yes."

"It's called a phone book."

Damn. Maybe she wasn't fit to drive. Less than ten minutes later, he turned into her neighborhood. He headed down her street, and she pointed to her duplex. "You'll have to park in front." The place didn't have a garage and she shared the drive with her neighbor who had parked both of his cars there already. Maybe tomorrow, she'd speak with him about what sharing meant.

Stone cut the engine, came to her side, and helped her out. The air had chilled since the funeral and she shivered. Without a word, Stone wrapped an arm around her shoulder. She was so tired that when she found herself at her own front door with

Stone holding out his hand for the key, she barely remembered walking up the porch steps. She opened her purse and fumbled through it. "Damn."

"Come on, tiger, let me look." He lifted her purse from her fingers, quickly located the key, and with one twist opened the door. "It's okay. You've had a hard day." Had he not smiled she might have punched him.

She yearned for her demons to disappear and for someone to erase the emptiness residing in her gut, but to rely on him wasn't right.

Once she stepped into the familiar surroundings, the tension eased a bit. She inhaled. "Do you smell how fruity it is in here?" *Yuck*. It was her mom's cologne. The overpowering scent had lingered. "I'll be right back."

She stalked to the bathroom, picked up the room deodorizer, and returned. She spritzed the hallway and living room using a light touch, not wanting to make things worse. She inhaled and decided it was a lot better.

Without asking, Stone plopped onto the sofa and pulled out his phone. "What kind of pizza do you want?"

She'd made too many decisions today already. "You choose."

He looked as if he was trying to contain a smile. "Oh, no you don't. If I order pepperoni, you'll say I didn't give you a choice and that I was trying to tell you what to eat."

Stone wasn't the macho type—at least not when he was around her. He'd acted like a pit bull with the detective though, and she found it suited him. If the Cade Carter had been here instead, she bet he would have ordered without regards to what she wanted.

"How about veggie?" she suggested.

"Works for me."

While he called the pizza place, she ducked into the kitchen and prepared coffee for Stone and hot tea for herself. She remembered he liked a lot of sugar and located a few packets in the cupboard.

When his hands touched her shoulders, she jumped.

"Easy. I just wanted to see if I can help."

She faced him. "You don't have to be so nice. I'm not used to it."

He cocked a brow. "Does it make you uncomfortable?"

Through her overtired brain, she tried to figure out what it was about him that was a bit unsettling. "I'm not sure."

He stepped back. "Have a lot of people treated you like crap?"

"No." Or did she have nothing to compare it to? Maybe she sucked at picking men, but she refused to be like some women who blamed all men because of a few rotten apples. Hell, maybe it was seeing her mom again that brought back too many bad childhood memories.

The whistle on the teapot blew, and she poured the water into her cup. The coffee finished brewing a minute later, and she fixed his drink.

He took a sip as they walked into the living room. "Perfect."

His comment pleased her. When Stone returned to his seat on the sofa, she sat across from him, wanting to watch him instead of craning her neck.

Even holding her hot tea, she felt awkward. Except for when Stone told her about his friend dying in the war, she knew little about him. But what to ask? "Tell me about your hobbies." She thought it was only fair since she'd shared hers.

With stretched out legs, Stone leaned back and drank his coffee then set it on the table in front of him. "I do work a lot, but when I do get out, I love to ski, ride horses, rock climb, bowl—if you can believe that—and at night, I love to read a good science fiction."

She wouldn't have put that mix together. "You don't devour detective novels?"

His eyes shone. "I think I get enough of the real life stuff from Cade. Plus, I want an escape from my reality, too."

She could understand that. That was why she read romance novels. She loved happily ever afters. He'd commented a while back about how he desired to travel. "What was your last vacation and where did you go?" *Yeesh.* She sounded like a game show host.

He jabbed his tongue in his cheek then blew out a breath. "It was so long ago it's hard to recall. The last time I left town for a few days was when I went to Black Hawk, Colorado."

She wasn't familiar with the place but she liked the sound of the name. "What's there?"

"Casinos. But what I really enjoyed was the side trip to Georgetown where they have a train ride that takes you over a tall gorge. If you're queasy at all about heights, don't go."

She had no problem with being high up. "I bet the view of the mountains would be wonderful. I grew up in Oklahoma City where it's flat." It was one of the things she loved about Rock Hard. The terrain was rugged, varied, raw.

"That part of Colorado is definitely not flat."

She enjoyed hearing about his life and wanted to know more. "Tell me about your job."

He told her about a few of the more intense fires they'd had over the years, along with the more harrowing rescues. A half hour later, Stone was halfway through his story when the doorbell rang. Both of them jumped up. The way he glanced at her forced her to sit back down. He'd want to pay.

As soon as Stone stepped inside, the aroma from the pizza made her mouth water.

He closed her door then waved the box in the air. "You want to eat at the dining room table or in the living room?"

"Table." It would be more intimate, and right now she needed the companionship.

Part of her had died with Chris's death, and too often, bits of reality would sneak in and stab her belly when she least expected it. Then at the oddest times waves of depression, mixed with the sensation of being overwhelmed, would crash down on her. She tried to think of her patients and how they handled their own anxieties but decided maybe she was just weak. Stone seemed to prevent those wicked, cruel sensations from entering her thoughts.

It was ironic. Being there for others was easy. Sucking up her own grief was damned hard.

"…napkins?" Stone asked.

She'd gone off again. Maybe she did need him here. "I'll get them."

Amber's job depended on her staying focused, but her ability to think clearly right now seemed to have evaporated. Once they were seated, they both dove in.

"I really needed this," he said.

"It's the best food I've tasted. Ever." She was pleased she was able to eat.

In no time, the pizza disappeared. Stone stood and picked up the carton. "Let me have your napkin."

"I can do it." He hesitated then nodded as if he could see she was on the verge of tears. Cleaning up gave her a sense of normalcy, but it also tired her out. A cabinet door opened behind her and she spun around. "What are you looking for?"

"Wine. I thought you could use a drink."

Boy could she, though it might put her to sleep. "In the fridge. There's a bottle of red wine already open."

He cocked a brow at her choice of storage location. Seconds later, he escorted her to the sofa and sat next to her. "Here." He handed her a nearly full glass.

On the first fruity sip, her taut muscles began to unbind. As much as she didn't want to think about anything that had happened today, she needed to hear what Stone thought about the interrogation.

"Do you think Cade thinks I'm guilty?" She was pleased her voice hadn't cracked.

He brought the glass to his lips and drank a third of the wine. "Hard to tell. I do know he wants to find the killer so bad he'll keep digging until he does."

"He already dug deep and couldn't find anything on me."

"True. Do you have any idea who might have harmed all those patients?"

She shook her head. "No. Trust me, all during Chris's service, I tried to picture each nurse and doctor, wondering who could put Emma and Chris out of their misery, but I came up empty-handed." She twisted toward him. "Don't get me wrong. We all hate seeing anyone suffer, but we respect life too much not to let the natural order of things rule."

"No one is particularly soft-hearted?"

"That would be half the staff."

He put his near-empty glass on the coffee table. "How about someone who cares for you? Is there anyone who would hate to see you suffer and kill for you?"

That was ridiculous. "And then blame me by signing my name to the drug sign out sheet?" A small laugh escaped.

"I see your point. Let's assume the person didn't think anyone would check."

She couldn't imagine anyone doing something that terrible, even if it was in the name of love. "Sad to say, other than Chris, there was no one who ever loved me enough to do that." Pity slid across his face. She waited a second for him to say the usual platitude about how her mom loved her, but he thankfully kept quiet, so she continued. "As for the hospital employees, I don't believe in dating people I work with. The only person I'm really close to at work is Jamie, and she'd never harm anyone. Especially Chris. She cared for him too much."

"She seemed to."

The conversation made Amber's stomach-churning return.

"Not to sound rude, but I'd like to crawl into bed and read a little." She placed her glass on the coffee table. "I can't thank you enough for being with me today." She would have asked him to drive her to the funeral home to pick up her car, but she wasn't in the right frame of mind to deal with it now. She'd ask her neighbor to give her a lift tomorrow.

"You need your rest. Two traumas in one day are more than anyone should have to bear."

His support helped so much. As she stood, she glanced over at the chair Chris always sat in. He'd picked that one because it squarely faced the television. Never again would she wag a finger at him to remind him to apply to school, or wait up for him on a Saturday night. An involuntary sob escaped, and a tear ran down her cheek.

Stone shot to his feet and pulled her to his chest. "Come here, you."

She didn't reject his offer. When he cradled her in his arms, it felt right. She sniffled then leaned back. "I'm good now." She swiped a finger under her eye.

He rubbed a thumb across her lips and confusion rippled through her.

"You don't have to be in control all the time, you know, tiger."

"I haven't been in control at all lately."

"I know just what you need." Next thing she knew he lifted her in his arms. "Sleep, and lots of it," he said.

She agreed, but having him carry her seemed odd. "I can walk," she said when he reached the hallway.

"No doubt you can, but I want to make your life easier." The hint of a smile relaxed her.

Stone Benson was an amazing man, but if he walked out of her life right now, she'd be even more devastated.

Chapter Eight

Amber was light as a feather. Stone worried about her not eating enough. The best thing would be to tuck her into bed and slip out. Tomorrow he had to be back at work, and that meant a 3:15 A.M. wake-up time. Drake had taken Stone's shift when he'd needed to be with Amber, and now he had to return the favor.

There were two doors on the right side of the hallway. One must be Amber's room and the other Chris's. Stone didn't want to make a mistake and walk into the wrong one, stirring additional grief.

"Which room, baby?"

"The second door." She wiggled in his arms as if she didn't want to be a burden, but from the way she'd wrapped an arm around his neck, she enjoyed being held.

He nudged open the door with his hip. As soon as he stepped in, she reached behind them and flicked on a switch. A delicate pink lamp lit up next to her bed.

He set her on her feet but kept a hand on her back until he was convinced she was steady. He expected her to turn, thank him again, and walk him to the door. Instead, she stared as if confused, looking lost like a small child.

Now what? "Let's get you into some pajamas."

He fully anticipated rebellion on her part, but instead, she stepped to the side as if she'd lost her balance again. Whether it was from the alcohol or exhaustion, he couldn't tell. All he knew was she wasn't fully there. She might have hidden her sleepwear under the pillow, but he walked over to the only dresser in the room and opened the top drawer. Panties and bras. *Wrong one.* The second drawer held T-shirts and shorts. The last one gave him what he was looking for—flannel nightgowns. Given it was summer, they might be too warm.

"What do you wear to bed?"

"Um. A tank and panties."

Shit. He should probably walk out now, but as a paramedic, he'd removed more than his share of clothing from a victim and had always remained professional. He could do that now.

Or so he hoped.

He located a fairly conservative tank top and tossed it on the bed. "Come sit down."

As if on autopilot, she did as he asked. He almost missed the feistiness she'd exhibited with Cade. To be honest, he'd never seen a woman go off on his roommate like that. Had it been under better circumstances, he might have enjoyed it.

Cade was always in control. When Amber had challenged him, his roommate looked startled and a bit guilty. Maybe there was hope for him after all.

Stone knelt, tugged off her shoes, and set them next to the door he assumed was the closet. She wore a black dress under a fitted gray jacket that didn't have any buttons and which came slightly below her breasts. Her makeup was minimal, probably because most had washed off with the tears.

He slipped her jacket from her shoulders, stepped over to a door that turned out to be the closet, and hung it up.

"Go ahead and take off your dress, baby."

As if he didn't exist, she stood and reached behind her to unzip the back but struggled with the zipper tab.

He rushed to her side. "Let me help."

He turned her back to him and unzipped her. Stone was worried. A few minutes ago, she was asking him about his hobbies and where he'd last traveled. Now, she appeared as if she'd gone to some new place. He hoped it was nicer there.

Steeling himself against her allure, he dragged the dress down her shoulders until the material pooled at her ankles.

Don't look.

"Step out of this."

She lifted her foot, moved to the side, and repeated with the other leg. Then she sat back on the bed. "Will you stay with me?"

Her voice came out so thin, his gut twisted. "I don't think that's a good idea." He picked up her dress and hung it next to the jacket. If he stayed, he'd want to hold her, soothe her, and love her. Under the circumstances, that wouldn't be fair to her.

The tank lay beside her. In a quick motion, she unhooked her bra and tossed it on the floor. His cock went rigid.

Leave. Now.

Staying would only cause more problems, but could he abandon her? He glanced down at the gorgeous woman. *Jesus.* He'd have to be made of steel not to be affected. Her breasts were small and high—delicate and tender looking.

Don't be a pervert.

Stone turned to the side instead of facing away from her because he didn't want her to think he was rejecting her. Didn't she know being together after what she'd been through wasn't right?

"Stone?"

Her voice cracked again, and he faced her. She wore her tank top, but her nipples still protruded. "Yes, baby?"

She turned around, pulled down the covers, and slipped in. Relief poured over him. "Can you stay with me for a while?"

She'd been through so much. "Sure." He sat on the side of the bed and brushed an errant hair from her face. "Go to sleep."

"Hold me?"

He was afraid she'd want more, and he couldn't say no. "For a few minutes."

He kicked off his dress shoes, and the relief was instant. Nothing else was coming off though. He stood, tugged down the spread, and crawled in next to her. Her subtle perfume had a hint of roses that filled his nostrils. He could only hope his thick slacks hid his erection. Amber turned on her side, her back to him, and snuggled closer. He worked hard not to let his groan escape.

He'd promised to hold her, and hold her he would. Once he gathered her in his arms, his lips met the top of her head. When every inch of her fit snuggly against him, a cloud of contentment filled him. She wiggled her butt, hopefully just to get comfortable, and his testosterone levels soared.

He closed his eyes and pictured her injured brother. His cock softened by half. Then she twisted around in his arms and faced him. *Not good.* "Amber?" He wouldn't have said anything had her hand not rested on his cock.

"Yes?" She looked up at him. Her eyes were wide and her bottom lip drawn in.

"What are you doing?" He worked to keep his words even.

She fumbled with his buckle and he shot his hand between them to stop her.

"Please, Stone. I need to feel alive. I'm so dead inside."

Christ. The one glass of wine must have gone to his head, because it sounded like she wanted him to make love to her. He wanted nothing more than to oblige, but as stupid as it sounded, he didn't want her to hate him in the morning—or rather hate herself.

✧ ✧ ✧

Amber admitted she was probably being rash asking a man to make love to her, but she not only needed him, she wanted him. Stone had been so nice and comforting, and right now, there was nothing that could help the ache go away faster than feeling him all over her body.

She reached up and kissed him before he had the chance to turn away. The moment their lips made contact, heat seared her, and her body exploded with need. The urge to grab his cock again was strong, but she feared he'd leave if she did.

Wanting more, she reached down, clasped his hand in hers and dragged it up between them. Even though she was the one placing his palm on her breast, her nipple puckered.

"Amber, you'll regret this."

She liked it better when he called her baby. It sounded nicer and more caring. "No, I won't." She wouldn't. She knew better.

His fingers suddenly shot to life, and when he plucked a sensitive nub, all sorts of erotic reactions stimulated her. She wanted more. If she could have slid her hands down his pants and touched his hard dick she would have. Instead, she pressed her palms against his chest and thrilled at his muscular hardness.

His lips captured hers, and this time his tongue teased her mouth open. She couldn't tell if it was her heart banging against her chest or if Stone's also added to the intensity, but she'd never been more alive.

Their tongues met and, like a starving animal, she dove in.

Stone pulled back seconds later. "I can't."

Disappointment collided with shock. Before she could stop him, he dragged back the covers and sat up. He bent down to slip on his shoes.

When she found she could speak again she asked, "You're leaving me?" How could he do that?

He froze then slowly turned around. "I won't lie. I want you—bad—but I have to demand a rain check. The next time will be the right time. I promise."

"Now's the right time." She sounded petulant, but today had sucked, and the only way to made it better would be to have a naked Stone hold her tight.

His face softened, and his beautiful green eyes changed to a lighter color. "You have to trust me on this." He returned to putting on his shoes. In a flash he stood. "I have to be at work by 4:00 A.M. I'll be in touch, but know you can call me anytime if you need me."

She needed him now. Wanting to escort him to the door, she sat up and her head swam. Dizziness swamped her.

He knelt back on the bed and lowered her down. "There you go." He leaned over and kissed her forehead then brushed her lips. "Sleep."

As if he had some supernatural power, he disappeared. Seconds later, the soft click of the front door closing reached her. "Damn you, Stone Benson."

She buried her head in her pillow and let out all of the anxiety, frustration, and fear that had consumed her in the last few days. She pounded the mattress until she tired and fitful sleep consumed her.

Cade sank back in his chair when he spotted Emma Luther's parents come through the station door. His failure at finding their daughter's killer left a bitter taste in his mouth that never seemed to lessen. He stood and held out his hand. Mr. Luther shook his. The mother did not. He had no visitor chairs in front of his desk, so he slid his own to the side and motioned for the mother to sit.

Mrs. Luther took the offer and wove her fingers together. "I heard another person was murdered at the hospital. A young man who'd been paralyzed." She blinked and her chin wobbled.

"Yes."

"Are their deaths connected?" Mr. Luther's voice sounded raw as if he and his wife had spent endless hours talking.

Cade believed so. "I'm afraid I'm not at liberty to discuss the second case either." The parents wanted details, and he couldn't blame them, but rules prevented him from telling them more.

"What can you tell us? Are you still working on Emma's

case?" The father stiffened, acting like he wanted to do battle.

Over the last month, both of Emma's parents had suffered terribly. Whereas Mr. Luther looked gaunt, Mrs. Luther seemed to have ballooned. His aunt had done the same thing when Tanya had been killed.

"I swear to you, I'm working night and day on this case. It's as important to me as it is to you." He knew that wouldn't satisfy them, but it was all he could give them.

Mr. Luther's hands fisted. "Bullshit. And you know it. Emma was our daughter. You never even knew her." His lip curled.

Having a shouting match in the precinct, or anywhere, wouldn't do anyone any good. Cade held up his hands. "You're right. I didn't know Emma, but I have personal reasons for wanting to solve this case. I never meant to imply something else."

"Come on, Diane." Mr. Luther helped his wife up. "We'll be back, detective."

Cade had no doubt they would. As soon as they left, he dragged his chair back to his desk and dropped down more defeated than ever. He really had no idea where to look next. The thought of waiting until another patient died shredded his gut.

The hard strike of boot heels slapping the entryway tile made him look up. Stone. He rarely came to the station. Cade studied his best friend's expression but couldn't tell what he was thinking. Their hours hadn't meshed in the last few days, though in all honesty, he got the sense Stone was avoiding him. After Cade brought Amber in, he'd expected a response, though why Stone hadn't confronted him these past few days was anyone's guess—unless Stone needed time to calm down.

"Cade." His roommate planted his palms on his desk.

Here it comes. "Shouldn't you be at work?" He wasn't ready to talk about Amber yet or that interview fiasco. Cade knew Stone had been her pillar of strength, and from his newfound serious demeanor, he had strong feelings for her.

Stone's eyes widened. "I work the four to four shift four days a week. Haven't you paid attention?" He straightened. "Don't answer that. Ever since that young girl died, you've not been yourself."

"I know." The image of his cousin refused to leave his mind, too. "Emma reminds me of Tanya."

"I'm aware of that, but you can't let that cloud your vision."

"You came here to be my nursemaid?" He cocked a brow. A tiny part of him recognized he just might need the help.

Stone shoved his thumbs into his pockets. A glint of a smile surfaced and Cade's blood pressure lowered. The tension that constantly surrounded him had skyrocketed in the last few weeks.

"What you need is a six-pack of beer and a bunch of women to fuck." Stone didn't bother looking around to see a few heads turn.

"You know where I can find a few?" He was kidding, but it felt good not to have the blanket of hostility hanging between them for a change.

Ever since Emma Luther's murder, his life had been hell. He and Stone shared everything, including women, but of late Stone made sure their contact had been kept to a minimum. He knew what and who precipitated the change between them—Amber Delacroix—though even he could see his actions added to the divide.

Maybe if he got out and forgot about the case for a few hours, the lead that was niggling at him might surface.

"I know of one woman you might like."

Cade bet he was referring to Amber. He couldn't even entertain the idea. She was a suspect.

Even though he'd been distracted, Cade had noticed his roommate had changed. One-night stands had been the norm, but not recently. Cade sensed that ever since Stone had met Amber, he wanted more. Hell, Cade did, too.

Cade leaned back in his chair trying to give off an air of

confidence. "I have to say I like the change in you. What happened? I thought you'd come in to punch me, not offer me some entertainment."

His jaw hardened. "Amber is not entertainment."

"Sorry. I hadn't meant to imply she was."

Stone straightened. "I saw your face in the interrogation room and thought long and hard about it. You really don't think Amber is guilty, do you?"

It was time to be honest. "No." He dropped the façade and shoved a hand through his hair. "But fuck me if I can find another suspect. Amend that. There are about fifty people who are capable and have the ability to put someone out of his misery, but I don't have hard evidence on any of them."

"This might be selfish on my part, but I think you owe Amber an apology."

He chuckled at that comment even though he saw no humor in it. "I don't think Ms. Delacroix would let me get close enough to say I'm sorry. Besides, until I have the murderer in custody, I can't say those words."

"I figured you'd tell me that. So find the bastard."

"Like I'm not trying?"

Stone shrugged. "I thought you should be aware that while you're doing your job, I plan on being there for her."

That wasn't news, but there was an added cockiness he hadn't seen in Stone before. Cade leaned closer. "You didn't—" Asking his roommate if he'd slept with her within earshot of his colleagues wouldn't be cool.

"Not yet, but when the time's right, I will."

Stone had lost his mind. "She just lost her brother." Even if she killed him, which he seriously doubted, she'd still be grieving.

"That's why I walked out last night. Just wanted to let you know you should hurry." With that, he spun on his heels and strode out.

God help him if Cade didn't crack this case soon.

Chapter Nine

Just knowing she'd soon spend time with her friends for their weekly happy hour had kept Amber sane for the last few days. She hadn't made the last two get-togethers, and she'd really missed the camaraderie. All of her friends, as well as Stone, told her having a routine would help her regain a sense of normalcy. So, here she was on her way to the weekly affair.

Not that she believed the grieving was over, but she was beginning to put a few things in perspective. Or at least she wanted to believe she was succeeding. For starters, she was keeping a more careful watch over her terminally ill patients. Any time a doctor came in, or a therapist showed up, she tried to remain nearby. Having someone else die under her care would be too much to bear. She could only hope that Chris was the last victim.

When she wasn't in protection mode, she thought of Stone. Yes, she was embarrassed for having propositioned him, but he'd been willing. In retrospect, he'd also been right. She wasn't ready to be with a man yet. But with each passing day, she'd felt a little more like her old self.

Stone called almost every night, mostly to talk, but they had gone out to dinner twice. Both times he'd brought her home and made some excuse why he shouldn't come in. He said when the time was right, he'd know.

Why was he the only one to decide?

She parked on Second and Peak, a block and a half away from Banner's Bar, where she was meeting her friends. From the number of cars, it looked like it was going to be a busy night.

That's it. Jamie said something about the owners bringing in woman to teach line dancing. Amber hurried inside where the air smelled of beer and peanuts, and the noise and music were loud. She totally loved it.

Jamie waved. "Over here!"

She was with Becky Andrews, the nurse who often manned the desk on the third floor; Zoey Donovan, the hospital's psychologist; and Melissa Williams from gynecology.

"Am I late?" Amber pulled out a seat. She poured herself a glass from the half-empty pitcher of sangria sitting in the middle of the table then waved the container, "I can see I am."

They chatted a bit and then Zoey leaned forward. "I heard you're dating Stone Benson. He's such a catch, girl." She wiggled her brows in an obvious attempt to keep the conversation upbeat.

A quick shot of jealousy filled her. "You've been out with him?" She wouldn't have been surprised if the fiery redhead had.

Zoey dropped her chin and looked up at her. "No, but from your reaction you are rather far gone."

Now she saw through the hospital psychologist's ploy. Zoey was trying to take Amber's mind off the recent tragedy. "Your shrink hat is on backwards. Stone Benson is… a friend." Both Jamie and Becky cleared their throats. "Okay, he might be a bit more than that, but trust me, we haven't slept together."

On that note, she picked up the pitcher and noticed both her glass and the large container were empty. She hadn't even remembered drinking hers. Abby, the waitress, came over with a refill. When had her friends even placed the order? She definitely needed to get her head in the game.

Becky looked up and nodded toward the entrance. "Okay,

now there's someone I could sink my teeth into."

Everyone at the table turned, and Amber's heart nearly stopped.

✧ ✧ ✧

Cade had needed to get away from the precinct. He was supposed to get off work an hour ago, but he went over the two cases one more time, searching for that elusive clue he was positive was there.

As he stepped into Banner's Bar, lots of giggling, along with one big whoop, caught his attention. He spotted the owners, Justin and Brandon, moving some tables to the side. The big banner announcing Jillian Dwaine, the line dance instructor, glared out at him. Her picture looked hot. Usually the sight of something that pretty would have sparked his interest, but not tonight.

As he made his way to the bar, he let his gaze drift to the area where all of the giggling originated. The second he saw Amber Delacroix, a rush of emotions flashed through him—no doubt part was guilt, and some was from the connection he'd felt between them despite the bad circumstances. As much as he didn't want to admit it, he was experiencing some honest to goodness lust, and he hated himself for that weakness.

Her chin lifted and when their eyes met, the distaste radiating from her doused his burgeoning erection. *Thank you, Amber, for that.*

He swiveled onto the stool and waved to Adam, the bartender.

"Long time no see, stranger." Adam pulled the cloth from his shoulder and polished the wet splotch on the bar in front of him. "Where have you been, man? The dart games aren't the same without you."

"You hear about the murders at the hospital?" He wasn't in

the mood for small talk.

Adam's cheer disappeared. "A real shame, though if I were that far gone it might be a blessing in disguise to have someone help me reach the other side faster."

Cade felt the same way, but the law didn't think so. "Anyone else you know have that same opinion?"

His hand stilled. "Oh, fuck. You don't think I had anything to do with those deaths? I haven't stepped foot in the hospital since Brandon had an appendectomy three years ago."

"No, but if anyone comes in bragging about helping someone bite the dust, let me know, will ya?"

"Sure." Adam nodded to the table. "By the way, the pretty brunette over at the big table has been staring at you since you walked in." Adam leaned on his elbows and bent close. "I bet you could get lucky if you played your cards right."

Cade glanced at the table to see if perhaps more than Amber was a brunette. Two of the girls were, but only Amber was shooting him lethal stares. "Even if I had fifty-two aces in my hand, I bet I wouldn't win anything with her."

Another roar came up from their table. "How long have they been here?" From what Stone said, Amber rarely drank more than one glass of wine.

"About an hour and a half. So what can I get you?"

"Whatever ale you have on draft."

"Coming right up."

Against his better judgment, he twisted around and studied the room. The line-dancing instructor, who didn't quite look as good as her picture, was speaking with Justin. From the way she was gesturing unhappily and pointing, Cade guessed it was about the music that was rather loud. When he swung his gaze over to Amber, she was actually laughing. She looked real pretty when she had a smile on her face.

Two men walked in and looked around. Cade shot to high alert. One was Rob Gardner, who had a record for petty theft.

The other "gentleman" was Sam Richland. If his ex-wife could be believed, he liked to sweep women off their feet with a lot of promises then abuse them. That sounded like Cade's old man except for the abuse part.

Both cowboys were in the mid-thirties and appeared to be on the prowl.

"Here's your drink, Cade."

He wasn't a beat cop anymore and should probably mind his own business. He spun back around and polished off half the glass in one long chug. God that tasted good. Maybe Stone was right—he should get out more.

The music struck up and the instructor invited newbies and experienced alike to come on up and try the line dance.

Adam served two more customers then headed back to him. "I still think you should ask the brunette to dance."

"Amber would rather take on a buffalo than me."

"Ouch. Sorry man. Didn't know you knew her that well."

Her laughter rose above the country music. He turned to find Sam leaning over the table with Amber's face tilted up toward him, a smile on her face.

Damn. Sam was a snake. He was tempted to grab the guy by the neck and toss him out, but so far he'd done nothing wrong, and Amber seemed taken by him. If Stone's sister could be believed, Sam Richland was a good-looking man with the devil of a heart. Amber was too naïve to see what kind of man he was.

She scooted back her chair, and Sam grabbed her hand to escort her to the dance floor. For a second, Cade was tempted to ask someone, too, just so he could be on the floor with her. Amber needed the protection.

To hell with it. It was her life. She and Stone didn't have a permanent relationship, so there was no reason to interfere. She was a grown woman and a professional to boot.

"Another one?" Adam asked.

"Sure. Why not?" He wasn't on duty.

The song ended and Sam escorted Amber back to her table. Cade faced the bar again and had knocked back half of his ale when his cell rang. He debated not answering it, but his work ethic refused him the luxury. Slowly, he extracted his phone from his pocket, thinking it was probably Stone wanting him to join a few of the firefighters for drinks or maybe even a couple of games of pool.

Wrong. It was Dan Hartwick, his boss.

"Carter."

"Cade, I'm afraid one of the doctors at the hospital is certain one of her patients was murdered."

Cade's gut churned, and his anger grew as Dan rattled on, giving him the name of the patient and the attending physician.

"When did this occur?" His heart jumped around inside his chest like his ribs were playing hot potato.

"Forty-five minutes ago."

"I'll be right there."

The ramification of that struck him hard. If this woman died less than an hour ago, and Amber had been at Banner's Bar long before that, then she couldn't have been the killer. It was possible she had a hand in the first two deaths, but that probability was slim.

This reeked of a serial killer. *Shit.* He'd been wrong. So very, very wrong. He doubted any words he said would appease her, but he had to offer them.

As he turned to find Amber so he could apologize, all of her friends were at the table, except her. His pulse spiked. Sam was gone, too. *Fuck.*

Cade reached into his pocket and dropped a ten on the counter for Adam. "When did Amber leave?"

"While you were on the phone."

"Thanks."

Cade slid off the stool and strode toward the door, his mind splintering. His attention raced between Amber and the recent death.

Hartwick's words continued to rattle in his brain. Rock Hard had its first serial killer—assuming the same person executed all three murders—and Cade's blood ran cold. It was close to seven on a Thursday night. He could be so lucky the time frame would narrow down the suspects.

He stepped outside and turned left toward Peak where he'd parked. He passed Nancy's Fabrics and halted. Two people were arguing a block and a half away. He didn't have time to intervene, but when he drew closer and saw it was Amber, his blood pressure rose. As if the sequence of events were frames in a slow motion movie, Cade watched Sam grab Amber and shove her hard against the car.

"Sam," Amber yelled. "Stop. Get off me." She grasped his arms and pushed him, but the man didn't budge. He outweighed her by almost a hundred pounds.

Cade went ballistic, and he was beside her in seconds.

Without asking what was going on, he shoved Sam back. "What the fuck is your problem?" His breath rushed out, and he got in the man's face. "When a lady says stop, it means stop."

Sam held up his hands. "Easy, detective. Inside Banner's, the little woman was asking for it." He lowered his arms and faced her. "Next time, don't act like you want a real man to fuck you then say no."

He glared at Cade and stormed off. Cade returned his attention to Amber. Her arms were crossed and her gaze unfocused, as if she was about to break.

"You okay?" *No, dumb fuck. She's just been attacked.*

"I think so." She still didn't look at him. His gut swam. She drew in a large breath. "Thank you. I tried to fight him off but he kept pushing me and I—"

"No thanks necessary. Keep breathing. It'll be okay." A strong urge to enfold her in his arms took over, but he refrained. She still thought he hated her. Making sure not to get too close, he opened her car door. "Do you want me to follow you home?"

When she finally made eye contact, her brows were pinched. "Why did you even stop? You think I'm a killer. Do you always come to the rescue of evil people?" Her voice had sharpened with each word.

He was pleased she'd snapped out of whatever place she'd withdrawn to.

"No. I stopped when I saw it was you." He inhaled. "Listen. About my accusation and the interrogation. I need to apologize."

"Hell yeah, you do." Her body froze and her eyes widened. "You caught the killer?"

He wished with his whole heart that he could say yes. "No. There's been another death at the hospital though."

"People often die there."

He placed a hand on the hood of her car, trying to decide how much to tell her. "One of the doctors believed her patient was murdered tonight."

She grabbed his arm. "Who?"

News would get out soon enough. "Her name was Stephanie Osmond. She died an hour ago."

Amber sank back against the car, and when her knees buckled, he ignored his early warning and clasped her shoulders. She wasn't fit to go anywhere. "Stay here. Okay?"

She stared straight ahead. "Stephanie?"

"Did you know her?"

"Not personally, but every death is tragic."

Other than when his grandparents had passed, he wasn't an expert on dying, but he wouldn't be surprised if she was reliving her brother's death right now. "Can you walk a block?" He couldn't leave her.

Her legs straightened, and he let go. "Yes."

"You're coming with me."

She pulled out of his grasp. "I thought you said I wasn't a suspect anymore."

Why did he keep royally fucking things up with her? "I don't. I thought I'd take you home."

She squinted. "What about the murder?"

"It can wait. I don't want you driving by yourself."

She lifted her chin. "I'm not going home. I need to be at the hospital. Whoever was Stephanie's nurse will be upset. I know what she's going through."

She wasn't going to give in. "Come on then." It might be against department policy to bring a civilian to a crime scene, but he bet she could help.

"Where?"

From her tentative tone, she probably had no idea about his agenda. He faced her, working hard to keep his voice calm. "I could really use your help. You said you wanted to go to the hospital, and I'd feel better with you by my side." That didn't come out right. "I don't want Sam to start drinking and decide he needs to teach you a lesson." That sounded even worse.

She bristled. "You think he would?"

His shoulders slumped. "No. I just said that. I'm sorry. Nothing is coming out right. Can we go and talk later?" *She's reduced me to pleading.*

"Sure."

She seemed to have recovered because her strides kept up with his. Once they reached his SUV, he opened the passenger door and helped her in. When he leaned close to make sure she was in safely, her light rose scent stirred something inside him. It was the same reaction he'd had the first time he'd interviewed her, before he'd gotten carried away and thought she might be guilty.

He climbed in the front seat, jammed the key in the ignition, and prayed this time he'd find the bastard.

Chapter Ten

At the thought of what Sam could have done to her, Amber squeezed her thighs together. She was more shaken than she wanted to let on. Having two horrible events happen at the same time threw her way off balance. She'd only had a glass and a half of sangria when she'd spotted Cade entering the bar. She'd wanted to show him that his terrible interrogation hadn't stopped her from living again. She wasn't guilty of murder, and she told herself she deserved to have a good time.

Sam was a good-looking man, but he didn't excite her in the least. Stone did.

Be honest. Okay, Cade did too, but in a different way. The detective was big, hard, stern, and powerful. She shouldn't have been drawn to someone who thought so little of her or who believed she was capable of murder. But she was. Maybe if Stone hadn't told her what a great guy his roommate was, she might have felt differently.

Then, when she'd feared she'd walk up to Cade and tell him what a jerk he was for drawing unwarranted conclusions, she left. Sam had followed her out. Even after she told the guy she wasn't interested, he didn't seem to care.

She shivered at the thought of that creep's hands on her. She needed to forget about him and think how Cade had come to her defense instead.

"You okay?" he asked.

She glanced over at him, realizing she was in his car. "Yes. Do you know anything else about the new murder?" Thinking about the death was almost more preferable to focusing on what Sam might have done to her had Cade not intervened.

His lips thinned. "No. It's enough that a woman is dead and having it occur in a hospital makes it worse."

"Why?"

"It's the perfect place for a murder to go undetected. People are going in and out of rooms all the time. If he or she was wearing a uniform, no one would have even noticed." He slammed his palm against the wheel.

Unfortunately, his assessment was true. Nurses drew blood and took vitals all hours of the day and night. The arrival of a doctor was less common, but they did check on their patients when necessary. "Do you know what floor she was on?" She prayed it wasn't the fourth.

"Third."

For the rest of the trip, Amber tried to sober up, though Sam's attack had done a good job of that. Less than ten minutes later, Cade pulled close to the Emergency Entrance and parked. In case he told her to stay in the car, she pushed open the door before he could stop her. He was there in a flash with his hand extended. He did act as if he truly believed she was innocent. It sucked that it took another murder to prove she wasn't guilty.

He blew out a breath after he helped her stand. "Let's do this."

She walked by his side, working hard to keep up with his long stride. "How can you do this day in and day out, if every call means a dead body?"

He cocked a brow. "Whoa. Until last month, Rock Hard had only one murder all year. I work mostly thefts, burglaries, and some assaults. The low murder rate was one of the reasons why

I never went to a large city."

As soon as they stepped into the trauma bay, Cade held out his badge, although she bet everyone knew him without the ID. When they arrived on the third floor, the atmosphere seemed drastically different—no loud chatter, only hushed voices that seemed hurried.

A tall policeman, standing in front of the reception desk, directed them. "Victim's in 324."

As they headed down the hall, the creases around Cade's eyes tightened. When they reached the victim's room, he faced her. "Maybe you should wait out here."

"I've seen dead bodies. More times than I can count." She didn't want to be shut out.

"I'm sure you have, but there are rules." He exhaled and tilted his head. "You could help me a lot by asking around. See what people know. The workers don't like to volunteer anything to cops."

That part was true. When Emma Luther had been killed, a few of the staff had been hesitant to speak. "I'll do my best."

"Thanks." He reached out a hand and gently clasped her shoulder. "I mean it."

His gratitude broke the tentative barrier that existed between them.

Amber nodded. Once Cade slipped into the dead woman's room, she forced herself to push aside the horrible death and focus on finding out who might have killed her.

Fewer nurses than normal were rushing about, so she went into the break room. Dr. Wendy Harrison, a gynecologist, had her head in her hands. Three other nurses were gathered around her, whispering and patting her hand. Now probably wasn't the time to disturb her. Her heart pulled in a tug of war.

Amber turned on her heels to leave when Doug Lambert, an OB-GYN nurse, came up to her. "You hear about Wendy's patient?" he asked.

"You mean Stephanie Osmond?" Doug nodded. She leaned closer. "What exactly happened?"

He shrugged. "From what the doc said, the woman had an allergic reaction from the Flagyl she gave her, which caused Stephanie to suffer from Guillain-Barré syndrome."

"That's like one in one-hundred thousand cases."

"I know, but Stephanie was the rare exception."

Something had been niggling at her since she'd heard about the death. "How did Wendy know she'd been murdered?"

"I don't know." He tapped his watch. "I need to get back to work."

Not having any idea how long an investigation like this took, Amber wanted to ask Cade to text her when he was ready to go. She could have asked one of the staff to drive her back to her car, but she wanted to learn what he'd found out.

When she reached room 324, the same tall policeman who'd been posted by the reception desk stood by the door. "Is Detective Carter inside?" she asked.

"He is." His brow cocked.

"Could you have him text me when he's ready to leave?" He nodded. "I'm Amber."

"I know."

Really? She wondered what Cade told the man about her. It didn't matter except if he'd said she'd been a suspect. Her reputation meant the world to her.

Amber was halfway back to the break room when she realized she hadn't let Stone know what happened. She texted him about Stephanie's death, the fact both she and Cade had been in the bar when the murder occurred, and that Cade admitted she was no longer a suspect. She knew Stone would be happy for her. Amber decided to leave out the whole Sam Richland event until she spoke with Stone in person.

No one was in the break room when she returned. Darn. There goes any chance of learning more. She fixed herself a cup of tea, then plopped down on the sofa and browsed through some of the medical journals to help pass the time.

Less than half an hour later, her cell buzzed. It was a text from Cade asking her to meet him by the reception desk. She gathered her purse and headed to the front.

When she rounded the corner, Cade was scribbling something into a folder. She doubted he'd tell her much about the ongoing investigation, but he might share something. "Well?" Hell, she probably knew more than he did.

"The woman is indeed dead."

Amber thought she caught a bit of police humor skate across his face. "Not funny." She quickly sobered and leaned closer. "How did they know it was *murder*?"

"I see your mind's been active." A muscle tightened around his eye as if he debated telling her. "This is not for publication."

Publication. Right. "I won't tell anyone." He lowered his chin as if he didn't believe her. "I promise." She held up three fingers as if she were back in Girl Scouts.

"There was an empty vial that had contained a neuromuscular blocker under the bed."

She gasped and then her breath whooshed out. "So that's how Wendy knew. The killer must have believed he or she was about to be caught and dropped it."

"Or else the person was just careless." Cade leaned back against the desk. Dark shadows circled his eyes. He pushed off from the counter. "I've got a hankering for a thick steak. I haven't eaten since breakfast. Care to join me? It's on me for the way I've treated you."

Taken unaware, she studied his eyes. Whereas Stone's were a beautiful spring green, Cade's were closer to blue. Maybe even turquoise. Sincerity shone, but they also were tinged with something that looked liked regret.

She had three choices. *Yes, no, and some other time.*

Cade had come to her rescue when he didn't have to. He

also was Stone's best friend, and she certainly didn't want to cause a problem between them.

Admit it. You're intrigued by him.

"Yes. Thank you." This was his way of erasing his guilt—a payback of sorts and nothing more.

The tall cop returned and nodded to Cade. "Got a sec?" he asked and motioned they step to the opposite side of the hallway.

Cade walked ten feet and huddled with the other cop. Keeping his back to her, she couldn't hear their conversation. *Damn.*

Within seconds, he returned. "Ready?"

Hunger pains had periodically stabbed at her in the last hour, so she was actually looking forward to the food. "Yes."

The drive to Third and Wakefield didn't take long. When she asked him another question about the case, he gave her the standard response about not being able to talk about it. She didn't press him since she really didn't want to dwell on the horror anymore either.

As luck would have it, he found a spot in front of the Steerhouse Restaurant. Cade cut the engine, strode to her side, and opened her door. Maybe it was only men in uniform who were overly polite, but she enjoyed the attention.

She'd never eaten at the Steerhouse before. "You come here often?" she asked.

"Not as often as I'd like even though I can attest to the fact they have the best steak in town." He placed a palm on her back and some strange sensation rippled up her spine. She'd spent days disliking this man, yet this person was totally different.

They stepped inside and she glanced around. The lattice back chairs, low-hung lights, and bar added to the cozy atmosphere. "I like the wooden vaulted ceiling. It gives the place a rustic look."

"I like it in here, too."

Once the waitress seated them, Amber sank back against the

booth and tried to push aside the recent shocks.

It finally occurred to her that since Cade was in the middle of an investigation that he probably should be working right now. "I thought a detective usually spoke with the family after... you know." She didn't want to say "murder" in a restaurant.

"My partner is doing the honors."

Stone never mentioned Cade worked with anyone. "I thought you were a solo guy."

A small smile appeared then quickly evaporated. "I prefer it that way, but I do make an exception every now and then." A twinkle shone in his eyes.

Okay. Why did she get the feeling he wasn't talking about his job anymore? Fortunately, the server came over and took their drink orders before she could figure out the double entendre.

"I'll have a sweet tea."

"Ale," Cade added.

She was pleased he didn't try to convince her to have a drink. After the day she'd had, she didn't need any more alcohol.

As long as she had to sit through dinner with a man she hardly knew, she might as well find out more about him. If he and Stone lived together, at some point their paths would cross.

"Why did you decide to become a detective?" Her question sounded corny and a bit stiff as soon as the words left her mouth, but she really wanted the details.

"I was a beat cop first, and then worked my way up to being a detective."

That didn't explain why he chose to go into law enforcement. "Were you ever in the military?" His dark hair was cut short, and he seemed to be a big rule follower. Perhaps he was an MP or something, which would make becoming a detective a natural course.

"Four years in the Army. Got out. Went to college and returned. End of story."

"Wow. Your whole life told in what...twelve words? I don't

think I could do that."

This time he did smile and *wham*. She hadn't expected such an intense reaction. Her heart skipped a beat and tingles raced up her spine. Cade Carter was lethal, but she immediately reminded herself Stone was whom she was attracted to.

Sure, a few of her friends were in ménage relationships and seemed to love it, but she wasn't the type to engage in something like that. Hell, she couldn't keep one man happy let alone two. Besides, no woman goes from having slept with a total of four men in her life to doing two at a time.

Nope. Not going to happen.

Besides, Cade didn't seem the type to share. He was too controlling, too solitary.

Stop thinking about sex.

The server arrived with their drinks and asked if they were ready to order. "I know what I want," Cade said. "Have you had time to look?" He'd softened his tone when he spoke with her.

She'd only glanced at the menu. "Give me a second."

The waiter nodded. While she thought about how to open up the close-mouthed man, she scanned the selections. She loved fish and was presented with about ten great options. She looked up at their server. "The salmon in the dill sauce."

"Excellent choice."

As soon as Cade gave his order, the waiter disappeared. She leaned on her elbows. "Let me ask you this. What motivated you to go into law enforcement in the first place?"

He sat back and stretched his arms across the top of the padded booth, but he didn't look comfortable. It was almost as if he wanted her to believe he had nothing to hide. "You won't stop will you?"

At least he hadn't bristled, but she wouldn't go so far as to say he was eager to answer either. "No, so spill, soldier." She tried to lighten the mood.

He blew out a breath, but there was no hint of humor in his

expression. "I imagine Stone will tell you the story sooner or later, so I'll give you my take."

She sat up straight, her gaze on him. "I'm listening."

"My father, Scott Carter, was a very charismatic man. Charming most would say. Good looking, my mother always claimed."

"Do you look like him?" *Crap.* That sounded like she thought he was attractive. Okay, he was, but she didn't want him to believe she was interested in him as a man.

"My mother said I did."

She waved a hand. "Go on."

He sat up and wrapped his large hands around his glass. For a second she thought about those hands and what they could do with her body. At that thought, she mentally shook her head. It would serve no one any good for her thoughts to head down that path.

"My mother, Miranda Wentworth, came from high society. Her father was an oilman in Texas. She was spoiled, and although she attended junior college, she really had no interest in furthering her education. When my dad passed through her town one day, he spotted her and immediately knew she was the woman for him."

The story was very sweet. "Was it love at first sight?"

He cocked a brow and sipped his ale. "You're a romantic, I see."

She was, but she wasn't sure she felt comfortable with him finding out that much about her. "Continue with your story, please."

"As nice as it sounded, it was not love at first sight, though my dad convinced my mother it was. He was attracted to her because of her family money."

The bitterness jumped across the table and nearly burned her.

"After my father swept her off her feet, he convinced her to move back to Rock Hard where he lived."

She couldn't imagine a wealthy woman giving up her life to move to this harsh climate.

You did.

"Did your father's family have money?"

"No, but once more he was able to persuade my mother he was a wealthy realtor and that he'd give her everything she wanted so she could live in the same manner as before."

"He must have been a magician." Poor men couldn't just produce wealth.

"If you call robbing banks magic, then yes."

A gasp escaped. His words had come out painfully hard, and he leveled her with a stare as if he expected her to think less of him. She didn't. "A bank robber, huh. How did that work out for him?" She was being facetious, but she didn't know what else to say.

This time when Cade leaned back, the tension in his face diminished. "Quite well for a while. Dad actually was a realtor in between *jobs*. He'd get a few sales, but that wasn't enough for Mom to remain happy. She needed money not only for herself but for me, too. When she complained she needed more, he and his partner would rob another bank."

"Did your mom know what your dad did?"

"No. At least not at first."

Something else didn't add up. "How many banks were there in Rock Hard back in the days?"

He actually chuckled, though it held no mirth. "Dad was smart enough not to rob banks around here. He and his partner traveled around to most of the western states. Dad told us he wanted to learn about the real estate in other parts of the country, which was why he was gone for a month at a time. I was too small to understand, but my mom seemed oblivious to it all, enjoying her cushy life."

It didn't sound like he had much respect for her, but perhaps the topic of his mother was also a painful one. "I take it he was caught?"

"Actually no, but he was shot in the leg during one of the heists. Somehow, he managed to make it back home. It was then he came clean to my mother. She was horrified at first, then decided as long as he didn't shoot anyone, it would be okay. After all, the banks were insured."

Seriously? What kind of mother was she? Cade's mom sounded as calloused as her own, but she had no right to judge his.

"Problem was, he refused to turn himself in, which meant he couldn't go to a hospital to have the bullet removed. By the time my mom realized his leg had become infected it was too late. He passed away a short while later."

"I'm so sorry."

"Me, too."

She hissed in a breath. "How did your mom deal with his death?"

"She was devastated. She truly loved him, for richer or poorer, as they say. After the money stopped coming in, she fell ill and couldn't afford proper care. A few days after I turned eighteen, she passed."

What could Amber say? The man had suffered terribly. "Why didn't she move back to Texas?" Her parents were wealthy and might have been willing to provide for her.

"She was too proud to go home. No one likes to admit they've been a fool."

That sounds like me.

"When did you find out about your dad's past?"

"My dad died when I was ten, but probably because I worshipped him, my mom waited until my fifteenth birthday before revealing what kind of man he truly was."

She couldn't imagine what that betrayal did to him. He still hadn't answered her question about law enforcement, but she could fill in the blanks. "With few choices, I guess it made sense to go into the service."

"Yes. It's what gave me my sense of direction, not to mention they paid for my education." He finished his beer. "What my dad did was wrong." A twitch caught his bottom lip.

Something else remained hidden behind his words. Then it hit her. "Are you trying to atone for his sins?" If that were true, what a horrible burden to bear.

He worked his mouth. "Maybe."

Their food arrived and instead of asking more probing questions, she dug into her meal. The salmon was divine. "You're right. This is a great place to eat."

Now a grin appeared, one big enough for his dimples to crease his cheeks. Who would have thought Cade Carter would have dimples? Maybe he wasn't the uber tough man she first believed him to be.

He was almost through with his steak when he set his fork down and waved to the waiter.

When the man trotted over, Cade ordered a coffee. "You want another tea?" He cocked a brow and looked as if he'd like to stay a bit longer.

"Sure." She was enjoying herself and wouldn't mind prolonging their "date."

"So tell me why you became an oncology nurse." He winced. "I hope it wasn't because someone in your family died of cancer."

"No, and I'm very thankful for that." She told him about her superstar brother who was now a doctor, and her accomplished mom who was a cardiac surgeon.

"It seems as if your whole family is into helping others."

She wasn't sure about her mom, but her brother was. "I guess."

"Stone said you moved here a year ago from Oklahoma City. Why Rock Hard?"

This sounded like a reverse of what she'd asked him about his mom. "I got a job offer that was very good." *Plus, I wanted to get as far away from my site of humiliation as I could.*

Chapter Eleven

From the slow way Cade was taking his time finishing the last few bites of his steak, his mind was spinning. He finally looked up. "Why not stay in Oklahoma? I imagine as an oncology nurse, you could have had your choice of locations. It's harsh here. From what I can tell, it doesn't look like some man lured you here with the promise of riches."

Far from it. Amber almost grinned. "I can see you don't work for the tourist bureau."

He waved a fork at her. "Touché. But I'm serious. Why come here?"

She didn't know how she knew, but it was as if the man could see right through her. "To be honest, I didn't want to be near my ex-husband anymore. Nor did I enjoy being around Mom. She disapproved of everything I did." Everyone in Amber's circles back home knew about Rich, but she'd only told Jamie why the marriage really ended. "I guess I should back up."

"Please."

"After I received my nursing degree, I met Rich Larson. He was a charming man who paid attention to me. I was quite inexperienced and fell for him. Within three months we were married."

She hadn't told Stone about her past. Not only didn't she want him to think of her as a failure, it was damn embarrassing.

She might not have told Jamie had the two of them not tied one on one night. Why she was sharing this with Cade she didn't know, except that he'd been forthcoming with her. It couldn't be easy to be a cop and admit his father had been a thief.

Ever since she left home, she'd bottled up her frustrations, anxieties, and insecurities until it had bubbled to the surface and eaten away at her. That was when she had leaked her past to her friend.

"Did he become abusive?" His scowl scared even her.

"Oh, no. Never."

The server set her glass of tea in front of her. "Can I get you anything else?"

"No, thank you," she said.

Cade just shook his head and then faced her. "I know I'm being nosy, and you certainly don't have to share, but it seems as if this break-up still bothers you."

Now she was a bit uneasy. "Do you read minds?"

"No, but many have asked me that question. I'm observant, that's all. For example, when you mentioned your home, your fingers tightened around your knife." He tapped the side of his eye. "And you get this cute little tic when you're thinking of something particularly bad."

She set her knife down and placed her hands on her lap unable to respond.

He smiled. "It won't matter if you put your hands on your lap or close your eyes, your body language tells me your thoughts."

"You're trying to psych me out, aren't you, detective?"

"Am I?"

She shifted in her seat then stilled, thinking maybe that action told him something. Damn him for putting such doubt in her brain.

"There's nothing you can do, sugar. Your eyes, your lips, the way you tilt your head are all tells. You might as well reveal your secrets because I'll drag the truth out of you eventually." He winked, but the memory of the interrogation intruded, and her stomach clenched.

Who was this man? He seemed to have a sixth sense. Actually, she had told him the truth when he'd questioned her about Chris's death. It was just that he hadn't been ready to believe her answers.

Regardless of his mistake, he seemed deeply sincere now. Something about him instilled confidence, too. *Whoa.* Where had that thought come from? A few hours ago, she thought Cade Carter was the devil incarnate, but now that she'd seen him in action, she actually…well, liked him.

You more than like him. Maybe it was because he'd shared his family history with her. She doubted he'd told many people about his past.

If he could confess his father was a bank robber, she might as well tell him her tale. After all, she'd have to spill the proverbial beans to Stone at some point.

She'd already finished her fish and pushed the plate to the side. She grasped her glass in both hands and leaned back. If he thought her action meant something, too bad.

"As I've said, my relationship with my family isn't the best. Except for Chris, we were never close." She inhaled. This was harder than she thought. "I went to college for four years and then applied to med school. I spent the year after college studying for the MCAT—that's the entrance exam for medical school. It's all I did. I was consumed with the need to get in."

"You were living at home, I take it?"

"Yes. I didn't have time to get a job, so it made financial sense. Mom worked a lot and Thomas was doing his residency by then, so I mostly had the house to myself." She sipped more of her tea, mostly to give herself time to figure out how to word what came next. "I took the test and didn't make as high a score as I'd hoped."

His cheeks caved a bit. "How did that make you feel?"

He sounded like a shrink. "Like what you'd expect. A failure. A real loser. The hardest part was that my mother emotionally pulled away even more."

He shook his head in apparent sympathy. "What did you do?"

"I went to nursing school. Mom pretended like she was proud, but I could tell she'd wanted a second doctor in the family."

"And afterwards?"

With each question, his tone became more urgent. His lack of judgment meant the world to her. "In walked Richard Larson." A small smile escaped. "Rich was a hedge fund manager who was quite wealthy, although the similarities ended there. He was the total opposite of my mom. I'm not sure whether it was because he was super nice or if I was desperate for someone to love me, but after a very short courtship, we were married."

"You were happy though."

Her stomach twisted a bit at the memory. "Yes. For a while." Her face heated. Telling someone about her inadequacies in bed wasn't a topic she wanted to bring up, but this would be a good rehearsal for when she approached Stone. "As time passed, I began to suspect my beloved husband wasn't interested in sex—at least not with me."

His brows furrowed. "It wasn't because of you."

His matter-of-fact statement bolstered her confidence. "Apparently it was. I was in total denial the entire year we were married. Then one day Rich came home and gave me the old, *we need to have a talk*."

Cade nodded. "Been there, done that."

Had he been on the receiving or the giving end? "Anyway, Rich said he was very sorry, but that he was leaving me. He'd only married me so he wouldn't be *found out*."

His mouth opened. "This Rich character was gay?" He jerked his head around, probably realizing his voice had come out rather loud.

"Yup. A month after our divorce was final, I heard he married Paul Wayfair."

Cade finished his drink. "I bet by then you'd applied for another job and were winging your way to Rock Hard."

"You got it."

"What did your mom think about that?"

She tucked her chin. "Are you kidding? She has no idea. At least I don't think she does. She's not in those circles."

"Did you tell Stone?"

She shook her head. "Not yet, but I will. I've been a little preoccupied, what with being the main suspect in a string of murders." She looked up and this time she winked. He had the courtesy to turn the slightest shade of red.

The waiter stopped by, dropped off the check, and picked up their dishes. She leaned back in her seat, amazed at how relaxed she felt for telling him. Not having that elephant on her shoulder was amazing. She thought any man who learned about her marriage would be put off, but Cade didn't seem to be. Stone would understand, too, as soon as she told him.

Cade nodded to her near-empty glass. "Ready to leave?"

"Yes. And thank you for dinner. That was very nice of you."

"My way of saying I'm sorry."

On their way out, Cade paid. As they headed back to his car, her overwhelming need to give him a hug startled her. They'd each shared something deep and personal tonight. As much she didn't want to admit it, she felt closer to Cade than to anyone else at this moment. She'd had those same thoughts about Stone, too, but he wasn't here.

What's wrong with you, girl? You're a one man at a time girl, and Stone's your man.

It might have been from that startling thought, her attack, or

Stephanie's death, but she became a little light-headed and nearly tripped over a paver.

Cade steadied her. "You okay?"

"I'm good." She inhaled, took two more steps, and felt a little better.

"Got some strong coffee at home? You might want to switch from tea."

"I can't stand the taste, though I did buy some of my mother's favorite blend for when she came for the funeral, but she didn't stay long enough to drink any."

Once they were on the road and reached the Gold Avenue intersection, he turned left onto SR25. He must have remembered her address from when he'd questioned her.

He'd driven about half a mile when she remembered her car. "Wait. I'm parked at the bar."

"I don't think you're in any shape mentally to drive."

That pissed her off. "I'm not drunk." He sounded like his roommate.

"Didn't say you were. Stone or I will pick you up early tomorrow morning and take you to your car if need be."

She didn't want to owe him. "I'll hitch a ride with my neighbor." *Again*. "Thanks anyway." Roger worked at Jiffy Lube in town, and the bar was on route to his job, so it shouldn't be a problem. Cade turned down her street.

"That's my house. It's the duplex. I'm on the left." As soon as he pulled in the drive, she faced him. "Thanks again for dinner and for saving me."

She pushed open her door and rushed up her steps. Amber couldn't to wait to get inside. Maybe if she went over the evening, she'd be able to sort things through. As she fumbled for her key, Cade seemed to materialize behind her and she jumped.

"Let me."

She debated swatting his hand away, but he managed to extract the key and open the door before she could protest.

Guess he was like Stone in more ways than one.

Uh-oh. Was he expecting a goodnight kiss? *Don't be stupid.* Dinner was just his way to apologize. He's not interested.

But you want him to kiss you. You told Stone you wanted to feel alive. That you wanted to be loved.

Oh, shit. Now what was she going to do?

Cade probably shouldn't be thinking about sex, but he was. While Amber was no longer a suspect, and his roommate was highly attracted to her, Cade wasn't sure his own attraction to her was wise. He worked late hours, and he'd been told numerous times that a woman wanted a man to be there for her at all times.

Hell, that's why you believe in ménage relationships.

If he was busy, Stone could pick up the slack, and vice versa. But would Amber want that? She wasn't experienced, or so she'd led him to believe.

Still, he had this urge to help her find her passion and make her yearn for something more. His mind had shifted to a threesome the moment he sat across from her at dinner. When she'd spoken about how her husband had deceived her, and the way her mother had treated her, he'd wanted more than anything to erase the pain in her voice.

And when he'd told her about his past, she'd listened and seen him for who he was. No one had ever called him on his need to atone before. Not until Amber.

To be fair, the only other person who knew about his background was Stone. Correction. He'd told one other woman—one he thought he loved—and she'd taken off before he could finish explaining his dad wasn't a bad man, just a misguided one.

Sure, Amber made a little joke out of what his father had done to make money, but with each piece of the puzzle he filled in for her, her interest had grown, not diminished. They'd connected on a deeper level, and he was positive she felt it, too.

He held open the door for her to go in. "After you."

The average Rock Hard woman was friendly enough to ask him in, but he understood why Amber would be hesitant—she liked Stone, and he appreciated her integrity.

Her gaze shot downward, and she rubbed her hands on her pants in a nervous gesture, probably unsure of her next move. He almost felt sorry for putting her in this position.

"May I come in?" That would take away any indecision on her part. "I'd like to discuss something with you." He had to be upfront about how he and Stone shared. Hopefully, that would lessen any anxiety she'd have over being with him.

He'd seen the excitement in her eyes a few times tonight, like when he'd placed his hand on her back and again when she'd leaned forward to listen to him.

She drew in her bottom lip as if she needed time to think about it. "Okay."

At her hesitation, his ego took a hit, but he didn't mind. This was Amber. Cute Amber who made him want to nibble on the lip she'd just sucked.

He followed her inside. Stone had described her place as being neat but rather minimal. To him, it had more charm than he'd anticipated. What looked like child paintings were neatly framed on the wall and made the place cozy.

He nodded toward a particularly vivid one to the left of the television. "Your artwork?"

"No." She smiled, but her chin shook. The memory must have been bittersweet. "Regina Drake painted it. She was only eight when leukemia claimed her. Bravest little girl ever. These paintings help me stay grounded."

"Nice." He walked up to one of a bird flying in front of the sun. "I like this one. It's happy."

"Me, too." Once more, she drew her gaze downward.

A painted rock sat on an end table. The brightly colored frog drew his eye.

"Holly Mitchell painted that."

"Nice." He loved how she seemed to cherish the ties she'd made with her patients, yet there was an awkwardness he wanted to wash away. "Got any of that coffee?"

Her shoulders rose and her eyes widened. She was such an innocent little thing. *Damn.* He enjoyed making love with an eager woman, but what would Amber be like? She was a tiger when it came to the care of her patients, but given her history, she might be shy in bed. The real question was whether she'd agree to be with him. Six hours ago she'd glared at him with an intensity that still bothered him.

He probably should walk out, but damn it, being with her was inevitable—at least if he had a say so. After what they shared tonight, they both deserved some happiness.

He followed her into the kitchen and leaned a hip against the counter. With incredible efficiency, she fixed a teapot for herself, filled up the coffeemaker with a blend from Starbucks, and then added the water.

"Do you drink coffee?" He'd only seen her order tea.

"No, but I keep it because Jamie and Ben like it." Her breath hitched. "And now Stone."

He hadn't known she was so close with those two. He'd spoken with Jamie during the Emma Luther investigation, and Ben Ford was one of the pharmaceutical technicians. "You see them often?"

"Yes. They come over all the time. The four of us watch movies, eat popcorn, and on rare occasion, get drunk."

"The four of you?" The missing person couldn't have been Stone. The timing wasn't right. A streak of jealousy raced up his spine.

"Chris and me."

He relaxed back, hoping she hadn't seen a change in his

demeanor. "I'm sorry."

"Me, too." Tears shimmered on the brim of her eyelid. She looked so lost. So lonely.

Something inside him broke, and he closed the gap between them. He gathered her in his arms, and when she didn't stiffen, some other part of his anatomy did.

You're a pig, Cade Carter. She needs time to heal.

He couldn't help it. No man could resist her. It was in his genes to give comfort.

No, it's in your genes to right the wrong your father caused.

Well, Amber brought out his better side. Her slightly curly hair flowed around her delicate face and her eyes appeared almost too big. Add in a perfect mouth, small pointed breasts, and he didn't want to stay away.

She leaned back and he let go. "Um, cream?" she asked.

"No. Black. Stone's the cream man." He smiled. "A real wuss."

She opened her mouth. "No, he's not."

He laughed. Amber poured him a cup and handed it to him. Once she fixed her tea, she led them back to the living room. So as not to make her uncomfortable, he sat in the chair opposite the sofa. Never before had he been at a loss for words.

Tell her about you and Stone.

She sipped her tea. "Are the police going to do anything about protecting our patients?"

While he needed to discuss Stone, if her thoughts were focused on the case, he wanted to remove her concern. "I plan to set up a task force. There will be a few uniformed officers—probably one on each floor—but I want to have several people go undercover, too."

She blew a breath over her tea. "That would be wonderful."

For the next minute, they both seemed lost in thought. It was time to tell her. "Amber, we need to talk."

Chapter Twelve

Amber stilled. She had no idea what he wanted to discuss, but right now her mental acuity was shot. "Talk about what?" Her heart thudded. She didn't like his serious tone.

"I want to discuss Stone and me. What we want. What we like."

Oh, my God. He's gay. Shit. This couldn't be happening again. First Rich, then Stone and Cade. No wonder Stone didn't want to spend the night with her.

You're a nurse. Nurses don't jump to conclusions. "What do you want?" She was pleased she'd managed to keep her voice steady. Inside, her stomach was flipping.

"First, let me ask you this. Do you like Stone? Really like him?"

Her pulse raced. "You know I do." But did it matter about her needs if he was gay?

"I'm glad. You've lived in Rock Hard for a year. Are you aware of the large number of ménage relationships?"

Her heart pounded. "Yes." Zoey had mentioned she'd been in one—sort of.

"Great, because Stone and I like to... *share.*" He wove his fingers together, and this time he was the one with the slight tic around his eye.

Share. She sank back into the sofa. Thank goodness it wasn't what she first thought, but the idea of the same woman appealing to both Stone and Cade seemed unlikely. In the beginning, Cade had been distant and Stone had been so kind. She hadn't thought the two could even be friends, let alone like the same person.

Say something.

"You do?" She didn't know why she needed to repeat what he'd just stated.

"Yes. Does that bother you?"

Why was he gazing at her so intently? What if she said it didn't bother her? Would he think she was a slut? Stone probably had told him how she'd begged him to make love to her. Cade would know his roommate had turned her down. Her ego couldn't take two rejections. Not now.

"No, though you should know, I'm not that kind of woman." *Then why is your heart racing?*

He stood, moved in front of her, and held out his hand. "Come here, Amber."

She didn't want to obey, but she couldn't help it. Placing her hand in his, she let him pull her to a stand. His crystal blue eyes penetrated her deeply. Conflict collided. Part of her wanted to feel Cade's strength and warmth inside her. He had such a strong direction in life and seemed to know what he wanted. And she'd like for him to guide her there. But was it wrong to want him when she had such affection for Stone? Did it matter since they shared?

Cade seemed to believe it was okay, but could she handle both men? Her insides contracted and spasmed. Her body seemed to betray her mind. *Is this what you want?*

God, she was so confused.

Amber had never been good with any man, let alone two. The stronger he appeared, the weaker she became. With her patients, she was aggressive, firm, helpful. But when it came time to care for her own needs, she faltered. Her friends said it was her mother's fault, but she knew better. She just needed more strength.

With the way his gaze bored into her, he did seem to want her. She swallowed hard. "If you and Stone share, tell me exactly how that works." Her comment wasn't just to stall. She wanted to know.

The corner of his lips lifted. "How do you think it works?" He moved closer. His hips and lips were inches from her.

Her insides clenched with what she could only identify as lust. He was much taller than she was, forcing her to look up.

"I know what a ménage is by definition, but I'm not sure how you deal with it. Do you ever get jealous of one another?"

"Only if Stone monopolizes the woman too much. But the details aren't important right now." He cupped her face. Panic and excitement rushed through her. "Rest assured we will never do anything to make you uncomfortable, though we might push your boundaries a little every once in a while."

She wasn't sure how to respond. After the devastating blow from Rich, this past year had been one of soul cleansing—figuring out who she was and how to best achieve her goals. While she'd dated a few men in Rock Hard, she hadn't slept with any of them. It hadn't felt right. When Stone had given her so much comfort, she'd been drawn to him. And now she wanted Cade.

He leaned closer. "Resistance is futile, sugar. I can tell by your eyes you want me." His hand reached up and brushed a thumb across a distended nipple poking through her shirt.

Even though the logical side of her told her to pull back, she couldn't. She liked being in his arms, liked being the center of his attention. Her pulse soared and her mouth turned dry. When he told her they shared, Cade had basically removed her only excuse—her feelings for Stone. Still. She had reservations. "Shouldn't we ask Stone?"

"By all means, but he's not here. Be assured the two of us have discussed this."

When? A few hours ago, he didn't even like her, thought her a murderer, but she didn't question him because she wanted to believe what he said was true.

Cade placed his hands on her waist and moved her backward until her knees hit the sofa. Time and the tea had sobered her—but Cade had confused her all over again.

She dropped onto the cushion and looked up at him. "I don't do casual very well." That came out wrong. "I mean, I'm not the type who sleeps with a man—or two—unless I think there is hope for something more."

He sat next to her, their thighs touching, and her heart raced. He lowered his head, and when she thought he might kiss her, her tongue darted out in anticipation of tasting him. That was what she really needed.

In one smooth move, he lifted her hips and dragged her onto his lap. His arm supported her back as he leaned over and kissed her. Thoroughly, sweetly, wonderfully. He was hungry, but then so was she, and as much as she wanted to dart in and devour him, Cade was in command. The thought made her even wetter—made her forget everything except him.

As his tongue slickened her closed lips, his hard cock pressed up against her bottom. "Let me in, sugar."

She opened for him. Her tongue reached out to make contact, but he dove in first. The brush was slow and sensual and unyielding. From the way his breath sped up, he needed her as much as she needed him. That heady knowledge gave her the confidence to caress his face. He groaned as soon as her fingers stroked his cheek.

He pulled back, his lips slack, his eyes dreamy. "I want you."

She stilled and sat up. This was the moment of truth. "I can't." She blurted out the refusal without thinking.

"Sugar?" The devastation in his voice tore at her.

"Be with two men that is." At least she didn't think she

could be with both at the same time. Her traitorous pussy contracted.

He smoothed the hair out of her face. "I can tell your passions run deep. That you're the type of woman who needs to be loved by two men." With her in his arms, he stood.

"What are you doing?"

"Showing you who you really are inside."

She should stop him, but when he looked down at her with such intensity, it was like bolts of electricity had charged through her body. Other than the sound of his booted heels smacking against the hallway in a hard, even rhythm, only the blood pounding in her ears registered. She didn't remember telling him which door was her bedroom, but suddenly he set her on her feet in front of her bed. He'd even managed to flick the wall switch on his way in.

Cade stepped back and ran a lingering gaze over her body. Tingles pricked her skin and she shifted her weight.

"You like it when I look at you, don't you?"

The thought of him seeing her naked made her even hotter. "It's uncomfortable." Disconcerting even, yet exciting at the same time.

He stepped toward her. It had been a long time since she'd been with a real man. She figured he wanted her naked, so she raised her hands to undo the first button on her shirt.

"Sugar."

The strong command stilled her, and she had to swallow past the lump in her throat. "Yes?" She almost didn't want to ask.

"I want to be the one to take off your clothes. One piece at a time. I want you to think about what will happen when I have you naked. Vulnerable. Open."

More spasms rippled between her legs. Never before had she been this excited. Keeping his gaze on her, he pushed the top button through the hole, and his fingers brushed her skin, nearly burning her. When he'd made it halfway down her shirt, she couldn't take it anymore and reached out to undo his belt buckle. This slow undressing had pushed her too hard.

The second her fingers yanked on the leather strap, it was as if she'd dropped a match onto a pool of accelerant.

"Jesus, Amber. What you do to me."

His mouth descended and he demanded entrance. She yielded and let his tongue dip and take her. The man tasted divine. Their breaths collided as she ripped off the belt and fumbled with his button and zipper. *Come on, come on.*

This was taking too long. She stepped back. "Please, Cade." She kicked off her shoes and tore off her pants. To her delight, he worked faster than she did.

Was she being hasty? Maybe. But after years of not being wanted, she needed Cade, needed his hard cock.

What seemed like a lifetime later, they were naked, and she soaked him in. *Wow.* The man was huge. And hard. His vein pulsed from balls to tip. Reality dawned. He'd never fit.

"So beautiful." His gaze lingered over her small breasts then traveled downward until he stopped at her naked pussy. "I like." His grin spread wide.

Keeping his gaze on her, he squatted next to his pants and extracted his wallet. When he located the condom, he tore open the package and slipped the rubber on.

Looking regal, he rose and hovered over her. Every one of her senses shot to high alert.

Cade leaned over and dragged kisses down her neck. "I like the way you smell." His voice came out husky and full of promise. He reached around her, drew one of her hands forward, and placed it on his dick. "Can you see how much I desire you?"

"Yes." It was almost too good to be true.

Don't question it.

With one hand on her breast and the other hand squeezing her rear, he walked her backward. When his cock pressed against her belly, she placed her arms around his neck and kissed him. He moaned in her mouth and her body lit up.

As soon as her rear bumped against the closed door, he dragged her legs open with his foot, and a torrent of sparks shot between her thighs. Dear God what the man did to her. He'd been an ass, so why was she even here with him? *Because he turns you on.* Deep down, Cade Carter was a good man, but was that enough?

Shut up and take what you want.

Before she had the chance to pull his lips near again, he dropped to his knees and inhaled. "I want to drink in your sweet nectar."

Now, she was the one to moan. He didn't give her the chance to even anticipate the swipe. When his tongue swirled and dipped into her opening, her pulse soared as streaks of pleasure bombarded her. She clamped her hands on his head and dug her fingers into his scalp. When he slid a finger into her, she gasped and rose on her toes. "Cade! Now."

As if he'd been waiting for her request, he stood and kissed her hard, his thumbs brushing her nipples. He grabbed her ass and lifted her. "Wrap your legs around me."

Yes! She did as he asked, crossing her ankles to secure her. To keep from falling backward, she slid her hands under his arms and latched onto his muscular back. She kissed him, exploring his mouth with all the pent up desire she'd suppressed for too long.

He guided his cock between them and dragged his hands down to her waist. The moment his long shaft breached her opening and slid in an inch, her eyes widened. *Holy fuck.* She was wet, and the slick condom helped, but he was really wide. His girth stretched her to the max.

"Breathe, sugar."

He then captured her mouth again. Their tongues dueled and parried, and lust catapulted over the edge. She sank down onto him taking his entire cock inside. She tossed all objections away, and said what was in her heart. "Fuck me hard."

"My pleasure."

Chapter Thirteen

Cade couldn't believe how amazing Amber was. Never would he have imagined he'd met his match. She was sexy, feisty, and fit him perfectly.

But he needed more. Holding her hips still, he withdrew and drove up into her again. Her gasp urged him on. Cade stepped a foot away from the wall and placed a palm between her shoulder blades to keep her from falling. "Lean back for me, sugar. I need your tits real bad."

She moved her hands to his shoulders and dropped back her head, exposing her precious breasts. They called to him. With his cock lodged deeply inside her, he sucked on the taut nipples. When her nails dug into his skin, her passionate side set him on fire.

He alternated between each tit, but then returned to her luscious lips, kissing her with desire and passion. His balls drew up tight. It didn't matter he was a fucking lawman and had spent all those years in the Special Forces. This woman made him lose control.

Their moans and grunts blended as he plunged in fast and furiously. Christ but she was hot.

"Come for me," he said between breaths. *I'm not going to last.*

As her pussy walls pressed down on him, Amber squeezed her eyes shut and let out a loud groan. Her climax shoved him over the limit. With one final stroke he buried himself deep and let the cum fly. Her passionate scream reverberated in his head and drove him wild.

He held her long and hard. When her hold loosened, he set her on the ground and withdrew. "Be right back."

The attached bath made for easy access. He ripped off the condom, wet a towel, and returned. Amber looked well-loved but ready to collapse. Her eyes were closed and her breathing shallow. He couldn't be more pleased that he'd satisfied her.

As soon as he drew the towel between her legs, her eyes opened. She looked down, her lips parted. "I can do that."

Amber would want the control. This time he'd let her. When she finished, he took the towel and dumped it back in the bathroom.

"How about we get some shuteye?"

Amber was overwhelmed with what had just happened. Never would she have believed she was capable of letting go like that. All those years of suppressing her desires had finally surfaced.

She'd suspected Cade to be a man full of hunger and lustful need, but she hadn't anticipated he'd take her to heaven and back. He strode over to the bed and pulled back the comforter. She looked down. Her nipples were red, and the rest of her body was vibrating. She bet her lips looked puffy from all the kissing. She usually slept in pajamas, but since Cade was naked, she might as well sleep that way, too.

He looked at her, waiting. "Coming?"

She slid into bed and scooted to the side. Cade joined her and drew her near. He gently kissed her nose, then her chin, and finally her mouth, but he didn't linger. "As much as I want to have a repeat performance, I think you need a break."

Who was this man? Where had the stern cop gone? "I'm

afraid you're right."

In one smooth move, he rolled her over and tugged her close. "Sleep." He placed another kiss on top of her head.

Right. Sleep. Her mind raced. Having made love with Cade had been fantastic, but now they were finished, the guilt returned. What would Stone say? Cade claimed his roommate would be fine, but she wasn't sure. Would he be upset when he found out? She hoped she hadn't ruined things with him.

"What's wrong, sugar?" She must have been twisting and turning.

She rolled over and faced him knowing she couldn't hide her feelings any longer. "Are you going to tell Stone about us?"

He smiled. "Hell yeah, I am. Stone will want to celebrate when he learns about us."

Now he was exaggerating. "He'll be angry with me. If I were him, I'd be." Amber begged Stone to sleep with her and then turned around and slept with his best friend. Who wanted a woman like that?

Cade stroked her face. "No. He won't. That's what sharing means. He wants you bad, but he'll be okay that we worked things out between us. It had to happen this way."

She chewed on her bottom lip. "Are you sure?" She wanted to believe what he said.

"Positive." He nodded to the clock. "If it will put you at ease, I'll find Stone right now and tell him the good news."

She dropped onto her back and shook her head. "It's late."

"Not to him. He's probably at work. He'll want to know." Cade slipped out of bed. "The sooner I tell him, the sooner we can be together. I don't want you having any regrets."

She rolled back over and propped her head up. "I won't." *Maybe.*

"Why don't I buy that?" He sat back on the bed and stroked her face. "You aren't from around here where ménage relationships are the norm. I know it seems strange to have made love with me. I'm Stone's best friend."

She winced. He'd nailed it. "You're right, but I'll feel better when I talk with him."

"I know, sugar, but I promise you, this is the start of something great."

That's what all the men say. It never took long before things went south.

Don't think such negative thoughts.

She wanted him to stay. "Why not just call him?"

"It's better in person. I'll be able to judge his reaction."

That made sense. He turned on the bedside lamp. As he buttoned up his shirt, she admired how handsome he was. "When will I see you again?" Hopefully, he hadn't heard the slight hitch in her voice.

"Very soon. I promise." Cade tied his shoes, stood, and then kissed her again with lips that were soft and assuring. "Thank you for understanding and for listening."

She figured he was talking about the accusation, and then the revelation about his father. "You're welcome." She sighed and closed her eyes, happy once more.

He shut off the light and then he was gone. Her doubts stormed in. *Damn.* Why couldn't she be like her friends? Settled, happy, and sure.

As soon as Cade left Amber's house, he dialed Stone. It didn't matter it was one in the morning. Either Stone would be asleep at their house or on the job. As long as he wasn't in the middle of rescuing someone, he'd answer. Someday, Cade would figure out his roommate's crazy schedule.

"Cade? What's wrong?"

Stone sounded awake. Given the clanging in the background, he was probably at the fire station. "You at work? We need to talk."

"Yeah, but I'll be home in three hours. Can it wait?"

Cade had to be up at six. "No. Because of tonight, everything's changed."

"Oh, fuck. Did something happen to Amber?"

"Only something good. I'll be right there." He disconnected and tried to focus on the deserted road and not on the amazing night he'd had. How in hell had he thought such a sweet woman could be capable of murder?

At least he found out the truth in time. He turned north on Gold Avenue then left on Third Street. At this hour, a ton of parking spaces were vacant in front of the station. He cut the engine, rushed out, and jogged up to the well-lit building.

Trevor, one of the firemen, was washing the truck. "Hey, Cade. If you're looking for Stone, he's in the break room."

"Thanks."

He found his roommate with his fellow paramedic partner, Drake Longworth.

Stone stood. "That didn't take you long."

"Can we speak someplace private?" The room was empty except for Drake and them.

Stone's partner stood. "I've got to check on the groceries in the kitchen. I'm next up to buy."

That was bogus, but he appreciated Drake's willingness to give them space.

As soon as Drake left, Stone squared his shoulders as if readying for a fight. "Tell me you didn't further piss off Amber."

"Why would you think that? I told you it was good news." Cade motioned they take the two chairs in the corner.

"Tell me."

"I'll start from the beginning," Cade said. "I went to Banner's Bar to clear my head, and who should be there but Amber and her girlfriends."

Stone blew out a breath. "I bet she wasn't happy you crashed her weekly happy hour."

"If I'd known, I wouldn't have gone there. She sent me glares so potent they hurt." He held up his hand. "Wait. It gets worse. Sam Richland came in and tried to put the moves on her."

Stone's hands fisted. "I don't like that fucker. You told him to leave her alone, right? That she's ours?"

Cade winced. "I'm not proud of my reaction. I did nothing because she was flirting with him. I think she was trying to piss me off."

Stone leaned back. "That doesn't sound like Amber. Then again, maybe it does. She can be rather aggressive when she wants something."

That was an understatement. Cade still couldn't believe how she'd practically torn the clothes from his body and then stripped off hers. He swallowed a smile at the thought. "At the bar, her signals were clear. She didn't want anything to do with me." Damn. He should have asked her why she'd flirted with Sam, but he'd been too busy worrying over the attack, Stephanie Osmond's death, and his terrible misjudgment of Amber. "I have no idea why Amber was acting out of character."

Stone's brows furrowed. "Wait a minute. Was she flirting with Sam before or after you realized she wasn't a killer?"

Cade winced. "So you know?"

"Amber texted me."

That was good, because now he didn't have to put his failure into words. "Before. Right after she danced one song with the man, she left the bar, and Sam followed her. It was then that I got the call about a third murder at the hospital and realized Amber was innocent. I immediately rushed out, not only because I had to go to the crime scene, but I'd hoped to catch up with her and tell her I was sorry. A block down the street, I saw Sam grab Amber's arm with force. She yelled at him to stop, but he didn't let go."

Stone leaned forward, his face flushed with concern. "Is she okay?"

"She's fine. After some ugly words, Sam stalked away. One of us should check in with her as often as we can. I don't trust the guy not to seek revenge."

Stone's jaw tightened. "That makes sense, especially with his history. What was her state of mind?"

"Shaken, then mad. At least she seemed relieved I'd come along. Because she appeared disoriented, I didn't want her driving home."

"I'm glad. What did you do?"

"I brought her with me to the hospital. She was actually very helpful. The other nurses were willing to talk with her."

Stone sat back. "That's it? You came all the way out here to tell me nothing happened to her?"

Cade shook his head. "There's more. A lot more. After I finished up with the crime scene, we went out to dinner. It was my way of apologizing. Plus, I was starving." Their time together had really changed him. "I told her about my father and what kind of man he was."

Stone whistled. "How did she take it?"

"In stride. Then she confided in me." He told Stone how her ex-husband had fooled her into thinking he loved her. "You should have seen her. She was devastated when he told her he was gay."

"Gay? Fuck. That would have hurt her terribly, especially after having a mother who had emotionally abandoned her." Stone ran a hand down his jaw. "I wonder why she never let me know."

"Embarrassed perhaps?" Cade shrugged. "I drove her straight home to make sure she was safe, and one thing led to another." Cade watched Stone carefully, hoping he hadn't misjudged his roommate.

A few seconds later Stone jumped up, his face contorted. He

punched Cade in the shoulder. "You fucked her?"

Cade pushed back his chair and jutted out his chest. "I didn't *fuck* her. I made love with her." He took two slow breaths. "Ease off. I told her that we shared."

Stone's breath seemed to rush out. Hope filled his face. "What did she say?"

"I think she might be amenable."

Stone shook his head. "Amber wouldn't agree to that. Was she drunk?"

"No. Not anymore, but she was hesitant because of how you'd react."

"Did she say why?"

"She adores you, but when the chemistry between us took over, we did what seemed right at the moment. Then afterward, she feared she'd ruined everything with you."

"But you told her we shared."

"Yes, but I don't think she believed me." He sat down again and Stone did, too. "We need a plan. We need to show her that it's all right for the three of us to be together."

"Should I go over there now?"

"It's two in the morning. Tomorrow will be soon enough." His mind spun. "I got it. We'll take her to Katie's birthday party on Saturday. Show her the three of us are meant to be together."

"Oh, shit. I forgot."

Cade almost smiled. "You forgot your sister's birthday?"

"What with everything that happened to Amber, and me working extra this week, I did. Crap. I need a present."

"Ask Amber to help you shop, tomorrow—or rather later today."

Stone finally smiled. "You know, sometimes you have good ideas."

"Gee, thanks, buddy." Cade stood, his body weary. "Remember, we have to show her that we aren't petty and we don't get jealous."

Stone stood, too. "I'll call her. I'll tell her you spoke with me and that I'm good."

"Don't wait too long. We don't need her second guessing herself."

Drake rushed in. "Stone. We gotta go. Fire out on Mountain View Road."

His roommate took off with a start. Cade huffed. This better work.

Chapter Fourteen

Stone remained by the ambulance as the firemen fought the blaze. Even at this distance the intense heat made him sweat, and the smoke saturated his clothes. The burn looked bad, but he prayed Trevor, Marshall, and Donner were able to get the victims out of the house. The rest of the men were manning the trucks, trying to put out the fire.

Shouts sounded and he returned for the gurney, readying it for whoever needed aid. Trevor rushed out with someone in his arms, and from the way he was sprinting, the person was alive—or so he hoped.

Drake took the young girl from him and placed her on the gurney. "I think I got her in time," Trevor panted.

"Thanks." As much as he wanted to find out the condition of the other victims, both he and Drake rushed to assess her injuries.

He looked down at the frail body. Smoke inhalation was their worst fear. As Drake hooked up the IV-drip, Stone checked her out. She didn't look older than seven or eight. His gut twisted, but he forced himself to remain calm and do what he did best—help others.

Stone placed a hand on her shoulder to get her attention. "Hi, honey. I'm Stone. Did the fire touch you?"

Her eyes widened and he listened to her breathing. "No.

Where're Mommy and Connor?"

Connor must be her brother. "They're working on bringing them out. We need to get you to the hospital, okay?"

Tears streamed down her face. He wanted to hold her and give comfort, but now wasn't the time. Her chin trembled and she twisted behind her to see the house. She didn't need those terrible memories, and he rotated her face toward him.

Drake nodded. "One, two, three."

On three, they lifted the gurney into the back. He then jumped in. Drake closed the doors and ran around to get into the passenger's seat. Seconds later, the driver took off, sirens blaring. They were fifteen minutes out, and he did what he could to ease her ragged breathing. She looked strong, and he hoped the only battle she'd have to face would be getting clean.

As soon as they arrived at the hospital, he and Drake brought the young girl into the trauma bay. The team knew they could be receiving a few more, and they efficiently took over. Once he and Drake made sure the child was in good hands, they both returned to the ambulance and caught a ride back to the station.

Stone was exhausted. He'd worked non-stop for the past week, and he had the next three days off. He wanted to sleep and then call Amber. He probably wouldn't learn the outcome of the blaze and the condition of the little girl's mother and brother for another few hours anyway. He'd have to check later.

Bleary-eyed, he signed out and drove home. He went inside and headed straight for the shower. Cade would be asleep so Stone tried to be quiet. He still couldn't believe Amber had softened toward his roommate. That must have been some dinner conversation.

Stone undressed and stepped into the bathroom to wash off the day's grime. As soon as he finished, he went back to the kitchen to grab a bite to eat. He made the easiest thing possible—scrambled eggs and bacon—and yawned through the entire meal. If he didn't get some shut-eye, he wouldn't be fit to talk with anyone.

After eating, he placed the dishes in the dishwasher and headed back to his room, hoping for a good night's sleep.

While he adjusted his pillow just so, his mind refused to calm. He was thrilled Cade and Amber had patched things up, but he was worried she'd change her mind about being with both of them.

Eventually, he dozed. Close to one in the afternoon, he roused. His stomach grumbled, and after he tossed on his jeans and a comfortable shirt, he made his way out to the kitchen to prepare another meal. He opened the fridge and saw the food supply was woefully lacking. Since he had to go shopping for Katie's present today, it would make sense to stop at the store afterwards.

He was about to make a shopping list when his phone rang. He picked up his cell from the counter and let out a big breath when he saw who was calling. It wasn't the station. Knowing this wouldn't be short, he ambled over to the sofa and dropped down. "Hi, Mom."

"I saw that house fire on television. I wanted to see if you were all right."

He swore she believed he actually ran into the flames. "I am. All I had to do was transport a young girl who'd been trapped in the burning house to the hospital." He knew her next question. "Don't worry. She wasn't burned. She'll be okay." *Physically at least.*

"I'm so glad." She inhaled. "The reason I called is to make certain you remembered it was Katie's birthday tomorrow."

"Have I ever missed one of her parties?"

"No. Cade's coming, right?"

"He sure is." His mother loved Cade. Once she'd found out his mom had died when he was eighteen, she had kind of adopted his roommate. Stone swore she fussed over Cade more than she did him.

"What time should we be there?"

"Two. And bring that nurse you've been seeing."

Wow. He was just about to ask if she minded if he brought someone. He would have asked how she knew about Amber, but he really didn't want to know the extent of her gossip grapevine.

"We'll be there. All three of us." It felt good to say that.

He disconnected and stabbed his fingers through his hair. Now, he just had to convince Amber to attend. Then he'd figure out what to get for Katie. His sister worked as a paralegal and was very picky about what she wore. To make matters worse, buying presents for women had never been his forte. He stood and paced as he dialed Amber's number. His breath quickened.

"Stone?"

Uh-oh. He didn't like her hesitation. "Hey, baby." Should he first tell her about his conversation with Cade or ask her to the party then tell her? "I have a favor to ask."

"Sure." Now she sounded more like herself.

"Remember I told you about my sister, Katie, the one who was so sick as a child?"

"She had acute leukemia, and if it hadn't been for your quilt-loving aunt, your life would have been even more miserable."

Amber was amazing. "You got it. Well, it's Katie's birthday tomorrow and we've been invited to a party at my parents. I thought if I could convince you to go, I'd see about borrowing dad's horses and taking you for a ride." The way his words rushed out made him sound a bit desperate. *You are.*

She squealed then sucked in a breath. "I'd love to." He swore he heard a hitch in her voice. She had to be wondering if he knew about her and Cade.

He wanted to get it out in the open. "Cade's going to be there, too."

Silence met him. "Have you talked with him?"

The pain in her voice cut straight through him. "Yes, baby, and it's all good."

"Really? You mean that?" The excitement in her voice returned.

He laughed. "Yes. I will admit I was a little disappointed not to be first, but that just means when we do have time to be together, it will have to be extra special."

"You sure?"

"Positive." Voices sounded in the background, which implied she was at work. *Damn.*

"What did you get your sister for her birthday?" She acted as if she had all the time in the world and that he was important. It helped calm his frustration.

She sounded like the Amber he knew. "Nothing yet and that's part of the problem. I'm clueless."

"You don't have much time."

He huffed out a laugh. "Tell me about it."

"Okay. Let me think. What are her hobbies?"

He liked how she must have thought knowing a person's hobbies helped define him. "Sad to say, I don't know. She works all the time like someone else I know." Amber chuckled and the foreign sound elevated his mood.

"Well, what did she like to do when she was younger?"

He racked his brain. "She liked to crochet."

"Perfect. Then get her a bag to hold her crochet needles. You can go to JoAnn's on First and Arbor Way. They'll have everything you could want."

He wouldn't know a crochet needle from a knitting needle. "Any chance I can bribe you into coming with me? I'll throw in dinner." He held his breath not convinced that she really wanted to be with both of them.

"I'd love to. I get off work at five. JoAnn's is open late on Friday night. Trust me on that."

Amber was something else. "I'll pick you up at five. Where?"

"How about I meet you at the third floor reception desk? It'll be easier than me trying to battle the crowds in the main lobby."

They'd still have to exit through there, but he wasn't going to say anything about her plan. "I'll be there."

When she disconnected, he almost felt light-headed. She was willing to help him pick out a present for his sister, come to a party with strangers, and ride the trails with him. She made him believe she might be willing to be with both him and Cade. His day just got better.

Chapter Fifteen

Amber wanted to check on her patient, Jennifer Seely, one more time before signing out and helping Stone shop. Most likely the woman would be moved to hospice care tomorrow. Poor Jenn. Her brain cancer had spread throughout her body.

Amber's heart ached as she stepped inside the dimly lit room. Because she had the next two days off, she might not have the chance to say goodbye.

"Hey, Jennifer." Amber moved closer and hoped her voice sounded encouraging.

The woman opened her eyes. She might be fifty-two, but she looked a lot older. Her eyes were sunken and her skin ashen.

"Amber!" She reached out her hand.

"I can only stay a few minutes." She didn't want Jennifer to think she was abandoning her without a good reason. "Guess what? I have a date." She put as much enthusiasm as she could into her voice, wanting to douse the room in hope.

"With your hot paramedic?" Jenn's eyes actually brightened.

Amber had spoken about Stone mostly because it seemed to make Jennifer happy to hear about a man treating a woman nicely. Amber's affair with Cade had been too recent, and the amazing sex had yet to sink in. No way was she ready to discuss how she'd given in to Cade after she'd told Jennifer how much she liked Stone. Not to mention, she didn't need to be discussing her future with a woman who'd been battered by her ex-husband then been given the terrible news about her cancer having spread.

Jennifer had been a fighter, but in the end she'd lost the war. Amber firmed her lips, not wanting to show any sadness.

"Yes. We're birthday shopping for his sister then having dinner together. I've never met Katie, but the party tomorrow should be fun."

Jenn's smile looked like it took effort. "Cherish your time with family. Before my parents passed, Larry had been so supportive." She glanced off to the side. "Then he changed."

According to Jennifer, he'd changed because her parents hadn't left them any money. From what he'd told her, he'd stayed with her because he believed she was his ticket to easy street.

"I'll stop by and see you when I come back on Monday."

"Okay."

Both knew that might not happen. Damn cancer. Needing to leave, Amber hurried out the door and nearly ran into Larry Seely. He'd tried to get in to see his ex-wife before, but the orderly on duty had stopped him.

"Mr. Seely." She used her sternest tone.

"Move. I need to see my wife."

"Your *ex-wife* is too weak to see you." Surely he hadn't forgotten Jenn had a restraining order out on him.

"Bullshit. Let me by."

"No." Amber inhaled and moved closer, trying to intimidate the six-foot tall man with her five-foot-four inch frame.

He grabbed her shoulders and shoved her to the side. Next thing she knew, Larry flew backward and Stone had shoved him against the wall. "Leave, or I'll call the cops."

Larry punched Stone, but Stone was quick enough for the blow to bounce off his chin instead of hitting him square on.

Amber's heart nearly stopped. She'd seen the bruises the man had inflicted on Jennifer's face and body when she'd arrived at the hospital for her treatments a few months back. The man was brutal.

Larry got in Stone's face. "Fuck off, buddy. I have every right to see my wife." He started toward the door again, when Stone pushed the man back.

"Leave."

Another nurse edged close but didn't cross behind them, probably for fear she'd get hurt in the fray.

"Stone, Jennifer is his ex-wife." Amber put the emphasis on the "ex" part. "She has a restraining order out on him."

Larry glared at her. "Fuck you, bitch. I'm going to tell your supervisor about you." He stormed off. *Good luck with that. Tammy White won't give you the time of day. She knows all about you and your antics.*

Stone immediately turned and gathered her in his arms. "You okay, baby?"

She reached up and tilted his slightly red chin to the side. "I'm fine, but you might be black and blue by tomorrow."

"Men don't feel pain." He puffed out his chest for a second then exhaled. When he followed his macho demonstration with a smile, her heart twisted.

Amber finally gave up trying to figure out how she could be so physically and emotionally attracted to both him and Cade. They were very different, but each had stolen a piece of her heart.

"Let me inform security about Mr. Seely, and then we can shop for your sister. Okay?"

"Do you want me to call Cade and see if the Rock Hard Police can send a man to watch her door?"

"You're a good man, Stone Benson, but that's what our security is for. While it doesn't happen often, we have our share of crazies."

"As long as they don't bother you, I'm good."

Leaving her car in the lot, she went with Stone. By the time they arrived at the craft-fabric store, Amber had a better idea about what kind of person Katie was. Like Stone, she was sensitive and just as ambitious.

Instead of opening her own car door, Amber let Stone come around to her side and help her out. As soon as she stepped inside her favorite place, a large amount of tension released. The inside smelled of fresh fabric, yarn, and wood. "I love JoAnn's. I can spend hours browsing."

"I've never been inside one of these places. It looks like Home Depot for chicks."

She laughed. "Spoken like a true man."

When they passed the cutting table, one of the workers waved. "Hi, Ms. Amber."

"Hi, Mildred," she shot back.

"I take it this is where you get your quilting supplies?"

"Yup." She led him over to the crochet section. "Take a look at these canvas totes." She lifted one up. "See the pockets inside? That's to hold the yarn." She raised a back flap that had a row of fabric tabs. "In here, she'll put her hooks. Does she have yarn? Or do we need to make a starter kit?"

"Starter kit?"

Amber laughed. "When was the last time she made something?"

He pulled back his bottom lip, enough to show teeth. "No clue."

She smiled. "Okay. Get a shopping basket, and I'll pick out a few things."

He was gone in a flash. After finding the perfect satchel, she walked over to the yarn section.

"Got it." Stone waved the carry-all.

"I'll take that. Why don't you find some wrapping paper? They have a small selection of cards near the front window, too."

He stilled. "Did I tell you that you are the best?"

"You're only saying that because you need me."

He glanced to the ceiling. "Maybe." He grinned and took off again.

By the time he returned, she'd picked out a great selection of different yarns, along with a pattern book.

"Got the paper." He waved his find. "Looks like you bought out the store."

Oh, crap. "I guess I forgot to ask how much you wanted to spend."

He took the basket from her hands. "It's all good. Ready?" Once they paid, he escorted her to his vehicle, stored the present in the back, and slid in. "I have a plan." He faced her. "What do you say we stop at the grocery store to pick up some food, and I'll prepare you a dinner you won't forget?"

"You cook?" When he'd offered dinner, she hadn't imagined he'd prepare it.

His eyes went ridiculously wide. "I told you my mom is an amazing chef. Just so happens, I inherited her cooking genes."

Rich claimed he was a great cook, too, but unfortunately, his menu was limited to three items. "This I'd like to see."

What a refreshing change it was to be with Stone now that the heaviness of her brother's death and her possible involvement in the murders had been lifted. Part of her still felt guilty over having slept with Cade, but she leaned back to enjoy the upcoming adventure. Before she knew it, he'd pulled into the grocery store lot.

Stone twisted toward her. "Is something wrong, baby? You've been real quiet. Are you thinking about that man at the hospital?"

That had not even crossed her mind. "No. I'm good." She forced a smile. At some point, she wanted to bring up Cade again, but now didn't seem like a good time.

"Great."

Once inside, she pulled out the cart. "I'll push." She liked to have something to do with her hands. "So what are we having?"

"It's a surprise." Then he stopped. "Maybe I should ask if you like Italian."

"I eat pretty much everything." She was surprised he hadn't figured that out since they'd been to dinner a few times.

"Good."

With amazing efficiency, Stone whipped through the store and picked up the ingredients as if he'd memorized what was on each aisle. The only items he actually took the time to examine were what went into the salad.

When they headed down the baking aisle, Stone picked up a box. "How about brownies for dessert? You like those?"

"Love them." This was going to be some dinner. "Can we buy ice cream to put on top?" She raised her brows.

"Anything you want, baby."

Stone was such a nice man. "How about I pay for the ingredients since you're cooking?"

"Nice try." He shook his head.

She'd tried. After she picked out her favorite brand of ice cream, Stone insisted on chocolate syrup and whipped cream. It was as if he could tell where her mind was headed.

Yes!

On the way home, he told her about the fire and that when he'd called earlier, he found out all three had made it out safely. "I don't think I'd keep my cool if I saw someone burned and screaming," she said.

"It's hard, but when I save someone, I feel good inside."

She smiled. "Me, too, but my efforts take a long time."

After they unloaded the groceries, Stone sorted through each bag and separated the items into groups.

She nodded to the piles. "I thought only I did that."

"Makes cooking easier."

That was her reasoning, too, though she suspected hers might have had something to do with her need for control. Her mom always insisted the family do everything her way and Amber had rebelled.

Stop thinking about Mom. It's a libido killer. "What can I do?"

He furrowed his brows as if he was deciding how she could help without ruining his masterpiece. "How are you with salads?"

"The best."

Stone pulled out a bowl. For the main meal, he found a large casserole dish along with a pot for the pasta. From the ingredients he'd purchased, they were having lasagna.

She washed the lettuce, tomatoes, olives, and then peeled the cucumber. "I'm surprised Cade's not home."

"He texted me and said he was working on some assault case. He'll be home later."

That might be for the best. Amber debated bringing up the whole ménage thing again but decided she'd rather talk about that sensitive topic after dinner, like when they were making brownies.

"Do you two ever get to eat together?" With them being frequently on call, she doubted their work schedules lined up very often. If that was the case how did they manage to even share?

"When we can. If I'm on day shift, we see each other more often."

"That makes sense."

Trying to find some clues about them, she glanced around the living room and kitchen area. Everything looked picked up. Did they have a maid, or was one neater than the other? Her money was on Stone for doing the cleaning.

While he worked on the lasagna, she finished making the salad. Anticipation raced through her. Stone was everything she wanted in a man and more. Add in Cade, and she'd definitely have her hands full.

Once Stone dumped in the noodles, he prepared the vegetables. By the time he cut off the ends of the beans and rinsed them, the noodles had finished cooking.

"Now for the preparation of the final masterpiece." He looked over at her and smiled. "Watch carefully. Just so you know, if I wasn't in such a hurry to eat and spend time with you, I would have made homemade tomato sauce."

She moaned at the idea of him being in a hurry. "Maybe you can teach me to cook someday." She knew the basics, but not much else.

"I'd be happy to." After making a big show of layering the noodles with the ricotta, Mozzarella cheese, and the sauce, he topped the dish with Parmesan cheese and shoved the finished dish in the oven. After dumping the beans into a pot of boiling water, he guided her into the dining room. "We need to wrap Katie's present."

"Okay." She glanced around. "Where did you put it?" While their home was neat, it didn't look like either had really taken the time to decorate it. Most of the furniture ran toward the black and brown tones. It needed color. And a woman's touch.

The thought surprised her. She might be moving too fast, but she wasn't a raw kid out of college anymore. Rarely had she met anyone, let alone two people, who she bonded with so quickly.

"I set it down in the living room. I'll get it."

She watched him hustle to the chair across from the sofa. Her attraction to Stone was easy to understand. He'd been there for her in her darkest hour. But there was more. He was a strong man, who like herself, cared about others.

Stone handed her the present and the wrapping paper. "You any good at this?"

She refocused on the task at hand. "As a matter of fact, one of my favorite times of year is Christmas. I take great pride in making the exterior of the present as nice as the inside."

"I suck at wrapping, just so you know. A piece of tape here, a piece of tape there, and all is good."

She laughed. "Chris used to ask me to wrap his gifts to Mom and Thomas. I loved to measure twice and cut once, as they say."

"A real perfectionist."

There was no offense in his tone. "It works for me."

He grinned. "I'll get the tape."

While he rooted through a kitchen drawer, she spread out the paper to figure out how much was needed. "It'll be easier if we put all the yarn and hooks in the bag."

"Whatever you think is best."

She smiled. She liked his "a piece of tape here, a piece there" comment. Sad to say, she didn't know all that much about Stone other than he was caring, wonderful, and great to look at. "What was your best present growing up?" She prided herself on the good segue since she was wrapping a present for Katie.

He slowly walked back with the tape. "It might have been the GI Joe helicopter." He drew in his bottom lip. "But I didn't get to play with it much because Katie, who was two at the time, decided to see how well it held up under her plastic hammer."

"Ouch." She could picture the rotors all bent. "That's so sad."

He nodded. "Yeah. Worse, was what happened to GI Joe."

She enjoyed his reminiscing. "Don't tell me she hurt him, too?"

"It was nothing short of murder. She decided to play tug of war with the dog. She grabbed GI Joe's legs, and Molly, our Pug, took the head."

She grimaced. "Joe didn't make it, I take it?"

"Nope."

"I'm sorry to have brought up your childhood nightmare. Any presents she didn't destroy?" Amber spread out the wrapping and placed the bag on top so she could measure.

"I'd been given the usual red wagon, water guns, a mountain bike, and even a train set, but I think it was the mini chemistry lab that my mom bought me I liked the best."

She hadn't seen that coming. "What did you do with that?" He was just a kid. She cut the paper and folded it over the bag.

"Are you kidding me?"

She looked up. "I took chemistry in high school and college, but I never had any test tubes or Bunsen Burners at home."

His eyes shone. "Mom wouldn't let me heat anything at home, either. She said it wasn't safe. All I could really do was make crystals out of alum and make clear liquid turn red. I loved to experiment to see which chemicals created which reactions."

That did sound like fun. "Did Katie get near your precious gift?" She held out her hand. "A one-inch strip of tape please." She pressed her finger on the present. He ripped off a piece that was a good three inches in length instead of one, and aimed it below where she held her finger. She said nothing about his measurement or placement.

"She did, but it was mostly to watch. Dolls were more her thing."

"And your younger brother?"

"He was too young."

She chuckled. "My bad. I meant what is he doing now?"

"Craig? He lives in Philadelphia. He's at Drexel University getting his masters in photography."

She would have guessed business. "Is your dad disappointed no one is going into the hardware profession?" She finished folding over the last piece. "Put your finger here, please."

He shook his head. "Dad just wants us to be happy."

What a refreshing change from how she grew up. The final piece of tape needed to be neat. She pulled off the correct amount and placed it on the point. "Perfect." If they'd had a bow it would have looked amazing.

The oven timer dinged and Stone smiled. "Now for my creation."

She couldn't wait to eat, but she so looked forward to dessert.

Chapter Sixteen

After eating what seemed like a week's worth of food, Amber leaned back and moaned. "That was fantastic." She hadn't wanted to stuff herself, but somehow Stone's lasagna was better than anything she'd tasted in a long time. Now she had no room for dessert.

"Tea?" he asked.

She'd had two glasses already. "Have any red wine?"

"Sure." He went back into the kitchen and opened a cabinet. "You didn't tell me what your favorite present was growing up."

He hadn't asked. "That would be when my dad bought me Sandalwood."

He placed the glasses on the counter and pulled a bottle from the wine rack. "That some kind of perfume?"

She laughed. "No. Sorry, she was my pony."

His hand stilled. "Your parents gave you a horse for your birthday?" He didn't have to sound so surprised. She'd told him her mom was a surgeon, and that her dad had been a lawyer.

"My parents were together back then." Not that her comment really explained anything.

"Did you live on a ranch?"

"No. We kept the horse in the country club stables." Now she sounded like a snob.

"I see." He poured them each a glass of wine and brought

the drinks over. "Here ya go. Let's sit in the living room. It'll be more comfortable." She chose the sofa and Stone sat next to her. "You want to ask me anything else?" He stretched his legs in front of him and wrapped an arm along the back of the sofa, looking totally at ease.

She didn't know if he was referring to his childhood or the act of sharing. He and Cade had convinced her they were okay with being a threesome, but she wasn't so sure she was. The logistics confused her.

She nodded behind her to the kitchen. "How do you and Cade decide who cleans?"

He cocked a brow and lifted the wine to his lips as if he wanted to give himself a moment. "I clean."

"Do you share a bathroom?" That sounded so dumb, but it was those types of things that might be important later.

"No. I'm a health care professional. I have this crazy need for cleanliness, and Cade's would never meet any standard for sterility. Besides, we have three bathrooms, so we each have our own."

He was a man after her own heart. Maybe she'd avoid Cade's bathroom, though she'd bet Stone was exaggerating. She wanted to ask about whether the women they'd shared spent equal time with the men. If Stone needed to go to bed early because of his shift, and Cade didn't even get home until say, nine, would he expect her to stay up with him until two in the morning when he decided to hit the hay? What if she had to be up by six?

Stone removed the still-full glass from her hands and set both hers and his on the coffee table. "You're thinking way too much about something. How about helping me make the brownies."

Maybe she had spent too many hours in the hospital, but these men seemed to be able to read her mind. She followed him into the kitchen, glad not to have to think about practical matters when she had such a nice man in front of her.

He located a large bowl and placed it on the counter. "How about I line up the ingredients and you pour and stir?"

She liked the teamwork. "Okay." She checked the back of the mix and turned the stove to the proper temperature.

He set out the eggs, oil, and filled the measuring cup with water. "I'll get the pan ready."

When she lived at home, she and her mom never cooked together. That was the job of the hired help. She missed out on what could have been quality time. "Did you help your mom cook?"

His eyes widened slightly. "Only when she needed help. I actually learned in the service."

So much for genetics. With a wooden spoon in hand, she tossed in the ingredients and stirred until they were mixed. Once Stone greased the pan, she poured in the mixture, scraping the bowl mostly clean. He placed the brownies in the oven and set the timer.

She ran the spatula over the little bit of batter that was left. "Want a taste?" She waved the dollop of chocolate at him.

With his gaze plastered on her, he moved close and slowly licked his side of the rubber scrapper. She did the same, and their noses almost touched. Her body ignited at the closeness.

Once the extra batter was gone, he leaned back. "I have something else you might like." He retrieved the can of whipped cream from the fridge and carried it with him into the living room. "Come on."

"What are you going to do with that?" She followed him.

"I don't want to wait for the best part." He raised a brow. "You didn't think I was going to waste this on the brownies, did you?" He grinned and her heart smiled.

"Oh, surely not." Whipped cream was good for a lot more than a dessert topping.

He took her hand and dragged her down to the sofa. Stone shook the can and uncapped the lid. "Open up."

This was going to get messy, but she obeyed. He pressed down the nozzle and swirled cold cream on her tongue. It tickled. She laughed as she swallowed the sweetness. The aftertaste was divine.

"Turnabout's fair play." Without waiting for him to hand over the can, she took it. "Open up, please." She squirted the whipped cream into his mouth, purposefully missing.

He made an exaggerated motion of swallowing all of it, but a bit of cream remained right above his top lip. "You missed some." Before he had a chance to lick it away, she swiped the cream from his lips and slipped her finger into his mouth. His eyes sparkled as he clamped down on her finger and ran his tongue around and around. Shards of electric shocks splintered along her spine.

Holy shit, the man was potent. Before he turned her on too much, she lowered her hand. "All clean." She had to say something.

He took the can back, and instead of aiming for her mouth, he squirted some over her right breast. "Whoops."

"Stone!" The shirt was a cotton blend, and the cream would wash out, but what was she to do now?

"I'm sorry, baby. Let me help you." He dragged a thumb across her nipple but that only made the smear bigger. "That didn't work, did it?" He gave her an exaggerated frown. When his mouth latched onto her breast, she cupped the back of his head. She groaned. Damned bra. She could barely feel his tongue.

He sat up. "I think I made it worse. I know. I'll wash it for you. Off it goes."

Without giving her a chance to agree or object, he lifted the shirt over her head. Good thing she already decided she wanted to make love with him.

His cheery tone disappeared. "Holy fuck, baby. You are hot."

Now it was her turn to smile. "What were you expecting?"

"I don't know. Not something this perfect." He leaned back. "No wonder Cade lost all control around you."

She tossed him a coy smile. "It's not all about physical attraction, you know. I want a man to see me as a person, to want me for who I am." *Damn.* She hadn't meant to get all philosophical on him. She'd been trying to keep things light.

He winced. "I fucked this up, didn't I? I haven't stopped thinking about you, and now that I'm with you, I'm making a mess of things."

"No. I was kidding. Though I admit I want a man to appreciate what's inside here." She tapped a finger over her heart.

"I do appreciate you." Stone clasped her hands in his. "You are an incredible person. Remarkable, in fact. You're strong, brave, kind, and good-hearted. You are the cream on top of a brownie sundae."

Now that made her laugh. "Okay. You're forgiven."

Stone pulled her into his arms and kissed her. Nothing was tentative about the way he took her. She didn't wait for him to ask permission and opened up, needing to explore him. Their tongues collided and danced, sending joy straight through her. He tasted of spicy tomato topped with sweet cream, and she couldn't get enough of him.

He broke the kiss and sucked in a breath. "God, but I've wanted to do that for so long."

His kindness and considerate nature poured out of him. "Me, too."

His thumb rubbed across her damp bra, and she wanted him to touch her heated skin. Just as she reached out to undo the buttons on his jeans, the damned timer sounded.

"Already?" They said in unison then laughed.

"Hold that thought, baby, while I take the brownies out to cool."

It would give her a chance to gather her wits. He opened the oven and placed the dessert on the counter. The rich aroma of chocolate filled the air and her stomach grumbled. But she'd forego the pleasure of the brownies if she could taste Stone.

Within seconds, he returned. Keeping his gaze on her, he leaned her onto her back and stretched out on top of her. "I want you. Now." He slipped his hands under her and kissed her again. This time, he nibbled her lips, drawing her bottom lip between his teeth. The slits in his eyes narrowed. "What I'd like to do is dribble cream all over your body and lick you clean."

"Uh-uh. I'll get all sticky, but if I put cream on your cock, it'll be easy to wash off."

"I say we try it."

The cock part or the cream all over my body part?

She squealed when he unhooked her bra and dragged the straps down her arms. He then dropped it on top of the table, barely missing her wine glass.

"Oh, yeah, baby, that's what I'm talking about." His gaze raked across her breasts and his mere look made the tips harden into peaks. He pressed a finger to her nipple and smiled when the pink crest bounced back. "So nice."

"I have a mind, too, you know."

He tilted his head. "If I could kiss and touch your brain, I would."

"That's better." She tried to give him her sexiest look, though she'd been out of practice for so long, she might have looked goofy. Fortunately, Stone didn't act like he thought so.

"Hold on." He lifted the can of whipped cream and spritzed a glob on top of her nipple.

"Ooh. Cold." The end stood up even more.

"I'll warm you up."

Leaning over, he captured the tight bud in his mouth and ran his tongue around several times until heat raced through her. When she arched her back for more contact, he captured the other breast in his palm then twirled the taut peak. The double sensation had her wanting more.

"You are so sweet," he whispered. "I need you."

Stone sat up and drew her legs on top of his lap. With quick movements, he pulled off her boots and socks.

He smiled. "Aw. You even have pink toenail polish. I like it."

He seemed to notice everything. She wiggled her toes for him. He deftly undid her pants as if he'd removed a woman's clothing many times before, and slipped hers off with ease, leaving only her thong undies in place.

He whistled. "This keeps getting better and better."

Amber lifted up on her elbows and reached out her hand, wiggling her fingers. "How about showing me something?"

He scooted out from under her legs and stood. Stone shucked off his boots then placed his hands behind his head. "Have at me."

Yes! When she'd been with Cade, they'd been in too big of a hurry to finish undressing each other. She wouldn't miss out this time. Even though she was almost naked, she sat up and undid the buttons on his pants. Wanting to tease him, she placed a hand over his bulging crotch. "Hmm. I wonder what's underneath here."

"You'll have to unwrap it and see."

Careful not to drag down his briefs, she lowered his jeans until they bunched at the knees. "How about you step out of them?"

She could have crouched low, but then she'd have been tempted to suck on his cock, and she wanted to explore other parts of him first.

He obliged then tossed off his socks. She stood. "I want to see what's under this shirt." A paramedic had to be strong to lift those gurneys into the ambulance and would be solid. He raised his arms, and she drew the material over his chest. Inch by inch she revealed highly defined muscles that prominently bulged at his pecs. His abs were sculpted and led to a narrow waist. "Nice." She ran her fingers along his tight belly with one hand and tossed his shirt next to her bra with the other.

"I'm glad you like it."

She touched a scar along one rib. "What happened here?"

"Got that two years ago. Some kid, high on drugs, had been stabbed, which was why we'd been called out. The kid didn't even seem to be aware he was close to bleeding out. When I tried to subdue him, he stabbed me."

Her breath caught. "I didn't realize your job could be so dangerous."

He enfolded her in his arms and kissed the top of her head. "It's not. Not usually. That was a one-time occurrence."

She wasn't sure he was telling her the truth, but a healthy Stone was standing in front of her, and that was all that mattered now. She glanced up at him. "Any other injuries I should know about?" She stepped back and ran her hands up and down his chest, pretending to examine him closely.

"You might have to go a little lower."

She wasn't going to give in so quickly. "Turn around. I need to check out your back."

He obliged. *Perfect.* His shoulders V'd to a tight waist and tapered hips. His ass was round and full, just the way she liked it. "Do you work out a lot?"

He chuckled. "Enough."

She couldn't help but squeeze his rear. In a flash, he flipped back around. "Enough, young lady. It's my turn to check you out."

She could only imagine what nooks and crannies he'd try to get into. His thumbs rubbed her nipples, and the light pressure tickled. "No war wounds there," she said.

As if he really was looking for scars, he ran his palms over her breasts and down her belly. She held her breath as he checked out her body.

"Baby, baby. You are more than my wildest dreams ever envisioned."

She exhaled. "I'm glad you're pleased."

"I'll have to taste her and probe her to be sure, though."

She loved the way his mind worked. He dropped to his knees and eased her thong lower. She thought he'd take her panties completely off, but instead he left them around her thighs. Stone clasped her hips, leaned in, and ran a tongue along the top of her mound.

Lick me lower. Here she thought Stone would be different and not tease her. *Wrong.*

His tongue moved downward with each swipe, driving her crazy. She clamped a palm on his head, trying to guide him to explore her wet pussy.

His hands slipped to her thighs. He dragged off her panties and shoved them to the side. He then opened her legs wide. "Hold that pose."

Shivers of delight raced up her body. He licked the inside of her leg in slow sensual circles. Amber swallowed a groan. Her arousal was strong. Couldn't he tell she was ready for him? She was a little sore and swollen from having been with Cade last night, but that wasn't going to prevent her from making love with Stone.

Any thought Stone might not want to be with her had long disappeared.

With one hand, he opened her folds and slipped two fingers into her opening. She went straight up on her toes. Ripples of joy ran up her spine. "Yes."

"So sensitive."

"I need more." Her breath rushed out.

"Don't worry. I'll give you plenty." Stone reached up and pinched a nipple, and heat shot straight to her core.

He continued to flick his tongue over her clit. She wouldn't be able to last if he didn't hurry and take her. She clamped down on his fingers. As waves of lust washed over her, she shut her eyes and drew in a large breath. If she told him to suck harder on her beaded nub, he'd probably find another sensitive part of her body to torture.

A key turned in the front door and she stiffened.

Chapter Seventeen

"Easy, baby. It's just Cade."

Just Cade? "I'm naked," Amber said, as she crossed her arms over her chest.

Stone withdrew his fingers and stood. Feet sounded on the tiled floor behind her. "All the better to greet him," he whispered. "Now go see if you can seduce him." He patted her butt lightly and turned her around.

Oh, shit. "I can't do this." While she might have jumped Cade's bones last night, she wasn't comfortable being with both men at the same time.

Cade glanced over at her. "Can't do what, sugar?"

His voice came out nonchalantly, as if it was an everyday occurrence to walk into his house and find a naked woman in his roommate's arms. She lowered one hand to between her legs. "Be so casual." If she took the plunge, she wanted to know they both really cared.

He shrugged out of his coat and strode over to her. "Casual? You call what we shared last night *casual*?"

Now she'd offended him. Everything they did last night had felt very real and important, maybe even long lasting. "I don't know." Being in the presence of these two men jumbled her brain.

Cade moved closer and lifted her chin. "Maybe we need to

have a repeat performance so I can convince you how good it is between us."

Stone captured her wrists and drew her arms behind her, enabling Cade to see all of her. He smiled and her pussy cramped. He looked like a hungry tiger ready to pounce.

Cade adjusted his pants. "Jesus, Amber. I'm hard just looking at you."

He sounded as if he meant it. "Remember, I'm new to this." She wanted to be with both men, but was she ready for a ménage relationship? *You should have thought of that before you slept with Cade.*

He leaned closer. "I remember. We'll go slow. I promise."

Never taking his gaze from her eyes, Cade stepped back and discarded his shoes, then removed his white button-down shirt and charcoal gray slacks.

She cleared her throat and nodded to his briefs. "You look good in black."

"Oh, yeah?" Cade tossed them off and winked, cutting the tension in the air.

In the bright light, Cade was more magnificent than she remembered him. As she stared at him, Stone reached around and fondled her breasts. He plucked her nipples, sending sparks straight to her clit.

Cade approached. "Don't do that, buddy. I'm hard enough." He ran a thumb down her cheek. "I'm thinking that for your first time, we need to show you how we care for someone so delicate."

The delicate word rubbed her the wrong way. She arched her back. "I'm not *delicate*." She was a dedicated, hardened oncology nurse.

Cade slipped three fingers into her weeping opening and finger-fucked her. As lust slammed into her, her breath caught, and she had to close her legs to keep from losing it. He withdrew his hand.

He smiled. "I see Stone hasn't satisfied you yet."

She tilted her chin up. "You interrupted us." She debated grabbing his cock to see how he'd respond, but instead twisted around and wrapped her arms around Stone's neck. "You ready to show Cade what you can do?"

He laughed. "Hear that, Cade? Our woman wants to pit us against each other."

With his hands on her waist, Cade tugged her out of Stone's grasp. A second later, she was upside down over his bare shoulder.

Cade patted her ass. "What are we going to do with you?"

She could have told him to stop, but every inch of her skin was vibrating with need. She trusted these men to do right by her.

"Take her to my room," Stone said.

She figured he made that suggestion because his bed would be made. When Cade entered the near dark room, she couldn't tell what it really looked like. Before her eyes adjusted to the dim hallway light, Cade placed her on the bed then crawled on top of her. Now, she didn't want to look at anything but him. Resting on his elbows, he kissed her thoroughly. The slow exploration of her mouth made her moan and wiggle beneath him. He was different from the desperate man yesterday.

Stone tapped Cade on the shoulder. "Don't hog her."

In a flash, Cade rolled onto his side, supporting his head with his palm. He dragged a finger from her belly button up to her nipple. "You are so beautiful." Even without him touching the tip, the peak puckered. He then slipped a finger into her and her body quivered. That was just what she needed.

Stone placed a knee on the bed and rolled her over to face him. "Cade, how about I enjoy her breasts and you can have her pussy? Oral only. My cock has yet to experience her." He dragged a rough knuckle down her face.

"No problem," Cade said. "There will be plenty of time for

both of us."

"I'm a bit sore from yesterday." She glanced behind her. "I'm not made of Teflon, you know."

Stone tapped her nose and returned her attention to him. "I'll take it easy on you, baby."

"It might help if I lick your cock first." She drew in her bottom lip, trying to entice him. "If it's wet, it'll go in easier."

From behind, Cade wrapped his arms around her, tugged her close, and whispered, "Go right ahead. I want to see how well he holds up under your masterful mouth."

She looked over her shoulder again. "How do you know if I have a masterful mouth, as you so nicely put it? I never got to suck on yours."

Stone laughed. "She got you there, buddy."

Cade tapped her hip. "Do Stone first."

Cade probably knew he'd never last if she started with him. She sat up and swung her legs over the edge of the bed. "Ready, Stone?" She gave him her best come-hither look.

She bet the glare he gave Cade was for her benefit. Stone stepped out of his briefs. As he approached, Cade rose to his knees behind her and lifted her breasts.

She exhaled and looked behind her. "How can I concentrate if you're going to play with me?"

Cade pinched her nipples, almost as if to remind her of the heated passion they'd shared last night. *Men.* She would have commented had her pussy not tingled a moment later. *Fine.* She'd show them she could handle both.

Stone approached. *Wow.* His cock was huge, maybe even bigger than Cade's, and that worried her. He might not fit.

Then you better do a damned fine job of exciting him so he won't take long before exploding. She ran her thumb over his balls. "I like how they're nice and hard."

Cade twirled her nipples then ran a palm down her belly. "Don't worry about me, sugar. I'm just enjoying your fine body." Anticipation shot through her as she recalled the amazingly hot sex they'd had last night. *Christ.* If he turned her on any more, she'd never be able to do a satisfactory job with Stone. Was that Cade's intent?

"Amber?" Stone tapped her head.

Focus. As she gently squeezed Stone's balls, he clasped her wrist, slid her hand upward, and placed her palm on his rigid cock.

"It needs you here more."

She swallowed a laugh. *Note to self—he can't take the teasing.* She planned to use that to her advantage in a moment. Licking the tip, she ran her tongue through his salty slit where a bit of cum had already oozed out. Having Stone lose control before he was ready was going to be a piece of cake.

With one hand holding his sac and the other on his dick, she traced a line with her tongue up his shaft until she bumped into the mushroom-shaped head.

"Suck on him, baby."

You are so going down. She eased her mouth over him. Stone pressed on her head as if he needed more friction. She obliged. The sooner he neared his climax, the sooner she'd get his cock, and given what Cade was now doing with her clit, she'd need him soon.

Amber only managed a few strong strokes with her mouth before Stone pulled back. "Enough."

Aha. Cade tugged her back and lifted her legs onto the bed. "My turn."

Stone dropped onto the bed next to her. "We'll try not to excite you too fast."

Too late. The thrill of what was to come had her body zinging with pleasure.

"Close your eyes and let us love you," Cade said with a softness she hadn't expected.

She shut her eyes. The bed dipped and when one of them

rubbed her nipples and the other spread her legs wide, her breath hissed out of her. Her skin caught fire.

With what seemed like practiced precision, the men performed a mouth assault on her body. Cade licked her slit while Stone nabbed her nipple. Tongues swirled, causing waves of lust to fill every vein. She bucked her hips.

"Don't move." Cade planted a hand on her belly and nabbed her tiny bud. Electric sparks shot through her with such speed her heart hammered in her chest.

"Please." Begging wasn't her style, but then again, she'd never been in such a needy state before.

"Patience," Cade said.

Patience, my ass. He certainly hadn't had any yesterday. To be fair, neither had she. Next time, she'd insist on sucking Cade's cock long and hard. She'd prove to him he had no patience either.

He lifted his mouth and threaded two fingers into her wet channel. When he pressed on her G-spot, she moaned. In a flash, she was turned over and lifted onto her elbows and knees.

"Condom. Nightstand," Stone commanded.

Cade moved to the head of the bed. The drawer squeaked open then foil tore. The snap of a condom made her juices flow harder. This was it—the time when she'd make love with two men.

Chapter Eighteen

Stone ran his hands up and down Amber's back. "You are so hot."

She opened her eyes to see Cade kneeling in front of her, his big cock inches from her mouth. Now she'd get to prove to the great Cade Carter that he wasn't as immune as he claimed to be.

As she reached out to pull his dick toward her, Cade clasped her wrist. "Wait. I want you to experience Stone without getting too distracted by what I'm about to do to you."

What was he talking about? She was the one about to give him a blowjob.

Stone grunted. "You're full of shit, Cade. Baby, don't listen to him. Torture him like you did me."

She let out a breath, realizing this was their way of calming her down. They were truly special men to understand this was a big leap of faith for her to love both of them.

Stone rubbed her back with one hand as he pressed his hard tip against her opening. His full inhale made her smile. He'd only eased in an inch when she gasped. His cock was huge, or else her inner walls were swollen from last night.

"I've changed my mind. Suck on it, sugar. It'll take your mind off Stone."

She wanted to revel in making love with Stone, but when

Cade twirled her nipples, she forgot everything. So that was what he meant by him doing something. The tension and slight pain caused her juices to increase, easing the way for Stone's cock.

He leaned over her back and kissed her neck. Having him in contact with most of her body, both inside and out, seemed so right. Stone slid in another inch, and when Cade presented her with his throbbing dick, she grabbed it. He moaned—loudly. *Good.*

As much as she wanted to drag her tongue up and down Cade's length, she bet she could bring him to the edge closer if she sucked on him hard. Amber drew her lips around the head and drove down on him.

"Jesus, Amber."

Her heart sang from his reaction. She swirled her tongue around and around. She only stopped when he pinched her nipples. Her breath caught, but she didn't open her mouth and lose the suction.

Stone took advantage of her lull and eased into her all the way.

"God, you're so fucking tight."

Surely, he knew why. Cade tapped her head and she resumed tormenting him. But the harder she sucked, the more pressure he applied to her nipples. Then Stone pulled out and drove back into her with equal intensity. The combination was mind-blowing. Heat bubbled inside her as her climax gained momentum.

Don't come.

She wanted to show her men she could be as strong as they were. But then, Stone dragged a hand down her belly and pressed on her clit. That was her Achilles' heel. Damn him.

Cade placed his hand over hers and pumped her fist up and down faster and faster. She leaned her hips back, needing Stone to take her over the edge now. All three groaned and moaned until it sounded like a bad orchestra warming up. Cade lost it first. Hot jism coated her throat and she lifted her head to swallow his tangy brew. He pulled back his hips but kept his fingers firmly on her breasts as if he didn't want to lose contact.

Stone increased his pistoning. "Come for me, baby," he cried out.

His plea, along with the next strong thrust that filled her to the hilt, took her over the edge. Her body pulsed and zinged as her climax swooped in. When she pressed her hips back for more, his cock expanded and pulsed, stretching her so hard, she had to open her mouth to bring in more air. When Stone finally finished letting loose, he grabbed her by the waist and rolled her over. His cock popped out.

Cade left the bed but returned moments later with a warm, wet cloth. This time, she welcomed him cleaning her.

On his knees, Cade faced her and brushed her hair out of her face. "Was it okay for you?"

"It was more than okay. It was fantastic, brilliant, amazing."

He grinned, and she knew she'd made the right choice. Two was definitely better than one.

Stone tapped her nose. "Anyone up for brownies?"

"If I can feed them to you both, I'm game." She smiled but had no energy to even move. *Oh, boy.*

✧ ✧ ✧

After making love with Amber the previous night and having Cade join in, Stone wanted to race to the highest mountain and shout about the wonderful Amber Delacroix. But now he was worried about bringing her to Katie's birthday party. His dad could be tough. No doubt his father would question her about what she did and where she grew up. Both of his parents could be a little overzealous sometimes, but he believed she'd win them over as soon as they met her.

For years, his mom had tried to find him a woman even

though he'd told her he and Cade shared. She'd been shocked at first, but eventually, she'd come to accept that lifestyle, especially as more people in town embraced the concept.

Cade had driven separately to the birthday party. Given the nature of his job, he said he was more comfortable having a car in case an emergency popped up. Because Stone didn't want anything to interfere with his time with Amber, he agreed.

She tapped the present she held on her lap. "Do you think Katie will really like what you got her?"

He thought it cute that she worried. "She'll think it's wonderful. Katie lives each day like it's her last. You'll love her."

The trip to the edge of town didn't take long. His family's home wasn't grand by any means, but the land it was built on had a wonderful view of the mountains. Dad owned a few horses, some cattle, and even raised chickens for family consumption. Stone hoped his mom didn't mention the occasional slaughter to soft-hearted Amber. She'd be too sympathetic about them eating the livestock.

He pulled in front of the house and she sighed. "It's lovely." Sincerity rang from her voice.

"I'm sure you lived in a bigger home growing up."

"Bigger but more sterile. I love log cabin style homes."

Dust billowed behind them as Cade pulled in next to them. Stone retrieved the package from Amber's lap, and together the three of them marched up to the front door. They then had to fight their way through the balloons attached to the handle.

Amber looked up and smiled. "I like your family already."

He could only hope. Stone pushed open the door and let Amber go first. Cade stepped in behind him.

"Mom?"

Footsteps sounded, and his mother rounded the corner. As expected, her gaze latched onto Amber. She smiled and rushed toward her. The hug seemed to take Amber by surprise. *Damn.* He should have warned her how affectionate his parents could be.

His mom held Amber out at arm's length and ran her gaze down her. "Well, well. You must be Amber. I'm so happy to meet you."

"You, too, Mrs. Benson."

"Call me Ellie. Everyone does." She reached out for the presents he and Cade were carrying. "Let me take those from you. I'll put them on the sideboard with the rest of the gifts. Stone, bring Amber into the living room. Everyone's here."

Everyone? They rounded the corner and to his delight his younger brother Craig was standing there. "Hey, little brother." The two embraced. "Let me look at you. Philadelphia seems to agree with you. You didn't tell me you were coming."

"It was a surprise for Katie." He stepped to the side and hugged Cade, too. After all, Cade had been there for Craig as much as Stone had been.

Katie stood and wrapped her arms around him then held out her hand to Amber. "I'm Katie."

"Amber." Her eyes sparkled when she smiled.

Christ. Where was his head? He should have introduced her to everyone, but seeing his brother took him by surprise. He wrapped an arm around Amber's waist. "The old fart on the chair is my dad."

She lightly punched him and tossed him an adorable pout. "That's a terrible thing to say." They walked over to his father, and Amber held out her hand. "I'm Amber Delacroix. Stone helped one of my family members, and I'm eternally grateful."

"Nice meeting you, Amber. What do you do for a living?"

Stone didn't want his dad to grill her. "You can put her through the grinder later, Dad. Let's let her relax for a second."

His father harrumphed. "It's not everyday I get to meet a beautiful woman." He glanced over at Mom. "Present company excluded."

His mom smiled.

Katie sidled up to them and nodded to the sofa farthest from the television. "Come sit with me, Amber. The testosterone level is strong enough to wash you away."

Amber smiled. "Nice meeting you, Mr. Benson."

"My pleasure."

Stone watched Amber follow his sister to the sofa. "Don't tell her any lies about me, Shorty," Stone called out.

Katie grinned. "I make no promises."

Leaving them alone might not be smart, but he wanted to catch up with his brother. After learning about Craig's newest camera, he nodded to Dad. "How about you and Cade keep him company, while I make sure Katie doesn't tell Amber anything that will make her bolt?" Sure, he was exaggerating, but he wanted to spend time with both her and his sister.

"Will do."

Stone crossed the room.

"—hand puppets," Katie said.

Stone came in on the tail end of that conversation. "What about hand puppets?"

His sister faced him. "Don't you remember when I was so sick in the hospital and you made me a hand puppet? Even sewed on eyes out of buttons and made a mouth out of an old scrap of cloth."

Amber looked over at him. "That's so adorable."

He groaned. Being adorable wasn't his life's ambition. He'd rather focus on what his sister did for him. "Remember the time I broke my leg racing my bike, and you spent hours painting flowers on my cast?"

Katie grinned. "I heard you got an endless amount of shit from everyone in school over those designs." Instantly, her hand clamped over her mouth, and her gaze shot to Mom.

He laughed. "It's okay. She didn't hear you swear."

A few minutes after their mother ducked into the kitchen, he decided to give her a hand. Stone stood and wagged a finger at

Katie. "Only good stuff, okay?"

Katie crossed her heart. "I promise."

As soon as he left, he knew his sister would be extracting as much information from Amber as she could. Poor Amber.

"Need help?" he asked his mom.

"You can turn the burner to low and cook the gravy."

He stepped to the stove and sniffed to see if he could figure out what was cooking in the oven. "What are we having?"

"What we have every year. Meatloaf. It's Katie's favorite."

He loved how she cherished tradition. He picked up a wooden spoon to stir the sauce. "So what do you think?"

"About what?" His mom continued to dice the salad ingredients.

She knew what he was talking about but apparently wanted to make him ask directly. "About Amber."

She stopped chopping. "She's lovely. The real question is what do you think about her? You and Cade have never brought a woman home before." She faced him. "You and Cade are both dating her, right?"

"For an old-fashioned mom, you're all right."

She grinned. "Now answer my question."

He couldn't get anything past her. "Yes." He inhaled. "I've only known her a month, but I can't stop thinking about her. She's good, kind, compassionate, an—"

"Oh, my. You have it bad, don't you?"

There was no use in denying it. "Yes."

The oven timer dinged, and she removed the meatloaf. "If the sauce is warm, pour it into the gravy boat and set it on the table. Then tell everyone the food is ready."

Once he did as she asked, the family took their regular seats but left enough room for Amber to sit between him and Cade. After his mom said grace, they passed around the food. Amber smiled the whole time, intently listening to whoever was talking. When he thought back to the way she described her family, he was glad to show her a family who interacted with love and compassion.

The meal, as usual, was delicious. The conversation was directed equally between Craig, Katie, and Amber. The more they conversed, the more comfortable she appeared.

Finally, when they'd finished, his mother stood. "As soon as I clear the plates, we'll bring out dessert and then we can open the presents."

Amber pushed back her chair. "I want to help."

His mom smiled. "I'd like that."

Normally, Katie would have volunteered, but it was a rule in the house that on a person's birthday, he or she didn't have to lift a finger. His mom and Amber carried the first load into the kitchen.

He nodded to Cade. "Let's help. It'll go faster."

Cade cocked a brow. "Me?"

"You want my mother filling Amber's head with what a jerk you can be?"

Both Craig and Dad laughed. Cade pushed back his chair and picked up some plates. They moved between the kitchen and dining room so swiftly that his mother wasn't given the chance to tell Amber anything bad about either one of them.

When they finished, his mom brought out a lit cake and they all sang happy birthday. Amber's voice was clear and on key—probably the only one in the room who was.

As Katie blew out the candles, he leaned over to Amber. "I'm guessing her wish is to be here next year."

Amber swallowed then smiled. "She will be."

That was what he wanted to hear. The chocolate cake seemed to taste better this year, most likely because Amber was sharing it with them.

His mom stood. "Let's open the presents now. I'll pick up the plates later."

They all convened back into the living room where Katie

received a protective cover for her laptop from Craig, a gift certificate to the Apple Store from Dad, and a pretty scarf from Mom.

Katie shook the present from Cade. "What's this?" She glanced at his roommate.

"Got to open it to find out."

Stone hadn't even asked what it was.

When she unwrapped the small box, her eyes went wide. "Oh, Cade. It's gorgeous." She held up a green stone pendant.

Amber moved next to Katie. "This is amazing."

When Amber fingered the well-crafted item and smiled, Stone tried to remember if he'd ever seen her wear jewelry like that. He didn't.

Cade grinned. "Trish Duggen is now making jewelry."

"Next time I see her, I'll have to thank her," Katie said.

"Open our present," Stone nodded to the remaining gift. "This is from me and Amber."

Amber twisted toward him and slightly shook her head. He smiled. He wanted her to feel part of the family. Katie picked up the package and shook it. "I can't imagine what it is."

"Open it." This came from Amber.

His sister ripped the paper, and he loved watching Amber wince at seeing her artwork torn to pieces. When Katie held up the canvas bag and lifted the flap she gasped.

She glanced between them. "I can't believe it. Mom, look!" She pulled out the yarn and showed her the needles.

"That's wonderful, dear. Why, you haven't crocheted anything in years."

"I know, but I've been thinking about picking it back up again. It really relaxes me." She leaned over and hugged Amber.

At first, Amber stiffened, but after a moment, she hugged his sister back. Stone's heart both warmed and ached at the lack of love Amber had in her life. He vowed to make it better if it was the last thing he did.

Chapter Nineteen

After the birthday party, Cade and Stone took Amber riding. It had been a long time since she'd been on a horse and now every inch of her body was sore. Part was because of her activity with her men last night, but the rest was because of the need to hold on for dear life. She used muscles she hadn't needed in years.

Cade had spent so much time at the Benson ranch he'd learned how to ride well, though not quite as expertly as Stone. Several times, the two had raced in front of her, turned around, and then hauled ass back. She never was quite sure what the bet had been, but they had her laughing with their antics.

After two hours of showing off, they must have been able to tell when enough was enough because they guided her back to the barn at a leisurely pace. Once they brushed the horses down and put them in their stalls, she made them promise to take her out again.

While her time outside had been wonderful, she was ready to get home and relax. As Stone pulled in front of her house, she unbuckled her seatbelt and faced him. "I'd love for you to come in, but I need—"

He smiled. "I know. You need a little down time, not only to think things through, but to rest." His gaze dropped between her legs and heat rushed to her cheeks.

She laughed. It was dumb to be embarrassed after their amazing love session. She still couldn't believe these men wanted her.

He clasped her hand. "Let me walk you to the door."

"As long as I get a goodnight kiss."

"Promise." He helped her out of the truck and escorted her up the steps. After she unlocked the door, she faced him for her reward.

Stone dragged a knuckle down her cheek. "I'll call you tomorrow."

She slipped her hands around his neck. "You better."

Stone leaned in and brushed his lips across hers then tapped her nose. "I can't get started, or you know what will happen."

Wetness had already pooled between her legs. She had it bad. "That I do."

She waited at the steps until he entered his car. As soon as he drove off, she went inside. Needing some girlfriend time, she called Jamie. It always helped to have a sounding board. Amber had called her yesterday morning and told her about birthday shopping for Stone's sister and the party. While Jamie already knew she'd been with Cade, Amber hadn't divulged she'd slept with them both, yet.

Jamie had told her Ben would be playing poker tonight with some of the other pharmaceutical techs. Apparently, one of the men's brothers was some gambling pro, and he was here for a visit. Personally, she didn't see Ben as the type to play cards, but maybe he was ready for a guy's night out after everything that had been going on at the hospital.

She called and Jamie answered on the second ring. "Hey, girlfriend. How did the birthday party go? Hold it. Why aren't you with your men?"

"I'll see them tomorrow." She let out a laugh that sounded fake even to her ears. "I needed a break to digest all that's happened." Wasn't that the truth? Witnessing how a real family acted had given her pause. Ellie's warmth only served to highlight how cold her mother was. The hugs, the smiles, along with everyone's willingness to help clean up showed her what she'd missed growing up. Yes, she'd had Chris, but he had his own friends, his own dreams.

"I can only imagine." Jamie's comment mentally brought her back.

"Want to come over for some girl time?" She swiped the tear threatening to spill, praying her voice hadn't divulged the extent of her dark thoughts.

She should be ecstatic right now. After all, she'd watched Stone and Cade interact like they were teenagers again, and the sex they'd shared had been beyond her wildest dreams. But in the back of her mind, she kept waiting for the proverbial shoe to drop. Everyone in her life had abandoned her—her dad, her mom, and then Rich. Why should anything be different now?

"Are you kidding? Hell yeah. I'll even bring the popcorn."

"Give me half an hour. I have to shower." *And gather my thoughts.*

"Perfect."

Refusing to let her pity party ruin her visit with Jamie, she forced herself to think only positive thoughts. Once Amber stepped into the shower, she let the heat pour over her body and soothe her aching muscles. Being with the Benson family had been amazing and eye opening. Riding with her men had given her a tremendous sense of freedom that she cherished.

As she scrubbed clean, she daydreamed about having made love with two men. Given how her mother had raised her, she should be embarrassed for wanting two men, but she wasn't. The incredible sensations still ran through her veins.

When the water cooled, she shut off the valve and stepped out. Jamie would be here in a few minutes. Amber wanted to chill, so she tossed on flannel pajamas and slippers and went back to the living room to gather the needed items for the evening—wine and cheese.

The doorbell rang within minutes, and she ushered Jamie inside. "Thanks for coming over." She wrapped her arms around her, glad for the company.

Jamie waved the popcorn. "How about we pop first and then you spill?"

"Spill?"

"You haven't had a chance to tell me what happened with the birthday present shopping."

That seemed like forever ago. They walked into the kitchen. "Stone knew nothing about crocheting." Amber told her about picking out a really cool bag and all the accessories. "Then we went grocery shopping, and Stone and I made dinner together."

"That's so romantic."

"I know."

"Did you two talk about Cade?"

"More or less. Stone insisted he wasn't upset and said he was happy Cade and I had patched things up."

The microwave dinged signaling the popcorn was done. Once she'd dumped it in a bowl, they walked into the living room where she curled up on the sofa next to Jamie. Amber handed the bowl to her. "So after we ate, one thing led to another."

Jamie's mouth opened. "You made love with him? Was it amazing? How would you compare him to Cade?"

She laughed. "I refuse to compare them. They're different in a lot of ways."

"Start from the beginning."

Amber inhaled. "So Stone and I were in the living room—naked—when Cade walked in."

Jamie's eyes widened. "What did you guys do?"

"Let him join in."

Jamie clamped a hand over her mouth. "Benny would never allow me to do anything like that, not that I want to, but sometimes…"

Amber had never seen any doubt in Jamie's eyes before. "Sometimes what?"

Jamie stuffed popcorn into her mouth and chewed. Finally, she finished. "Benny is almost too perfect. Too kind."

Amber knew that. Everyone did. "What's the problem?"

"Please don't think less of me, but I kind have been interested in trying a little kink—not the two men kind of kink—but something a little more than vanilla. I brought it up once, but Benny just sighed. He said he could never hurt me."

"What did you ask him to do?" Jamie seemed too sweet to be adventurous.

Her friend shook her head. "All I asked for him to tie me up with a scarf or something, and maybe get a little spanking. Nothing major."

"He couldn't think a scarf would hurt, would he?"

Jamie sighed. "A spanking might. It doesn't matter. Benny won't go for it. You know how Benny hates to see anyone suffer. You weren't in Rock Hard yet, but I had this mutt I loved with my whole being. He was old and had cancer, but he was my best friend. When I came back from work one night, Beau had died. I lost it and called Benny. We weren't even dating at the time, but he'd told me how much he loved animals."

"What did he do?"

"He rushed right over. He'd never met Beau, but he held me and wept along with me. Then with more care than possible, he wrapped him up, placed him in his doggie bed, and drove him to the vet's."

Amber poured the wine she'd set on the coffee table. "That's so like Ben. He's a keeper." She clasped Jamie's hand. "By the way, there's nothing wrong with vanilla sex."

"I know, but I want more passion."

Amber smiled at the erotic image of Cade plastering her against the door and taking her hard.

"What is it?" Jamie asked.

"I can't talk about being tied up or being spanked, but I can tell you about passion."

✧ ✧ ✧

The next few days went by in a blur. Amber occasionally spotted a detective at the hospital asking questions about Stephanie Osmond, but so far she hadn't seen Cade there. He'd called her Sunday, Monday, and Tuesday, each time to apologize for having to work late. Stone phoned, too, but his days off didn't fit into her schedule. It was highly frustrating.

When her cell rang Thursday morning, excitement raced through her. She was just finishing with a patient, so the timing was perfect. Smiling, she ducked into the hallway and strolled toward the break room. "Hey, stranger."

"I only have a minute to talk." Cade kept his voice low. "Are you free Friday after you get off work?"

"I am."

"I want us to be together."

Music to my ears. "Me, too."

"I wish it were sooner though. I miss you."

She chuckled. "Back at you." His sentimental attitude never ceased to amaze her. "What about Stone?" She held her breath.

"Sorry, sugar. He pulled the late shift, but he'll be free on Saturday. Maybe the three of us can come up with something to do then."

The practical side of a ménage relationship was exposing its ugly head. "That works for me."

"How about I pick you up at your house at six on Friday?"

"Perfect."

She was about to ask where they were going so she'd know how to dress, but someone called his name. He disconnected before she had the chance. Darn. She missed him already.

Friday night? Uh-oh. Two days ago, Cade said he had something to do that night, so she'd made tentative plans to be with Jamie and Ben. Now she had to cancel. It sucked, but Jamie hadn't been sure if they could make it anyway.

Since she had a few minutes free, she took the elevator to the hospice floor to let Jamie know. Before she found her friend, she wanted to see how Jennifer Seely was doing today. Amber sucked in a breath and squared her shoulders.

She'd stopped by Monday and again yesterday, but each visit became harder than the last knowing this was the end. Jenn had been one of her favorite patients. As she headed down the hallway, she dared a glance into the rooms. Most of the patients appeared to be asleep. It was sad enough when the person was old, but it was even harder when that person hadn't fully lived her life.

As she passed the room right before Jenn's, she slowed then backed up. The door was slightly ajar and she caught a glimpse of Ben's bright red hair. "Knock, knock." She peeked in at him bending over someone. She hadn't realized he knew any of the hospice patients.

Ben turned around and looked a bit startled. "Oh, hey, Amber. What are you doing here?"

That was what she was about to ask him. She could understand why he'd question her though. She rarely came on this floor. "I wanted to see how Jennifer Seely was doing. She transferred up here a couple of days ago."

He strode toward her. "Oh."

"I also came up to find Jamie, but I can tell you instead. I have to cancel on Friday."

He ushered her out the door and closed it. "Why? Hot date?" He winked as if he knew about what she, Cade, and Stone had done.

"As a matter of fact, yes. Is that okay? I promise we'll get together soon." She hadn't had both of them over since Chris had died.

"No problem. We never committed anyway. We might have to visit with Jamie's aunt. I'll let her know."

He turned to leave, but Amber clasped his shoulder and nodded to the woman inside. "Who is she?"

His eyes slightly widened. "That's my cousin. Real shame. She only has a few days to live."

"Your cousin?" She thought she knew everything about Ben.

"I never mentioned her because we drifted apart after mom died. She only moved back to Rock Hard after she found out she was sick."

"I'm sorry. I'm surprised Jamie never mentioned her."

"She doesn't know." He placed a finger to his lips. "Shh. I want to spare her. She goes through enough." He checked his watch. "Listen. My break's over and I gotta go, but we'll reschedule for sure." Ben looked down the hallway then back at her. He barely made eye contact. "Have fun with your man."

"Will do." She watched him stride down the hallway with hurried steps—and Ben never hurried. Amber shook her head. Maybe he was upset and needed to get away.

She stepped next door and found Jennifer asleep. Her breathing was raspy and shallow. Not wanting to disturb her, Amber backed out and headed to the stairs. She could use the exercise to help clear her head. Only this morning had her inner thigh muscles recovered. And they'd been tight from more than riding the horse. At that thought, a smile formed. She sure was a lucky woman.

Chapter Twenty

At six o'clock on the dot, Cade knocked on her front door and Amber answered. He was dressed in a pair of black slacks and a fitted white shirt open at the throat. *Oh, my*. "Come in."

He ran his gaze up and down her body. "You look amazing."

She smiled, glad she'd taken the extra care to impress him. "So do you."

Without a word, Cade drew her into a tight embrace and kissed her. Not only did his hard chest make contact, his hips did, too. Without thinking where this could lead, she hooked her arms around his back and tugged him close. When their tongues met, they dueled and sparred as if this might be their last kiss—ever. His desperation made her blood soar.

Reason intruded, and she palmed his chest. "We shouldn't get started."

"Why not?" He nibbled that wonderfully sensitive spot below her ear. "You don't want to ride me?"

She laughed as his tongue tickled her neck. "Yes, but after we eat."

He stepped away, looking amused. "Then food it shall be." He tapped her nose. "Where's your coat?"

She plucked it from the sofa and he led her out. After she locked the front door, Amber slipped into the front seat and buckled up.

Cade slid in. "You good with Thai food?"

"Love it." She'd mentioned in passing how much she liked Asian cuisine.

"Excellent."

Now she was glad she'd dressed up.

As he turned down Gold Avenue, she stared out the window, her hand aimlessly lifting and lowering her jacket zipper.

"—wrong?"

She turned her attention back to Cade. "Sorry, what?"

"Are you okay?"

"Yes. I was thinking about Jamie and Ben."

Cade glanced at her. "What about them?"

"I hadn't wanted to mention this, but I made tentative plans to watch a movie at my house tonight with them—assuming they could have made it."

"Shit, sugar. We could have rescheduled. Why didn't you tell me before?"

She let out an exasperated sigh. "Because it's hard enough for us to find time to be together, and I can go out with Ben and Jamie any time. Kind of like we did when Chris had been alive." She continued to fiddle with the zipper on her jacket. "Besides, our plans were up in the air." She looked down at her fingers, fighting some tears. "I'm not sure I'm ready to pretend everything is back to normal."

"It takes time."

"I know." He understood. Cade had lost both of his parents.

"You always play with your zipper when something's really bothering you, though. Did Jamie say something to upset you? Is that why they aren't coming over?"

She let go of the pull tab. "No. I cancelled." *Damn.* She sounded too defensive.

"If not Jamie, was it Ben?"

"No." She smoothed the hair behind her ear. "Ben's… fine."

"Sugar? You can tell me anything, you know."

"There's nothing to tell." So as not to fidget anymore, she clasped her hands on her lap, but her damn leg wouldn't stop bouncing. *Tell him something. Anything to shut him up.* "When I went up to the hospice floor to cancel the date with Jamie, Ben was visiting a sick relative." She inhaled deeply. "There's no crime in that."

He draped a wrist over the wheel, looking overly casual. "You seem bothered by this."

"I'm not bothered." She flattened her palms on her thighs so he wouldn't say her actions implied something.

He glanced at her again. "I get the sense you have a concern about something you saw."

"I didn't see Ben do anything."

His brow cocked. "I know Ben's and Jamie's friendship mean a lot to you. I also know that you don't want to betray their trust or do anything that would hurt them."

"No, I don't." She swiped the moisture from under her eye.

"Your patients' well-being is one of your deepest convictions. You could never knowingly allow anything to happen to them either, could you?"

A ray of hope seeped in. He did understand. "No, I couldn't."

"Sometimes, conflict results between those two needs. That's why I'd like to ask you a couple of questions."

He was back to his cop mode. "About what?" She sniffled.

"I want to help you ensure your patients stay safe. What does your gut say about what Ben was doing?"

Chills danced up her spine. Trying to act casual, she shrugged. "Like I told you. He was checking up on a sick relative."

"That's good. What was he wearing?"

Her leg stopped moving. "What?"

"Was he in his usual lab coat like he'd come from the pharmacy, or was he dressed in a T-shirt and jeans?"

"He was dressed for work. I don't see what difference it makes."

A large truck lumbered down the two-way highway in front of them, forcing Cade to slow.

He was acting like she was hiding something? She wasn't.

"Okay," Cade said. "Ben was visiting his cousin. Did he see you?"

She didn't mind answering that. "Yes."

"Did he wave you in and introduce you, or had you met his cousin before?"

Her stomach flipped. "No and no." She then told him how Ben had rushed out of the room most likely because he didn't want their talking to disturb the woman.

Cade inhaled deeply then let out a big exhale. "What are your instincts telling you about why he was in such a hurry?"

Her pulse sped up and sweat beaded on her forehead. "They're not telling me anything." She focused on the road ahead and ran her hands down her thighs. She faced him. "Have you been to this Thai House before? I know you love steak, but do they have something you like?"

"Amber. I can hear you're upset. You don't want anything bad to happen to Ben any more than I do."

"I'm not upset. Why should I be upset?" Her neck itched, and she scratched it, glad to have something to distract her.

"Amber. Sugar."

"What?"" She pressed her lips together and faced him, wishing he'd disappear.

"When Ben came out of the room, did he do something? Like touch you inappropriately?" There was a possessive grating to his voice.

"No! He kept his hand in his pocket the whole time."

Acid rose to her throat. How dare he think Ben would ever cheat on Jamie. The image of him surfaced. She had to admit he looked kind of funny with his lab coat pulled tight against his body and his belly protruding. Usually, if he was just chatting in the hallway, he'd stand with both thumbs in his jeans pockets, looking casual.

"Just one hand?" Cade's fingers unclenched from the wheel.

"I don't remember." She'd kept her gaze on Ben's right wrist, which was at an odd angle. It was almost as if he was hiding something in his pocket.

"Amber?"

"Yes. One hand."

She squeezed her eyes shut trying to picture Ben as he hovered over his cousin. He had acted a bit strange when he left the room, but it could have been because he was upset over her near death.

Then why did you look up the name of the patient to see if the two were related? A tear leaked out.

Cade turned down First Avenue and slowed as he neared the restaurant entrance. He parked, cut the engine, and reached out to her. "Sugar. Please. This is hurting me, too." His voice shook. "I think all this protesting is a cry for help. You want to tell yourself something, but fear is stopping you."

Tears ran down her cheeks. "Why did Ben lie?" The words burned in her throat. "The woman he said was he cousin wasn't his cousin." Cade didn't respond. He just held her hand. She choked out a sob. "He tells me everything. So why didn't he tell me about his cousin—or whoever she was?"

Amber pulled away from Cade's grip and dropped her head in her hands. She cried even though she wasn't sure why. Cade rubbed her back and let her grieve for the crack in their friendship. She finally sat up.

"Sugar. What is it that you can't say out loud? It must be painful."

Her body ached. Her brain screamed, *no, no, no.* Ben wasn't supposed to be in the room. Her heart lurched. She wouldn't go down that path. It was too dark, too terrible.

She sealed her lips, but the burgeoning doubt burst out. "He wouldn't harm anyone, would he?" She paused. Every muscle tensed. "Do you think Ben was in the room to hurt that woman?" She grabbed her zipper again.

He held her gaze for an eternity. "I don't know, sugar. Why don't you tell me more about why your sixth sense is leading you there?"

She shook her head over and over again. "He ran away. And Ben never moves fast." She hiccupped as she sucked in a breath. "Oh, no." Her gaze raced around. "That's why he asked me about the Ativan dosage." The reality of it all was too much. "Could he have been hiding a syringe in his pocket?"

Amber didn't wait for Cade to answer. She pushed open the car door and ran out, tears streaming down her face. She didn't want to consider it. Ben was a good man. Noisy cars racing down the road made it hard to think.

Just run! As fast she could go in her stupid heels, she rushed down the sidewalk, not having any destination in mind.

Footsteps pounded behind her. "Sugar?" A second later, Cade scooped her into his arms. Her feet kept kicking as he dangled her off the ground. "Shh."

He set her down, turned her to face him, and held her tight. Amber lowered her face onto his shoulder. After having to deal with weeks of frustration over Chris's accident and death, Sam Richland's attack, and the possibility of Ben being a murderer, the dam broke. Sobs tore through her body, ripping her up inside.

"Oh, sugar." Cade just held her and rubbed her back. "Shh. It'll be okay."

The tears wouldn't stop, but Cade never let her go. Amber stood there a long time. Eventually, the fight eased out of her.

Her bottom lip trembled. "I don't want Ben to be guilty." Her insides shook. Ben had to be innocent. He just had to be.

He leaned back and swiped his thumb under her eye. "Don't worry. We'll figure it all out together."

Chapter Twenty-One

Once she was more or less composed, Amber looked up at him. "I'm sorry I ruined the evening." She ran her hands down his chest. The soft material over the hard planes of his chest helped unbunch the knots in her stomach.

"You did no such thing." He pulled out a handkerchief and dabbed what was probably mascara all over her face. "You had doubts about a good friend. That's all."

Is that all they were? Doubts? She hadn't seen Ben doing anything illegal, so maybe her imagination had gone crazy from the stress. That's all.

She took the cloth from Cade's hand, extracted a mirror from her purse, and checked her appearance. "Dear God."

He smoothed her flyaway hair. "You are a wonderful friend, Amber Delacroix. The best. You fought a good battle. You wouldn't have tried so hard to keep from suspecting him unless deep in your heart you believed Ben wanted to help those people so much that he put them to sleep."

She shook her head, and then placed her cheek on his muscular chest. "If Ben is guilty, murder is still murder, but I'm not sure if he did anything."

"I have to say all of your evidence is circumstantial."

She wanted to believe him. "You're right."

He smiled. "That doesn't mean I won't be looking into his activities."

It was his job to find the killer. "I know."

Cade wrapped a comforting arm around her waist. "What do you say we shelve the investigation until I've had another chance to look into this and have a nice dinner?"

She leaned into him and wiped her eyes again. "I'm good with that." She prayed he found nothing concrete against Ben. Besides Cade and Stone, Ben and Jamie were all she had.

Cade walked her back through the parking lot. He opened the restaurant door and ushered her in. She hoped she could stop drawing any more terrible conclusions for the rest of the evening. Inhaling, she lifted her head high and walked in.

"Oh." This was better than sitting in the car with her dark thoughts. Much better.

The Thai restaurant had subdued lighting, with warm-colored wall coverings. A large fish tank that lent serenity to the surroundings sat in the center of the restaurant. A pretty waitress in a red silk sheath showed them to a table nestled between two potted ferns. It was cozy and rather romantic.

Amber slid into the booth, and Cade sat across from her.

He stretched an arm along the back. "So, have you recovered from all of our racing around on the horses last week?"

A small smile lifted her lips, and she let out a long breath. She appreciated his effort to take her mind off her meltdown. "Today was the first time I felt normal. I had no idea I was so out of shape." She pressed a hand under one of her thighs, which it was still a little tender.

He leaned forward. "I'll be honest. I was a bit sore, too. To keep fit, we should go out a few more times before it gets too cold to ride."

"I'd love that." Nothing soothed her soul better than being outdoors.

The server came by for their drink orders. Given Amber's

recent mental lapse, she ordered a hot green tea instead of wine. Cade asked for an ale.

He tapped his fingers on the table. "I like you Amber Delacroix. A lot. You have integrity, and that means a lot to me." Cade studied her for a moment, but she wasn't uncomfortable with his scrutiny. "I want to know what makes you tick. What drives you?"

He probably wanted to understand why an in-control oncology nurse almost had a psychotic break. "What drives me?" She shrugged. "I never thought about it."

Kindness washed over his face. "How about if you tell me one thing that scares you." He looked deep into her eyes.

Thinking Ben might really have harmed Chris. "What does that have to do with what motivates me?" She kept her voice low.

"I just want to get to know you better." He leaned forward. "How about this? Tell me an event that happened a long time ago that you feel contributed to who you are today." He unrolled the linen napkin and placed it on his lap. "It might have been something fantastic and inspiring, or an event you want to forget, but can't."

She'd already exposed a part of herself that was still so raw that nothing she said now could further hurt her. "You mean like a secret?" Telling him about Rich had been hard, but she could think of only one other event that had scarred her for life. Hell, she was the first to believe honesty was at the core of everything. Look at Rich and how they'd failed. If only he'd been truthful sooner, the pain wouldn't have been so bad.

"Yes." Cade exhaled very slowly. "You know, sugar, being in a relationship with one man can be challenging. Being with two doubles it. I want to understand who you are in here." He tapped his chest. "And up here." He placed a finger on the side of his head.

The server came over and set a tea cup, a pot of hot water, and a teabag in front of Amber and an empty glass along with a bottle of ale in front of Cade. "Have you decided?"

"Give us a few minutes," Cade said. The server nodded and left.

Needing a moment to compose her thoughts, Amber dunked her teabag in the pot of hot water and swirled it around. She didn't meet his gaze. Instead, she continued to stir her tea. "I was twelve and Chris was six. He wanted to play hide and seek." She glanced to the ceiling for a second. "It was his favorite game, mostly because I'd usually let him win." She dipped the teabag again. "We were down by the river one afternoon where we often played. So as not to know where he hid, I would close my eyes, plug my ears, and count to one-hundred."

"A six-year-old boy could get into a lot of trouble in that amount of time."

"I found that out." She drew in her bottom lip. She'd been careless, reckless, stupid. "This one time, I shut my eyes and began counting. When I finished, I went to his usual hiding places but couldn't find him."

"You must have been in a panic."

"You have no idea." She sucked on her cheek. "I was convinced my parents would lock me up for life if I let anything happen to my little brother. I promised my mom I'd watch Chris, and I didn't." Her damned chin quivered.

"But you found him."

She sniffled. "Eventually. I spotted his shoes by the river and figured out what must have happened. I ran along the banks, shouting and crying. Then I spotted him wedged between two rocks." She blinked back tears. "He was unconscious." Her hand shook at the memory. It had been a long time since she'd thought about that day.

"Oh, sugar."

Cade's sympathy helped her heart to slow. "Later, Chris told me he'd spotted a fish jump in the river. Since it was summer, the water was merely cold, not freezing. He took off his shoes and waded into the middle. The problem was that the water rushed over the rocks really fast there. That was why he got knocked over and hit his head." Her stomach churned.

Cade clasped his bottle with both hands. "I bet he was terrified."

She shook her head. "Not Chris. Nothing bothered him."

"Did you hear him scream?"

"No. My ears were plugged, and I was counting out loud."

"Jesus, Amber."

She tried to smile, but her lips wouldn't stop trembling. "His mouth and nose were fortunately above water."

Cade slowly shook his head as if he couldn't imagine what she'd gone through. "You were so young. What did you do?"

"It wasn't like we had cell phones or anything. I screamed for him to get up, but he didn't. We were too far from the house for anyone to hear, so I waded in and managed to drag Chris to shore." She shut her eyes, and the same movie replayed in her head. She shouldn't be upset. This happened a long time ago. She opened her eyes to continue. "I ran home for help. Dad was there. He rushed back and carried Chris home. By then, he'd roused, but Mom insisted they go to the hospital."

"But he was okay, right?"

"He had a concussion, but he recovered." She looked at the fish slowly swimming in the tank. "My mother changed after that." Amber returned her focus to Cade. "It was as if the thought of losing one of us was so great she retreated to some dark place. It got worse after Dad left."

"She was afraid."

"Probably, but I was afraid, too. It was my fault that Chris almost died." A tear escaped. Was it for the six-year-old Chris or the man who was no longer?

"It was an accident."

She tapped her temple. "My head knows that but not my

heart." Other than her family, Amber had told no one that story, but even after all this time, it helped to say the words. "What about you? Got any secrets, besides your father's indiscretions?" She swiped the white linen napkin across her eyes.

All hint of cheer evaporated. "Do you promise under penalty of death to keep what I tell you between us?" The concern he'd shown a moment ago had turned hard.

Did Stone know about Cade's big secret? "Promise."

He nodded. "I'd mentioned that on my fifteenth birthday, my mom told me my dad had been a bank robber."

"Yes. Which was what motivated you to go into law enforcement."

"Mostly. But there was another trigger. There was this skinny kid in my advanced algebra class. His name was Leonard Bird. He didn't talk much and didn't have many friends."

"That's sad." If it weren't for her support system, she'd be a total mess. "But you became his friend?"

"Not at first. I didn't want to get close to anyone back then."

As a nurse, she'd met a lot of teenagers who were withdrawn. "Were you afraid he'd find out about your dad if you hung around together?"

"Yes, and the fact Mom and I were poor."

"What about Stone?" She tried to picture what they were like back then. Was Cade a macho kid and a bit of a bully, or had his stern exterior developed later?

"We didn't hang out together in high school. He was two years younger."

Her tea finished steeping, and she removed the bag. She blew on the steam rising off the top.

Clearly, Leonard was an important part of his story. "Was Leonard ever mean to you? Is that why you didn't want him to learn about your background?" It would be terrible if Leonard let it out that Cade's dad had been a criminal.

He shook his head. "No. I didn't tell anyone about my family. Until Stone. And then you." Her heart soared that he trusted her so much. Cade drank from his bottle as if he needed a moment. "It was early in the year, and I'd come to math class without my expensive calculator. It was the kind that drew graphs. I had worked at a gas station all summer to save for it. Then one day it disappeared. For some reason I thought Leonard had taken mine."

She tried to put herself in his shoes. Cade would be too proud to tell the teacher. "Did you steal his?"

He winced. "Yes. I thought if my dad could steal, why couldn't I?"

She pressed her lips together. Poor Cade. "I'm sorry."

He dragged a thumbnail down the label to peel it off. "Not noble. I know."

"Did Leonard suspect you?"

"He didn't say anything. About a week later, I was rummaging through my locker and found mine under a pile of papers. I felt like shit. We'd had a test that week, and Leonard had to take it without his calculator. He failed it, and I never forgave myself. When I placed the one I'd taken back on Leonard's desk, I thought he hadn't seen me. But he had."

Her heart went out to both boys. "What did he say?"

"That his mom couldn't afford to buy him a new one, but that he knew I needed it more." He looked away. "That's when I knew stealing was really wrong. It was then that I decided to atone for all the people my father hurt."

Now it was her turn to place her hand on his. "Whatever happened to Leonard?"

"We became best friends, but he didn't come back his junior year—don't know why—and I never heard from him again."

"Why didn't you look for him?"

His chin drew in. "I was a kid. I honestly had other issues I was facing back then."

"Why not now? Maybe you can reconnect on Facebook.

There can't be too many Leonard Bird's, especially if he listed Rock Hard as his high school."

He smiled and her insides lit up. "See? You are a romantic."

"Well, if that happened to me, I'd want to learn my friend's fate." She wouldn't blame Cade if didn't believe her, especially given her recent suspicion. She prided herself on being a true friend, but clearly, with Ben, she'd turned into a Judas. The guilt tore her up.

"Maybe I'll check him out." He nodded to the menu when the server returned. "See anything you like?"

She studied her choices and selected the Pad Thai. Cade ordered the same.

All through dinner she thought back to how one small event in a person's life could stick with him for a very long time. As an adult, she knew it wasn't her fault her daredevil brother had gone into the stream to chase the jumping fish. She was equally convinced her parents should have warned them about the dangers of playing in the water. Still, she felt guilty Chris had nearly drowned.

Their meal arrived and they dug in. Cade made cute little moaning sounds with each bite.

She chuckled. "Don't you eat well?"

He glanced up at her. "When do I have time? Remember, I suck at cooking."

"Stone is a great cook."

"When he cooks. He mostly eats at the station."

Then how could they possibly think they had time for a woman in their life? Would they fit her in when they could? Did they even want something permanent? At some point, she'd have to ask them, but right now she wanted to enjoy everything about Cade Carter and Stone Benson as possible.

After dinner, Cade paid. He held out his hand and helped her from the booth.

"Next time, I'm paying."

He cocked a brow. "That would be a no."

She was a strong believer in equality. "I make good money, you know." At least compared to a public servant.

He escorted her outside and into his car. "I never said you didn't. It's not about that." He walked to the other side and folded himself onto the seat. "Taking you out makes me feel good. Okay?"

She wasn't going to argue for now. "Okay."

He started the engine and drove out of town. Cade tapped his fingers on the wheel. "Maybe you should consider leaving a bag of clothes at our house for when you spend the night."

"Really?" Excitement laced her tone at the implication.

"You sound surprised."

How did one respond to that comment? "I'm just cautious."

"In that case, I need to show you just how good it can be between us."

Chapter Twenty-Two

Amber thought they'd go back to Cade's place, but instead he drove to her house. Maybe he planned on spending the night and thought it would be easier on her in the morning. That was nice in theory, but it would mean when Stone returned home in the middle of the night, he couldn't crawl into bed with them. *Darn.* She missed him already. Though to be honest, if she had to discuss her suspicions about Ben to Stone so soon after her revelation to Cade, she might crack, and she wasn't ready to shed another bucket of tears.

Cade pulled into her drive. "It's a shame Stone couldn't have joined us," he said.

"I know." With each passing day, the idea of being with two men was sinking in. "I would have enjoyed hearing more about Stone's life." She wanted all three of them to connect on a deeper level.

Next time.

When they stepped into her house, she headed to the kitchen. "I bought some ale for you."

"You didn't have to do that." Cade followed behind her. "Do you have a Coke?"

That surprised her. "Sure do."

She grabbed two cans, one for him and one for herself. On her way home from work, she'd stopped at the store and bought snacks—not because she thought Cade would come back here after dinner, but because she liked to have some on hand. It was her comfort food. "I can make popcorn. I also have some leftover cheese and crackers."

"Great."

As she handed him the can, her cell rang. She set down her drink and located her phone in her purse. Her heart nearly stopped. "It's Ben." She looked up at him.

"Let it go to voicemail."

Her mind raced. "But I always answer. He'll think it strange if I don't." Her heart pounded.

Cade lifted the phone from her fingers. "Next time you see him, you can say we were making love."

His logic helped settle her nerves. "Okay." Another round of reality struck her. "What am I going to say when I finally talk to him? What if he and Jamie come over next weekend? Do you think he knows that I—"

Cade gathered her in his arms. "Shh. It'll be okay. Let's think about this." He guided her to the sofa. "Here's what you're going to do. If he or Jamie asks you to meet them, for the first few times, tell them you have a date with either Stone or me."

"I can do that." Amber certainly had complained enough to Jamie about not having enough time to be with the men because of their crazy schedules. "What if he stops me in the hospital hallway?"

"You talk with him. Sugar, if—and that's a big if—Ben is guilty, you have to pretend he's innocent. Don't give him any reason to think you suspect him."

She was happy he didn't add that Ben might harm her. She knew better. Ben wouldn't. Hell, he couldn't even tie up Jamie or spank her for fear of causing her pain. Amber relaxed. "Okay."

He pulled out his cell. "I'm texting Stone to let him know where I am. I'm not leaving you in this state of mind."

He hadn't planned to spend the night? She knew better.

"Who are you fooling? You can't leave without some booty." He glanced up at her and chuckled. The sound was a balm to her tormented soul.

"You up for that? 'Cause if you're too upset, I'll be happy to hold you all night. I'm not going to let anyone hurt you. Ever." He dragged his knuckle down her cheek.

"Thank you, but if you think you are getting out of making love with me, you are sorely mistaken."

He pulled her close. "That so? Just so you know, I will always *want* to make love with you." They both leaned forward at the same time and kissed. Every cell in her body heated. He sat back. "I can't get started. I have to text Stone now or I'll forget."

While he left his message, she placed the popcorn in the microwave. Doing a menial chore helped settle her stomach. When she returned to the living room, Cade was stretched on the sofa.

"I need to change," she told him. From all the anxiety and emotional upheaval, she'd perspired heavily.

He grinned. "Don't put too much back on. I'm just going to have to take it off."

His words skimmed over her skin and made her simmer. She planted a knee on the sofa and kissed his cheek, then rushed to her room. It was only eight, so she figured they could relax before engaging in mind-blowing sex. She quickly put on a tank top and comfortable bottoms. After she washed off the streaks of mascara, she dragged the damp cloth over her armpits. Fearing she might become emotional again tonight, she didn't put back on any makeup.

She headed out. Cade had taken off his boots and socks and unbuttoned his shirt halfway. No man deserved to look that sexy.

Amber nodded to the television. "Pick out something to watch while I get the cheese and crackers." He picked up the remote and turned it to Netflix. The microwave dinged. "Good timing," she said more to herself than to Cade.

She removed the bag and inhaled, loving the buttery smell. She dumped the contents into a bowl, grabbed a roll of paper towels and the saltshaker. The aroma made her very full stomach grumble.

He was scrolling through the movies as she plopped next to him. "Anything look good?" she asked.

"How about The Twelve Dates of Christmas?"

She laughed. "That's a chick flick."

He held a palm upward. "So? You don't like romantic comedies? I find that hard to believe since you're such a romantic."

She laughed. "I like them fine. I thought you'd want something starring the Rock or Tom Cruise or a movie where people battle to their death. You know, a tough guy film."

He set the remote down. "Sugar, I appreciate that you see me that way, and while I admit I'm focused, ambitious, and hard working, that's my job. Hopefully, those things don't define me. What my dad did to me and my mom might be my motivation for working hard, but I have a lot of other facets. Sometimes, I like to forget. I can even be silly." He raised his brows up and down fast, and she laughed appreciatively.

"Me, too." She stuck out her tongue. "Like to forget, that is." While it felt good to let loose, she needed a lot more than that to help douse her demons tonight. She snuggled close. "I want you to make love with me. Now."

This was what she'd yearned for. But it was incomplete. Stone should be here, but for now, she'd enjoy Cade to the fullest.

"Oh, sugar." Cade stood in front of her and pulled her up. "If you're good with letting this hot popcorn go to waste, I'll be happy to oblige."

"Mind if I take a quick shower?" She'd purchased candles, too, and wanted a moment to light them. "Give me a few minutes before coming in, okay?"

"Hurry." He kissed her.

When his lips lingered, she pulled away then rushed down the hallway. For the first time today, hope filled her.

✧ ✧ ✧

Wanting to give her all the time she needed, Cade paced. Had this been under different circumstances, he'd have rushed down the hall after her, stripping his clothes on the way. After everything she'd been through tonight, Cade didn't want to move too fast, but the butt plug was burning a hole in his pocket. When it came to Amber, he had no control. He wanted her—bad. After seeing her struggle with the ethical question of what to do about her good friend, Ben, his admiration for her grew. Never before had doing right by her seemed so important.

If he were honest, he'd acknowledge that he had never taken his time to really understand any woman well. Why? He never saw the relationship lasting more than a few nights or at most, a couple of weeks. Yet the older he became, the more he wanted what Stone's family had. Love. Stability. Friendship.

Amber had nailed him the first time she met him. She could see his need to atone, but now he understood no matter how many people he brought to justice, he'd never make up for his father's wrong doing. Like Amber, he needed to do what he believed was right.

That meant loving her the best he could. If he fucked up this relationship then he might never get another chance at having something this wonderful again. He had to be on his most sensitive behavior—reading her every breath, understanding her every move. It didn't matter their time together had been short. They'd connected.

He couldn't wait any longer.

With strong strides, he ate up the space between here and her room, stopping only when he reached her closed door. Not only did he need his heartbeat to slow, he wanted to give Amber time to think about tonight. It was going to be amazing, not only between the two of them, but between all three of them soon.

Cade stepped in. The room was bathed in candlelight and he smiled. The woman was all heart. The bathroom door stood ajar, and he imagined her wet, naked body.

Once he set the lube and plug on the dresser, he opened the bathroom door. *Fuck me.* She'd just stepped onto the bathmat, and his balls drew up tight at the sight of her. Glistening, she was a true vision.

Her eyes widened and she grabbed the towel and placed it over her front. "I'm not ready."

"Sugar, you don't need to be shy around me." He stepped toward her and lifted the material from her grasp. "Allow me." He turned her around and dried her back, her delicious butt, and her shapely legs. He wanted her needy. "Turn around." She obliged. "You are magnificent." As much as he wanted to take his time, he couldn't wait. In a flash, she was in his arms.

"I'm still wet."

He grinned. "Then I guess I'll just have to lick off every drop of water."

She giggled, and he fell for her even more. Once in the bedroom, he pulled down the comforter and gently placed her on the bed. The flickering candles danced over the walls, creating a womb-like environment, and he couldn't wait to take her.

He debated how to make tonight extra special. One thing he knew about his woman. She liked it when he talked dirty. "Is your pussy wet and ready for my big cock?"

"I'm not sure." When she dipped a finger into her opening, his cock turned to steel. Dear God in heaven, she'd be his death.

She then waved her finger, and he nearly lost it. Two buttons later, his shirt was history. The belt came next and then the trousers. Amber sat up as if she wanted to make sure not to miss the show.

She grinned. "Keep going."

He stepped over to the bed, needing her hands on him. "How about you finishing?"

Perhaps he shouldn't have offered his cock so quickly. He was weak when he was with her, but she did seem to enjoy tempting him to come. Using a light touch, she guided his briefs up and over his cock. When his dick popped out at her, she squealed. Her pleasure thrilled him.

"Hurry." He hadn't meant for the one word to come out strangled.

If he let her tease him for too long, he'd never last long enough to put the butt plug in her.

She looked up at him. "Hurry? Uh-uh. I'm going to take my time. Make you beg for my pussy."

God he adored this woman. "So you think you have all the control?" She did, but he wasn't ready to tell her that just yet.

She touched her tits then dragged a hand between her legs. "I got these."

Cade shook his head. She was taking this too far. He stepped back and shucked his briefs before moving closer. "Suck on him."

"Yes, sir." She had the nerve to salute him.

With the tips of her fingers, she drew his rigid shaft toward her with slightly jerking movements, acting like this was her first blowjob.

The second her tongue touched his cock, high-voltage power shot up his body. His heart pounded. He could be on a stakeout for hours never taking his gaze off a building, but put Amber in front of him, and he lost all focus. He lowered his arms and dragged his fingers through her hair, helping to guide her down his cock. With her free hand, she clasped his balls. The combination of her tongue, hand, and magic fingers, had him hissing in a breath.

Don't come.

They had so much loving ahead of them. Showing Amber about pleasure would be his one gift to her, though she was bestowing a lot of joy on him right now.

When she sucked hard and tightened her grip, he closed his eyes, trying not to lose it. Her tongue swirled and her fingers danced along his cock. He pulled away. “Enough play time.” Even though he’d used his toughest voice, she looked up, cocked a brow, and grinned.

Oh, crap. He’d just open the gate and given her free reign. His heart was doomed.

Chapter Twenty-Three

Amber had achieved her first goal—that of pushing Cade way past his limit. He might act like some kind of macho man, but when she had her mouth on his cock, he folded like a collapsible chair.

He tapped her head. "Get on your hands and knees for me." His stern command held a tender undertone.

She loved teasing him, but she honestly hadn't thought she'd be able to get him so riled up that he had to make love with her this fast. She hoped this didn't cut short foreplay. She wanted to be brought to the edge of her climax many times before finally giving in.

"You do understand the mechanics of a ménage, right, Amber?"

Her mind raced to her butt and she clenched her cheeks. "Yes." She'd told him that before. "But I've never had a cock back there."

"I know. That's why I need to stretch you out first."

She caught the slight lowering of his tone. It was almost as if he was waiting for her to tell him no. Well, she wouldn't. She wanted Cade Carter—all of him. Everywhere. She had to feel alive tonight. "Okay."

While she wasn't facing him, she bet he had that cute grin on his face. His feet padded across the carpet and metal sounded against glass, like he was unscrewing a lid. As she thought about what it would be like to have something cold and hard in her ass, shivers tripped up her spine. At least when it was Cade's cock, he'd be warm and pliable.

She liked something stiff as much as the next woman, but not when it was plastic. "Can't I skip this step and go straight to the real deal?"

She hadn't expected him to laugh. "Oh, sugar. You lighten my darkest days. You're tiny, and my dick is well, big."

That was true. At least she'd asked. The bed dipped and his hands massaged her shoulders—not the area she thought he'd focus on, but after thirty seconds of his strong hands working her muscles, the tension eased out of her body. "I like that." She just hoped his massage wouldn't lull her to sleep.

As if he read her mind, he stopped. A citrusy scent filled the air. The brush of cold goo on her anus caused her to lean forward. *Yikes.* Reading about plugs, dildos, and anal gels hadn't really prepared her for this moment.

An arm swept under her belly. "Come back here, you. Relax. I'll make sure you like it."

He said that in such a calm way that she thought maybe she'd overreacted. "I was surprised, that's all."

When he ran a hand up her belly and captured her breast, she exhaled and closed her eyes. This was where she wanted to be. He continued to play with her tits, swirling his finger around each areola in a slow seductive manner that made her lower half clench with desire. With his other hand, he ran his thumb around her tight, muscled back hole in an attempt to get her to relax. He hadn't shown her the plug, but no matter the size, she bet her asshole wasn't wide enough.

He kept up a steady rhythm, and her body finally gave in. Cade pinched one of her hardened nipples, and her body sprang back to life. She moaned, waiting for the glorious pleasure to follow.

He seemed to take advantage of her distraction and eased his thumb into her ass. *Whoa.* She tightened her muscles again.

"Amber. If you want my cock in your pussy sometime to-night, you can't do that." His voice remained soft, as if he knew this was difficult for her.

"I'm sorry."

"There's nothing to be sorry about. Just try to let go. Trust me."

She did. More lube scented the air and this time his index finger entered her. When he added a second digit, her breath caught. While the sensation only slightly pinched, she was more embarrassed than in pain.

Angry at herself for being such a wuss, she did her best to stay loose, and forced her mind to go blank, to enjoy every twirl and dip of his finger. After a while, the ache turned to pleasure, and she wiggled her butt for more.

"You ready, sugar?"

She wished he hadn't asked and just impaled her. "Yes."

He pressed the hard, slippery object against her ass and twisted the tip. Her breath caught at the newness of it all. "Push out as I press in," he instructed.

She did and the plug slid in halfway, causing her ass to burn a little. "Ooh." When he drove the piece of plastic in farther, he must have hit a few erotic nerves and she moaned. She wasn't even aware her ass could feel such enjoyment.

"Do you see the potential now?"

"Yes." Who would have thought?

He rubbed her ass with one hand while he rotated the plug into her asshole. While it made her feel full, she liked the pressure. It turned her on.

"You're doing great."

He tapped the end, and a quick bolt of joy darted straight to her pussy. She never expected that. He lifted her up and eased her onto her back. The change in angle created all new areas of stimulation. "Whoa."

He smiled. She reached up to run her hands down his chest, and he immediately captured her wrists and drew them over her head.

"Let's leave the touching to me, shall we? Keep your hands right there."

A delicious shiver traced a path from her nipples to her thighs. Why did his commands turn her on so much? *Because Cade was doing the asking.* As he climbed on top of her, he nudged open her thighs. Once again, the change in position sent the butt plug deeper into her ass. *Holy shit.*

He grinned. "I see you understand the workings of that tiny piece of plastic."

"Tiny?" The man was crazy.

He lowered his body until his massive chest was sealed against her breasts. Then he kissed her, possessing her with his lips. They both opened up and greeted each other. The tip of his cock was at her opening making it hard to concentrate. He'd put on a condom, but she didn't remember him donning it.

Their tongues twirled like two ice skaters in a pairs' competition, sometimes touching, sometimes exploring on their own. They'd each had the peanut based dish for dinner, but he tasted more like Coke—tangy and sweet.

When his thumbs reached between them and rubbed her nipples, her cream dripped. Amber clenched her fists, wanting to run her hands down his back, to feel the ripple of his muscles as his body flexed with each movement, but she wouldn't disobey him. Not being able to do what she wanted gave her a different kind of thrill. She arched her back to get more pressure, and her butt lit up. The plug sure could travel far.

He broke the kiss and slid lower on her body. Anticipation sent sparks all through her. When his mouth latched onto one nipple, she moaned and spread her legs wider, hoping he'd impale her now. With the plug in her butt and him tormenting her tits, she needed him badly.

Just don't come too soon. She wanted to show him she had control. He pulled her nipple taut and her cry escaped. "Oh, yes."

He alternated between her tits, nabbing each nipple faster and faster. God, what the man could do to her.

He sniffed then smiled. "Someone's excited."

What did he expect? He was driving her crazy, turning her body to mush. Cade dragged his tongue down her belly, coming closer and closer to her needy opening. She lifted her hips in offering.

"Keep still or that ass plug will put you over the edge before I've had a chance to love your pretty little pussy."

He rubbed his thumb across the top of her pubis then opened her folds with one finger.

Touch me more.

Cade slid lower on his stomach. His thumbs dug into her thighs, but he then did nothing more. His lack of attention to her clit and swollen opening ratcheted her desire. She lifted her head.

He was staring right between her legs, his mouth twisting to the side, as if he was trying to decide which part to torment first. He smiled then dipped a finger into her wet opening. The friction, while small, jacked up her hormones. "More. Please."

He looked up at her. "Are you trying to tell me how to make love to you?" There was a slight steely edge to his tone, but she thought he did that to heighten her arousal. Well, it had worked.

"No."

"Good. Now relax and let me take you to another time and place."

She wanted that. Needed it for her soul to heal. The first swipe of his tongue had her reeling. She dug her nails into her palms. She'd never last if he didn't take her soon. "Please, Cade."

Her plea must have had an effect on him because he dipped three fingers into her and swirled them around fast. Sparks of need raced up and down her spine, building her climax. If she didn't get his thick shaft soon she'd lose it.

When he drew her clit between his teeth, she yelled. "Damn you. Give me your cock."

He laughed—actually laughed. "Sugar, sugar. I've only just begun."

She should let loose and come, but then he'd believe that when the time came for the three of them to be together, she couldn't handle two cocks—and she could. She squeezed her eyes shut and pictured Stone beside her, playing with her breasts while Cade loved on her pussy.

His tongue circled her clit until the tiny nub swelled. It was too much. "Oh, oh, oh."

She lifted her hips, loving how the plug in her ass hit new nerves every time she shifted. Then Cade's heavy body was on top of hers, and his lips found her mouth. His kiss came out hard. Demanding. Needy. She lowered her hands. To hell with not touching him. She threaded her fingers through his hair and planted her feet on the mattress. Cade pressed his cock against her opening and plunged in. Stars burst behind her lids. *Oh. My. God.* There was no room. The plug took up too much space, yet the added size from his dick tripled the pleasure.

He'd unleashed her inner beast, and she scraped her nails down his back. After he drove his cock to the hilt, he kissed her with more passion than she thought possible. As if he knew she'd be overwhelmed, he waited. Pulses radiated in every direction and her pussy cramped with need. It was as if he had his finger in the dam. If he moved even the slightest bit, she'd burst.

"Amber, what you do to me." His words came out on a breath. The kiss that followed spoke of a future. Of hope.

She held on tight, and together they soared upward. Her juices flowed as she encased his cock, holding him hostage and loving him hard. He dipped his head and murmured something she couldn't decipher. As he thrust his cock inside her again, he moaned, and they both burst at the same time. Her screams and his wild cry collided. Her climax tore through her, and she lost her sight, her breath, her heart. Cade Carter had done what he'd promised—taken her somewhere she'd never been before.

How long he held her, she couldn't say, since no thoughts entered her brain other than those of pure delight. Eventually, he withdrew, stepped away from the bed, and returned with a warm cloth.

After he wiped her clean, she reached around to take out the plug. His hand snapped on her wrist. "Leave it in for another hour."

"Why?"

"Because I said so."

She mouthed his phrase back to him. He laughed, dropped down next to her and kissed her again. Life with Cade would never be dull.

Chapter Twenty-Four

When Amber roused, the smell of eggs filled the house, causing her stomach to grumble. After eating a big dinner, and then munching on popcorn and cheese after a night of sexual bliss, she was surprised she had any desire to eat ever again.

She cracked open an eye and wondered when Cade had risen. A shower would have to wait. Breakfast came first.

She was naked and didn't feel comfortable walking around the house that way, so she tossed on her tank and flannel bottoms and padded out.

Cade was dressed in his slacks and had his white shirt untucked. She slipped behind him and dragged her hands up his naked chest. "I thought you didn't cook."

He looked over his shoulder and smiled. "I can do simple."

"Simple is good. What can I do?"

"I couldn't find the coffee."

"It's hidden." From the cabinet next to the fridge, she pulled out the bag of Starbucks coffee, but pushed back the reason why she'd purchased it.

He removed the eggs from the burner. "Plates?"

"I'll get them." Once she set them next to the stove, she brewed the tea and fixed the coffee. The plate of eggs didn't look very substantial for a man Cade's size. "If I had known you were coming over, I would have bought some bacon." And muffins and whatever else a real man ate.

"I'm fine with this."

While he placed the food on the table, she prepared the beverages. Once they were seated, both scarfed down their food. "You said both you and Stone were free today. What are we doing?"

"He said he was taking charge of the activities, so I don't know."

Before she had a chance to discuss possible outings, Cade's cell rang.

He grimaced before pulling out his phone and checking the caller ID. "Fuck. Sorry, sugar. It's work."

She sank back against her chair. She didn't get called in often, but when she did, she had to go.

His fingers tightened their grip. "Where? When? I'll be there." He set his phone down. "I am so sorry. There's been an attempt on a patient's life."

She grabbed the back of the chair. "Attempt?" Who was doing this?

"I don't know much more than that."

"Do you want me to come?"

"It's your day off. Stone will be so disappointed if he can't be with you."

Would it always be like this? Would she be constantly disappointed because the three of them couldn't be together? "Do you think Stone will still want to go out with me?"

He pushed back his chair, lifted her out of hers, and cupped her face. "I can guarantee it. Just don't have too much fun without me."

"I'll try." Despite the horrible situation, a small chuckle escaped.

He bent down and kissed her. Knowing Cade had to leave, she kept the contact light.

"I'll call you," he said, as he stepped toward the door.

As soon as he left, the air thinned. Boy, did she have it bad.

✧ ✧ ✧

When Cade arrived at the hospital, he rushed up to the fourth floor. His sometime partner, Ethan Harper, met him at the reception desk.

Ethan's tie was loose and his shirt wrinkled. "Have you been here long?" Cade asked.

"I was here on duty on the fifth floor when I got the call from Hartwick."

Cade nodded. "What do you know?"

"Edgar Mulholland's monitor went off, indicating he'd stopped breathing, and his nurse rushed in with a crash cart. She must have gotten there quickly, because she managed to revive him. The man has ALS—that's Lou Gherig's disease."

"I know what it is." Cade's gut clenched.

"He's in the late stages of the disease."

The thought of anyone suffocating in his own fluids was chilling. "How do we know it was attempted murder?"

"Edgar told his nurse."

His heart pounded hard for a couple of beats. "Can he identify this person?"

Ethan shook his head. "Said he was asleep when he felt the port wiggle and woke up."

"What did he see?"

"Edgar said it was still dark in the room, and since his eyesight is terrible, he could only make out the shape of a person. The muscles in his eyes don't work well."

"Could he tell if it was a man or a woman?" He knew from experience, someone else could be guilty, too.

"All he recalled was that the person was hunched over him, so he couldn't tell. When I spoke with him, he wasn't fully awake. He might remember more details later."

Cade's mind whirred. "I wonder why the killer didn't think about the alarm, or give him enough drugs to prevent resuscitation."

"I can think of a couple of reasons. One, when the alarm went off, he or she panicked and didn't give the second drug—assuming it's the same person."

Ethan's assumption was reasonable. "And two?"

"Maybe he couldn't get enough Ativan without arousing suspicion."

Something wasn't right. "How do you know it was Ativan?"

"Found the vial."

Cade huffed out a breath. "Fuck. That's the second time a vial has been left. No one is that careless, unless—"

"Unless he wants to get caught?" Now it was Ethan who raised his brows. "Not buying it."

"I trust you sent the evidence to the lab to see if there are any fingerprints?"

"Sure did, but there weren't any on the vial for Stephanie Osmond, so I'm not getting my hopes up."

"I wouldn't either, especially since everyone wears gloves around here."

Dan Hartwick strode up to them and faced Ethan. "What can you tell me?"

Ethan filled his boss in on the details. Hartwick squared his shoulders. The man looked more tired than usual. He hadn't shaved, and if Cade's memory served him right, the boss wore the same suit yesterday. He had no room to talk though. He was in the same boat.

Hartwick dragged a hand down his jaw. "Seems like the killer is escalating. Cade, do a timeline to see if we can anticipate when he might strike again."

Cade's gut swirled. He hadn't wanted to believe the boyfriend of Amber's best friend could be involved, but he had to tell them her suspicions. "I'll do that. You should know that one of the nurses, Amber Delacroix, has a theory."

"What would that be?"

He told Dan and Ethan about her gut feeling. "Everything's circumstantial, but Ben had the means and possibly the motive."

"Ethan," Hartwick said. "Check out his alibi. See if he's at the hospital now. If not, find him and speak with him."

"On it, boss."

Cade tensed. "Don't mention Amber's name. I don't want retribution in case he's involved."

"Got it." Ethan trotted off.

Dan glanced at Cade. "We stationed cops on every floor. How did this happen?"

"The killer's good, despite appearing quite careless." His sixth sense told him the dropped vials were for show. While he didn't know Ben other than when he'd questioned him in the Emma Luther case, from the way Amber spoke of him, he didn't seem the type to need recognition for his good deed. Then again, Cade was no shrink.

Dan nodded. "Check to see if there's any security footage for this floor."

He'd done that for the Luther case. "The hospital only has cameras in public places, like the parking lot and the cafeteria."

Dan looked up as if he expected to point to one. "I swore I saw some around in other places."

"Can't have them in the rooms for privacy issues." He thought back to what one of the staff members had told him. "There are cameras in the ICUs and other critical care units, as well as some for the rooms housing those mentally unstable, but not on this floor."

"Shit."

"My thoughts exactly."

✧ ✧ ✧

After arriving home seven hours ago, and managing a few hours of sleep, Stone was still a little groggy. Thank God, he had three days off. He planned to spend them with Amber and Cade. His roommate had been with her more than he had, and that sucked. He bet the two of them were chomping at the bit to get on with the adventure he'd planned.

While Amber might be out of her element, he wanted to see how she adapted to hiking. Next time, he'd introduce her to rock climbing.

To make sure she was agreeable, he called her cell.

"Hey, Stone."

Her voice wasn't as cheery as he'd hoped. "What's wrong?"

"Cade had to go into work."

Shit. That wasn't the end of the world, but the three of them needed to do things together in order to bond. She sure was getting a good view of what things might be like in the future though.

The future. He liked those two words. It was crazy he'd fallen for Amber so fast, but her spirit, ambition, and open mind had caught his attention. Add in her loving nature, and he'd been hooked. Cade, too, was falling for her, too, which made it almost too good to be true.

"The two of us can still get together if you're up for it." He held his breath.

"I'd love that. Cade said you had something planned."

"I thought we could go hiking. I even put together a little something to eat." Stone had a backup plan in place in case she wasn't up for it.

"We're having a picnic?" He hadn't expected her to sound so excited.

"Yup. Can you be ready in twenty?"

"Sure can."

"You have sturdy boots, right?"

"Of course I do. I live in Montana now. Haven't used them

much, though."

He chuckled to himself. He'd have to take it slow. As soon as he disconnected, Stone grabbed his backpack from the garage. He retrieved the food he'd bought before he went into work yesterday from the fridge and stuffed everything inside, making sure to grab extra water bottles for Amber. While he was disappointed Cade had to work, he was anxious to spend quality time with her.

His cell rang. Cade. "Hey."

"Look, I have to cancel."

He appreciated the heads up. "Amber told me."

"Did she mention about last night?"

Instead of cheer, Cade's voice held a lot of tension. Stone leaned against the counter and grabbed the edge. "Did something happen?"

Cade told him about her near breakdown and that she suspected Ben might be the serial killer. "Be careful with her, okay? She's really fragile."

Shit. "I will, but Ben? He's such a nice guy."

"So she said."

Stone blew out a big breath. Ben and Jamie meant the world to her. While Stone hadn't spent much time with her friend, from the eulogy Ben delivered at Chris's funeral, he was a caring person—more so than most. Stone actually thought Ben was a bit weak and that Jamie was the one in control. Ben just didn't seem to be the killer type.

Stone drew a palm down his chin. "Amber didn't see him harm anyone, did she?" Amber had been through too much already. Having Ben guilty would destroy her. With no supportive family to speak of, Jamie and Ben had become her life.

"No. Watching Amber struggle with the conflict was one of the worst times of my life and really tore me up."

"What do you think? Is he guilty?"

"I don't know, which is why we need to be careful. Let Amber bring up the topic first, okay?"

He could feel her pain. "I won't say anything unless she mentions it."

"Good. I doubt she will. She's still trying to process everything. Ethan and I are checking into Ben's whereabouts. Let's wait and see if there is any substance to her claim before we have another heart to heart. If Ben is guilty, she'll need a lot of comfort."

Stone pushed off from the counter and walked into the living room. "I'm taking her hiking today. Maybe that will help keep her mind off her troubles."

"Great. Keep her safe." Voices sounded in the background. "I gotta go." Cade hung up.

"This sucks." Stone grabbed his keys and headed out.

Fifteen minutes later, he pulled up in her drive. The day was perfect—temp almost near eighty—which for Rock Hard, Montana was a rarity. They'd get hot climbing, but what he had planned at the top would take care of that.

As he slipped from his truck, the front door opened, and beautiful Amber emerged. She was thankfully wearing proper hiking boots and carrying a daypack. He was worried she might bring a purse or something. From the way her long sleeve shirt was bunched in places, he suspected she'd layered for the day. Smart girl.

"Hey." Stone ran up and embraced her.

Having her in his arms set his body on fire. He hugged her tight then loosened his grip. If he had his way, he'd never let her go. His lips yearned to taste her, and he captured her delicious mouth. She was pure sweetness. Her arms slipped over his shoulders and wrapped them around his neck. When his stiff cock pressed against her body, he leaned back, chuckled, and adjusted his balls.

"It's up to you how we play this, baby, but do you want to hike then make love or make love then hike?"

She looked at the sky. "Seeing how clear it is, I say hike, *shower*, then make love."

He smiled. "Come on then."

He helped her into the cab of his truck before slipping into the driver's side.

Amber snapped her seatbelt into place. "So where are we going?"

"Harmes National Forest."

Her brows furrowed. "Oh."

"Don't worry. We won't be hiking any paths that are too steep. And there will be a reward at the end."

Her mouth made the prettiest "o" shape. "I like rewards."

For the rest of the trip, she gazed out the window.

"Wait until we reach the top," Stone said. "You won't believe the view."

"It's pretty here, too."

She sounded better. Good. He turned off the paved surface and onto a fire road. While his truck bucked and bounced on the rutted path, Amber didn't complain. He liked she was made of sturdy stuff, but perhaps she was mentally so far away that she wasn't aware of the ride at all.

The road ended at a boulder. "Far as she goes." He glanced over at her. She was smiling. *Yes!* "Ready?"

She jumped out, not waiting for him to open her door. He got his pack out of the bed of his truck and slipped it on.

She donned her small daypack and checked out his gear. "You need something that big? We're just having lunch, right?"

"I want to be prepared for every contingency. Come on." He didn't need her to ask what that might entail. "Why don't you lead? I tend to walk fast."

She stuck out her tongue. "Braggart. I know you're in better shape."

He pounded his chest and laughed, inhaling the clean air. For the next twenty minutes, he enjoyed the fabulous scenery of

Amber's ass moving and swaying in front of him. Her pace was steady and sure.

She stopped suddenly to pick a purple flower. "This is beautiful." She inhaled and closed her eyes. "And sweet."

"Like you." He vowed to keep that look of wide-eyed wonder on her face forever. "It's called a fairy slipper."

The strongest urge to protect her against everything bad came over him. He never wanted her to be sad again.

Her shoulders sagged. "Now I wished I'd brought my camera."

"You don't have your cell?"

"Honestly? I didn't want to chance getting called in."

He never left home without his. While reception was spotty in the mountains, the camera would work just fine. "I have mine. Hold the flower up to your face and I'll take your picture." After he located his phone, she posed and he snapped away. This would be one he'd keep forever.

"Take one of us both," she said, excitement lacing her voice.

As soon as she moved next to him and smiled, he held out his arm and snapped. "Let's check it out," he said. She leaned over as he scrolled to the picture. "Look at you." Amber was tiny and beautiful. "It's a keeper."

"Send me a copy?"

"Will do." He stashed the phone back in his pack and patted her butt. "Let's get moving."

After another twenty minutes, Stone made her stop to drink water. Never once during the hike had she complained, not even when she had to climb over some large boulders.

When her pace began to slow and she kept wiping her brow, it appeared as if her interest in hiking as waning. "We're almost there, baby."

She looked back and smiled. "I'm good." Her breath had quickened.

He didn't want her too exhausted. He had plans. Because the

turn off to the lake could be tricky, he decided to take the lead. "I need to find the spot where we cut in."

After three false attempts, he found the overgrown path. He held out his hand to help guide her. "Watch out for low branches."

Once they wove their way through the tunnel of trees, they came upon a secluded spot overlooking a huge lake with the view of the mountains as a backdrop.

She stilled. "Oh, Stone. This is amazing! We don't have anything like this in Oklahoma."

He grinned and gathered her in his arms. "I love it here, too." And not just because of the vista. "Let's follow the ridge. I know of a nice spot where we can have our picnic."

And make love.

Chapter Twenty-Five

Amber had ridden the flat plains of the Benson ranch that had a view of these mountains from a distance, but it was a lot different this close to the peaks. The fresh air, the hint of sage, the majestic trees, and magnificent vista overwhelmed her senses.

She wrapped her arms around her shoulders. “I think if I had a home right here, I’d never leave.” She gazed over the placid lake.

“I’d love that, too, but with my job, I fear too many people would die by the time I hiked down the mountain and drove to the fire station.”

She punched him. “That was assuming I didn’t work. I wouldn’t want to commute either.” He acted like she was suggesting they should live together in her imaginary house. While she might like that, she didn’t want to get her hopes up.

He nudged her and nodded to the water. “Let’s try it out. What do you say?” He dropped his pack.

She twisted toward him. Stone stepped back, untied his boots, and kicked them off. “What are you doing? You’re actually going for a swim?”

“Yup.” He then stepped out of his pants.

“I bet the water’s freezing.” It didn’t make a difference that she was sweating and the air temperature was somewhere in the seventies.

"Chicken?"

He knew how to push her buttons. "No." While most of her efforts had been in indoor heated pools, she prided herself on being a strong swimmer.

Not one to turn down a challenge, she shucked off her pack, then her shoes, and all of her outerwear. A sudden breeze raised goose bumps on her arms and legs, but she was determined to do this. She thought he'd stop at his underwear, but no. He got naked. While his cock wasn't erect, it wasn't soft either. She bet that would change as soon as he hit the chilly water.

He nodded to her attire. "You sure you don't want to take off your sports bra and undies? Or did you bring a spare?"

Now he was being ridiculous. "No. You didn't tell me we were going swimming."

"You know those undies won't keep you warm in the water. After you swim, you'll be happy you have something dry to change into."

He had a point. Wet sports bras sucked. She looked around. "What if someone comes?"

"It's pretty isolated up here." He grinned.

"But what if they do?"

He ran his hands down her bare shoulders. "Would it bother you if someone saw you naked?"

"Yes." She wasn't an exhibitionist.

He leaned in close. "Or would it *excite* you?" The mere presence of his bare body had her hormones flying through her veins.

This wasn't like Stone to push her. *Unless.* She bet Cade had told him about last night, and he was trying to keep her distracted. Well it worked.

She glanced around. "No one's coming, right?"

"No, baby. I just didn't want you to freak if it happened." He ran his gaze down her.

Now he was the caring man she was falling in love with. She latched onto his beautiful green eyes that seemed to have taken on the shade of the pine trees around them. Her inner walls clenched at the thought of doing something this unorthodox.

As if her fingers had a will of their own, she pulled the bra off over her head. Even sweaty, the cool air pebbled her nipples. He reached out and caressed a breast. All thoughts of anyone seeing her vanished.

"So beautiful. I've missed you so much." He had the nerve to step back and nod to her panties. "Those, too."

"I'm getting there. These things take time." Going braless was one thing, but being buck-naked was something else altogether. She hesitated before lowering her bottoms one inch at a time. His gaze followed her movements. She stepped out of her panties and placed them on top of her pack. Without warning, he lifted her and rushed toward the water.

"We need to go in slowly, Stone."

He dropped back his head and laughed. "Hell, no. We'll chicken out if we do. It's all or nothing. Ready?" His feet were already at the edge of the lake.

"Like I have a choice?"

"Not anymore."

He ran in. She waited to see the shock on his face from the cold, but none came. This mountain lake might not be as chilly as she anticipated.

The second her ass dipped into the lake water, she knew she couldn't have been more wrong. "Oh, shit."

Down they went. *Holy hell.* He dunked her up to her neck. "It's like an ice bath." Her breath literally caught in her throat and no more words escaped.

Stone set her down and her feet landed on soft sand. "Race you to the middle," he said.

Damn him. He knew how she'd respond to that challenge. At least the swim would heat her up. "You're on."

As long as she was this wet, she might as well go in all the way. She dove in and swam underwater until her breath gave out. When she surfaced, Stone was by her side taking long, even strokes, not even looking winded. So much for beating him—unless she cheated.

Normally, she wasn't one to bend the rules, but she believed this constituted an exception. She grabbed his ankle and jumped on his back. After the intense swim, the water didn't feel so bad.

He laughed and rolled over. Now she was straddling him. "Better watch out, little girl. Something could happen in here."

The freezing water temperature would negate him from being able to carry out the warning. "I dare you."

She flipped and swam as hard and as fast as she could toward shore. Less than fifteen feet into her retreat, he grabbed her waist. "Oh, no you don't. I'm not letting you get away that easily."

He turned her around and when he stood, she automatically wrapped her legs around his waist. The kiss that followed removed all thoughts of the cold water. Now refreshed from the swim, her energy had returned and she kissed him with everything she had. He probed her mouth while his thumbs danced across her hard, budding nipples.

"Someone's cold." With her holding on tightly, Stone walked them onto the banks. "I brought a towel."

"I'm glad you came prepared."

He smiled as he placed her on a somewhat smooth surface. Amber jumped up and down, trying to stay warm while he rummaged through his pack.

"Tada!" He waved a striped beach towel. "Allow me."

Even though he was dripping wet and had to be cold, he ran the towel over every inch of her body. And she meant "every" inch. When it came to her tits, pussy, and, ass, he lingered.

"I'm good. Now it's my turn." She snatched the towel from him.

He cocked a brow. "Only because I tossed you into the lake will I allow you to return the favor."

She widened her eyes on purpose. "You don't like me touching you?"

"You know better, but you'll take your time, and I have other plans."

"Ooh." She hurried to remove most of the water off his rippling body. He then drew her into a strong embrace.

"Now, I'm going to make love to you. I've yet to have you for myself."

She tucked in her chin. "You think we're going to make love in the open where anyone can come upon us? Human and animal alike?"

He tapped her nose. "That's why I have a tent."

Her amazement for this man grew. "You're kidding."

He bent over and pulled out a one-foot long nylon bag from his pack. "I'll show you in a minute. Put some clothes on but be prepared to be stripped as soon as we're inside."

They both dressed quickly. The clothes warmed her right away.

He held out the tent. "How about you carry this—it only weighs five pounds—and I'll bring the rest. I know a nice spot a little way from here where it's more secluded."

She grabbed her small pack and the tent and followed him. Never once had she dreamed about making love outdoors, especially with someone as wonderful as Stone, but here she was.

While a part of her felt guilty for enjoying him so much when Cade wasn't there, she figured that was what the ménage lifestyle was about. Adore the person you were with at the time.

They'd walked about five hundred feet when they came to a romantic clearing snuggled among the tall trees. "Nice." The pine-needled-covered ground would make for a soft floor for the tent.

He set down his pack, removed the tent from her hands, and

opened one shock-corded pole. "Everything is color-coded. Thread the pole through the same-colored loop and I'll take it from there."

She did as he instructed and found the design easy and practical. Four poles later, the tent was erected.

"Very cool."

He nodded. "I thought we'd eat in the open and then convene inside for some *dessert*."

She laughed at his way with words. He unhooked an insulated pad from his pack and spread it out. She sat down and then helped him with the food. "Wow. You really went all out." He had hummus and vegetables, cheese and crackers—her favorite—and three different kinds of sandwiches.

"And more water. You can't be too hydrated when you're hiking."

Amber was thirsty and drank half of the bottle. She'd shared quite a bit of time with Cade and learned a lot about him, but when she and Stone had been together, he'd spent most of the time comforting her. He was a caring man with deep convictions. While she'd met his wonderful family, she wanted to learn more about the man himself and keep the emphasis off herself, which was what she needed right now.

She picked up a ham and cheese sandwich and bit into it. "What was your most difficult call as a paramedic?"

"Most difficult case in what sense?"

"Good question." *Hmm.* "Okay. Was there one call you wished you'd handled differently?"

"I try not to second guess myself. Usually when we arrive, we assess the scene for safety before we act. Mostly though, by the time we get there, the scene has already been secured."

"It didn't sound like the scene had been secured when you helped the kid who stabbed you."

"I'm afraid in that case, the ambulance got there minutes before the cops." He blew out a breath. "But my worse case, huh? I guess it would have been two winters ago when the search and rescue team needed backup. The mountains around Rock Hard sure can get some mean avalanches."

She didn't like that he had to go into ravines or climb mountains to save people. That seemed so dangerous.

"This time an avalanche had crushed a mountain cabin, and a family had been trapped inside. A few days later, a ski patroller spotted a smokestack sticking above the snow. He yelled down the chimney and heard a faint response. Unable to do more on his own, he raced down the mountain for help. We had no idea what we'd find when we got there."

She couldn't imagine the panic of being trapped inside. She wrapped her arms around her as if she was fending off the cold herself.

"The victims needed help to arrive as fast as possible. Our job was to stabilize them so S&R could bring them down safely. Transporting someone down the mountain can be tricky. By the time we managed to reach the people, the man was already dead, and his wife was barely hanging on. Huddled between them was their year-old baby. My heart almost broke, but by some miracle the child was still alive."

Amber shook her head.

"We stabilized the wife. Her condition was too critical to carry her out, so we called for a copter rescue."

That was so sad. She couldn't imagine what it would be like to watch your husband die lying next to you.

"We wrapped the man in plastic and brought him down on a sled. I prayed the whole time we wouldn't have another avalanche." He looked to the side. "Unfortunately, the mom lost both her feet from frostbite, but the baby was fine." Stone cleared his throat and nodded to all their food. "Eat up." He wagged a finger at her. "And no more sad stories."

She agreed, but it was a testament to the type of man Stone was that he still seemed shaken by the tragedy. As they dug in, she swore each bite tasted better than the last. "Guess what?" She kept her voice more cheery than she felt. Her mind was still on that poor woman losing her husband and then her feet.

"What?"

"I'm making a quilt for you and Cade."

He set down his drink. "Oh, baby. That's so nice of you."

"It's nothing fancy, but I want you to think of me every time you look at it." Stone gathered the rest of the food and stuffed it back in his sac. She laughed at his frantic pace. "Is there a fire?" She thought her comment witty.

"I'm hoping to start one. With you." He winked.

Aw. With the food safely stored, he slid the pad into the tent, and she crawled in after him. It smelled like new plastic. "Did you just buy this?"

"No, but I haven't had a chance to use it. I was waiting for someone special to share it with."

"You are so sweet."

He grinned. "That's me."

Because it wasn't more than three feet high, she could barely sit up in it. Stone located a second pad and placed it next to the other one. The two together took up the entire width of the tent.

"This way, no matter what we do, we won't fall off." He sat on his heels and lifted off her shirt.

Her damp hair from the swim chilled her. She wrapped her arms around her chest. "Brr."

He grinned. "You don't have to worry about being cold for long, baby. I'm going to warm you up inside and out."

"I bet you are." And she couldn't wait.

Chapter Twenty-Six

Stone rolled the damp towel and placed it at the head of her mat. "I want you to be comfortable." He gently pressed on her shoulder, and Amber lay down, her gaze never leaving his face. While the air was a lot warmer in the tent than outside, she was still chilled.

She'd already ditched her shoes, so all he had to do to get her naked was tug off her pants, panties and sports bra.

He stared. "I don't know where to begin. You are almost too much for my senses." He snapped his fingers then looked to the side. He dragged his pack closer, opened it, and extracted a condom. "Now, I need you naked." With care, he removed her clothes below her waist. He fingered the material. "We need these to dry a little more."

While he found a place for them, she removed her sports bra. "This is kind of wet, too." She dangled the material from a finger.

Stone took her bra, set it out to dry and then removed his shirt. He placed it over her chest. "This is to keep you warm until I have you naked and under me."

"Ooh. I can't wait." It seemed a lifetime since she'd made love with Stone. This was going to be unique and wonderful.

When he finished undressing, he slid next to her and pulled her to his chest. "I've been waiting forever for this."

Their kiss started out hard and then softened to a tender caress. As his tongue dipped in and out of her mouth, she ran her hands down his back, loving the feel of his muscles. Stone rolled over and dragged her on top of him. His hard cock that she wanted to taste pressed against her belly.

She reached under her and ran a finger along his hard shaft. "I want to lick it."

He hesitated. "Be good."

Not if she could help it. While there wasn't much room to maneuver in the small space, she was able to sit on her heels between his legs. Bending over, she grabbed his cock. This was going to be so much fun. With a small amount of pressure, she lifted her palm up and down, loving the bumpy ride.

"Suck on him, baby."

"I will when I'm ready." She'd always been accused of pushing a person's limits—at least she did when it came to caring for her patients, but would she take it too far with Stone?

Fine. She flicked her tongue down the middle of his cock, zigzagging back and forth. He moaned. This was good. When she reached the tip, she ran her tongue under the lip, increasing the pressure each time she circled him.

A dollop of his tangy cum surfaced. "Excited?" A giggle escaped.

"Keep that up and you'll be on the receiving end of a geyser."

"Uh-huh." Carefully capturing the head of his cock, she dragged her mouth down as far as she could go. She swirled her tongue around his length and slowly massaged his balls while she rubbed his thick shaft.

"Oh, baby. Take it easy. I'm getting too close."

She lifted her head. "You wouldn't." To test his resolve, she pumped harder and sucked longer. She swallowed to open her throat so she could take in more of him.

Stone grabbed her hair and tugged. "Fuck!" His cry came a

second before hot jism squirted into her mouth.

He let go of his tight hold and she lifted her head, drinking in his tangy nectar. When he finished, she sat up. "I can't believe you went off like that."

Stone dragged a hand down his cheek. "I told you to take it easy."

She dropped mouth open. "Me? It's my fault?"

He grinned. "Totally."

She'd get him hard again if it was the last thing she did. As much as she didn't want to admit it, he'd need some time to recover. "How about trying to make me come?"

"That'll be so easy."

Now he'd insulted her. "Oh, yeah?"

He raised his brows. "You willing to wager something?"

"Nothing more than hot sex."

Stone laughed. "Love it."

Not having a lot of room in the tent, they changed positions. Stone twirled a finger around her folds but didn't open them. He leaned back on his heels and pressed her feet closer to her butt. "Open your knees wide for me."

She opened her pussy completely to him. *Oh, my God.* Her cream was already seeping. One thing became obvious. She liked being vulnerable and at his mercy.

His brows rose. "I'm glad I've earned your trust."

The moment you came to speak with Chris you had my trust—and my heart. "You have."

"Then let me see if I can excite you."

He was being silly because in this small space, she'd already perfumed the air. Stone leaned over and ran his tongue right across her opening. The first swipe had her stomach clenching.

"I love your sensitivity."

"I liked your sensitivity, too." It had been exhilarating to make him lose control.

He slipped a finger into her and slowly withdrew it. She

waited for him to continue. When he didn't make any more contact, she lifted up on her elbows. "I love when you touch me." She hoped he'd do more with encouragement.

Instead of fingering her, he slid next to her and removed his shirt from her chest, exposing her breasts. "So pretty."

He ran his finger around a puckered nipple in a teasing fashion. Amber firmed her lips, but he didn't seem to get the hint. She glanced at his cock. It was actually hard again, and from the way the vein was throbbing, he'd recovered completely from his climax.

Stone stopped touching her. "What are you thinking about, baby? I just rubbed your other nipple and you didn't respond. Bored already?"

"Hardly. I was focusing on your cock."

He laughed. "Thank you for being honest."

As soon as he kissed her again, desire swamped her senses. Stone's hand on her breast warmed her from the inside out. He had a way of exciting her with the lightest of touches. Instead of diving into her mouth, he nibbled around the edges, pulling out her bottom lip between his teeth. Then he kissed her again. Damn Stone Benson. Her pussy throbbed.

"I'm ready," she said.

"Not yet." Stone used his free hand to swipe her damp hair from her face. "I could watch you all day. I love how your emotions flash across your face."

She tried to keep her expression blank, and he laughed. He was trying to psych her out. She inhaled to lift her breasts. "My tits are needy."

He grinned and dipped his head, sucking on one nipple while he twirled and pressed on the other one. She tried not to make any noise, but she failed miserably. He went back and forth between them. With each pass, her pussy clenched and cramped.

"Sto—ne," she whispered.

He slipped a hand between her legs and cupped her mound. Slowly, his hand came to life—first with one finger, then two, and finally three. When he curled his fingers and hit her most sensitive spot, she squeezed her eyes shut. Maybe if she didn't see the passion all over his face, she might calm down.

Wrong. Her body caught fire. Just as she about to give up and come, he stopped, and her eyes flew open.

"Condom." In seconds, he picked it up and ripped open the foil. He stilled. "Shit."

"What?"

"Hear that?"

Blood was thrumming through her veins so fast, she heard nothing for a moment. Then laughter sounded, and they both bolted upright.

Stone groaned. "Might be time to pack up and head back to town." He cocked a brow. "Unless you want to walk out naked and scare them away."

"I'm not that brave." Besides, the voices sounded like kids. That wasn't good, but at least they were inside the tent. Had these hikers come up thirty minutes earlier, they'd have gotten an eyeful with them swimming naked.

"Get dressed so we can pack."

Damn, damn, damn. She'd been so close.

The trip down the mountain didn't take long. Neither spoke much, because they were in too much of a hurry to reach the car. She for one was anticipating finishing their lovemaking at the house.

Unfortunately, close to town, his cell rang. He glanced at the number. "Shit. Sorry." He listened for a bit. "How bad? What about Drake? Colter? Brett? Where? I'll be right there, sir." He tossed his phone on the seat. "I can't tell you how sorry I am."

"Another fire?"

"Eight car accident. It's over in Drumfield. They're really short-handed and our captain offered our services."

"I understand." If it wasn't Cade rushing off for a case, it was Stone racing to rescue someone. Maybe she was destined to get her heart broken.

✧ ✧ ✧

Cade and Ethan returned to the station to make phone calls and to check out Ben's alibi.

Hartwick showed up an hour later. "Anything?"

Cade shook his head. "Nothing yet on Ben Ford. But take a look at this." He'd created a timeline for when the killer struck and twisted his computer screen toward his boss.

Hartwick studied the entries and whistled. "I'm not liking this. The killer's escalating." He pointed to the last entry. "What's this?"

Cade wasn't sure if he should have included the woman Ben had visited, which was why he'd shaded it a different color. "This might have been an aborted attempt." He reminded Hartwick about Amber possibly interrupting Ben.

"I'm wondering if the murders are well-thought out and the timing planned, or if he has a mental list of the people who are suffering, and then takes advantage of a lull in security."

The idea was sound. "Our men have been posing as doctors and nurses but haven't spotted anything suspicious so far," Cade said. "That makes me think it's a staff member. Whoever is doing this is good at not attracting attention."

"That scares me. Put more men around this Ben guy."

Cade nodded. He and Ethan had been discussing one option. "Ethan and I have come up with a way to draw out the killer, Captain."

Dan quirked a brow. "What do you mean?"

"We'll send in a cop to pose as a sick patient. We can say he has pancreatic cancer and has only a few weeks to live. Make him in pain—a lot of pain. That way when the nurse tells everyone about her really sick patient and how much it hurts her to see him this way, the killer might strike."

Dan nodded appreciatively then sobered. "Wouldn't our guy be in hospice at that point?"

Cade scrubbed a hand down his jaw. "Maybe not yet."

"Who should we bring in?"

Cade and Ethan had battled over who should be his caregiver. They'd gone back and forth about whether Amber should be the nurse in charge. He didn't want to put her in danger, but the killer had yet to harm a staff member. He figured when she was in the room she'd be safe.

Still, Cade had agonized over the decision. If he had his way, he'd keep Amber away from the hospital until the killer was behind bars. Knowing her, she wouldn't agree. If he chose someone else to be the nurse, there would be less chance this person's complaints would reach Ben—assuming he was guilty. What Cade wanted would hold little weight to Amber. She'd insist on doing this, if only to prove her suspicion about her friend's guilt was false.

"We thought we'd ask Amber Delacroix to be his pretend nurse, and even bring in a shrink to make it appear more legit. Twice now, the person has targeted people Amber has been associated with—Emma Luther and Amber's own brother."

"Yes, but three times he's killed or attempted to kill other patients."

Cade blew out a breath. "If I could see into the killer's head, I'd know what to say, but we have to act fast, Captain."

Hartwick threaded a hand through his hair. "Tell me about it. The mayor is riding my ass."

"If you'll give us the green light, we'll set it up."

Dan drew in his bottom lip. "Go. We have to get this guy."

"Thanks. If he keeps to schedule, he'll strike by the end of the week."

"You better hope it's our undercover agent he tries to kill

next."

"Amen." He and Ethan already had discussed the agent wearing protective sleeves to prevent the killer from jabbing him with a needle. There would be a fake port in his arm if he decided to go that route. Cade prayed this worked, because he hated putting Amber through any more emotional turmoil.

Ethan strode in. "Sorry. I was on the phone." He dragged a chair across the aisle and sat down. "So? Did Dan go for it?"

"Yes, thank God."

Ethan nodded. "Who do you think would be a good undercover guy?"

He'd looked over the rosters to find a match. "Thad Dalton or Mark Eagan. Both are strong enough to wrestle a needle out of the guy's hand."

"Thad is faster than shit and could run the killer down, but a cancer patient in late stages should be pale and thin."

Cade held up a finger. "Ah. That's the beauty of makeup. I figure if they can make it look real in the movies, why can't we?"

Probably because he was so tired, he could picture Thad in his hospital gown chasing after the perp with his bare ass hanging out.

"What are you smiling at?"

Cade sobered. "Nothing. Let's go find Thad and give him his new assignment."

"You do know he'll not be pleased. He's used to chasing after gang members. Lying in bed for a week will drive him up a wall."

"He'll do it if it means catching a killer."

Chapter Twenty-Seven

It took most of Sunday for Cade and Ethan to set up the sting operation. As Ethan had claimed, Thad was less than enthusiastic about his undercover assignment. In the end, he'd relented.

After calling Amber to make sure she was home, Cade headed over. Stone's truck was in the drive. Lucky bastard. As soon as she opened the door, the reason for working these extra hours sunk in. He wanted Amber to be happy.

She looked worried. "Come in. You mentioned something about a sting operation?"

"Yes." Cade ushered both her and Stone into the living room and outlined the plan. If he was way off base about having Amber participate, Stone would set him straight.

She twisted her fingers into a knot. "What if I blow it?"

Cade cradled her in his arms. "You won't."

Stone leaned forward. "What exactly are you asking her to do?"

He expected the concern from Stone. "Talk to the other nurses about Thad's condition." He faced Amber. "All I want you to do is pretend he's another Emma Luther. Whoever is guilty will find out about your distress. Either he'll not want you to suffer or desire to put poor Thad out of his misery."

She took a moment before answering. "What about my

other patients?"

She was such a caring woman. "Go about your job as normal. That's all." He kissed her forehead. "But be careful and stay alert."

Stone stood and walked over to the kitchen, no doubt keeping an ear open.

She suspected Ben Ford, so she would be cautious around him. If her friend was innocent, Cade prayed she didn't let her guard down around the other staff members. Amber was a trusting person by nature, and he hoped that wouldn't be her undoing.

She sat up straight. "When do I start?"

He did love this woman. Her spunk and determination was a good match to his nature. "We should have Thad ready to go by tomorrow morning at the latest."

"So all I have to do is act upset in the break room and say what a sad case I have?"

"That's about it. You'll have to go into Thad's room and pretend to do your thing."

"My *thing*?"

Crap. He needed to learn more what she did. "Yes."

While she seemed to relax back, her gaze remained on some unspecified spot on the far wall.

She then faced him. "Maybe this undercover cop could have a wife who's pregnant. That would add to the authenticity of my anguish. What do you think?"

Cade smiled. "Brilliant." This might actually work. He mentally searched the list of female employees. "One of our officers, Nancy Trillion, is about to pop right now." She was on leave, but perhaps she wouldn't mind making an unscheduled visit. "She can visit Thad and act as his grieving wife. I'm sure she'd love to help bring down this killer."

"Hmm."

Amber worried the buttons on her shirt, a sure tell of her

distress. His heart squeezed. "Sugar?"

"What does Nancy's real husband do?"

That was an odd question, but one he could answer. "He's an investment banker. Why?"

"Maybe her real husband could pretend to be her brother or Thad's brother. That way she won't ever be alone. It would minimize any danger to her."

Her need to protect seemed to be as strong as his. "It's a good plan."

Stone placed a Coke in front of Cade and an iced tea for Amber. "I'd like to help if I can."

Cade cocked a brow. "What are you thinking?"

He shrugged. "People don't blink an eye at a paramedic walking around. I don't work Monday, and for the rest of the week, I don't go in until four in the afternoon. I could stop in from say noon to four to make sure Amber isn't alone with anyone for long."

She shook her head. "As much as I appreciate that, the killer isn't after me. Remember, all of his cases have been mercy killings."

"Except for Stephanie Osmond."

"The killer didn't know she would get better," she shot back.

Cade nodded. "Which implies a doctor isn't involved. And probably not a nurse, either."

Her shoulders sagged. While she didn't mention it could be Ben, he bet she was thinking it.

Cade stood. "As much as I'd like to stay and enjoy your company, I've got to get back." He leaned over and kissed her.

She looked up at him with the most soulful eyes. "You can't stay a little longer?"

He blew out a breath. "I promise when this is over, we'll do something special—just the three of us."

The smile he received in return made his day.

The moment he stepped outside, however, his gut churned.

God, he better not be making a mistake by having Amber involved. Stone had only offered minimal resistance. He, too, must have realized that if his people watched Thad's room twenty-four-seven, she'd be safer than if she went about her normal routine.

Once he arrived at the station, Cade strode up to Ethan who was speaking with the makeup artist. As soon as they finished, he turned to Cade. "We're still planning on getting the psychologist, Dr. Donovan, on board, right?"

There were a shitload of details to take care of. "Yes. How about you handle it? Tell her she'll need a few scheduled visits to make this look legit. I've already touched base with Dr. Zachery Stanfield, and he agreed to act as Thad's doctor."

"What about Amber?"

"She's a go."

"Good. When's Thad arriving at the hospital?"

"He'll be *transferred* here from Helena this afternoon, supposedly because Dr. Stanfield is an old family friend who they hope can do his magic on Thad."

Ethan stood. "Then I guess we're set."

"Yup."

As soon as Ethan left for the hospital to ask for Dr. Donovan's help, Cade compared the schedules of all the nurses and doctors. Patient assisted death was legal in Montana, but so far, the killer hadn't made it look like suicide. Cade wasn't ready to rule out a physician, but it was looking more like someone who had access to the drugs but not the complete knowledge how to use them. That narrowed the possible suspects.

Ben Ford was climbing to the top of that list.

✧ ✧ ✧

Now that this whole sting operation was in full swing, Amber worried about Cade. He had called her each night to see how her shift had gone, but he hadn't stopped over. He had to work on "the" case. He'd stayed away from the hospital because he feared if he showed up, it might tip off the killer.

She'd asked Stone when Cade slept, and from what Stone could tell, Cade only came home to shower and grab a bite to eat.

In one of Cade's weaker moments, Stone had been able to convince him to go bowling on Saturday night with them. It would be the first day Stone had free, and while Amber sucked at bowling, she might be willing to jump out of a plane if it meant she could be with both her men at the same time. Unfortunately, it was close to that time of the month and she was bloated, but she wasn't going to be the one to cancel.

Stone said he and Cade would pick her up at six, and that they would eat at the bowling alley. She'd never been to these lanes before, but if it was like the ones she went to in high school, all they had was greasy pizza and questionable hamburgers. It was the together time that really mattered.

She wore capris with a slight stretch to them and a long-sleeved top that would allow her to move. Her form was so rusty, however, it wouldn't matter what she wore.

Right on time, the doorbell rang, and she rushed to let them in. Her heart lurched. "I can't believe I get both of you." She expected one of them to have gotten called in.

"Ready?" Stone asked.

"What? No hello kiss?" She hadn't seen them for days.

Both descended at the same time and made her giggle.

"You had her last," Cade said. He picked her up and kissed her hard.

Their bodies lined up perfectly, and his cock hardened as their kiss progressed.

"My turn," Stone said.

She could see this could become a problem. After Stone thoroughly kissed her, her body was hot for them. "We can't."

She patted her stomach and scrunched up her nose.

Stone immediately sobered. "You sure you even want to go out? We can stay in and I can fix you something to eat."

Now she chuckled. "No. I'll be fine. I think it's mostly stress. Although other factors are about to occur, too."

Cade wrapped an arm around her. "To take the pressure off you, I say it's me and you against Stone then."

"What?" Stone laughed, as he opened the door.

"Works for me." This date would help take her mind off everything that was happening. Hopefully, it would help Cade, too. Stone had driven, so the three of them squished into his front seat. "Ooh. It's a ménage sandwich. I'm the meat and you two are the bread," she said.

Cade picked up her hand and kissed her knuckles. Her heart swooned at his tenderness. She loved how he could go from tough guy to romantic in a flash.

"You are so going to experience more than that afterwards."

Suddenly, she wasn't feeling so bad. "Promises, promises." She wouldn't ask if there were two cocks in her future. If nothing else, tonight should help move their relationship forward.

Stone pulled into the lot. "Here we are at Rock Hard's famous bowling alley. Pinarama," Stone said with pride lacing his tone.

The outside appeared to be a little seedy. Having two of the three "a's" unlit didn't help. Cade piled out and helped her. From the back Stone retrieved a bag.

She grunted. "Don't tell me you have your own ball and shoes?"

"Okay, I won't." He grinned.

Both men grabbed her hand and they entered the fray. The place was packed. Women bowlers had taken half the lanes. Teams wore matching shirts, which implied tonight was league night.

"Cade," Stone said. "How about getting us a lane while I help our woman find a ball?"

She liked the "our woman" part.

Cade nodded and headed to the counter. Stone ran his gaze up and down her. "I'm thinking you're the eight-pound type."

In high school, she'd used a ten-pound ball, but her fingers might not be as strong any more. He made her pick up at least five of them before she found one that seemed right. "This is good."

Cade came over. "Lane four." He picked up a ball and set it down. He nodded to Stone's bag. "What weight you got in there?"

"Fourteen, but the house balls tend to be a little heavier. I'd try a twelve or a thirteen."

Amber was curious how this duel would end. Cade tried a few balls and finally chose a fourteen pounder. *Men.*

Stone grinned as if he knew Cade had been fooled. "Let's get you shoes."

By the time they made it to their lane and set up the electronic scoring, it was close to seven and she was starving. Her stomach grumbled.

"Oh, baby. We need to get you something to eat. Pizza? Hotdogs? Hamburger? What?"

Her stomach churned at the thought of the greasy fare. "How about we split a pizza?"

"What kind do you like?" Stone asked.

"Whatever." She just needed food or she'd get a headache.

"I'll go," Cade said. "Amber. Beer?"

"Coke." The carbonation might settle her stomach better.

Stone nodded to her ball on the rack. "Why don't you take a practice throw?"

She shook her head. "You just want to check out your competition. I hope you're prepared for Cade and I plan to outscore you."

He laughed. "You think? What's the bet?" She loved the twinkle in his eye.

Cade came back with a Coke and two beers. "Pizza will be up in a bit." He looked between them. "What?"

"Stone doesn't think we can beat him. We can, can't we?"

She thought she'd see the look of victory on his face. "Oh, sugar. I was only kidding back at the house. We don't stand a chance unless you're a superstar."

She shot a gaze at Stone. "You're that good?"

He shrugged. "Me and the guys used to be on a league. Took second place two years in a row."

She waved a hand. "Well, then, there's still hope for us."

Stone chuckled and shook his head. He sat at the scoring table and pointed to the monitor above them. "You're up first, baby. Show us what you've got."

No pressure here. She picked up her ball, did her three-step approach, and eased it down the lane. It thumped all the way to the end. While the ball hit the three pin, it only nicked the head pin. The slow speed garnered her a six. She turned around, not wanting to see the disappointment on Cade's face.

He was beaming. "Way to go!"

Okay. So this wasn't a real competition. She figured no matter who won or lost, they'd end up in bed, which was exactly where she wanted to be—assuming her stomach improved.

Her next throw took out two more pins for a total of eight. Not bad for not having bowled in years.

"Cade. You're next, man."

Cade stood and swaggered to the ball return. If she hadn't known, she never would have guessed he was a rather up-tight cop with a serial killer on his hands. He picked up the ball, stepped to the line, and looked right and left like she'd seen the pro-bowlers do on television. He rolled the ball down the lane so hard it barely had time to curve. One pin dropped.

"Good shot, man."

Cade turned around. Instead of a sneer, he smiled. "I meant to do that."

The ball returned, and he stepped up to the line again. This time, Cade seemed a little more serious and eased up on the throw. He knocked down seven more and raised his hands in victory. He even did a silly little dance, which had her laughing.

"We are so going to win." She glanced at Stone and grinned.

"You wish."

Cade nodded to the bar behind the pool tables. "Food's up." He jogged up there.

Amber nodded to the lane. "Stone, take your turn, and then we'll eat."

Stone was rather nonchalant as he approached the lane. He held the ball for a few seconds, as if he needed to center himself, then tossed it with smooth precision. Pins flew everywhere, but one remained. His shoulders tensed for a second. He, too, seemed to have high standards.

The ball returned just as Cade set the food on a table behind the lanes. Stone aimed and then rolled the ball softly. The ball headed down the middle, curved left, and then knocked down the pin.

She clapped. "A spare! Good job."

He turned back and smiled, but it didn't reach his eyes. Boy, he was serious.

"Let's eat," he said.

They put the game on hold and chowed. The men fought over the pizza, but she only ate two pieces before she was full. A small ache started behind her eye. *Damn.* She didn't need a headache. Not now. The timing couldn't have been any worse.

Caffeine usually helped, so she guzzled her Coke and plastered on a smile. "Let's go beat him, Cade."

He nodded. "Let's do it."

The rest of the game was neck and neck. In the end, Stone beat them by five pins.

"Rematch," Cade demanded.

The smell of the oils on the lane or the building's mold increased her headache, but she refused to have anything interfere with their fun. "You're on."

This time Stone started. He let the ball fly and held his pose for a second before standing and swaying as if he was urging the ball to turn this way and that. "Strike!" he shouted.

She and Cade clapped. She stood and a sharp spike stabbed her eye. A few times, she debated asking the men to take her home, but they seemed to be enjoying themselves too much. *Damn.* Their huge sexual experience might have to be put on hold if the headache didn't ease up.

Amber threw an eight on the first toss, but missed the spare by a hair. Cade made up for her lack by knocking down all the pins. The race was on.

Forty-minutes later, she and Cade were victorious and hugs were shared all around.

"Tiebreaker?" Stone asked.

This time she had to speak up. "Not for me. I've got a killer headache."

Their cheer disappeared in a heartbeat. "Sugar, why didn't you tell us sooner?"

"I was having fun." Now they'd fuss at her.

"Next time, let us know sooner."

She nodded. Stone removed his shoes, and she and Cade followed suit. Cade paid and then escorted her out.

"I'm sorry, guys."

Cade opened the passenger side door. "It's not your fault. I had fun. We'll have to do it again."

"Hell, yeah," Stone joined in. "A tie is not acceptable."

Leave it to the men to make her laugh. When they arrived back at her place, Stone made her lean back on the sofa while he prepared a hot compress for her face.

"Can I fix you some tea, sugar?"

Cade probably had never made tea. She only used the loose stuff. The pitcher of iced tea was probably gone. "I'm good."

The men sat next to her as she placed the soothing cloth over her eyes. Stone rubbed her arms, while Cade massaged her feet.

When she awoke, they were both gone. *Crap.* She hadn't meant to fall asleep. A note sat on her stomach. She read it out loud and smiled. "Loved tonight. If we'd stayed, we never would have gotten any rest." Both men signed it. "Aw."

It was already past midnight so she didn't blame them for not hanging around. Even though they never got to bed, she had to say, she'd seen an incredible side of both men. She was falling fast and prayed they were, too.

Chapter Twenty-Eight

By the following Wednesday, over a week after the sting operation had begun, Amber's nerves were totally shot. Her three-day headache had finally disappeared, but it threatened to return every time she walked down the hospital halls. She couldn't help but study every staff member, wondering if one of them could be a killer. Sadly, she'd even jumped when Jamie came into the cafeteria and sat at her table.

"What's got you so uptight?"

Jamie didn't work on her floor, so Amber hadn't had the chance to tell her about Thad. She also hadn't shown up to this week's happy hour either. While she'd spoken with Jamie a couple of times on the phone, she wanted to see her friend in person before she brought up her concerns about Thad. "I'm good."

"You're like a jack rabbit with a hunter nearby."

Amber laughed. "I'm not that bad." She drank some of her tea then sobered. She cast her gaze downward for a moment before beginning. "Last Monday, a young man was brought in with pancreatic cancer. He's so sweet and brave, but his pain level is killing me."

Jamie's expression turned serious. "Isn't the doctor giving him morphine?"

"Yes, but it's not enough." She pressed her lips together and thought of Chris and his helpless situation. That made her eyes water for real. "His wife is eight months pregnant. She's out of her mind with grief."

Her friend shook her head. "Who's the doctor?"

"Zachery Stanfield. He's the best. He's going to try a new protocol for Thad. I pray it works, but I've seen his blood work and really don't think there's much hope."

Jamie clasped her hand. "I guess my floor will be getting a new patient soon."

"Maybe. Dr. Stanfield said it could be a month or more. To suffer that much breaks my heart."

"I hear ya."

They both ate their meal, but with the way Jamie was picking at her food, she was thinking about poor Thad, too. Amber hated lying to her best friend, but she told herself it was for the greater good.

Amber wanted to change the subject before she acted too much out of character. "I'm really looking forward to our get together tonight." It was just the girls.

Jamie's eyes opened. "What? No Cade or Stone?"

Her friend knew how much Amber was taken by them, and that she wanted to spend as much time with her men as their schedules allowed. "Both are working, so I'm free!"

"Good. I spoke with Becky. She can't make it, but I think Zoey and Melissa can."

"I so need this break. Lately, this place has been crazy. Everyone is on edge." That wasn't a lie.

Jamie nodded. "I think it's those murders."

"You're probably right." Amber studied Jamie, but she didn't seem to have any idea Amber suspected Ben.

As soon as they finished lunch, Amber went back to doing her rounds, checking to see the administered drugs were doing their job on her patients. Close to five, she passed Thad's room. Since the door was open, she peeked in. To her surprise, Zoey

Donovan was there.

"Hey!" *Crap.* She shouldn't have been so cheery.

Zoey was able to keep her professional demeanor and didn't smile back. "Thad and I are talking about end of life decisions."

Amber glanced at Thad. If she didn't know he was a robust undercover cop, she might think he was close to death. Someone had done a good makeup job. More than that, he looked, well, scared.

"How's it going, Thad?"

"I hate feeling like shit. I'm in so much pain, I want to die." He turned his head. She almost believed him.

"Hang in there." The man was good. She had to give him that. Amber made sure her back was to the door and kept her voice low. "You coming tonight?"

Zoey nodded. "Thad, I'll be back tomorrow. Stay positive for your wife."

He grunted.

Even though this was a sting operation, Amber felt bad for the guy. The young shouldn't die. At that thought, her mind went straight to Chris, and she sucked in a breath.

Zoey placed a hand on her arm. "You okay?"

Her eyes watered. "Thad reminds me of Chris. That's all."

"It'll take time, but if you need to talk, you know where to find me."

Zoey was good at her job and very sincere. "I will. See you in a few."

Once they parted, Amber couldn't wait to leave. She passed a few nurses and doctors she didn't remember seeing before and wondered if they might be undercover, too. She prayed Cade and Ethan's plan worked. It had to.

Amber had finished a glass of wine by the time Zoey finally

arrived at Banner's. Now the foursome was complete.

Zoey dropped onto her seat. "Sorry, ladies. I had a late walk-in.

Something in Zoey's eyes seemed different. "Want to share his name?"

Zoey laughed. "Why would you think it's a male?"

"By the look in your eyes. I get the sense the late appointment wasn't a real therapy session, but if I'm wrong, tell me to mind my own business."

"He's just an old friend who happens to be married. Sorry to disappoint you all." She leaned forward and looked right at Amber. "I want to know how your fireman and your super cop are doing."

Did the whole town know? "They're good."

Zoey cocked a brow. "Have the three of you found time to be together?"

That was an odd question. She told them about their bowling adventure. "But that seemed to be the exception. Stone is on night shift for the next month and Cade is working on a few cases that have interrupted our time together. Why?"

She shrugged. "Just asking. As you know, years ago I dated two men." She rolled her eyes. "It was bad enough one would never put the toilet seat down while the other was a slob."

Jamie sighed. "Benny never puts the seat down and is a slob. And that's only one man."

Once more, they all chuckled as Melissa picked up her glass. "You don't have to answer this, but do the men get jealous? I've only dated one guy at a time, but if I looked at another male, he'd freak!"

Amber and Zoey answered at the same time. Amber said no while Zoey said yes.

Melissa looked confused. "Care to explain?"

Amber nodded to Zoey. "Go ahead." Stone and Cade claimed they didn't get jealous, but she really hadn't been with them long enough to be sure.

"This stays between us girls, right?"

"Always," they said in unison.

"Dave and Mark were both amazing men. Dave was a dentist and Mark a psychiatrist. You'd think smart men like that wouldn't enter into a ménage relationship until they were willing to share."

"Right," Melissa said.

"If I was with Mark, Dave would demand I pay as much attention to him and vice versa." She waved a hand. "Not a subject I like to talk about." She turned to Melissa. "Tell us something fun you've done this week."

"Fun? I'm still reeling from Stephanie Osmond's death."

Zoey placed a hand over hers. "I'm sorry. I wasn't thinking."

Melissa had been Stephanie's nurse. Amber didn't want her night to end on a down note. "Guess what adventure I had since our last get together?" She couldn't wait to tell them about skinny-dipping, and how before she and Stone had finished making love, some hikers showed up. All eyes turned to her. "Listen closely, and I'll tell you a tale."

Stone hadn't had a chance to see Amber for days because of his intense schedule. Before he went to his supervisor and offered him his first born to switch to the day shift, he wanted to have a conversation with Cade. With his late hours, and Cade's obsession with finding the killer, they hadn't had a chance to talk about the direction of their relationship with her.

Because Stone didn't have to be at work for another two hours, he planned to speak with Cade then stop by and visit Amber. She had today and tomorrow off. Even just a hug and kiss would help him get through the day.

He texted Cade and immediately received a reply he could

spare a half hour. Something must have happened, because Cade was at the hospital. He'd claimed he didn't want to be seen hovering in the hallways.

Stone then checked to see if Amber was free at three. She, too, texted right back that she was. Perfect. He'd chat with Cade then drive to Amber's house before he headed into work.

In less than fifteen minutes, Stone was rushing up to the second floor to find his roommate. Because he was wearing his paramedic uniform, no one seemed to notice him. As a thought too horrible to even consider entered his mind, his steps faltered. A paramedic would be the perfect person to put these patients out of their misery. Both Ativan and succinylcholine were available to him in the ambulance.

Stone raced through the names of his co-workers, dismissing each one immediately. It wasn't possible. None of the men had become close enough emotionally to any of the patients to do this. Other than maybe Chris, whose condition had been severe, most of those he and his fellow paramedics delivered to the hospital were treated and on their way home in a few days. Firemen didn't deal very often with people with cancer, liver failure, and life-ending diseases.

When he caught sight of Cade, his roommate was speaking with a doctor. Stone waited until they finished their conversation before he went over. Cade's eyes were bloodshot and his posture less than straight.

Cade nodded. "Hey. What's up?"

Why Stone was nervous to have this conversation, he didn't know. "Got a minute to chat?" His roommate had said he was free, but his scheduled might have changed.

"Sure. Our prime suspect has the day off. That doesn't mean he can't slip in here, but mentally I've lowered the alert from red to orange."

"How did the interrogation go yesterday?" Cade mentioned he would be speaking with Ben, Jamie, and two other nurses again. The others were to make it look like the cops were just being thorough.

"Jamie acted nervous, and Ben was belligerent at first, then turned into a total mess, but he didn't confess if that's what you want to know."

Damn. "Did it help you narrow down your search?"

"No. We have to catch the person in the act."

"You aren't worried the real killer will lay low for a while?"

Cade ran a hand over his head. "It's possible. At this point, I've given up trying to guess the killer's next move. It's been close to two weeks, way longer than I thought he'd last."

"Want to grab a coffee?" Cade looked like he could use the break.

"Sure."

The cafeteria was on the other end of the wing. Cade didn't ask what this was about, but Stone bet his roommate could guess. Because Stone was about to head into work, he grabbed a coffee and a pastry. They picked a table along the wall and sat.

Stone inhaled. "I want to talk about Amber."

Tension crossed Cade's face. "What about her?"

"I'm about to go in and ask my supervisor for the day shift. I want to spend more time with her, but I need to know your intentions."

Cade barked out a small laugh. "You her dad now?"

That brought a smile to his lips. It did sound as if he wanted to make sure Cade had honorable intentions. *Shit.* He sucked at this. Stone wanted a permanent ménage relationship, and the three hadn't even engaged in a real three-way yet.

"Look. I know we've always kept what we do with our women casual, but Amber is different," Stone said.

Cade grabbed his mug with two hands and sipped the steaming brew. "I know. She's special."

"So how serious are you?" They'd never had this conversation before and Stone feared he'd fuck it up.

Cade cocked a brow. "As serious as you are."

That didn't answer Stone's question. "I think she might be the one for us."

A slow, tired smile spread across Cade's face. "My thoughts exactly."

Relief washed through him. "Then you better catch the son of a bitch who's taking these lives so we can get on with ours."

"Don't I know it." Cade leaned forward. "When this is over, we need to tell Amber we want her. All this last minute cancelling of dates along with only one of us being free for her doesn't do anyone any good."

Stone couldn't believe his ears. "I couldn't agree more, but we do have jobs and that can't be helped."

"I know, but we can work together to minimize the disturbance." He looked away for a moment. "I want a family. A real family. Like what your parents have." Cade leaned back, looking as if he'd needed to get that off his chest.

Stone stuffed the pastry in his mouth and grinned. Amber had actually done it—tamed the great Cade Carter. He'd thought the day would never come.

✧ ✧ ✧

Amber wanted nothing more than to see her men, but Cade said he planned to spend every waking hour at work until the killer was caught. Stupid man. He'd put himself in an early grave if he wasn't careful. However, it was his determination that she admired most about him. She loved his dedication, his concern for justice, and his *never give up* attitude.

When Stone had texted her to ask if he could stop over in an hour for a few minutes, she said she'd love the company. He'd come by the hospital a few times this week, but that only served to add to the frustration. Not being able to hug and kiss him was driving her crazy.

Now she had to hurry. She dumped a six-pack of ale into her already too full grocery cart. She'd been so busy she hadn't had time to even shop. Her mind raced to what Stone and Cade might like to eat when they did come over. She immediately scratched pizza off the list. They needed something more nutritious like fish, chicken, or good old grass fed Montana beef. As she headed to the meat aisle, her cell rang. It was Jamie. This was a busy day.

"Hey, girl."

"Amber." Her voice came out shaky. "Is there any way we can meet?"

She pulled the cart to the side of the aisle so she didn't block traffic. "Sure. What's wrong?" She bet Stone would be in and out in before Jamie could even stop by.

"I broke up with Benny." The sob that escaped ripped Amber up. Her mind jumped to all sorts of bad scenarios. Had Benny told her something?

"Oh, honey. I'm at the store but can be home in fifteen minutes. Meet me there, okay?" *Damn.* Her kisses with Stone would have to be quick. Her talk with Jamie wouldn't be.

"Okay," she choked out.

Before Amber could extract more information from her friend, Jamie disconnected. Dear God. Even though Jamie had been acting a little distant lately, Amber hadn't seen this coming.

She wondered if Jamie suspected Ben of the murders, too. No. Jamie would have come to her with that horrible thought before she spoke with Ben—or so she hoped.

Stomach churning, Amber rushed to the check out. It was just her luck it took eons to get through the line. One item didn't have a label and the cashier had to send someone to check the price. Amber had been tempted not buy the can of peas, but the kid had already run off. *Aargh.* Murphy's Law seemed to be in full force today.

When she finally paid, she rushed to her car and stored her

four bags in the trunk. When she reached her drive, she was pleased she'd beaten Jamie there. She grabbed one of the bags, and as quickly as she could, rushed up the steps. She opened the door, set her groceries on the counter, and raced back out again. Waiting this long between shopping trips hadn't been smart. As it was, she'd have to go back tomorrow for the fish and chicken she didn't have time to buy today.

She loaded up both arms, traipsed back inside, and set the packages down. "One more to go," she huffed.

As she turned around, Ben was standing in her open door.

"Hello, Amber."

Oh, shit. He was pointing a gun straight at her chest.

Chapter Twenty-Nine

Amber covered her mouth with both hands. Her throat clogged as adrenaline zipped through her. She shook her head. *This can't be happening.*

Ben stepped into the living room, and she scrambled backward. When her leg bumped against something hard, her feet flew out from under her. *Oh, fuck.* Arms flapping, she landed on her ass, and pain tripped up her spine.

Get out of here!

Heels scraping against the floor, she tried to scoot away from him. Ben's mouth moved, but the blood pounding in her ears prevented her from hearing anything. She had to escape. Had to get away from him.

Amber flipped over and propelled forward on all fours as she tried to gain traction on the slippery hardwood floors. Needing to call for help, she made it to her feet and raced toward the counter.

Footsteps pounded behind her. "Amber. Stop."

She'd heard his words but didn't obey them and dove for the cell. With shaking fingers she dialed the nine and then the one.

"Amber!" A shot sounded and a bullet hit the wall next to her head, sending sharp bits of plaster into her cheek. Blood dripped. Her ears rung. Then the pain registered, but she pushed aside the throbbing ache.

Press the one again.

Suddenly she was in the air, flying across the room. Heart in her throat, she couldn't focus. She landed with a thump on the sofa and banged her head on the sofa arm. *Fuck.*

"Give me that!" Ben ripped the cell from her hands and hurled it across the room. "Bitch." A crash sounded.

He backhanded her across the face and a streak of fire skated across her cheek. She tried to scream but only a croak escaped. Paralyzed with fear, she ran her gaze around the room, looking for a way out, but she kept coming back to one thing—the barrel of a gun pointed at her chest.

"Get up." He waved his weapon—a weapon that would kill her.

No matter how much she urged her muscles to work, her body refused to respond. He yanked her up by the arm and a wave of pain twisted in her joint and then raced through her jaw. He shoved her back across the living room.

She staggered to a stop and held up her hand. "Ben. Don't." The words erupted.

Amber swiped the blood from her split lip. Looking down, she spotted red splotches splattered across her pants. She wiggled her chin to see if he'd broken her jaw. It didn't really matter. She was going to die.

Ben stepped toward her, and her heart pounded harder. Only now did she notice his bloodshot eyes, and that he hadn't shaved in days. His wrinkled clothing implied he hadn't slept either.

Ben's lips curled as he waved the gun. "You. Ruined. My. Life."

His words entered her brain and rumbled around. *I ruined his life?* That didn't make any sense.

When her back hit the doorjamb leading to the hallway, she hadn't remembered moving. She rubbed her hands down her thighs. The stench of perspiration made her nose wrinkle.

Then Ben took two more steps toward her, and her legs weakened. Unable to stop, she slid to the ground, tears streaming down her cheeks. This was the end. After years of not finding love, she finally met Cade and Stone. Now, she'd never get to love her men the way she wanted. A giant sob escaped. She wanted children, too, but that would never be. "Oh, God." She hiccupped. She didn't want to die.

"Shut up." Ben paced. "Just shut the fuck up. I need to think."

At least that was what she thought he said. A tidal wave of pictures, sounds, and laughter filled her mind of when she was little. Suddenly, all the arguments she'd had with her mom seemed petty. Really petty. Amber wished she could tell her mother she really did love her. But that would never happen. Not now. She slumped.

Ben peered down at her and held the gun with both hands. "You convinced Jamie to leave me." His words dripped acid, his eyes glassy and hard.

She looked up at him, but he was no longer the Ben she knew. "Me? That's not true."

Wait. The grocery store. Jamie was upset. When was that? Her brain remained fogged.

He waved his gun again, his jaw hardening. Adrenaline accelerated her fear.

Stop it. You're a nurse.

She drew on her training and forced her pulse to slow. She had to stay alive. If not for herself, then for the relationship she wanted to have with him men, and the child she wanted to raise. She gasped at what her death would mean to them.

Her gaze shot to the splintered phone scattered on the floor and prayed the call had gone through.

He kicked her foot, jarring her back to him. "Don't lie to me. It was you who turned Jamie against me." He nearly spat out his words.

She swallowed past the lump in her throat. "I'm sure it's a misunderstanding." With tremendous effort, she pushed against the wall and edged her body upward.

He lowered his gun arm an inch. "Then you did talk to her?" He fisted his hand and walked back to the sofa. He spun around. "How did Jamie sound?" A hint of her old friend surfaced, which helped to lower her dangerously high blood pressure.

Her knees wobbled and she grasped the molding behind her. What had he asked? It was something about Jamie. Was it how she'd sounded?

"Good. I mean scared." *Fuck*. That didn't come out right. "Contrite." She added that for Ben's benefit.

"No she's not."

Damn. He didn't believe her. She glanced toward the kitchen, judging whether she could make it out the back door before he shot her. She'd have to run through the dining room and kitchen first. She'd never make it.

Come on, Jamie. Get here.

"Don't even think about it." Then he charged.

No! Her hand brushed against the side table and latched onto the painted rock one of her patients had decorated. Without thinking, she picked it up and hurled it at him. It hit him in the head and crashed to the floor.

For that split second, power surged through her. Hope soared.

He stopped and held his head. "You fucking bitch." He waved the gun and squinted at her.

Don't ever look at me like that again. The fire in her blood exploded. "For God's sake, Ben, put the gun down." She pushed off from the wall and came toward him. "I don't know what you think I've done or what I know, but you're wrong." Her heart continued to pound, and her vision turned white for moment as if she might pass out.

"No. Get back!"

He came at her again and shoved her with his palm, bruising her sternum. She stumbled but righted herself before she hit the wall again. Amber refused to go down. If she was going to die, she wanted it to be with dignity.

Ben got in her face and leveled the gun at her chest. "She said she wasn't in love with me anymore." He stepped back and paced again. She couldn't chance running because he kept glancing her way.

His love probably smothered Jamie. *Say something.* "That's not true. She told me she loved you." But that was six months ago.

"You poisoned her against me. You saw me with that woman and told her." His chest inflated, as if waiting to learn what she knew.

She needed to stall. "Your cousin? How is she?" She hissed in a breath, acting like she was waiting to hear the woman had passed.

His hand seemed to waver. "You don't get it. I needed to prove to Jamie that I loved her."

At first, she couldn't connect the dots. Then reality sunk in. *Oh, fuck. Please don't confess. Then he'll have to shoot me for sure.* "I don't know what you're saying."

He tapped his chest with his other hand. "I wanted to show Jamie that only *I* could take away her pain."

"You always take her pain away. She knows that. Remember, Beau? The dog?"

For a split second, his face softened and his gaze appeared unfocused. "Jamie was sad."

"Yes. And you helped her."

A creak sounded near the door. "Benny?" It was Jamie. A shot of hope soared through Amber's veins.

She prayed Jamie had heard Ben threaten her and had called the police.

He twisted toward her. "What are you doing here?" There

was little affection in his tone.

"Benny, what's going on?" Jamie moved closer to him and held up her hands. "Put down that gun so we can talk."

Amber wanted to tell her not to get near him, that he'd lost his mind, but she didn't want to say those words out loud.

Benny's eyes went cold as he raked his gaze over Jamie. "Stop. Don't get any closer."

Jamie's shoulders sagged and her face paled. She stopped. "Benny? It's me, Jamie." She kept her voice low and soothing. "We'll work this out. Together. Put down the gun."

Sweat dripped down Amber's arms, mixing with the caked blood. She didn't dare move, praying Jamie's words would reach him.

"No. It's too late." Bitterness colored his tone.

Jamie probably thought he was talking about their break-up.

"Talk to me, Benny. It can't be this bad." Jamie edged closer, and Amber let out a slow breath.

She prayed Ben wouldn't want to take her life with Jamie being a witness. He wouldn't want to cause the woman he loved any more pain.

"That woman was paralyzed." He shook the gun and his eyes went all dark. "She begged me."

Now Amber knew Ben had truly retreated to another place.

"Benny, please." Jamie stepped close.

"Don't." The gun shifted to Jamie.

"I love you, Benny. You love me."

His eyes softened, and Amber thought he might relent. Then like a dark cloud passing over the sun, he swung the gun back toward Amber. "Jamie won't tell, but you will."

Suddenly, Jamie sprinted toward Amber, ramming her shoulder into Amber's chest. She slammed into the wall. Pain and surprise ripped through her at the intensity. A gunshot went off as shock ripped through her. No sounds seemed to register in her brain. *Oh, no.*

Chapter Thirty

Just as Cade finished his coffee, Ethan rushed into the cafeteria. "Good. I found you." He glanced at Stone. "Hey." He pulled up a chair. "Look at this." Ethan shoved a piece of paper at Cade.

His roommate studied it with intensity. "Holy fuck."

"Tell me about it," Ethan said. "That pharmacy tech caved."

Not that Stone should be privy to any investigation, but if Amber was involved in any way, he wanted to know. If Cade couldn't tell him, he wouldn't press the issue.

Cade glanced up at him. "Seems like Ben Ford paid Derrick Thompson to work for him, but sign in as Ben."

Stone shook his head. "I don't get it."

"The times line up to the days and time of the murders."

Stone's pulse raced. "So Ben did kill those people?" He kept his voice to a whisper.

"Possibly. Shit, it's not enough." Cade turned to Ethan. "Where's Ford now?"

"Last time we checked, he was at home."

Cade pushed back his chair. "We need to find him."

Just as Cade stood, his cell dinged, indicating a text message. He pulled it out, and his face paled. "Fuck. It's from Jamie. It says, 'Ben's at Amber's. He's got a gun. Hurry.'"

Stone's heart almost stopped.

"Shit," Cade said. "This was sent a few minutes ago."

Neither said a word as they both sprinted out of the cafeteria. The smell of disinfectant seemed sharper and the image of Amber surfaced—naked, beautiful, loving.

"The cruiser's in the back," Cade called behind him.

Stone followed. No matter how fast they ran, it took too long to get outside. When they reached cruiser, they both hopped in. Cade jammed the key in the ignition and peeled out of the lot, the siren blaring.

Cade picked up the police radio and asked for backup at Amber's. He then jetted under I90 toward Gold Avenue.

"Drive faster, damn it." Stone punched the dashboard as they careened through town. His body shook and his gut was about to give up the roll he'd just eaten. Ben just might be insane. God help Amber.

"She'll be okay." Cade was patronizing him again, but thank God Cade looked determined.

"You don't fucking know that."

"Calm down."

"I am fucking calm." *Or not.*

✧ ✧ ✧

Heavy thuds reverberated on the floor as Ben came toward Jamie who was crumpled on the floor. "Oh, shit. Jamie. I didn't mean it. Baby, baby."

Amber gathered every ounce of energy and courage in her body and stood. Keeping her gaze on Ben, she helped Jamie to her feet. Her friend winced. Jamie's arm was covered in blood. The bullet meant for Amber had hit Jamie instead.

She straightened her back. "Benny. Stop." Her friend must have drawn on every ounce of reserve strength in her body to shout that command.

Like he'd been felled by a roundabout kick to the stomach,

Ben dropped to his knees, his gaze lowered, and a sob escaped. "I'm sorry. I never meant to hurt you."

Amber held her breath, waiting for the criminal side of Ben to return. Jamie nodded to Amber and inched toward Ben who still held the gun in his hand. Jamie leaned over. "I'm hurt, Benny. Real bad."

"Jamie?" He sounded like a pathetic little boy.

Faster than lightning, Jamie wrenched the gun from Ben's hands and scrambled backward, trying to level the weapon on him, but her arm wavered. She clamped her left hand over the wound and grunted.

Like a Phoenix rising, Ben stood and seemed to have garnered his control. He changed right before her eyes. "Jamie. Give me the gun. Amber must die. She knows too much." His voice came out deep and strong.

Amber snatched the weapon from Jamie's clenched fingers and edged in front of her. Amber kept the gun pointed at Ben's chest.

"You don't have the guts to pull that trigger," he said with a sneer.

Clearly, he had no idea that when challenged, Amber Lynn Delacroix never backed down.

✧ ✧ ✧

Ten long minutes later, Cade slammed on his breaks in front of Amber's house. He cut the engine, checked to make sure his weapon was secure, and pushed open his door. He nodded to Stone. "You take the back entrance, and I'll go through the front."

Stone's jaw tightened. "Got an extra piece?"

Cade reached into the glove compartment and handed him his spare. "Here." Now he was happy Stone had gotten his license.

Once Cade checked the scene, he'd make his move. He jetted out of the car. At least Stone had the sense not to shut his door hard. Not wanting to spook Ben, Cade waited for Stone to disappear behind the house before he eased up the front steps. Voices from inside sounded tense. Cade heard another woman's—probably Jamie's—and a male voice that must belong to Ben.

With gun in hand he peered through the living room window, hoping they'd be too preoccupied with what they were doing to notice him.

What the fuck? Amber held a gun in her hand and was pointing it at Ben. Caked blood coated the side of her face. His gut churned and he forced down his anger. Jamie was sitting on the floor, her arm streaked in red. Ben lurched toward them.

Go!

The door stood ajar. Cade bulldozed in and leveled his weapon at Ben. "Stop!" He looked over at her. "Amber?"

She lowered her arm. "Thank God you're here."

"What happened?" He kept his voice as even as possible as he moved closer to Ben.

Jamie answered. "Ben shot me, but he was aiming for Amber."

"Amber, set the gun down before someone gets hurt." He faced Ben. "Ford, get down on your knees and put your hands on your head." The man folded like an accordion. He didn't even claim he was the victim. "Amber, Stone's at the back door. Open it for him."

Amber ran through the kitchen. Right after he'd cuffed Ben, both stepped back into the living room.

"Hold still." Stone was checking out Amber.

"I'm fine," she said. "Jamie's been shot."

"Stone, call for help," Cade said. He would have called, but Stone could provide better intel.

Stone rushed to Jamie and looked her over. He then dialed

the station and gave them her vitals and described the scene. Sirens sounded in the background. *Good timing.* Moments later, two officers rushed in, weapons drawn. Cade gave them the lowdown. Cade nodded to Ben. "Get him out of here."

The officers dragged Ford to his feet. "Baby," he cried, as he struggled to get out of their hold, but failed. "I'm sorry, Jamie."

Jamie didn't even look at him.

Stone rushed into the kitchen and returned with two wet towels. He handed one to Amber and the other to Jamie. "Hold them over your wounds," he said to both.

Since Jamie seemed to be in the worst shape, Stone attended to her. Once he looked at her wound, he pressed on her fingertips to make sure she had good circulation.

Cade rushed over to Amber and led her over to the sofa. Blood had streaked her chin and cheek. *Jesus. What the fuck happened?* Her gaze remained focused straight ahead. As soon as she sat, she rocked back and forth. Cade slipped next to her and gathered her in his arms, careful not to press too hard. "What happened here, sugar?" He sat back needing to watch her expression.

"Ben came at me with a gun." A sob escaped.

He figured that much. "I bet you were scared, huh?"

She leaned back, sniffled, and glanced at him. Then she lightly punched him. "Was not."

At least half the tension left his body. His Amber was back. In a much steadier tone, she told him how she tried to get away and call for help. She nodded to the pieces of phone on the floor. After she told him how Ben had backhanded her, he wanted to kill the guy himself.

The medical team arrived before she finished her story.

Stone looked up. "Trevor, Marshall." Trevor rushed over to them, and Marshall joined Stone.

Cade moved out of the way to give Trevor room. He ran his hands up and down her spine and then along her jaw.

Marshall helped Jamie to her feet. "Can you walk to the ambulance?"

"I think so." She looked over at Amber. "Can she come with me? She's the only family I have."

Marshall placed a hand around her waist. "We have two ambulances so we can give each of you our undivided attention."

Trevor guided Amber to a stand, but she swatted away his hand. "I'm fine."

"Let Trevor do his job, sugar." *Stubborn woman.*

Stone walked up to Amber and guided her to the door. "I'll ride with her."

Trevor nodded.

Cade stood. "I'll meet you at the hospital. I have to wait for the forensic team.

✧ ✧ ✧

Amber's body ached. The tension had ripped her apart and a mean headache was brewing. Not to mention both her jaw and face ached like a bitch. She feared looking in a mirror. By tomorrow, her face would be swollen and a not-so-pretty combination of black, blues, greens, and yellows.

"Watch your step." Trevor helped her into the back of the ambulance.

Jamie's ambulance sped down the street. She looked for Stone. Seconds later, he appeared and hopped in back. The tension ripping through her body eased.

Trevor closed the back door. Seconds later, the passenger door slammed shut.

Stone placed one hand on her shoulder and the other on her back. "Lie back for me, baby, so I can examine you."

"Trevor already did that." Now that the police had hauled Ben off and Jamie was being tended to, the reality was finally seeping in.

Amber pressed her lips together and closed her eyes. "Poor Jamie. I can't imagine what she must be going through right now. Ben had been her life." It didn't matter that Jamie had wanted to end the relationship. She must still have feelings for him.

Stone rubbed a thumb over the back of her hand. "I know. I bet the betrayal to both of you has to be overwhelming."

She loved that he understood. "It is."

Stone lifted the clothe from her face, nodded, and replaced it. It seemed like they arrived at the hospital in only a few minutes. While Stone wheeled her in, once the nurse came, Stone kissed her forehead. "I'll be right outside."

Nurses and doctors came and went. They X-rayed her jaw and fortunately detected no cracks. Amber couldn't wait to get out of here and check on Jamie.

A different nurse came in and Amber questioned her. "Do you know how my friend Jamie Henderson is doing?"

The nurse smiled. "I'll check for you just as soon as I clean your facial wound." The nurse numbed her cheek. That hurt. She picked out the pieces of plaster and disinfected the wound. "There. I'll let the doctor know you're ready for your stitches. I'll go check on Jamie for you."

Finally. "Thank you."

The doctor came in and announced she was a plastic surgeon, for which Amber was grateful. "When you heal, you won't even be able to see where the cuts were."

In about fifteen minutes, the doctor said Amber was good to go, but to wait for the nurse to give her further instructions.

The nurse came back in. "I checked on Jamie. The doctor is removing the bullet now."

"Can I see her?"

"In a bit." She handed Amber some paperwork.

"Knock, knock."

She looked up, and her heart skipped a beat. Both Cade and

Stone rushed over to her. Stone studied the doctor's handiwork. "Nice. How does it feel?"

"Good." The numbing agent made her word sound slurred. "I want to see Jamie." Damn, it was hard to talk out of one side of her mouth.

Both men helped her up. "If she's awake, she'll be groggy, baby."

"That's okay. I need to see her."

With a shaking hand, Amber filled out the discharge papers. Since she worked here, all of her information was easily accessible.

The men brought her to Jamie's room. Eyes closed, her friend looked so peaceful. Amber looked up at Stone. "How long do you think she'll have to stay here?"

"I bet the doctors will release her tomorrow."

Amber walked over to the bed and moved the blonde strands from Jamie's eyes. "Hey, girlfriend." She kept her voice soft. "Can you hear me?" Amber squeezed her hand.

Jamie groaned and opened her eyes. "Hey." She wet her lips.

Like she had with Chris, Amber picked up the pitcher and brought the straw to Jamie's lips. "How are you feeling?"

Her friend glanced down at the bandage on her arm. "It's out?"

"Yup. All gone." Amber put the water back on the stand.

Jamie ran a gaze up and down Amber's face. "You look better."

Amber fingered the stitches. "Yeah. The doc did a good job patching me up."

Someone knocked on the door. "Hello?" Ethan, Cade's partner came in. "I'd like to take Ms. Henderson's statement now."

Cade nodded. "Amber, we should go."

She nodded then hugged Jamie goodbye. "I'm here for you. We'll get through this."

"When are you coming back?" A bit of fear crossed Jamie's face.

"Tomorrow morning."

Jamie's lids drooped. "Okay. See ya."

Cade wrapped an arm around Amber's waist and walked her out. "Anyone up for something to eat?"

As much as she wanted to crawl into bed and sleep for a few days, she needed food. It was dinnertime, and the men would be hungry. "How about Italian?" With her numb cheek, pasta might be the easiest to chew.

If there was one lesson she learned from coming so close to dying, it was that she loved her men. As soon as she was able, she wanted to show them just how much.

Chapter Thirty-One

Under the circumstances, last night had been as good as could have been expected. After a good dinner, Stone and Cade had brought Amber back to their house and made sure she was comfortable.

Once the Novocain had worn off, Amber had downed some Tylenol and went to bed. The medicine helped, but it was being cocooned between her men that worked best. The downer was they told her they'd keep their hands off her until she completely healed. That meant a week with no sex. *Ugh.*

Cade had driven back to her house and picked up a suitcase with her clothing. For not knowing exactly what she needed, he did a great job at picking out things.

When she woke this morning, she was sore from Ben having shoved her against the wall, but compared to Jamie, she was in good shape. Her cheek ached, but not as much as she'd expected.

The aroma of bacon and eggs drifted into the bedroom. While she figured her supervisor would insist she take some time off, Amber wasn't ready to sit and do nothing. Keeping busy would help her cope.

She stepped into the kitchen. Cade was at the stove dressed for work and looked devilishly handsome. "Good morning."

He looked up and winced. "Let me look your wound." He

studied her face. “Hmm.”

She’d checked out her appearance and had been quite upset at first, but she understood that with time, she’d heal. Compared to what her cancer patients went through, this was nothing. “It’s going to get worse before it gets better.”

“That’s true. Does it ache much?”

“It’s not too bad.” Amber didn’t want to discuss it anymore and nodded to the stove. “I can do that. You don’t want to get your shirt splattered with grease.”

He cocked a brow. “I’ll have you know, I am quite capable of staying clean.” Just then, the bacon popped and crackled, and he jumped back.

Amber laughed but immediately touched her cheek. She’d have to limit what she did today. “Suit yourself.” She busied herself setting the table. “Stone at work?”

“Yes. As soon as I drop you off home, I have to go into work, too.” He faced her. “Or do you need me to stay home with you? Because I will.”

How sweet was that? “I’m going to visit Jamie.” She held up a palm to halt his objection.” If the doctors wanted Jamie to stay another day, then Amber would do her rounds. That way she’d be near her friend. If they released Jamie, she’d spend the day with her.

Amber and the men had talked a lot last night about what had happened, and she was coming to grips with Ben’s breakdown, Jamie’s injury, and her near death experience. It certainly gave her a new perspective as to what cops must go through.

After they ate, Cade dropped her off at home. She changed into her scrubs and then drove to the hospital. As soon as she found out what room Jamie was in, she took the elevator to the second floor. The staff was actually smiling again and appeared a lot more relaxed. They must have heard Ben had been caught.

Amber knocked and entered Jamie’s room. Her friend was sitting on the bed, getting dressed. *Yes!*

"Hey, girlfriend. Should you be up so soon?" Jamie's hair was matted and her makeup streaked.

"Just got released, and boy am I happy." She lifted her good arm and smelled her armpit in an exaggerated fashion. "I stink."

"Could be the dried blood on your shirt. I came to be your chauffeur, seeing how you won't be driving for a while."

A spark lit in her eyes. "Awesome. I was just about to call a cab." She sighed. "You're dressed for work."

"I put them on in case you weren't released. I wanted to be nearby."

"Aw. Thank you."

Amber stepped over and helped Jamie button her shirt. "Did you sleep last night?" *Or did you have nightmares?*

"I couldn't turn my brain off. It was terrible." She yawned. "I finally asked for something to put me to sleep, but now I'm paying for it. I wish I could go to work, but with my arm the way it is, I can't really function. It sucks."

"You want me to see if I can find something clean for you to wear?" She might have a clean pair of scrubs in her locker.

"I just want to go home."

When Jamie stood, she wobbled a little. "You sure you've been released?"

Jamie firmed her lips. "Yes."

It was another half-hour before all the paperwork was complete, and forty-five minutes before they pulled into Amber's drive. While Jamie said for her to drop her off at home, Amber insisted she stay with her. "You can't drive your car home with one arm. Besides, what if you need something?"

Jamie looked to the side. *Way to go. She's probably thinking Ben would have helped.* "I haven't thought that far ahead. It sucks it's my good arm." She lifted it, winced, and then lowered her arm.

"I figure we might as well recuperate together."

Jamie leaned her head back against the seat. "As long as you don't mind me showering at your place and borrowing a shirt,

I'm game to be pampered."

Amber smiled. "Since you saved my life, it's a deal."

Jamie let out a small laugh and looked like her old self. While she had to reach across her body to open the car door, she moved rather well once she got out. Jamie said the bullet hadn't done too much damage for which Amber was thankful.

She unlocked the front door, and then walked Jamie back to her room to shower. Amber pulled out fresh towels and a clean shirt. "Here you go. I'm going to make us something to eat."

"Sounds wonderful."

"Do you want me to wrap your arm in plastic wrap so the bandage doesn't get wet?"

Jamie shook her head. "I'll just remove it."

"Suit yourself." Amber always carried plenty of first aid supplies as Chris was constantly injuring some part of his body. She pushed back the memory. "Take your time."

She went to the kitchen to prepare some sandwiches. To her delight, Cade had put her groceries away last night. Those two were unique men who were perfect for her. Mostly they'd witnessed a sad woman working hard to cope with what life had thrown her. With Ben behind bars, maybe she could move on and be the type of woman they deserved.

Amber fixed sandwiches along with some snacks. When Jamie finished showering, she came out looking refreshed.

"How do you feel?"

"Outside better. Inside the same. I'm still in shock."

Amber brought the food over to the coffee table. "Let's eat here."

They both dug in. Even though the stitches and bruising made it a bit painful to chew, Amber managed to eat. Right after she'd finished half a sandwich, she leaned back. "We never got to talk. How about you start from the beginning?" Her last phone call with Jamie had been about her breaking up with Ben.

Jamie heaved a heavy sigh. "I feel bad not telling you sooner, but I wasn't proud of what happened." She drew her knees to her chest and wrapped her good arm around them.

"What do you mean?"

"Benny and I have been dating for three years. He was my best friend. I really did love him."

"I know. When you and he used to come over, and we'd all watch TV and laugh, I couldn't imagine you with anyone else. What changed your mind?"

She shrugged. "I don't know. Benny had no ambition. He was becoming more and more dependent on me to make all the decisions in the relationship." Jamie stretched out her legs and leaned back. "I want a man who will take charge—at least in the bedroom." She looked over at her. "Maybe seeing the way Cade and Stone treated you made me realize what I wanted."

That made Amber smile, though a hint of guilt snuck in. "Be careful what you wish for."

Jamie nodded and a small smile lifted her lips. "I can't say when I noticed it, but Benny kind of got weird right before Emma died."

Amber bit into the other half of her ham and cheese even though her stomach was doing all sorts of acrobatics. "Weird how?" Poor Jamie. She must be thinking she could have stopped him had she known.

"He'd become distracted when I was talking to him. Once he even yelled at me for no good reason. Right after Emma died, he actually shoved me. That wasn't the Benny I fell in love with. He used to be the most gentle man alive, one who couldn't hurt a fly."

"Did you ask him what had changed?"

She nodded. "He said his supervisor was talking about letting go a few of the techs. He was really scared it would be him."

"I'd be nervous, too. Do you think that was what caused him to go off the deep end?"

Jamie wove her fingers together and shook her head. "Not

directly. I believe it was when I told him I didn't love him the same way he loved me."

Amber's breath caught. That would destroy Benny. She tried to put the pieces together. "He told me he wanted to prove to you how much he loved you. How could he think if he killed people who upset you, that you'd love him again?"

"I wish I knew." She looked up and grabbed Amber's hand. "He loved Chris. That death had nothing to do with me. I'm certain of that."

"You have to listen to me, and listen good. None of the deaths are your fault." She inhaled. "Ben was unstable."

Jamie's chin wobbled. "I keep telling myself that, but it's not working."

Amber squeezed Jamie's palm. "Why didn't you tell me sooner?" She worked hard not to sound accusatory.

"Like I said, I was embarrassed." She bit down on her bottom lip then released it. "It might seem like I was stringing him on, but I swear I wasn't. I loved Benny until he weirded out on me."

"Hey, you had to do what was right for you." Amber sipped on her Coke. "When you called me yesterday, were you planning on telling me you suspected Benny of the mercy killings?"

"Shit no. I never would have guessed in a million years he would harm anyone." Jamie picked up some chips and stuffed them in her mouth. "I called because two nights ago Benny asked me to marry him."

That was not what Amber expected her to say. "For real? Even after you told him your feelings for him weren't as strong anymore?"

"Yes, and trust me, I was shocked he asked. Maybe he thought I wanted a commitment or something. That I'd change my mind if he showed me a ring."

"If I'd been Benny, I might have gone that route, too."

Jamie shifted in her seat and winced. "When I said no, he got really, really mad."

Amber leaned back. "He must have wanted to blame someone and came after me."

"It's possible. I'm so sorry."

"It's not your fault." She seemed to be saying that a lot.

Jamie closed her eyes for a moment. "I still can't believe Benny really killed those people, especially Stephanie Osmond."

"I know. Her death made no sense. There had to be a point when he stopped thinking clearly." Wasn't that a kind way of saying Benny had lost his mind?

"Yeah."

Amber finished her sandwich, her mind speeding. She was sick how Ben had taken Chris's life in his own hands, but nothing could be done about it now. "My boss suggested I get some counseling, so I might go see Zoey."

"Seriously?" Jamie snagged another handful of chips even though she hadn't finished her sandwich. "Maybe I'll speak with her, too."

She was happy her friend agreed to receive some guidance. "I could probably spend a few months with her given all the shit that's happened in my life."

Now it was Jamie who placed a hand on her arm. "Speaking of shit, what are you going to tell your mom?"

Crap. Amber hadn't thought about that. "I'm not sure it will matter if she knows who killed her son, but I will let her know." Would her mother say it was Amber's fault for having chosen unstable friends? "All I know is if I'd killed someone, I'd never have been able to get up in front of a crowd of mourners and sing his praises."

"Amen."

More than anything, Amber wanted to put this in the past and move on.

Chapter Thirty-Two

For the next five days, Stone or Cade stopped by her house to keep her company, but other than a kiss, the men kept their distance. The bruising on her face had all but disappeared and just this afternoon, the doctor had finally removed her stitches. She couldn't wait to tell the men the moratorium on cuddling and making love was over.

On her way home from work, she called Cade, since his schedule seemed to be the most difficult to coordinate.

"Hey, sugar."

"I've been given a clean bill of health." She smiled at the excitement in her own voice. She'd told them about the appointment.

"Fantastic. Stone and I have everything planned. Tomorrow, we're going to take you someplace special."

"Just the three of us?" This would be a dream come true.

"Yup. Away from our cells, too. We've decided to drive to Glacier National Park. Might even hit the Canadian side. Our jobs can't reach us there." He paused. "I have to do a lot of catch up work tonight in order to take the time off, but tomorrow morning we'll pick you up at eight sharp. Can you be ready?"

"You bet."

✧ ✧ ✧

Amber bundled her coat tighter around her shoulders and gazed at Mount Gould looming over Swiftcurrent Lake. "This is amazing!"

The drive along the Going-To-The-Sun Road had been an experience of a lifetime, affording her spectacular views. But then again, any body of water near mountains always took her breath away.

This past week had moved both too fast and too slow. Waiting until she could spend quality time with Cade and Stone seemed to take forever, yet she'd been so busy at work time had flown by. Between seeing her patients and checking on Jamie, she hadn't had a minute free. Jamie had been a trouper despite being on the mend. After three days of staying home, Jamie had gone back to work, albeit in a limited capacity. She wasn't allowed to lift anything.

Stone placed a hand on Amber's back. "Let's head to the car, and we can drive to one of the trail heads."

Cade didn't seem as enthusiastic about running around outdoors, but with time, she bet he'd be as gung ho as Stone. Once they reached the beginning of the path to Iceberg Lake, they parked and grabbed their gear from the back. When they told her it was a five-hour round trip, her biggest fear was that by the time they returned to the hotel, she'd be too wiped out for sex.

You will find the strength.

Cade patted her butt. "Let's not dawdle. We've got a big night planned."

That helped her pick up the pace. They'd hiked for about an hour when Stone stopped. "Look up on the mountain. See all the sheep?" He wrapped his arms around her from behind, and pointed to the animals walking precariously on the overhangs.

"Oh, wow. That's incredible." He let her watch for a bit. The animals maneuvered across the landscape effortlessly.

He squeezed her shoulders. "Let's go. Don't freak if we yell or clap. It's to let the bears know we're around."

"Seriously?"

"I'm afraid so. Just stay with us and you'll be safe."

"Right. You probably brought me along so if a wild animal attacks, you can run and leave me for him to eat." Of course, she was joking, but the quick shot of fear that skated across Stone's face made her chuckle. "Kidding."

He ruffled her hair. "You'll pay for that."

For the rest of the trip, the scenery mesmerized her, in part because it was so diverse. One minute they'd be walking through a pine grove, and the next they were hiking around piles of snow interspersed with the prettiest patches of wildflowers she'd seen in a long time. Cade pointed to a moose off in the distance, and Stone spotted a grouse.

They finally arrived at their destination—a lake where icebergs bobbed in the water. She ran up to the edge to gaze at its beauty. "It's so blue."

Cade sidled up next to her. "It's really something."

Stone pulled off his pack. "Let's enjoy the view from this rock and eat lunch. I'm famished."

The day was clear with the sun high in the sky. After hiking at a good clip, she unbuttoned her jacket to cool off. She settled next to her men and inhaled the sweet mountain air. The peace and quiet had been fantastic until another group of tourists arrived. "Ugh."

"It happens," Stone said. "This is a really popular spot."

They finished eating and headed back to hopefully something even more thrilling. Between the company of her men and the glorious vistas, she couldn't have asked for a better start to the day.

As soon as they reached their vehicle, she was sweating. Cade helped her into the front seat.

"I, for one, need to shower," Cade said. "From the pictures on line, the bathroom at the hotel looks like it might hold two of us." He raised his brows.

"No you don't, buddy. It's all three or none at all," Stone shot back.

Cade burst out laughing. "I'll wrestle you for it."

She remembered what Zoey said about the two men she'd dated and how they always fought for her attention. "I'm up for a little squishing if you two hunks don't mind me rubbing my body against your muscled chests." *And down your asses.*

Stone glanced at her. "Oh, no. Not rubbing." He traced a line from her waist to her knee.

Amber lifted her chin. "How do you think you're going to prevent me from touching you in the shower?"

Cade placed his hand behind her shoulder and tugged her close. "We have our ways." He looked over at Stone. "You did bring the rope, paddles, nipple clamps, and chains, didn't you?"

"Funny, funny," she said.

"Fuck," Stone said with an exaggerated emphasis on the word. "The chains. I forgot them. Maybe we can find a store around here that has some."

They had to be joking. Right? When Cade grinned, she relaxed.

Less than a half-mile later, they pulled up to the Many Glacier Hotel. *Wow.* "This place is huge."

"From the pictures, the inside is even more impressive," Cade said.

She liked that they were exploring someplace new together. Stone parked. When she struggled dragging the suitcase on the gravel road, Cade helped. "I'll do that, sugar."

Her men were so nice.

When they stepped inside the hotel, she stood there for a minute, mesmerized. Wood was everywhere, shooting up three stories. At one end of the main room stood a mammoth fireplace, and in the center was a huge sitting area. "This is stunning."

"I can't wait to see our suite," Cade said.

"Suite?" These men were spoiling her.

Stone leaned over. "It was the only room with a king-sized bed. I figured we'd need it." He grinned and her insides fluttered.

Once they checked in, they headed upstairs. Jittery excitement filled her. Tonight would be her initiation into the world of a full-fledged ménage. While she'd had a plug in her ass, she imagined having Cade's thick cock in her butt would be a totally different experience. Adding Stone's dick might burst her to smithereens.

Stone let them in. The room was simple. A quilted spread topped the bed and the corner desk looked handmade.

"There's a second bedroom back there," Stone pointed, "but I'm thinking we all might want to share this one." He nodded to the king-sized bed.

"Totally," she said. What would have been the purpose of coming if not to spend the night deliciously pressed against one another?

The exposed pipes in the ceilings gave it a very rustic look. Right now, the big bed looked divine, but she figured the men weren't thinking about resting or sleeping. Stone and Cade placed their suitcases on the bed and placed hers on the luggage stand.

Because her pants were wet from hiking through a few piles of snow, she was a little chilled. She rubbed her arms up and down.

As soon as she warmed, she sat on the desk chair and tugged off one boot, looking forward to the hot shower.

Stone glanced over. "Your feet are red and look cold. Let me help." He knelt in front of her, and with strong but gentle hands, massaged her insoles.

"Ahh. That feels divine." She wiggled her toes, loving how he made the tired muscles relax.

Stone smiled and worked on the other foot. When her feet were no longer chilled, he stood. "We could warm you up faster if you're naked."

She could do that. "How would you boys like a strip tease?" She'd never done one before, but it wouldn't matter if she was good at it or not. Stone and Cade would like her act no matter what.

"Yes! We're going to get a show." Stone moved back to the bed.

Cade pulled the chair from behind her and sat. "Go ahead, sugar. Make us want you even more."

She walked up to Cade and leaned over, flaunting her chest. "Do I receive a big reward if by the end of my act your cocks are hard?"

Cade leaned back and grinned. "The biggest."

"If I had music," Stone said, "I'd play it for you. We can't sing you a tune because, well, we can't sing."

After Katie's happy birthday song, she could attest to that. She didn't care. She loved them no matter what.

Amber inhaled a deep, cleansing breath and stepped to the side so both men could watch her. All of a sudden, heat rose to her cheeks.

"Go on." Cade motioned with his hand. "We don't judge."

To set the scene, she slowly rotated her hips as if she was trying to keep a hula hoop going. At the same time, she lifted her shirt inch by inch. If she knew how to belly dance, she would have fluttered her stomach. Stone smiled, but Cade's expression remained fixed on her face. She wanted to break him. Make him grab her.

What a shame she wore another not-so-sexy sports bra, but there wasn't anything she could do about it now. As soon as her shirt cleared her breasts, she tossed the material in the air. She thought it would land between the two of them, but Cade reached out and grabbed it before it hit the floor. He brought the material to his face and inhaled.

A smile emerged, and his dimpled cheeks caused her panties to dampen. *Keep going.* To remove her hiking pants, she turned around, unbuttoned then unzipped them. Slowly, she eased the material over her butt. Since Cade seemed to be more of an ass man than Stone, she bent over at the waist and wiggled her rear for him. When she glanced behind him, she caught the grin. *This is working.*

Keeping her gaze on one then the other, she pushed down her pants and stepped out of them. As if they had some secret signal, they both stood and approached her.

"I call bottoms," Cade said.

Stone waved a hand. "Your loss. I get her glorious tits."

"I'm not done."

They didn't seem to care. In a flash, her panties and bra disappeared. Stone swung her up in his arms, walked her to the tiny bathroom, and then drew back the curtain. "Start without us. We'll be in there in a second." With that, he set her down then closed the door.

She stood for a moment trying to figure out what just happened. She thought her little performance had gone well, or had those wonderful adventures been a figment of her imagination?

No. They weren't.

Since she only had a short window to use the shower by herself, she turned on the water, and when it warmed, stepped in. The soap smelled like fresh mint. "Mmm." She'd just lathered her hands when Cade pulled back the curtain. Gloriously naked, he and Stone got in. So that was what they were doing.

Stone stood in front of her, the water bouncing off his back, and Cade was at the far end. They were so large they took up almost the entire tub. Cade picked up the shampoo and nodded for Stone to lift the handheld showerhead.

"How about you kneel, sugar, so I can wash your hair?"

The intimate act wasn't lost on her. Her pulse raced as she knelt on the rubber mat. *Ooh, nice.* Right at cock level. She ran her tongue over her lips then gazed at his hard dick.

"Don't even think about it." While Cade appeared to be trying to keep a straight face, he failed.

Damn. His cock was so nice and thick and erect—ready for

sucking. "How about one lick?"

Cade laughed. "Sugar, I don't think you can stop after one." He was right. "Besides, once you start, no telling if I'll get any shampoo on your head."

"Fine. I'll be good." For the moment.

"Stone, get her hair wet for me." Cade looked down at her. "Close your eyes."

She obeyed instantly, her heart beating rapidly in her chest. She'd been to salons and loved having her hair washed, but she'd never had a man lather her hair while she was on her knees—naked.

The water rained down on her for a few seconds, and then Stone turned off the faucet. The cool air immediately chilled her. She peeked up at him for a second. Cade palmed some shampoo, knelt in front of her on the hard porcelain, and rubbed the gel into her scalp. She inhaled the rich aroma. Peaches. Or maybe mango. His fingers moved over her scalp, and her muscles unbound. That was, until Stone knelt behind her and soaped up her breasts. She squeaked. His light touch tickled.

"Easy, baby. Let me clean you."

She'd already washed before those two entered the shower, but somehow she didn't think they cared. Stone rubbed her nipples, and her pelvic area tightened. He twisted the tips and pinched them over and over again until she was so hot, she might have to ask them to rinse her in cold water.

"Now for your pussy," Stone said. "Go ahead and sit, baby. Spread your legs wide so Cade can see how pretty you are."

She hesitated for a second, imagining the position. After the week she'd had, she wanted to give up control. It would be nice not to have to do anything but let them pamper her.

"Amber?" Concern filled Cade's voice.

She must have taken too long. "Sorry." Now they'd think she wasn't ready for them. And she was.

She sat and stretched her legs to the side.

"Mmm," Cade said. "If your beautiful breasts weren't all

soapy, I'd be sucking on them right now."

Then hurry. The tips ached for his rough tongue and wicked ways.

Stone grunted. "Watch it, Cade. They're mine for now."

The thrill of being wanted created such a high. Instead of touching her tits, Cade slipped a soapy finger into her opening, but the lack of friction had her yearning for more.

"It's so little." She hadn't meant to whine.

He laughed. "Wait until we finish. I'll show you something that isn't little."

"Now you're talking."

She wished Stone would finish rinsing her hair so she could open her eyes.

Stone tapped her shoulder. "Baby, stand up, face me, and bend over real far." She'd just sat down. She almost told them to make up their minds.

Stone helped her to her feet and she bent over as he requested. Then she looked behind her. Her ass was right where Cade could impale her. Was she ready? Her belly contracted as he stepped close. "Don't you need to use lube first?" she asked Cade.

"To rinse your hair?" Stone answered, obviously not realizing where Cade's cock was in relation to her back hole.

Whoops. "Never mind," she said sweetly.

As Stone finished up, Cade seemed to take great pleasure soaping her ass. Even when slick, his calloused palms scraped her sensitive skin. Cade took every opportunity to dip a thumb or finger into her tight muscled ring. Her memory kicked into gear, and she remembered how after the initial shock and pinch of the plug, she liked having something in her ass—as long as it was small.

Cade patted her butt. "Go ahead and stand. Now you get to work."

She flipped wet hair out of her eyes. "My turn, huh?" This was what she'd been waiting for.

Chapter Thirty-Three

Both men were already wet, so Amber grabbed the too-small bar of soap and rubbed Cade's chest, taking great care to make sure to run the soap over his flat nipples then down to his belly button. With every pass, his chest hair sprang back to life. She came close to his erect cock, but she figured he'd want her more if she didn't give him what he desired.

"Now, I'll do Stone's top half." She repeated the same procedure on him, loving how his muscles bulged and flexed with each swipe. "Both of you turn around so I can clean your backs." *And asses.*

Amber had so much fun letting her fingers roam over their gorgeous bodies. While both were well defined, Stone had a broader back, whereas Cade's thighs were rippled masses of power. She couldn't wait for him to drive into her hard. His ass was round and tight, whereas Stone's was a bit smaller but more muscular. Both should be models. They'd make a fortune.

As soon as the men rinsed, Stone lifted her out of the tub and set her down. "Don't move."

Steam fogged the mirror and carried with it the minty scent of the soap.

Cade stepped from the tub and stood in front of her. "Hold your arms out and spread your legs so we can dry you, sugar."

Cade helped guide her into position.

Dear Lord, but she was totally exposed. It didn't help that the row of bulbs above the sink illuminated every inch of her body. The room was so well lit, each hair of Cade's dark stubble as well as the flecks of dark blue and gold in his irises stood out. She shut her eyes to keep him from seeing into her soul.

"Don't shut me out, sugar." Cade ran a rough palm down her cheek.

She opened them and inhaled his clean scent. The first swipe of the terrycloth towel across her breasts made her nipples stand on end. Stone must have felt left out because he pressed his strong chest against her back, sending heat straight between her legs.

He clasped his hands right above her hips. "I love your tiny waist." He released her then polished her butt with a different towel. If he looked closely, he'd see it was her butt that was big, not that her waist was small.

Water from her wet hair dripped down her back and over her nipples—the spot Cade had just dried.

"You're getting everything wet again," Cade complained.

"Would you like me to wrap my hair?"

Cade handed her the towel he'd used. "Go for it."

After dipping her head, she twisted the terrycloth in a turban then stood. "Now it's my turn, right?"

Cade shook his head. "No."

They weren't being fair. "Why not?"

"Because we can't wait any longer." Stone lifted her and practically ran out of the bathroom. He was still dripping when he placed her on the bed. Stone leaned over and ran a hand over a breast. A quick shot of lust grabbed her right between the legs. "So pretty."

He then circled her nipple then dragged his finger down to her belly. Shivers of delight followed in its wake.

Cade crawled onto the bed next to her. "I want to touch and

lick you into oblivion. Only then can you appreciate how much we both love you." He ran a thumb over her closed folds. Tingles burst across her skin and danced up her spine.

Wait a minute. Did he just say they loved her? Or was it only a saying? She'd always failed when it came to finding real love. Why should now be an exception?

It can be if you let it. She didn't dare get her hopes up. She was bound to do something to mess this up.

"I can't wait to lick you." Cade's cock pulsed. He looked up at Stone. "Ready to love our woman?"

"You bet."

Damn Cade Carter for taking his time, rubbing the inside of her thighs with his thumbs while he licked the top of her pussy lips. He never quite dipped his tongue in far enough to give her satisfaction.

Amber lifted her hips, hoping he'd hurry.

"That's not going to work, sugar."

She knew that might be the case, but she had to try. Stone must have understood her need because he leaned over and kissed her with lips that were soft yet demanding. As soon as she let him in, they explored each other. His aggressive tenderness melted her from the inside out. She'd dip her tongue into his mouth, and he'd thrust fast into hers mimicking what was to come. With each touch, her hopes soared.

He lifted his head and smiled. "I want to taste so much of you. I can't wait for you to see what I can do for you."

She wanted to shout, "go for it," but instead she smiled. The words had flown out of her mind because at that moment, Cade slipped between her legs and delved his tongue straight into her wet opening.

Instinctively, she lifted her hips, but he placed a warm palm on her belly to still her. Amber wanted intense pressure and fast flicks but she received slow, lazy ones. Cade probably knew this would create havoc inside her. Damn him.

"Wouldn't one of you like my mouth on your cock?"

Cade ignored her question and flicked his tongue over her swelling clit. He finally looked up. His clear blue eyes darkened to navy. Desire swam in their depths. She guessed her request had been denied.

As if Cade's tormenting licks weren't enough to drive her over the edge, Stone moved into position and drew her hardened nipple into her mouth. One slow swipe at a time, he drove her crazy. She groaned but refused to beg. How could she be so weak with just foreplay?

She knew why. They were the experts and she the novice.

Stone smiled. "Would you like a little more pressure?"

"Yes, please." *Thank you, Stone.*

He sucked on one nipple and shards of blissful glory drove straight to her clit. As if that wasn't enough, Cade slipped a finger into her and swirled it around. He moved his finger fast and hard, sending her closer to her climax. Then Stone kissed her. Nothing was slow and tentative about the way he took her mouth. As soon as Stone sat up, she sucked in large mouthfuls of air.

"I think she's ready." Cade reached over to the table.

A jar unscrewed and lube scented the air. This was it. Getting to have Cade in her ass made her body heat. She wanted them both to hurry, to take her hard, to make her theirs.

"Cade," Stone said. "Let's have her ride me."

Cade nodded. In a flash, Stone stretched out on the bed and pulled her on top on him. His hot chest warmed her body, and the soft hairs almost tickled. Their kiss only lasted a few seconds before Cade bent her knees and lifted her shoulders.

"Why don't you lick him a little then ride him hard? Wear him out."

Stone laughed, but Amber just smiled. This was so perfect. Now she understood how this worked. She scooted between Stone's legs, bent over, and grabbed his hard shaft. With her ass in the air, Cade had every opportunity to get her ready for the big event. Shutting out the anxiety of the unknown, she shook her hips to let him know she wanted him to take her.

He patted her butt. "Remember not to tighten your ass or I won't fit."

Amber inhaled deeply and concentrated on relaxing every muscle, but her fast beating heart made it difficult. Stone's dick pulsed inches from her, and she focused on loving him the best way she knew how. She bent over, ready to drive him to the brink.

Uh-oh. What if he exploded again? Waiting for him to recover might ruin things. Decision made. She'd tease him only a little.

Holding his dick tight, she lowered her lips over his cock and swirled her tongue around his length. She loved his manly flavor—tangy with the slightest hint of the mint from the soap. As she sucked harder, Stone groaned. *Yes!* She pumped her hand up and down, and Cade graced her back hole with more lube. The urge to clench was great, but she forced herself to relax.

Stone threaded his fingers through her hair and guided her head down his cock. "That's it, baby. Take him deep."

Cade ran his thumb around her tight muscled ring. Could she handle his big cock in her ass? And if she could, how would Stone fit in her pussy?

The tip of Stone's cock reached the back of her throat at the same time Cade slipped a thumb into her anus. She wasn't as skittish as the first time. As he brushed against a few nerves, she enjoyed the tingly sensations. She must have been concentrating on what Cade was doing, because she tightened her grip on Stone's cock a bit too much. He lifted her head off his cock.

"I can't wait anymore. Sit on him." Stone grabbed a condom from the nightstand. He tore the top with his teeth, extracted the rubber, and slid it over his cock in one quick movement.

He tapped her knee, signaling he wanted her to straddle him. Her juices ran wild. Unfortunately, her ass was too low for Cade to play with.

Then Cade's muscular chest pressed against her back, and his fingers found her already swollen tits. "Let me have these a moment."

The first pinch made her lift her butt. She grabbed Stone's cock and drew it toward her opening. She hovered over the tip before easing downward. The first inch was divine until his girth became too much. Retrying, she slid down more easily, but his cock still stretched her wide.

"Come here." Stone guided her shoulders toward him, elevating her ass for Cade's pleasure.

Cade broke contact and released his hold on her tits. The loss made her devour Stone's lips. She needed him. Wanted him.

Another snap of a condom sounded behind her and more lube wafted toward her. She rose an inch then dropped down on Stone's cock, never breaking the kiss. She was in heaven.

When Cade's tip breached her back hole, she tensed, pressing down on Stone's dick.

"Don't do that," and "No," came from Stone and Cade respectively.

Cade squeezed one cheek hard. She relaxed—sort of. Realization dawned. They weren't going to fit. No way. No how. Cade was so much bigger than that plug he'd used.

Stone latched onto her hips and held her still as he thrust up into her. Her body soared and her honey dripped. This was exactly where she needed to be.

As Cade edged in, Stone almost completely withdrew. Cade took his time, moving in small increments. The burn was quite intense at first, but then it waned and edged toward pleasure. Stone returned quickly but pulled out right away as if he wanted to give her time to become accustomed to Cade. Her pussy tightened at the vacancy.

Stone massaged her breasts again as Cade made his way down her darkened channel. With each pass, her ass felt like it was going to burst apart, but she trusted him to know when she'd reached her limit.

"You are so fucking tight, sugar," Cade said. "My cock is loving this."

Amber tried to lower her body to encompass Stone, but his grip increased. They must know taking both at once would be a huge step for her. Finally, Cade reached the end and hit some nerves that lit her up.

She gulped in air. "Oh, my God."

The burn was gone, but the pressure remained intense. Then Cade eased out, and Stone drove in. Her eyes widened and her breath caught again.

"You okay, baby?"

She nodded.

Cade leaned over her back again and kissed her neck as he twisted and turned her hardened nipples. Electric bolts raced down her body, threatening to open the floodgates and let her climax in. She wanted to wait to celebrate together, but it was so hard to control the rush swamping her.

Gritting her teeth, she moved her hands from beside Stone's head down to his shoulders. His warm flesh excited her. She loved how with each breath, his muscles pulsed and flexed.

The second she pressed her nails into his skin, both men pistoned into her hard, and she let out a feral yell. Never before had something hit every erotic nerve in her body at the same time. Blood zoomed through her veins and the men went in and out together. The faster she gasped for breath, the stronger their thrusts, and the harder they took her. Like an oil well pump, they were in sync until Cade slid his hand down her belly and pressed on her clit.

Similar to a rocket's launch button, her climax descended like a tidal wave. Unable to stop it, she shouted their names. Both cocks exploded, pounding her ass and pussy to slightly different beats. The stretching took her higher, and then she seemed to be floating on a cloud, looking down at their three bodies entwined. This was how it was supposed to be.

She didn't remember how long they remained as one, but Cade was the first to pop out of her. He returned with a towel and wiped her clean. Had it not been for Stone lifting her off his cock, she wasn't sure she'd have been able to move.

Stone then left the bed for a short while and returned without a condom. They both slid next to her and held her tight. She'd never been so happy. Heaven only knew what they had in store for her tomorrow.

Chapter Thirty-Four

After two of the most fantastic days of her life, Amber hadn't want to return to Rock Hard, but duty called. As soon as she finished with one of her patients, she strode down the hospital corridor toward Zoey's office. Amber dreaded meeting her friend when she wore her psychologist's hat, but her supervisor, Tammy, had insisted. Sure, Amber was still dealing with her brother's death and with the betrayal of Ben, but Tammy believed it was having a gun pointed at her chest that was reason enough to get help. Maybe she was right.

Despite the therapy session looming, all day she'd floated from room to room, spreading cheer everywhere. Being with Stone and Cade had transformed her. For the first time in her life she felt like she belonged, that someone really wanted to be with her. The whole concept of two men loving her was pretty heady stuff. If she could put what happened with Chris and Ben into perspective, her life would be perfect.

Zoey Donovan's secretary looked up and smiled. "Hi, Amber. Zoey's finishing up with someone. Have a seat and she'll be right with you."

The small seating area was empty. Scattered on a table in the middle of the room was every type of magazine. She grabbed a Home Design and sat. Five minutes later, Zoey's client walked out and Zoey motioned her into her office.

When Amber took a seat on the leather chair opposite the desk, Zoey pulled her cushy chair off to the side and opened a folder. "I know this is a little awkward since we're friends but what you say here, stays here."

"I know." Zoey took her oath very seriously.

"From what your supervisor tells me, you seem to be handling all of your crises very well. I'm curious how you've dealt with Ben's betrayal."

Zoey certainly got right to the point. Jamie had been in to see Zoey, so Amber wouldn't be breaking any confidences. "Ben was fragile. A few years ago, he lost his mother to a horrendous disease. According to Jamie, Ben had been with his mom every step of the way." She imagined Jamie had already told Zoey this, but she wanted to make sure there were no misunderstandings. "His dad, too, hadn't been in the picture since he was a kid."

"Are you saying you understand why Ben did what he did?"

Amber leaned back. "In a way. You've heard me go on and on about my folks, how good it was until my dad left, and how my mother never really warmed up to me. I know what it's like to need affection. I think Ben was like that, too. With his mom gone, he focused his life on Jamie."

"I want you to know that Jamie has given me permission to speak freely to you."

"She told me she had."

Zoey steepled her hands. "Were you surprised when Jamie told you she didn't love Ben anymore?"

"Completely. It might have been the trigger that set him off." Jamie couldn't say for sure, but it made sense. "Was it right for her to finally admit it after all these years?" Amber shrugged. "People change. Do I understand how Ben might want to do anything to regain her love? Absolutely."

Zoey leaned back in her seat and made some notes. After a moment, she inhaled. "I have to say you have an amazing attitude. Many would be angry. In fact, I've seen women blame all men for what one did to them."

"That was the old me. I've been leery of men because of Rich, but then Stone and Cade came along. I've realized a person doesn't always get a second chance. I want to learn to forgive."

Zoey jotted more notes. "Tell me what it was like to have that gun aimed at you. What went through your mind? And did you believe Ben would harm you?"

"I was terrified, but I didn't want to believe Ben really wanted to kill me." She tapped her chest. "He was always kind and gentle to me—or at least he used to be. I knew nothing about the breakup, and because Stone and Jamie were on their way, I prayed everything would be okay." That might not be totally true. "Actually, Ben had turned cold, and he was no longer the person I knew. That was when I was really scared to death."

"I believe Ben shot at you and missed. He hit Jamie instead. How did that make you feel?"

"It all went down so fast. I'm not sure if I've processed all of it yet."

Zoey nodded. "That's quite normal." They talked about whether her relationship with Jamie had changed and how Amber was dealing with her newfound loves.

"I really feel good. Am I sad it happened? Absolutely, but I'm trying to find the silver lining."

Zoey smiled. "If you experience any problems sleeping or have an excessive change in weight, please consult a medical doctor."

She leaned forward. "I hate pills."

"I understand." Zoey made another short note. "I'm going to recommend you return in one month."

Her time was up? That went by fast. "As much as I love chatting with you, why?"

"Will you come back?"

That was evasive. "If you think I need to."

Zoey smiled and stood. "See you tomorrow at happy hour?"

"Wouldn't miss it."

As soon as she stepped out of Zoey's office, she ran into Stone and Cade. "Hey. What are you doing here?" It was four fifteen, so Stone would be off work, but Cade never left the station this early.

"We spoke with your supervisor," Cade said. "Tammy said it was okay if we whisk you away a little early."

"What's the occasion?"

Stone wrapped an arm around her waist. "Can't two men in love want to be with their woman?"

She loved the "love" part, but they'd never really said those three little words to her. "Let me grab my purse from the locker room."

They escorted her there. She picked up her bag and came right out. "Ready."

Outside, they walked her to Stone's truck where she piled in between them. She was about to ask if she could stop home and change out of her scrubs, but if they thought she needed to change, they'd probably suggest it.

Stone crossed under I90 and hopped on Gold Avenue. He drove straight through town. When he didn't turn on SR25, she figured out where they were going. "Are we finally having the picnic where all three of us can be together?"

Stone grinned. "You are a smart one. I wanted to erase any bad memories you might have of Harmes River. Besides, I did promise you a rain check."

"That you did." But she'd considered the picnic on top of the mountain great compensation.

Ten minutes later, he hooked a right into the park. On a Wednesday, most of the place was deserted. *Perfect.*

He parked in the lot and Cade helped her out. From the back, Stone lifted a wicker basket. "It might be a little early for dinner."

"I'm always up for eating."

She helped them set out the sandwiches, chips, and drinks while Cade put out the plates. The rushing water, the birds chirping, and the balmy air created the most peaceful setting.

Just as she was ready to chow, Cade and Stone moved behind her, twisted her around, and pulled her up.

"I thought we were eating." The delicious looking food had her stomach grumbling.

"We want to do something first," Stone said. He picked up her hand. "I know how much you've been through this last month or two, but something wonderful has come from it all."

She smiled. "I met you two."

"And we met the woman for us."

Stone's voice actually wobbled a bit, causing a lump to form in her throat. When they both dropped to one knee, her heart nearly burst. The implication was almost too much to bear.

Cade pulled a small box from his pocket. "As the elder of the two, and by far the better looking, Stone and I wanted to tell you since you've come into our lives, we've learned what love is. It may take some sacrifice at times on your part to put up with us, but being with you has filled us with the kind of joy I've never had in my life."

She never knew Cade was capable of such romance.

Stone nudged him. "Get on with it."

"As is the way in Rock Hard, Montana, while a woman may want to be with two men, technically she can only marry one of us. That would be me, as I am the oldest and wisest, but I'm afraid you'll be stuck with Stone anyway." Cade grinned.

Stone shook his head in apparent disgust. "What my roommate is very badly stating is that we both love you with our whole hearts, and it would be the greatest honor on earth if you would agree to marry us. What do you say?"

Tears welled. After the fiasco with Rich, she honestly thought she wasn't cut out to be loved. She glanced from Stone to Cade. "You really love me?" She'd never heard those words said with such sincerity.

Cade kissed her knuckles. "I love you more than you can know."

A tear dripped down her cheek. Stone picked up her other hand. "But I love you more."

She choked out a laugh. "Then yes and yes. I will marry you both." Her heart swelled.

Cade opened the velvet box and slipped a beautiful diamond on her left ring finger. "I wish it were bigger," Cade said, "but know this represents the tiniest fraction of our love."

Words wouldn't even form. Her love for them knew no bounds but putting that concept into a coherent sentence was impossible. She could face a man with a gun and speak quietly, but right now she was too overwhelmed.

Stone nudged Cade. "She seems to be in a trance. I think a kiss is in order."

Stone gently enfolded her in his arms and kissed her with tenderness, love, and passion.

She cleared her throat and then swiped a tear from her cheek. "I needed that."

Cade lightly shoved Stone out of the way. "My turn."

His kiss curled her toes and almost made her willing to strip and have her way with them right by the river. As luck would have it, a family of four chose that moment to drive up. *Damn.* "I guess we'll have to celebrate big time tonight."

Both men grinned.

✧ ✧ ✧

Three weeks later

Why she let Stone and Cade talk her into an engagement party she didn't know, as she wasn't good at throwing get-togethers. Jamie, bless her heart, had made a list of everything Amber needed to buy to make the party a success. Zoey and Melissa volunteered to bring the hors d'oeuvres. Because the men had asked her to move in with them, for the last week, Amber had spent every waking moment bringing over her clothes and a ton of her junk. She never knew she'd accumulated so much stuff in the year since moving to Rock Hard.

Between the hospital, moving, and trying to shop, she was exhausted.

Cade squeezed her shoulder. "Go get ready. Stone and I will make sure it's all perfect."

Amber glanced at the clock. "The guests will be here in thirty minutes. Yikes."

They both chuckled as she rushed down the hall to the master bedroom. She'd been thrilled they'd replaced the king-sized bed with two queens bolted together. Now all three of them had plenty of room to roll around while they slept. Had she been in a cramped bed, she would have been impossible to live with.

Amber had already showered, so all that was left to do was change into her party attire and put on makeup. Zoey had insisted they go shopping for something really special. In a boutique shop in the Rock Hard Mall, they'd found a form-fitting top to go with a long, flowing skirt. Add in the pair of cute matching pumps, and she thought she looked pretty good. Her neck was bare, but none of her jewelry really went with her blue shirt.

After she put on her makeup and fixed her hair, she inhaled and joined the men.

"Stone." Cade nodded toward her.

They'd been acting a little strange for the past few days, but she thought that was due to nerves. Getting engaged was a big step for all of them.

Both men approached. Because Stone had his hands behind his back, excitement flashed through her.

"Remember the birthday present Cade gave Katie?" he

asked.

"How could I forget that necklace? It was beautiful."

He brought his hand from behind his back and opened a case. Inside was a similar necklace, only the piece was a gorgeous, dark blue. "We thought this would look good on you."

"Oh, my God. This is amazing."

"Turn around," Stone said.

He slipped the necklace around her neck and Amber fingered the smooth stone. Her pulse soared. She turned back around and hugged and kissed both of her men.

Stone's cell rang. "Excuse me. It's Mom." He answered and paced over to the kitchen. "No problem." He returned a minute later. "My family is running a little late. Seems Dad popped a button off his shirt, and Mom had to sew it back on."

That was sweet. The loving relationship between his parents was what she yearned for.

The doorbell rang, and Cade and Stone exchanged glances. The party didn't start for another fifteen minutes. So who was it? Melissa or Zoey bringing the hors d'oeuvres? Or had Jamie wanted to see if she could help? Her arm had healed, but she wasn't supposed to lift anything heavy.

"I'll get it," Cade said.

She heard murmurs at the door. A second later, Amber's mother appeared with a present in hand. "Amber." Cade slipped the gift from her mom's fingers.

Her heart dropped to her stomach. "Mom? What are you doing here?" Okay, her voice didn't sound angry, but it was laced with a bit of shock.

"Your men invited me. I hope it's all right to crash your engagement party."

Stone and Cade had been in contact with the ice queen? She glanced at them, but they were only looking at her mother.

Something was wrong. Her mother had never given a hoot about her. Now that she was here, though, a bit of guilt surfaced.

Amber hadn't even told her about the big news. "Sure. It's okay."

Stone placed a hand on her mother's arm. "What can I get you to drink, Mrs. Delacroix?"

"Call me Madelyn. After all, I'm about to become your mother-in-law."

She almost sounded as if she approved. *Where had the real Madelyn Delacroix gone?*

"Wine perhaps?" Stone urged.

"White is perfect."

Other than when she was with Thomas, Amber had never seen her mom be…nice. She could do gracious but only when she was in a roomful of doctors. "Come sit down, Mom."

Amber was determined to find out what was going on. Her mom better not be here to try to talk her out of marrying Cade and Stone. She'd fail.

While Stone poured the wine, her mom sat on the sofa, her back straight, her fingers laced tight. "Thomas wanted to be here, but he wasn't able to make it."

"It was nice that he wanted to."

She nodded. "I want to tell you that I'm happy for you." Her mom swallowed hard at the "happy" word.

Now Amber knew an alien had possessed her mother. "Thank you." Her mom fiddled with her watch bracelet, twisting it around her wrist, an action Amber had never seen her do before. "What's going on?"

Stone set her mom's glass of wine on the coffee table then moved over to the side behind the sofa. He appeared to be standing guard, waiting to intervene in case things got ugly, but not so close as to eavesdrop. She loved him even more for that.

Her mom looked off to the side then back at her hands. "After Chris died, Thomas reminded me how empty my life had become when your dad left."

Her mom had never indicated Dad's departure affected her.

"We all suffered after that," Amber said.

Her mother nodded and finally met Amber's gaze. "I buried myself in my work and put myself above my children."

She admitted that? *Wow.* Amber wouldn't be petty and bring up the fact that she doted on Thomas and even seemed to put him above her job. But having faced the end of a gun had taught her one thing—it was better to leave some things in the past.

Not making eye contact, her mom's chin trembled. Her watch seemed to be the object of her attention. "I'm willing to admit now that I wasn't able to provide you with the kind of childhood a little girl needed." She finally glanced up, and tears shimmered in her eyes.

Amber studied her mother. Damn, but her mom actually believed what she was saying, but she wasn't ready to forgive her yet. "I think you're a little confused, Mom. You were able to provide me with what I needed, but you chose not to. That was the problem."

Her mom's mouth opened slightly. She then snapped her lips shut and shook her head. "I didn't provide for you, did I? I'm sorry." Her mother picked up Amber's hand, but the grip held little warmth. "But I do love you. You have to believe me." She inhaled, but Amber couldn't respond. "I want to know if I've lost my little girl for good."

Did her mother not have a clue how lonely Amber's life had become before she met her men? No matter how much her mom apologized, she couldn't bring back Amber's childhood.

"Mom. That ship sailed a long time ago." She drew on her inner calm. "You know what I missed the most growing up?"

"No." Her mother let go of Amber's hand. "What? I want to know."

"Getting to spend time with you learning how to cook, and not seeing the look of joy on your face when I hit a double at a softball game."

"I never went to one of your games, so how could I?"

"Precisely."

Her mom cast her gaze downward. "Oh."

Amber sniffled. "I've always wanted to know if you believed I wanted to go alone when I shopped for my prom dress?"

She slowly shook her head, her eyes racing back and forth. "I never thought about it."

"It's something mothers and daughters do together. It's a rite of passage." *And you were never there.*

Her mom glanced at her hands for moment. "I remember you brought home a pretty pink dress."

That was a small apology. "It was actually a blue satin dress with a pink sash." Amber wanted to forgive her, but couldn't. "If it was so pretty, why didn't you want to take a picture of me standing next to Charley? He might not have been my dream date, but at least he bought me a corsage." Amber turned to the side and swiped a finger under her eye.

Her mom's lips pressed together. "I probably don't deserve it, but if you have any forgiveness in your heart, I'd like to try to be more a part of your life." She placed a hand on Amber's wrist.

Her touch almost burned.

The image of Ben pointing that gun in her face surfaced, and how her regrets had flashed before her eyes. Was it time to let go of the past?

"You really want to be part of my life?" Amber didn't think her mother understood what that meant. "Because whether you do or don't, I'm going to be fine. I have a new life now with the two men I love."

That doesn't mean you can't give her your love, too.

Her mother stared.

Amber inhaled. "But I'm willing to let you show me, if you can, that you want to share future milestones."

I do love you, Mom. But it will take some time for me to show it.

"Tell me what I can do," her mom said. "I'm listening."

That was a first. "Our relationship has to be a two way street. It can't just be me caring about you or doing things that are convenient for you. My whole life, it's been about you and your career. Now it has to be about me and my two men, too. They've shown me what love is. I'm different now."

"I'm not sure I know how." Her mom's voice shook.

"Here's one way. When I call you, don't put me on hold right away. It always makes me feel like I'm not as important than who you're with at the time."

Her mom slapped a hand over her mouth, and her eyes ping ponged around. "I do that, don't I? Amber, I'm so sorry." Tears ran down her mother's cheeks. She opened her purse and actually had a tissue. She wiped her eyes.

Amber waited for her mother to say more, but even that small admission was a big step.

Her mom cleared her throat. "So, show me this ring the boys gave you."

Amber's heart pounded in her chest. For the sake of possibly forging a new relationship with her mother, she held out her hand. Cade and Stone would want her to. And she did, too.

"Not that I'm asking your permission, but you seem rather calm about me being with two men."

"It's beautiful." Her mother shifted her gaze to the side then back up at Amber. "I won't lie. I'm having a hard time dealing with the idea. It isn't natural, you know."

Amber counted to ten, waiting for her mother to ask what she was going to do when her patients and fellow doctors found out. But she never did, and Amber's pulse slowed. There might be hope.

The doorbell rang, and seconds later, Zoey and Melissa rushed in bearing trays of food. Jamie was right behind them.

"Excuse me. I have to see to my friends." When Amber turned away, a piece of her heart crumpled. Her mom looked so lost. With time, her mom might figure out how to do better.

If Amber ever had children—and she wanted a ton—she would be the best mom ever. Before she reached the girls, Stone got there first and hugged her friends while Cade wrapped an arm around Amber's waist.

He leaned over. "How did it go?"

"I've said my peace." To her surprise, expressing her opinion brought some closure.

"Good. Did you promise her mercy?"

Amber chuckled. "No need. I gave her some already." She glanced back at her mom who was sipping her wine, staring off into space.

Amber wanted to mend the wall that existed between them. For now, she wanted to love her men and love them hard.

Her mother set down her glass and stood. With straight shoulders, she strode toward them, looking like she used to so long ago.

"Amber, Cade, Stone. May I speak with you three for a moment?"

Amber's stomach tumbled. Would her mom dash Amber's hope of a possible healing between them? "Yes?"

Her mom closed her eyes for a moment then nodded. "I've come to ask if I could help you three plan your wedding?"

Goose bumps raced over Amber's body, and joy spread through her veins. "Oh, Mom. I'd love that." The tears she'd held at bay let loose.

Amber was filled up with hope and so much love. Her life just got better.

The End

About the author

I love to read, write, dream, and connect with people. A book with a happily ever after is a must, as is having characters I can relate to. My men are always wonderful, dynamic, smart, strong, and the best lovers in the world.

I love hearing from readers, too!!

You can contact me at:
velladayauthor@gmail.com

Visit my website at:
www.velladay.com

Check me out on facebook, too at:
www.facebook.com/vella.day.90

Follow me on twitter at:
www.twitter.com/velladay4

I also write as Melody Snow Monroe:
www.melodymonroe.com

Want to know more? Sign up for my newsletter:
http://eepurl.com/I0OX5

OTHER BOOKS BY THE AUTHOR

MONTANA PROMISES

GENRE: Medical Romance, Contemporary Western Romance, Erotica ménage romance, (MFM)

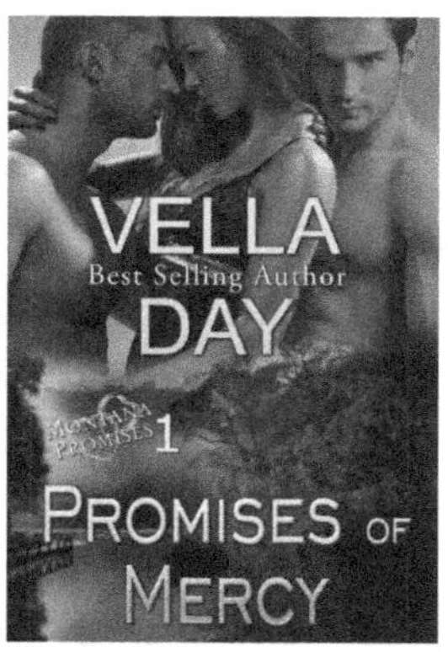

PROMISES OF MERCY (BOOK 1)

Killing is wrong. The reason doesn't matter.

When oncology nurse, Amber Delacroix, learns her reckless brother has been in a paralyzing motorcycle accident, sorrow fills her soul. He's murdered a few days later, and now she's utterly devastated. Adding to life's cruelty, the cowboy cop assigned to her brother's case brings her in for questioning.

Stone Benson, the paramedic who brought Amber's brother into the hospital, stays by her side throughout the tragedy. He treats her with kindness and compassion—something she hasn't experienced much in her life. Amber yearns for more than his comforting words, and they embark on a tremulous journey. Just when she feels that their relationship is at a turning point, he reveals that he likes to share his women with his good friend and roommate, Cade. That turns out to be a huge problem, because Cade is the cop who believes she's guilty of killing her brother.

As chance would have it, another murder occurs when both Cade and Amber are in the same location. Realizing she's not the mercy killer, Cade offers a heartfelt apology—one that includes dinner and a sharing of souls. When things heat up between them, she succumbs to his passionate ways. The big question that plagues her now is where does Stone fit in?

Stone knows exactly where Amber needs to be. Right between him and his best friend, Cade. He'll do whatever is necessary to convince her that she has finally met two men she can trust and build a life with.

Too bad the killer has other ideas. When he goes after Amber, what will the men need to do to save her in time to pursue a loving ménage relationship?

PUBLISHER'S NOTE: This adult contemporary romance contains explicit sexual content, graphic language, and situations that some readers may find objectionable (double penetration, ménage, violence). Not intended for those under the age of 18.

CAVEAT: But if you love medical erotica with a contemporary western setting, this book is for you.

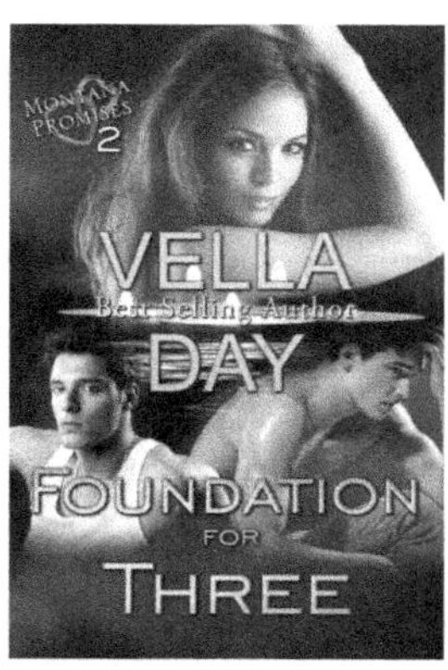

FOUNDATION FOR THREE (BOOK 2)

You aren't free to love until you realize you can't make someone love you back.

As builder Pete Banks is finishing a remodel for psychologist Zoey Donovan, she arrives home dazed, injured, and distraught. As he calms her down, she draws him in with her halting story of how Thad Dalton, a local cop and Pete's roommate, saved her life. When Pete learns Thad was shot, he's torn between staying with a woman in need and being there for his roommate.

Zoey never intended to blurt out to a man she's never met how she almost died, but Pete's understanding nature alters something inside her. Usually, she's the one trying to figure out her clients' needs, not the other way around. While Pete Banks is one of kind, she can't tear her mind from Thad, the man who risked his life for her.

Detective Thad Dalton was never so scared in his life when a madman grabs Zoey in the hospital corridor and threatens to kill her if his demands aren't met. Thad ends up taking a bullet to save her but would do it again if it means having her in his life.

When Zoey, Thad, and Pete attend Thad's parents' anniversary party sparks fly. She realizes she wants a more personal connection to these two men. While Thad's on board, Pete doesn't think he's worthy. His self-loathing forces him to retreat and casts doubt on their future together.

Zoey and Thad are justifiably both mad and hurt. It's going to take a miracle to patch this threesome back together for their happily ever after.

PUBLISHER'S NOTE: This adult contemporary romance contains explicit sexual content, graphic language, and situations that some readers may find objectionable (double penetration, ménage, violence). Not intended for those under the age of 18.

PACK WARS

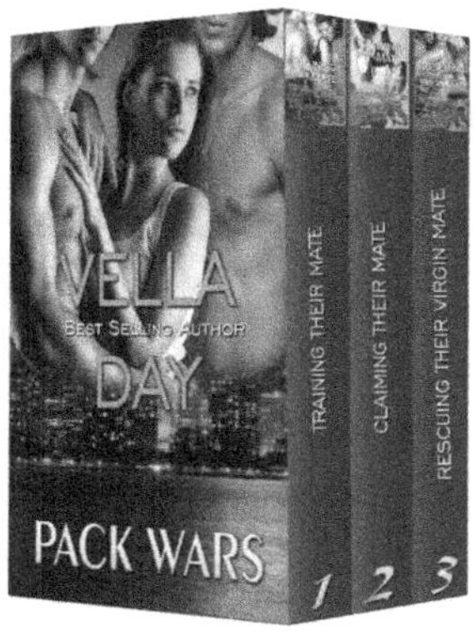

NOTE: These THREE novellas (50K each) were previously released as single titles.

GENRE: Paranormal Werewolf Romance, Paranormal Erotica, Paranormal Menage (MFM)

TRAINING THEIR MATE (BOOK 1)

She failed to stop him. Now he's coming after her.

Liz Wharton has one goal—to kill the man who raped her mother. Had she known Harvey Couch was a werewolf, she never would have tried to take him on by herself.

Determined to put an end to the pest bent on revenge, Harvey sends his goons after her. When two wolves attack her, Liz is sure she's hallucinating. Good thing Trax Field is there to stop them.

Trax and Dante Field, members of the Pack, have devoted their lives to stopping bad shifters like Harvey Couch. Saving Liz would have been just an ordinary day, but when Trax finds her huddled in an alley, bruised and shaken, he's convinced she's his mate.

To keep her safe, Trax and Dante hold her captive in their loft apartment. When they aren't searching for Couch, Trax and his brother spend the night training their future mate in the art of bondage and sensual pleasures. How will they be able to convert her into embracing not only their lifestyle but also their animalistic side?

CLAIMING THEIR MATE (BOOK 2)

She saw the killer. Now he wants her dead.

Realtor Chelsea Wilson enters a vacant home she wants to show and comes face-to-face with a dead man—and a killer. Freaked out, she runs, but the killer nabs her.

Ricardo Mendez, a werewolf who runs a drug operation, doesn't need a witness to the murder. He viciously attacks her, but the dead man's brother, werewolf Kurt Wendlick and his Pack partner, Drake Stanton stop the final assault.

When Kurt and Drake save Chelsea, they're certain she's their mate and will do anything to keep her safe. Her loving ways puts Kurt in a tailspin. He wants to claim her, but first he needs to avenge his brother's murder.

What can Chelsea do to help the tormented man? Will the three ever explore the world of BSDM together?

RESCUING THEIR VIRGIN MATE (BOOK 3)

She's sold into slavery. Now she's on the run.

All Elena Sanchez wanted was to get on the plane to Costa Rica and visit her parents. When the authorities tell her they need to search her, she finds herself drugged and caged by a sadistic bastard who plans to sell her virginity to the highest bidder.

Two Pack members, Clay Demmers and Dirk Tilton, learn that Elena, Harvey Couch's former secretary, is a victim of a human trafficking scheme. They go undercover and bid for her. As soon as they see her, they realize she's their mate. More determined than ever to save her, they buy her, but at what cost?

Elena doesn't know who to trust. They inform her they're werewolves, but is that any better than being sold into slavery to humans? With care, Clay and Dirk teach her how to embrace her submissive ways. The problem is this good Catholic girl likes it. Will the guilt from her upbringing prevent her from having the best ménage relationship possible or can she find a way to have both?

PUBLISHER'S NOTE: This adult contemporary romance contains explicit sexual content, graphic language, and situations that some readers may find objectionable (double penetration, ménage, violence). Not intended for those under the age of 18.

THE BURIED TRILOGY

NOTE: These books have been published previously under their separate titles.

GENRE: Romance, Mystery, Thriller, Suspense, Serial killer

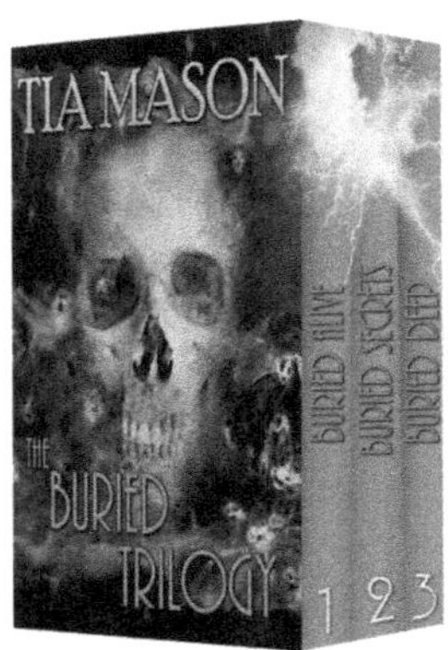

BURIED ALIVE (BOOK 1)

When loner homicide detective, Hunter Markum, finds the skeletons of four women in a mass grave just outside Tampa, Florida, he's distraught as hell. It leaves a bitter taste in his mouth, as it's a harsh reminder of his own sister's unsolved murder.

For the first time in his career, the usually detached Hunter feels a more personal connection to this case, and agrees to team up with Dr. Kerry Herlihy, a forensic anthropologist, in the hopes she can decipher the buried bones. Her compassion for these cold case victims draws her to him.

Kerry too finds Hunter's strong family attachment appealing, as her family abandoned her as a child, but she tamps down her desires. The case must come first.

Against their will, the attraction ignites, and their quest to find the killer soon reveals the identities of the victims and the chilling fact that each woman had been abused. When Kerry's work throws her directly in the killer's path, Hunter realizes how much she's come to mean to him. In a race against the clock, Hunter must apprehend the murderer if he hopes to save the woman he loves once she's buried alive.

BURIED SECRETS (BOOK 2)

When rookie Tampa Police Officer, Jenna Holliday, goes undercover at a local occult store to investigate a rash of grave robberies, she never expects to become the victim of a black magic death spell.

Dr. Sam Bonita, a forensic anthropologist, in search of answers regarding a headless body, visits the store where Jenna works and is enchanted by her.

Believing Sam holds the key to her case, Jenna tries to get close to him. When his house is burned to the ground, with both of them inside, she's unsure if her cover has been blown or if Sam is the object of some deranged killer.

Only after a series of murders, and a few death threats, do Jenna and Sam suspect a serial killer is on the loose and after both of them.

BURIED DEEP (BOOK 3)

When forensic anthropologist, Dr. Lara Romano, first examines the exhumed skeletons of two Native American men buried in Tampa, she has no idea she's caught the eye of a serial killer who's intent on dipping her in plaster and covering her in hot wax to complete a twisted ode to his Seminole mother.

Isolated by her profound hearing loss she suffered as a child,

Lara jumps at the chance to work in the field and prove she's as competent as any hearing scientist. Not even the easy-on-the-eyes cop bucking to work with her will distract her from her goal.

Missing Persons detective, Jake Kinsey, needs a high profile case to land him a job in Homicide. Though he suspects the attractive rookie scientist may hinder his success, he believes the cadavers in Lara's investigation are linked to his current case—eight missing men, all Native Americans, believed to be dead.

What Jake and Lara don't realize is that the missing bodies have been left in plain sight as part of a tableau constructed by the madman who plans to use Lara and Jake for his final scene.

www.ingramcontent.com/pod-product-compliance
Lightning Source LLC
Chambersburg PA
CBHW060520180626
46817CB00002B/427

* 9 7 8 0 9 8 9 9 7 5 9 2 6 *